ALL THE BLUE-EYED ANGELS

AN ERIN SOLOMON MYSTERY

D1453004

Praise for
ALL THE BLUE-EYED ANGELS

"Jen Blood has created my favorite narrator of the decade: the whip-smart, sassy, and delightfully stubborn Erin Solomon. The story she tells—with its hidden turns, dry humor, enthralling pace, persuasive complexity, and vivid setting—is absolutely unforgettable."

—Lewis Robinson, award-winning author of *Water Dogs* and *Officer Friendly and Other Stories*

"The pacing is flawless, building steadily to a riveting climax. The characters are complex, likable and expertly drawn. If you enjoy contemporary mysteries, then you don't want to pass on this one."

—Tahlia Newland, Awesome Indies Book Reviews

"In *All the Blue-Eyed Angels*, Blood has given us a powerful, emotionally complex story peopled with fully-realized characters and terrific, well-honed prose. Thankfully, this is but the first in the Erin Solomon mystery series. I'm very much looking forward to the others."

—Darcy Scott, author of *Hunter-Huntress* and *Matinicus*

"*All the Blue-Eyed Angels* grabbed me from the first few lines and wouldn't let me go... If you like mysteries with a strong plot filled with dark secrets and murder, and a kick a** setting, along with a romantic-triangle involving two vastly different men, then you'll love this book."

—DV Berkom, author of the bestselling Kate Jones thrillers and Leine Basso thrillers

ALL THE BLUE-EYED ANGELS

AN ERIN SOLOMON MYSTERY

JEN BLOOD

Adian Press
Maine

Adian Press
934 River Rd. #1
Cushing, Maine 04563
www.adianpress.com

Publisher: Adian Press
Cover Design: damonza.com
Author's Photograph: Amy Wilton Photography

Dedicated to my parents,
for their unwavering belief in the importance
of writers and the stories we tell.

AUGUST 22, 1990

ON MY TENTH BIRTHDAY, I am baptized by fire.

I race through a forest of smoke, ignoring the sting of blackberry brambles and pine branches on sensitive cheeks and bare arms. Up ahead, I catch a glimpse of my father's shirt, drenched and muddy, as he races through the woods. I follow blindly, too terrified to scream, too panicked to stop.

A figure in black chases us, gaining on me fast. At ten years old, raised in the church, I am certain that it is the devil himself. He wears a hooded cloak; I imagine him taking flight at my heels, reaching for me with gnarled fingers. I run faster, my breath high in my chest, trees speeding past. The air gets thicker and harder to breathe the closer we get to the fire, but I don't stop.

The Lord is my shepherd, I shall not want.

I can hear him behind me, three or four steps back at most, his breath coming hard and his hands getting closer.

I skid into the clearing certain that I'm safe now—I've reached the church. The church is always safe.

But today, nothing is safe. Flames climb the blackened walls of the chapel, firemen circling with hoses to keep the surrounding forest from burning. My father has arrived ahead of me—I find him kneeling in front of a pile of rubble just feet from the flames. His shoulders shake as he cries.

He maketh me to lie down in green pastures. He leadeth me beside the still waters.

I go to him because I know no one else will, and wrap my arms around his neck. When I scan the tree line, the man I felt behind me just moments before is gone. Now, there is no one but the firemen, the local constable, and my mother with her doctor's bag and no survivors to heal.

I pray in my father's ear, whispering words of comfort the way he always has for me. There is a smell that sticks in my throat and turns my stomach, but only when my mother comes for me, trying to pull me away, do I realize what that smell is.

He restoreth my soul. He leadeth me on a path of righteousness for His name's sake.

A coal black, claw-like hand reaches from beneath the pile of burned debris where my father weeps. A few feet beyond, I see a flash of soot-stained white feathers, china-blue eyes, and a painted smile that seems suddenly cruel. I stay there, fixated on the doll, until my mother takes me in her arms and forces me away.

She sets me on the wet grass and places a mask over my face so that I can breathe. The oxygen tastes like cold water after a long drought. I sit still while the rain washes over me and my father cries and the church burns to the ground.

I'm just beginning to calm when I feel a presence like warm breath at the back of my neck, and I turn once more toward the trees.

The cloaked man stands at the edge of the woods, his hood down around his shoulders. Rain plasters dark hair against his head. Water drips down high cheekbones and a thin, sharp nose.

Yea, though I walk through the valley of the shadow of death, I will fear no evil.

The words of my favorite Psalm stutter in my head—*Thy rod and thy staff, they comfort me.*

The man in black turns his head, his dark eyes fixing on mine.

My cup runneth over.

He puts a finger to his thin lips and whispers to me through the chaos.

"Sshhh."

More than twenty years will pass before I pray again.

1

I RETURNED TO MY hometown of Littlehope, Maine, on a wet afternoon when the town was locked in fog. A cold rain filled the potholes and pooled on the shoulder of coastal Route 1, ensuring that I hydroplaned most of the drive up from Boston. I hadn't set foot in Littlehope since my high school graduation, when I left the town behind in a beaten-to-hell Honda Civic with the vow that I would never return.

That was fifteen years ago.

Littlehope is a fishing village at the end of a peninsula on Penobscot Bay, about two hours from Portland. It's known for Bennett's Lobster Shanty, the Ladies Auxiliary Quilting League, and a small but determined band of drug runners who rule the harbor. Littlehope also happens to be ten miles as the crow flies from the island where thirty-four members of the Payson Church of Tomorrow burned to death and where, a decade later, my father hanged himself in their honor.

They say you can't go home again. In my case, it seems more apt to ask why the hell you'd ever want to.

I walked through the front door of the *Downeast Daily*

Tribune just after eleven o'clock that Wednesday morning. The *Trib* has delivered the news to three counties in the Midcoast for over fifty years, from an ugly concrete block of a building on Littlehope's main drag. Across the road, you'll find the Episcopal Church, the local medical clinic, and the only bar in town. My mother used to joke that the layout was intentional—locals could get plastered and beat the crap out of each other Saturday night, stumble next door to get patched up, and stop in to see the neighborhood preacher for redemption on Sunday morning.

The first job I ever had was as Girl Friday at the *Trib*, fetching coffee and making copies for the local newshounds, occasionally typing up copy when no one else was around or they were too lazy to do it themselves. Walking through the familiar halls that morning, I soaked in the smells of fresh ink and old newspapers, amazed at the things people are usually amazed at when they come home after a lifetime away: how small the building was, how outdated the décor, how it paled in comparison to my golden memories.

My comrade-in-arms, Einstein—part terrier, part Muppet, and so-named not for any propensity toward genius but rather for his unruly white curls—padded along beside me, ears and tail up, his nails clicking on the faded gray linoleum floor. Plaques and photos decorated the concrete walls, some dating back to my teenage days with the paper. I passed two closed doors before I reached the newsroom—the last door on the right, with yellowed Peanuts comics taped to the window and the sound of a BBC newscast coming from within. Einstein's tail started wagging, his body shimmying with the motion, the second he caught scent of the company we were about to keep.

"Settle, buddy," I said, my hand on the doorknob—

though in fairness the words were probably more for me than him. The dog glanced up at me and whined.

I opened the door and had only a second to get my bearings before I was spotted; it's hard to be stealthy when a bullet of fur precedes you into the room. Daniel Diggins—aka Diggs to almost everyone on the planet—greeted my mutt with more enthusiasm than I knew I would get, crouching low to fondle dogged ears and dodge a few canine kisses while I took stock of the old homestead.

The computers had been updated since I'd been there last, but were still out of date. The desks were the same, though: six hulking metal things with jagged edges and scratched surfaces, buried under the detritus of the newspaper biz—piles of paperwork, oversized computer monitors, and half-eaten bags of junk food. A couple of overweight, graying reporter-types were on cell phones on one side of the room, while Diggs and another man stood at a desk that had once been mine. Behind them, a wall-mounted TV was tuned to MSNBC.

Before Diggs straightened to say hello, the other half of the duo locked eyes with me. Though we'd never met face to face, it was clear from the man's pointed glare who he was—and that, unlike me, he had not been looking forward to this meeting.

"Are you planning on saying hello to me at all, or is this visit gonna be all about the dog?" I asked Diggs, if only to break the sudden tension in the room.

"It's always all about the dog," Diggs said. "You should know that by now." He stood and enveloped me in a warm hug. I held on tight, lost in a smell of wool and comfort that would forever be associated with the best parts of my youth.

"How're you doing, kiddo?" he asked. The words were

quiet, warm in my ear—a question between just the two of us before I got started. I stepped out of his embrace with what I hoped was a businesslike nod.

"Good. I'm good."

"Good," he said. "And the drive was…?"

"The drive was fine, Diggs."

He smiled—a slow grin that's been charming women around the globe for as long as I can remember. Though I hadn't visited Littlehope in over a decade, Diggs and I never lost touch. Our latest visit had been a few months before, but he looked no different than he always does: curly hair stylishly unkempt, his five o'clock shadow edging closer to a beard than I'd seen it in some time. He was toying with me now. Diggs likes that kind of thing.

When it became clear that I wasn't playing along, he nodded toward the other man at the desk.

"Noel," Diggs said. "This is Erin Solomon. Erin, Noel Hammond."

Hammond extended his hand to me like someone had a gun at his back, and we shook.

"Nice to finally meet you, Noel. Thanks for coming."

"Diggs didn't give me much choice."

So, Diggs had come through again—this time by delivering a much-needed source at my feet. "Yeah, well, he knew he'd have to put up with my bitching otherwise. It won't take long."

"This is about your book, then?" he asked.

I glanced at Diggs, making no effort to conceal my displeasure. "You heard about that?"

"The whole town's heard about that," Hammond said. "It was the lead story in the paper about a month back. The book deal, you inheriting Payson Isle… Everybody knows about it."

I raised an eyebrow at Diggs, who raised his hands in surrender. "It wasn't my call, Solomon—there was no way I could keep it quiet. I figured you'd rather I do the write-up than somebody else."

He was right about that, at least. Still, I wasn't thrilled to think the entire *Trib* readership was in on my business. I suppressed a sigh and told myself to get over it. I was sure it wouldn't be the last surprise I had in this investigation.

"So, where do you want to do this?" Hammond prompted me.

He was a lesson in how deceptive a phone voice can be. In the one telephone interview he'd granted me in the past three months, Hammond had been articulate and reserved during a conversation that had been anything but pleasant. Though I'd known he was a retired cop, I had still pictured an aging professor-type—someone the local fishermen would hate, and the women in the tiny library on the corner would fantasize about. I was wrong.

Though he had to be at least sixty-five, Noel Hammond was built more like a linebacker than a man bound for the geriatric set. Over six feet tall and easily two-hundred pounds, he looked like he could bench press a buffalo without breaking a sweat. His hands were callused, his grip stronger than I'd expected.

"Do you guys mind coming back to the dock to check things out with me?" I asked. "We can talk there."

"Actually, there's been a little change of plan," Diggs said. "I got a boat for you like you asked, but we took her out to the island and set the mooring already. Noel said we can take you out there together—make sure you get set up all right."

This had clearly been Diggs' idea, since Hammond looked like he'd rather hog-tie a rattlesnake than spend the afternoon hauling my ass around the harbor.

"That would be great," I said.

"Great," Hammond repeated, with a notable lack of enthusiasm. He was out the door before I could respond.

Five minutes later, Diggs and I were headed out when a grizzled fisherman in coveralls and an orange hunting cap stopped us in the hallway. I fought the urge to run in the other direction the moment I realized who it was.

"You got that paperwork I asked you for, Diggs?" he asked. He didn't give me so much as a sidelong glance.

"I was just on my way out, Joe—can I drop it off later?"

The man shook his head; he didn't look pleased. Joe Ashmont was the fire chief in Littlehope—or at least he had been, up until the Payson fire. A week after the church burned to the ground, Ashmont turned in his resignation. Though the reasons for that were never quite clear, he always seemed to hold my family personally responsible.

"I've gotta get that boat fixed or I'm screwed—the season's about to start, I can't have her leaking oil all over the bay. You said you'd help me," Ashmont pressed.

Diggs glanced at me in apology. "Yeah, all right. Just hang on a second and I'll grab it. You wanna wait in the office, Sol?"

I started to nod, but Ashmont interrupted. "She can wait here with me. I don't bite."

Ashmont was probably in his sixties, though he didn't look a day under seventy-five. Still, he was lean and mean and, despite his claim to the contrary, I suspected that biting was the very least I had to worry about from him. Since he'd had a front-row seat at the Payson fire, however, I knew I'd need to break the ice sooner or later if I wanted any information from him. I sent Diggs on his way.

Einstein growled low in his throat, and stood with his body blocking my legs—just in case I did something crazy and took a step toward the psychopath in the hallway. He didn't need to worry, though. I planned on staying put.

"It's good I run into you," Ashmont said the moment Diggs was out of sight. The way he said it gave me the uneasy feeling our meeting didn't have anything to do with luck.

"Oh?"

"Payson Isle belongs to you now, don't it? Word is Old Mal left it to you."

'Old Mal' was Malcolm Payson—brother of Isaac Payson, the preacher who had led the Payson Church until their untimely demise. Ashmont took a step toward me. I smelled whiskey and stale cigarettes on his breath.

"I guess it does."

"'I guess it does,'" he repeated, his voice up a tone to mimic me. "It does or it don't, right? I got fishing rights off that back cove—been pulling traps there for the past twenty years. Your old man didn't bother me, said I was welcome to it. Once he strung himself up, nobody said a word about it since."

My chest tightened at his words. "I'll look into it," I said.

A slow smile touched his lips. "You do that," he said. "You got your daddy's red hair, but you look just like your mum—you know that?" His eyes slid up and down my body, lingering on my chest. "You're littler than her—not much to you, is there?" I'm lucky to hit five-five in heels, and at the moment I felt about three feet shorter. "You got that fire in your eyes, though. A lot of secrets locked up tight in that busy head."

He took another step toward me, then leaned in more quickly than I would have thought possible. Einstein leapt for him, but he cuffed the dog in the side of the head with a swift, meaty-looking fist. Stein yelped and a split second later Ashmont's hand was wrapped around my upper arm, his mouth at my ear.

"Somebody might crack that pretty skull and let all those secrets spill out, you don't watch yourself. Go home, *Miss* Solomon. You got no business here."

Einstein was headed in for another go and Diggs was rounding the corner when Ashmont released me, turning on his heel.

"Mind that dog," he said, calling back over his shoulder as he reached the door. "A dog like that bites me, nobody'd say boo if I shot him where he stood."

I stared after him, too stunned to respond. As soon as Ashmont was gone, I knelt to check on Einstein.

"What the hell was that?" Diggs asked as he hurried to my side. The dog was fine, just a little shaken up; I hadn't fared so well.

"Did you see that? He hit my damn dog. Who does that? The son of a bitch actually *hit* my dog."

"What'd you say to him?"

Like it was my fault. I turned on him. Diggs held up his hands before I could light into him.

"Not that that justifies anything," he added quickly. "It's just—you know Ashmont."

That was true—I did know Ashmont. And it wasn't like I was actually *surprised* at his behavior, given the number of drunken brawls he'd started and hateful epithets he'd spewed in my family's direction when I was a teen. That didn't make it any more acceptable, however. I took a manila envelope from Diggs' hands.

"This is his?"

Diggs nodded. He didn't say anything when I tore the envelope open, and he did a fine job of keeping his amusement to himself while I skimmed the pile of paperwork inside.

"His boat broke down," he said. "There are a couple of places that offer financial assistance to lobstermen, but he was having a hard time with the paperwork. I told him I'd give him a hand."

Since I couldn't think of a fitting insult for this fairly innocuous revelation, I settled for a pointed glare as I returned the documents to the envelope and handed them back to Diggs.

"Newspaper man by day, guardian angel by night. What would Littlehope do without you?"

"I'm sure they'd muddle through."

A horn honked in the parking lot.

"That'll be Noel," Diggs said. "Not here half an hour and you've already got two men who'd just as soon watch you drown than toss you a line. Could be a new record."

"Give me time—I'm sure I can do better."

From the look on Diggs' face, that was exactly what he was afraid of.

2

DIGGS AND I FOLLOWED Hammond to the town landing in my car, navigating roads virtually unchanged since I'd been there last. We passed rundown houses in need of paint; stacks of lobster traps and brightly painted buoys in muddy yards; a full parking lot of pickups at the general store, gun racks mounted in the back windows and right-wing propaganda on the bumper stickers.

It was still raining when I inched my Jetta down the steep grade to the landing. I parked, then leaned back in my seat at sight of a harbor filled with fishing boats bobbing on choppy black water. Diggs watched me from the passenger's seat. I was transported back to afternoons at the newspaper with him, in the days when missing a deadline or misquoting the locals were my biggest worries.

"So, what happened to doing this next month, once spring has a firmer hold on things?"

And I had more time to recover, is what he meant.

"I'm fine, Diggs." I shrugged. "The divorce has been final for a while now—it's time to move on with my life."

"I don't know that a month qualifies as 'a while,'

technically. I think the boys at Wikipedia say it has to be at least two—maybe longer. And I wasn't talking about the divorce." He hesitated. "You were just in the hospital..."

I looked up sharply. The look on my face must have told him the topic was off limits, because Diggs fell silent.

"I told you, I'm fine. Now, let's get out there before Noel takes off without us."

"Yeah, because that'd be a tragedy."

I got out of the car before Diggs could stall any longer. He held out for maybe sixty seconds, silent and stubborn in the passenger's seat, before he joined me.

Between the rain and the gray day, it was impossible to make out the shape of even those islands closest to shore. Payson Isle, just over ten miles north-northeast of us, was nowhere to be seen. Hammond got out of a rabid-looking Dodge Ram loaded down with lobster traps, its grill smashed on the left side, and Diggs and I followed him down the slick boards of the town wharf. He stopped at a behemoth fishing boat with *Frankenstein's Bride* stenciled on the side in red letters, the body painted bright blue.

For the first time since leaving Boston, I felt something other than the staunch resolve that had fueled me night and day for the past several months. Hammond wasn't a friend, and he wouldn't be anxious to spill the secrets I knew he'd been keeping since the Payson fire. Somehow, I'd always pictured this interrogation happening somewhere more secure than on his boat riding stormy seas.

By the time I'd harnessed Einstein into his doggie life preserver—ignoring Diggs' mockery and Hammond's rolled eyes—and we'd loaded ourselves and our gear aboard, the storm had all but subsided. I pushed aside my growing unease. We motored out of the harbor with Hammond at the helm, his feet firm on deck and shoulder-width apart, riding the swells. He lit a cigarette and I breathed in the smoke, the smell diluted by the sweetness of the sea and the inescapable scent of bait soaked into the floorboards. I imitated his stance, standing in the doorway of the pilothouse with Diggs behind me.

"Are you really okay?" Diggs asked.

I leaned back and let him take my weight, just for a second or two. "Fine," I said. "It'll be good to get on with everything."

I doubted he believed me—I certainly didn't buy it. I was on my way to an island on which few had set foot since my father's body had been discovered hanging from a beam in the old Payson greenhouse, ten years after the fire that had taken everyone else in the Payson congregation. My six-year marriage was over, my body still recuperating from a loss that I had, as yet, refused to even acknowledge. And as soon as I could talk to Hammond without the roar of a diesel engine to drown us out, I knew things would only get more complicated.

So, was I okay?

Somehow, that didn't matter anymore. I was here. And, one way or another, I wouldn't leave Littlehope again until I knew the truth about Payson Isle.

●

It took just over an hour to reach the island. Hammond's boat was too big to dock at the precarious-looking wharf, so he pulled alongside the mooring Diggs had set earlier and dropped anchor. A cute little speedboat waited for us in the water below, dwarfed by Hammond's thirty-eight-foot

Cadillac of a lobster boat, but I wasn't interested in leaving yet. The engine hummed lower, idling in the waves. Fog hung over everything, the only sign of life a couple of lobster boats in the distance. Einstein sat on my foot. Hammond looked at Diggs, then at the horizon. After he'd avoided me for a solid minute or two, I cleared my throat.

"You're not coming with us to the island, I take it?" I said.

He shook his head. "I'm on my way out of town—need to get packed."

"You're leaving?"

"For a couple weeks. I've got some things to take care of back home."

Silence fell between us, thick with questions Hammond had yet to answer. Diggs watched our exchange curiously, but said nothing.

Finally, Hammond relented. "Maybe we can get together when I get back."

"Or maybe we can do this now," I said.

"Okay, I might not be the most intuitive man on the planet, but I'm sensing some tension," Diggs interrupted. "You mind giving me a little background here?"

Hammond cocked an eyebrow at me. I shrugged. Diggs was bound to find out sooner or later, anyway.

"You remember the stuff I told you about why I'm here?" I asked.

"To retrace the final weeks before the Payson suicide and write a book about your findings."

I considered that for a moment. It was definitely part of the story—just a fairly small part at this point. "Yeah, well…" I said. "I may have left a few things out."

Once I'd gotten him up to speed, Diggs stared at me in confusion. I could hardly blame the guy—I'd been equally confused when I saw the photos Noel Hammond had taken at the Payson crime scene twenty-two years ago.

"So, Malcolm Payson leaves the island to you out of nowhere," Diggs began.

I braced myself for the recap.

"And in with the junk Payson's lawyer sends to you, you find an envelope with crime scene photos from the fire."

"Crime scene photos nobody had ever seen before," I said. "I've seen all the original files—they're not with them."

"And the name written on the back of a couple of these photos is Noel Hammond," Diggs kept on. He looked at Hammond. "How do a police detective's shots of a crime scene just disappear?"

"I guess that's the question, isn't it?" I said, shooting my own pointed glare at our noble captain.

"I told you," Hammond said, his back up. "I wasn't working the case—I was just on vacation. I used to volunteer with the fire department in town whenever I was up. I responded when the call came in. It was just professional habit to take shots of the scene—they didn't have anything to do with the investigation."

Hammond bent down and picked up a clam shell from the deck, absently rubbing it between his thumb and forefinger before he whipped it into the ocean with a flick of his wrist.

"I left a week later," he continued. "My wife and I went back to Bridgeport, and I didn't really follow the case after that."

"That's bullshit," I said. "You never thought to check into it, considering the things you found at the site and the implications you must have known they had? They closed the books on the case after less than a month, saying it was coerced suicide with Isaac Payson to blame. Your photos would have proven them wrong."

Diggs intervened. "Take it easy, Sol. What exactly was in those photos that was so damning?"

I waited for Hammond to respond. When he didn't, I knelt and pulled a file folder from my backpack. Diggs studied the 8x10s I handed him.

"What is that?" he asked, when he came to the second photo.

I looked over his shoulder, though I knew exactly which one had prompted the question. All the photos were black and white, the light good and the images sharp. Hammond had taken more than his share of crime scene photos, if these were any indication. The one Diggs held was of a charred wooden door.

"Is that a...?"

"Padlock," I confirmed. "A *locked* padlock. On the outside of the door. Which means Payson's congregation couldn't exactly opt out of their little pact, since they probably didn't lock themselves in from the outside."

Suddenly, Hammond became inordinately interested in the landscape. He took a pack of Pall Malls from his pocket, then patted down his Carhartts until he found a lighter. Diggs continued studying the photos, but my attention had shifted back to Hammond. He offered me a cigarette, which I accepted. I waited.

Teeth clenched around his cigarette, he inhaled deeply, then spoke with the exhale. "So, what exactly do you want from me? You've got the pictures—you know as much as I do."

"I want to know how nobody ever heard about the padlock," I said.

"I didn't know they hadn't—as far as I knew, they had all the information I did. Wouldn't have been my place to fill them in on their own investigation."

Diggs looked up at that. His eyes slid from mine to Hammond's, his forehead furrowed. "You were a cop—isn't that what cops do? I don't care if it's not your case. This was a key piece of evidence that somehow got missed."

"You don't know what you're talking about," Hammond said. The hostility he'd barely subverted up to this point crept through. "I told you on that first phone call—this is ancient history. It doesn't have a damn thing to do with you."

"Doesn't have anything to do with me?" I took a step toward him. "Are you nuts? You think this is just idle curiosity on my part?" The frustration that had been building for the past three months tightened like a corkscrew in my chest. I advanced on Hammond until he was forced to take a step back. "The past twenty years, everything I've done, every move I've made—"

I stopped. Hammond stared at me with something dangerously close to pity, while Diggs held me back with a hand on my arm.

"Thirty-four people died in a locked chapel that day," I said. It took some effort to keep my voice even. "No one could do an effective tox screen because there was so little fluid left in the bodies to test, but they found traces of Scopolamine." Diggs raised an eyebrow in question. "From henbane," I explained, then hesitated. "My father grew it on the island—anyone would have had access."

"One person in particular comes to mind," Hammond said under his breath.

Our eyes met. I tried to read what he knew, thinking back to that day: my father and I racing through a forest of smoke, the church in flames, a pile of burned bodies and debris... And the cloaked man I'd only told my parents about, repeating the story until my mother insisted I stop, convincing me that he'd been a figment of my imagination; just more fallout from the Payson fire.

"You have a theory you want to share?" I pressed.

I thought for an instant that Hammond would tell me whatever it was he was holding back, but a second later he broke our stalemate and glanced at his watch.

"I need to get back."

When you're interviewing someone for a story, there inevitably comes a point when you hit a wall. At that point, no matter how much you plead, how often you rephrase the question or bribe or cajole, the interview is over; your source has dried up. After fifteen years as a reporter, I'd learned to recognize the look in someone's eyes when they hit that wall. That was the look in Hammond's eye. Short of handcuffs and water boarding, there wasn't a thing I could do to get him to stay put and keep talking.

I pushed away everything but the cold, clean air around me. Silence reigned on deck for another few seconds before Diggs spoke up.

"All right—so, we have the story... A very *small* part of the story, but it'll get us started. Now what?"

"Now, I find out what really happened," I said. Hammond wouldn't meet my eye. "And we start on the island."

The boat rocked on the waves. Payson Isle was closer to me than it had been since I was a teenager, fog blurring its edges, a study in gray landscape and blue-black sea. Wind-worn evergreens and birches lined the granite shore. From where I stood, just above sea level on a boat that was not my own, the island forest looked impenetrable.

I turned my back on Diggs and Hammond and wrapped my hands around the cold, steel boat railing. The water below was too dark and too deep to see anything in its depths. It made me think of sea monsters and shipwrecks and hauntings—all those things I'd left behind when I graduated high school and abandoned Littlehope. I was older now, ostensibly wiser, but it turned out those superstitions hadn't completely released their hold on me.

Diggs and I transferred Einstein and my things to the speedboat, and Hammond pulled up anchor and piloted away.

From the mooring, it took Diggs and me all of five minutes to reach Payson Isle. We tied the boat off at the neglected dock and climbed wooden steps that had been driven into the side of the island's rocky ledges back when my father still called this place home. It was an easier climb than I remembered, and a newly liberated Einstein scrambled past us. Another few yards of rocky terrain and we reached the top, where I found myself at the foot of an overgrown path leading into the woods.

I stood at the top of the cliff looking down at the ocean below. It was just after one o'clock. The sun appeared as a distant white haze behind the fog. Einstein reclaimed his position at my side, while Diggs forged ahead. I had the feeling that he wasn't satisfied with the answers he'd gotten from Hammond. More than that, though, I knew he was pissed that I hadn't told him sooner about the pictures—about the real reason I was here. I let him go, hoping he'd burn off some of his anger before our inevitable discussion about all the ways I'd shut him out of my life in the past few months.

The path steepened as we continued our journey. The boarding house that had served as home to the Payson congregation had been built at the highest point on the island, to take advantage of a million-dollar view of the ocean below. The old three-story barn that had doubled as the Payson church, on the other hand, was built with good old-fashioned common sense in mind. It sat in the valley below, where it had been sheltered from high winds and torrential rain for over one hundred years. Its placement, combined with heavy rain the day of the fire, was the only thing that had saved the entire island from going up like a tinderbox.

We were on a dark path, thick with sharp-needled pines and scrub-brush, when Diggs slowed his pace. I could tell he was cooling off when he took the time to hold branches out of the way for me. Einstein had his nose pressed to the back of my knee, and showed no inclination to stray. I was trying to see up ahead. Trying to focus. The deeper we got into the woods, the harder the simple act of breathing in and out became.

It wasn't until we reached the rusted, wrought-iron fence at the head of the boarding house path that our situation sank in. The gate couldn't have been six feet high—smaller than I remembered it as a child, but still impressive enough to inspire dread. It didn't close all the way anymore; rather than trying to force it from the mud and partially frozen ground, Diggs and I just squeezed through the opening.

Once we were on the path to the house, Diggs actually tried to start a conversation a couple of times. I wasn't in the mood for talking, though. I just wanted to move—to feel my legs, burn my lungs with the cold. Shut off my brain, even if it was only for a few minutes. There was a change in the air as we trudged up the steep incline—it seemed warmer, less biting somehow. I chalked it up to the physical exertion and the thick stand of pine and birch shielding us from the wind. Ignoring memories of ghost stories I'd been taunted with as a school kid (*There's a madman on Payson Isle who talks to God and lives with ghosts…*), I finally stopped to catch my breath.

I set my pack down and paused on the trail, doubling over at the waist with my hands on my knees. Diggs turned back when he realized I was no longer behind him. The bastard wasn't even winded.

"So, I guess you won't be joining me in the Littlehope Iron Man this year."

"Not unless you're carrying me."

"And you're smoking."

I met his gaze with a hard smile. "And apparently you're not. I'm thirty-three, Diggs. That's a decade older than you were when you first took me under your well-muscled wing at the *Trib*. And maybe while I've been married you've forgotten the places we went and the things we did before I ambled down the aisle, but I haven't. Don't play big brother with me."

My words hit their mark. Diggs' blue eyes flashed and his strong jaw tensed as he worked to recover his cool. He closed the distance between us. "I haven't forgotten a thing, ace," he said quietly. There was something dangerous about the way he looked at me. Despite the cold, I felt my blood begin to warm. I looked away, a dozen memories running in a loop through my mind. Almost none of them were fit for underage viewers.

As though sensing my train of thought, Diggs took a step back. "Hammond's pictures—those are the reason you went off the reservation three months ago?" he asked. "The reason you and Michael hit the skids?"

"Michael and I hit the skids because he was sleeping with every doe-eyed coed in greater Boston."

"Okay," he conceded. A hint of anger slid across his face. Diggs always hated Michael. "But the other stuff—the not sleeping and the not eating and the...thing I'm not supposed to talk about. That was because of the pictures?"

"I don't want to do this now."

"But you know we're gonna do it sometime, right? Come on, Solomon. Twenty-three years, and nobody ever hears about a fairly obvious padlock on the scene of one of the biggest tragedies in Maine history? I'm not a paranoid man, but if that doesn't scream conspiracy, I don't know what does."

I pulled out one of the cigarettes Hammond had grudgingly loaned me before he left, lit it, and inhaled deeply. Diggs was watching me.

"We should get up there," I said, avoiding his eye. "I don't want to waste any more daylight." I shouldered my pack and hit the trail. I could practically feel the frustration rolling off him when I left him behind. We walked on in silence.

3

IT WAS ROUGH GOING from there, in every way. The road leading up to the house was no more than a swath cut through the trees, buried beneath years of fallen branches, new tree growth, mud, and ice. Diggs fell behind after our exchange, either brooding himself or giving me space to do the same. I pushed his questions to the back of my mind and focused on my surroundings.

Like most Maine islands, Payson Isle is predominantly granite, the source of the original settlers' livelihoods as early as the 1820s. Back then, the islands of Maine were worlds unto themselves, complete with bars, bowling alleys, and dance halls. When the market for granite was displaced by cheaper, more accessible concrete, those same islands became ghost towns. Isaac Payson's grandfather bought the eight-hundred-acre island for the grand sum of six dollars and twenty cents, back in 1928. He abandoned the granite quarry on one end of the island, kept up a couple of outbuildings for hired hands, and turned the place into a breeding farm for prize-winning quarter horses.

I was so caught up in the history of the place that I didn't notice that the trail had gotten darker, the forest quieter. Something stopped me mid-step. A whisper of remembrance curled like a ribbon of smoke around my throat.

"Were Jack's magic beans yellow or green?"

A greenhouse that smells like soil and sunlight. My father: red hair, like mine. Quick wit, clear eyes. And me, always with the questions.

"Maybe they were both magic," he suggests.

"They could have been black beans. Or lentils. Jesus didn't believe in magic, you know. Only miracles," I tell him.

"Sometimes miracles are magic. Sometimes magic is a miracle." I roll my eyes. They are green, like my mother's. I know this only from the pictures in our room—at six years old, I have no memories of her. At six years old, my world is still my father. The church. This island.

"You can't have both," I say. "You have to choose. Isaac says magic is a trick of the devil. Miracles are the work of God."

He puts his arm around my shoulders and pulls me close. My hands are dirty, my jeans wet from kneeling in soil all morning. My father smells like he always smells—like hard work and damp earth and laughter and home-baked bread. My father smells like home.

"I think you are magic," he whispers to me. It is a secret, I know. "And a miracle. Not even Isaac can change my mind on that one, baby. You'll always be my magic bean."

"Solomon? You okay?"

The boarding house stood just twenty yards from us, but I was focused on the overgrown path at my feet. Diggs had rejoined me somewhere along the line. I'd forgotten about my cigarette, the ash now almost as long as the remaining filter.

"What is it?" he asked.

I indicated the path. "That's the… That's where he died."

"The greenhouse?"

I nodded. Like that, the anger was gone from Diggs' eyes.

"We could go back to my place. Come here tomorrow instead if you want."

I tried smiling, but my lips were dry and stuck to my teeth. "Will something change between now and then?"

"Probably not," he conceded.

"Then I guess we should do it now. If I can't even get in the house without losing it, what are the chances I'll be able to spend all day every day putting the pieces together out here?"

I whistled for Einstein, who'd decided it was a great time to tour the grounds. We were at the top of the island. In the valley below, I could just make out the remains of the burned-out Payson Church. That would have to come later, though—for now, I focused on the massive old boarding house that I had once called home. I had to start somewhere.

The original boarding house was a simple three-story saltbox design, with a one-story ell that members of the church had added on the north side. The windows were boarded with sheets of weathered plywood, and the white house paint had long since peeled away, leaving bare clapboards gone gray with age.

Before we set foot inside, Diggs and I teamed up to remove the plywood from the downstairs windows. He photographed the perimeter. I tossed a stick for Einstein. Eventually, we ran out of reasons not to go inside.

I fished the key the lawyer had presented to me three months earlier from my backpack and went to the side of the ell, leading the way to the kitchen entrance. The granite step leading up was split down the center from too many seasons of extremes, slick with moss and rain. I stood to the side and jammed the key in the old, rusted lock, jiggling it back and forth until it finally clicked.

I glanced at Diggs before I stepped past the threshold. "You want to go first?" I asked.

"I could." There wasn't a lot of confidence behind that statement.

"Forget it. Just be prepared to get out of the way if any hobgoblins jump out at us."

"If any hobgoblins jump out at us, the last thing you'll have to worry about is me getting out of the way, ace. Trust me."

I gave him a shaky smile, wet my lips, and gave the thick, oak door a final push.

Despite having removed plywood from the large window over the kitchen sink, decades of grime ensured that little light made its way inside. Diggs and I stood in the entryway squinting as our eyes adjusted to the dim room. Faded linoleum flooring had curled up at the edges, the vintage 1970s pattern obscured by layers of grime.

"Brady Bunch meets Amityville Horror," Diggs said. "Nice."

"Payson redid the kitchen in '76, when he first started the church," I told him, recalling another of the litany of random facts I'd learned about the Paysons over the years. "What you're seeing was *haute couture* during the Carter administration."

We were whispering. Einstein had taken off yet again, but I could hear him barking in the distance—which meant in all likelihood he was tormenting the island squirrels. I kept the door open for him to come and go as he pleased and walked deeper into the kitchen. There were rodent droppings and a fossilized mouse in the double sink, and the sideboard looked like it could crawl away of its own free will. I moved on, past the kitchen and through a narrow corridor with a steep staircase off to one side.

The cold settled somewhere deeper than my bones, but the chill I felt had nothing to do with the weather. I stood at the grand arch that opened into the Payson meeting room. This was where it all began, and two and a half decades hadn't done much to brighten the bizarre living area at the heart of the Payson boarding home.

A shaft of light cut through the dirt on two picture windows, a door centered between them. I snapped a couple of pictures, then Diggs went over to pry one of the windows open and get some air flowing. Six picnic tables dominated the expansive room, placed in pairs end to end. An antique hutch against one wall had fallen victim to dry rot, its shelves buckled and its contents—mismatched dishes of all shape and size—scattered on the floor.

"You think this is really how they left it?" I asked.

Diggs looked over his shoulder at me. He had one foot up on the windowsill for leverage, trying to drag the swollen old pane up.

"I don't know. If anyone has been here in the past twenty years, they sure as hell were lacking in the housekeeping department."

"Malcolm Payson's lawyer said he didn't let anyone in," I said. "Once the investigation was closed, he hired my father to watch the place. I doubt Dad ever came here after everybody was gone, though."

"What about after your father died? Who watched the place once Adam was gone?"

He finally got the window up with a screech of wood against wood that set my teeth on edge.

"Malcolm paid some of the local fishermen to keep an eye out—paid them well, too, from what I heard," I said. "They took the job seriously. Guns and ammo have never been in short supply around here; you know that."

"So, no keggers, make-out parties, or Ouija fests on the hallowed grounds?"

I looked around. No beer bottles, cigarette butts, used condoms. Not so much as a stray Little Debbie wrapper.

"Doesn't look that way."

Diggs abandoned the window and came to stand beside me, surveying the room. "So, this is where you lived. For how long again?"

"Nine years." It felt stranger than I'd expected to be back, trying to reconcile everything I'd known with the reality of what it was now. "I would've been here a lot longer if my mother hadn't come out and dragged me back to civilization."

"That's one way of looking at it."

I looked up when I realized he was staring at me. "And what's the other way of looking at it?"

"That your mother got you out of here before the shit hit the fan. If she hadn't, you and your father would have died along with everybody else."

I didn't have a response for that. I thought back to those years on the island with my father—the best years of my childhood, in most ways. Diggs wouldn't understand that, though. Hell, *I* didn't understand that. Before he started psychoanalyzing my early years, I went off in another direction.

"There are cabins here, too—half a dozen or so, I think,

on the other side of the island. The families in the church stayed there. Isaac shared the top floor of this house with his wife and kids." I went through the house in my mind, trying to remember the layout. "My father was the only man who lived here at the house, besides Isaac. The rest of the bedrooms were for the single women and their children."

Diggs nodded. I knew what he was thinking: Isaac had set it up so he'd have ready access to any of the women or children he wanted, on any given night. I didn't say anything. I wondered what kind of salacious hell he thought I'd lived through out here, before my mother swooped in and took me to the mainland.

While I went through the meeting room, Diggs excused himself to take a tour of the grounds. He said it was to get a look at the place, but I knew he was just giving me time to adjust to my haunted homestead. Either way, I appreciated the gesture. Without Diggs and Einstein on my heels, I continued exploring.

Isaac and his wife had been responsible for the interior decorating, though they could have used some pointers from the good folks at HGTV. There was the standard, Western ideal of Christ with lamb in his arms, brown eyes soft and forgiving, and another of the same Christ, a halo just visible through flecks of mold and mildew. A two-foot-tall, moth-eaten satin cross embroidered in gold with the words "Jesus Saves" hung by the door. Then, there were Isaac's personal touches: oil paintings done by the preacher himself, mounted in handmade frames throughout the house.

The painting above the fireplace was five feet across and maybe three feet high. I could remember standing in this spot when I was a kid, mesmerized by the scene Isaac had created: an ethereal Christ on the cross, a Mona Lisa smile on his wasted face, while in the background a thousand warriors burned. Their bodies were twisted and bloody, their eyes black with agony. The frame was partially rotted away, and the painting itself was stained in places and barely visible in others. It didn't matter, though—I still remembered every grotesque detail. Long before the fire, it had been the centerpiece in more than one childhood nightmare.

Isaac's twisted artistic sensibilities had also been the inspiration for the church's primary source of income. There were examples of these in the meeting room as well, though I wasn't nearly as tickled at sight of the marionettes as I'd once been. The adults in the church worked together to make the handcrafted angels, then sold them on the mainland at local shops and craft fairs.

One of the angels lay on the ground just a few feet from the fireplace. It was all but dust, the strings disintegrated, clothing and wings eaten away. Now, just a naked wooden body and a head with faded but strangely mesmerizing blue eyes were all that remained.

Before I could stash the doll from hell somewhere where the blue eyes would quit following me, there was a commotion outside. I knew something was up because Einstein was barking like a rabid banshee—the desperate, high-pitched bark usually reserved for creepy neighbors or suspicious-looking postal workers. I narrowly missed colliding with Diggs on my way out the door.

"I found something. Bring your camera."

He looked a little green around the gills, so I did as I was told, following him to the edge of the tree line behind the house. He'd tied a very unhappy Einstein to a birch nearby. At sight of me, my mutt howled in protest, nearly strangling himself to get free.

A moment later, I understood why Diggs had needed him out of the way.

The smell hit first—damp and sickly sweet, like meat long past its expiration date. I followed my nose to a mid-sized wooden box that definitely hadn't been there when we'd walked the grounds just half an hour before. The top had been removed. I peered inside, where a bloody mass swarming with flies was nestled in newspaper. I nudged the box with my foot. Once the flies had cleared and I wrapped my brain around what it was, my stomach turned.

"I think it's a lamb," Diggs said.

"A lamb's head, actually," I said. I looked around, but saw neither hide nor hair of the rest of the carcass. "Young, by the look of it—maybe newborn. Where the hell did it come from? Einstein ran the grounds up and down when we first got here—he would have caught the scent the second we passed the gate."

"It certainly begs the question, doesn't it?"

I knelt, the wet ground soaking through my denim-clad knees. Diggs stood with his head turned away, his arms crossed over his chest. Since he was being no help, I told him to go set Einstein loose before the mutt had a complete breakdown.

"There's something in its mouth," I called after him.

After my mother took me away from Payson Isle, she settled in Littlehope as the county physician. I was her not-so-eager assistant on more than one midnight call to patch up drunken fishermen or their wayward wives. A lamb's head, regardless of the shape it was in, didn't hold a candle to some of the things I'd seen by the time I was thirteen.

"How can you touch that thing?" Diggs called to me with a grimace.

"I'm not touching it. I'm just poking it a little."

Einstein raced to my side as soon as he was free. Diggs looked mildly annoyed, but I just gave the one order Stein knows by heart.

"Leave it."

The dog's tail dropped. His grin vanished. Dejected, he turned around, walked a few paces, and sat down. Despite everything, I could tell Diggs was impressed. I couldn't really take the credit, since Michael was the one who trained him.

Diggs went to stand beside Einstein as I continued my exam.

"Its neck was cut straight through—this is a clean cut, no ragged edges. No hesitation with the kerf marks."

"And you know this because…?"

"Research for a story I did a while back. I guess it's safe to assume this wasn't a natural death."

I turned the head over with a nearby stick. Underneath, maggots squirmed rice-white bodies along the exposed bone and viscera.

"Einstein was barking when we were inside," I recalled. "Someone must've left it here then."

Diggs finally ventured closer. "That's the only theory I could come up with. Which means whoever it was is probably still here. Or they haven't gone far." He hesitated. "I could go after them."

"And do what, exactly? Skewer them with your rapier wit?"

He shrugged, conceding the point easily.

"Anyway, it's probably just some local idiot playing a prank," I said. It was a fairly disgusting one, even by Littlehope standards. I wasn't ready to consider the alternative, though. "If you go after them, it could escalate—let's just let it be for now."

I returned my attention to the box at my feet. The lamb's eyes were open, with a milky film over them. I prodded at the tiny teeth with my trusty stick in an attempt to dislodge whatever was stuffed in the mouth.

"I think it's the heart."

"Christ," Diggs said. "You sure?"

"I wasn't exactly an all-star in biology at Wellesley, but I can see the chambers. It looks about the right size, too."

Diggs had gone quiet again, but finally he cleared his throat. I looked up to find him staring at me, his jaw set.

"What?"

"What the hell's going on?"

I didn't like his tone, but I couldn't necessarily blame him for it. "What do you mean?"

"I mean, *What the hell is going on?* You lost a baby not three months ago, your marriage just fell apart, and now you're on an island where thirty-four people burned to death and your father hanged himself over a bed of tulips. And now I find out that the story we've been given for twenty years about the fire that killed them was all lies, and you frankly don't seem all that surprised. And there's a fucking *lamb's head,*" his voice rose, "that's obviously been left by someone who's not completely in their right mind. So, I'll ask one more time before I turn around and go back to the mainland without you… What the hell is going on, Solomon?"

He'd come closer during his tirade. Einstein growled. The temperature was cooling as shadows grew longer and the day got later. I stared at the ground, thinking about everything he'd said. Bit my index fingernail, until I remembered that I'd stopped biting my nails years ago.

"My father wasn't with me that morning."

Diggs looked confused. "What morning?"

"The morning of the fire," I said. Impatience tinged my words. "When the Payson Church burned to the ground and thirty-four people burned with it. We spent the night before at a hotel…"

"For your birthday," he nodded. "I remember the story—it was your father's alibi."

I shook my head. I felt tears starting, much to my horror, and brushed them away roughly before Diggs could comment. "The phone rang in the night, or early morning—it was still dark outside. It woke me up."

I could see it all, suddenly: the hotel room my father had booked on the mainland so we could spend my birthday together, with the twin beds and the carpeting and the color TV bigger than any I'd seen before. We made homemade pizza in the little kitchenette. And then, deep in the night, came a phone call that woke me from a sound sleep. My father's voice had been low, uncharacteristically strained, when he spoke with whoever was on the other end of the line.

"So, who was it? Who called?" Diggs prompted when I didn't continue the story.

"I don't know—he wouldn't tell me. But he made me promise never to tell anyone that he'd left me alone that night. And that was it. I was at the hotel alone that whole morning."

I knelt and turned my attention back to the carnage at my feet, if only for something to keep me from bursting into tears—which would have been way worse than a decapitated lamb, as far as I was concerned. Diggs crouched beside me. He didn't touch me, and his voice held no pity when he spoke again.

"You thought he started the fire," he said. "You've thought it ever since that day."

"No," I said quickly, remembering the man who had chased me through the woods that day. "Not at first," I admitted. "Later, once I started looking into it more, I knew the Payson fire wasn't what they said… Once I started studying cults and cult behavior, I knew the Paysons didn't fit the profile. I knew mass suicide didn't make sense for who they were and what they believed."

"And now that you have proof someone else started the fire?"

I kept my eyes focused on the ground, my jaw clenched tight while I pulled myself together. Diggs touched my arm, but I shrugged him away. Cleared my throat.

"Whether it was my father or it wasn't, I need to know the truth. I can't spend the rest of my life wondering." If I was going to tell him about my pursuer on the island that day, now would be the time. *They'll put you away if you tell them what you saw—only crazy little girls think men in black cloaks are chasing them.* I heard my mother's voice, remembered her hard green eyes intent on mine. I kept quiet.

Diggs straightened and offered his hand. After a moment's hesitation, I took it and let him pull me up. When we were eye to eye again, his lips curled up in a determined smile.

"Okay, then," he said.

"Okay then, what?"

"Okay then, let's solve this thing. But first, stop playing with the gory fucking disembodied head, and come back to the mainland with me. You look like you haven't slept in weeks, and I've got deadlines to meet."

"And then…?"

"And then, we start doing the research. Go back in time, and figure out what the hell happened out here in the month or so before the fire that got thirty-four people killed and destroyed your father's life. And, just as interestingly, how the evidence that it was murder mysteriously vanished from a very public crime scene and no one ever noticed."

I managed a smile. "That easy, huh? Just go back in time."

He wrapped his arm around my shoulders and pulled me closer as we walked back up the path to the house.

"Easy as falling off a log. Just stick with me, kid, and we'll have this thing solved by the time summer traffic picks up."

If only it had been that simple.

JULY 20, 1990

THEY COME TO THE CHURCH in the night, hidden in a canoe beneath old blankets and a catch of fish whose oils soak through and seep into Rebecca's long, dark hair, so that for days afterward she reeks of it. Her son shifts beneath her. His hip is a sharp *v* in Rebecca's side, and she knows her weight on top of him must be stifling on this warm night. Still, the boy doesn't complain.

Their guide sits in the bow of the canoe, paddling in long, experienced strokes through the still ocean water. He is a tall, quiet redhead whom Rebecca has never met before, though Reverend Payson has told her about him. Adam, like the first man. Adam, who tends the church garden and never speaks of his past; whose daughter was recently taken from him, to live on the mainland with her mother. Rebecca touches her son's soft dark hair, unable to comprehend being parted from him that way.

When they reach shore, Adam flashes a beam of light into the woods. Though she has been warned against doing so, Rebecca moves the blanket just enough to see what's happening when she feels the craft coming aground. At Adam's signal, another man comes out into the open and helps him drag the canoe onto the shore.

"Stay where you are," Adam tells her. "Someone could be watching from the water. We'll carry the canoe into the woods, then you can get out."

Two more men appear, the four of them lifting the canoe like pallbearers. Rebecca kisses her son's head and he squirms. He mutters something that she can't make out, and then they wait in silence for the cover of trees to guarantee their safety.

Once they are in the woods, the men put the boat down and Adam helps mother and son to their feet. Zion, her boy, remains serious and silent, his eyes occasionally meeting his mother's, seeking reassurance. Though other boys might be self-conscious about being too close to their mothers at this age, Zion is not. At twelve years old, he has no reservations about standing with his arm around her, absorbing his new surroundings. He doesn't seem afraid. There have been many nights worse than this, and the relative calm of the strangers around them is a welcome change from the unpredictable ire of the men they have known.

And so they follow, Adam and one of the others leading while the remaining two trail behind. There is no moon, the night heavy with the wet heat of July, black as the bottom of a well. One of the men at their right flank shines a flashlight, though Rebecca and Zion are the only ones who need it. She hears the stumbling stealth of island deer in the distance, and draws comfort from the familiar sound.

They reach the barn. Rebecca has never seen it, but the Reverend has told her stories of this sacred space in the woods, blessed by God himself. She follows the men, taking a step up as the flashlight gives a fragmented shadow-story of the building. Inside, there is the sweet smell of hay, tinged with an underlying dampness inevitable in these old structures. Their footsteps echo against the wooden floorboards, and Zion's hand tightens in hers as they approach the stairs.

There is a faint golden glow coming from above, and the audible murmur of a near-silent mass. The trapdoor to the second floor stands open; they climb through to find themselves in the Payson chapel. The entire congregation is there, standing, facing them—families Rebecca has known from Littlehope who gave up their lives on the mainland to come here. Women, eyes down-turned, hold children who gaze at the newcomers without fear. Men stand beside their wives, their heads bowed as Rebecca passes. Each member of the congregation holds a candle; the entire scene is bathed in an ethereal light. Rebecca squeezes Zion's hand and he looks up at her. All she can see are those big eyes and she smiles, nods, and feels him relax.

The trapdoor they've come through is at the back of the chapel. As she and Zion follow the two men down the center aisle, the congregation turns and is seated. Rebecca thinks of her wedding: of her expectations before the day came, the vague hope of flowers and ceremony. If she had had her way, it would have been like this. It would have had weight, and ritual. If it had meant something then, perhaps it might mean more now.

A large wooden tub stands at the front of the chapel. Rebecca stops moving, and Zion comes to a halt beside her. Adam turns and nods to her.

"It's all right. You're safe here. Isaac will come soon."

Shadows play along the wooden walls. When Rebecca and Zion reach the end of the aisle, the four men leave them standing at the tub. No one speaks; no one moves—least of all Rebecca and her only child. One of the women in the front row comes to stand before her. The woman's hair is long and braided, and she wears an ankle-length floral dress that hangs like a sack on her thin frame. Rebecca wears old jeans and a flannel shirt that used to be her husband's. The thin woman offers a shy smile, and her fingers go to the buttons of Rebecca's shirt with clear trepidation.

Rebecca flinches. Her hand flies up with a will of its own, pushing the stranger away.

And then she hears him.

" 'The wilderness and the solitary place shall be glad for them, and the desert shall rejoice, and blossom as the rose. It shall blossom abundantly, and rejoice with joy and singing. The glory of Lebanon will be given to it, the excellency of Carmel and Sharon, they will see the glory of the Lord and the excellency of our God.' "

In the enclosed space, his voice carries, floats down, wraps around her. He comes closer, down the aisle, his silver hair aglow in the candlelight. He wears a flowing white robe, and he makes a single gesture, a sweep of his graceful hand. The woman beside Rebecca steps away, her head bowed.

" 'Strengthen ye the weak hands. Confirm the feeble knees. Say to them that are of a fearful heart—" his voice rises rather than softens as he approaches, and it feels as though an electrical current is traveling beneath her skin. "Be strong, fear not. Behold, your God will come with vengeance, with recompense. He will come, and he will save you.' "

He takes another step toward her. Rebecca recognizes that others are present, but they have become unimportant. The flame from the Reverend's candle dances so close that it burns a kiss into her arm. He holds it aside and instantly someone appears to take it away, as Isaac's fingers find the buttons of Rebecca's shirt. His eyes, a dazzling blue above high-cut cheekbones, never leave hers as he undresses her.

" 'Then the eyes of the blind shall be opened, and the ears of the deaf shall be unstopped. Then shall the lame man leap as a hart, and the tongue of the dumb shall sing. For in the wilderness shall waters break out, and streams in the desert. And the parched ground shall become a pool.' "

He slips the shirt from her shoulders. Her breasts feel heavy to her, cumbersome. Reverend Payson is tall like she is, never looking at her but never looking away. He kneels to unbutton her jeans, and she knows that Zion is watching this. There is an instant of resistance when Rebecca tries to remember why this is wrong, why this should be causing shame, but all she feels is warmth and love and a safety she hasn't known in years.

" '...and the thirsty land springs of water. In the habitation of dragons, where each lay, shall be grass with reeds and rushes.' "

She is completely naked now. They take Zion from her, and the boy follows two of the women to the pews. Rebecca sees him in her periphery, but for the first time since his birth, she can't focus on her son. Using a stepstool to climb over the edge of the tub, she steps into lukewarm water that swirls around her feet, up her legs, in tideless swells. The Reverend joins her, still wearing his robe. It billows around him, touching Rebecca's thigh and setting fire to it. Scorching it clean. He motions for her to kneel.

" 'And a highway shall be there, and it shall be called the way of holiness. And the wayfaring men, though fools, shall not err therein.' "

When she goes under, his voice is still above her, swimming around her, welcoming her to this new life.

" 'No lion shall be there, no ravenous beast will be found there, and the redeemed shall walk there.' " His voice rises again as she comes up for air, his fingers clenched so hard in her hair that it pulls at the sensitive skin at the back of her neck. The pain paints everything in vivid color.

" 'The ransomed of the Lord shall come to Zion with songs and everlasting joy upon their heads. They shall obtain joy and gladness, and sorrow and sighing shall flee away.' "

Isaac kneels in the water beside her, his robe against her wet, naked body. She falls into the feel of his lips on her forehead.

"Welcome home, Rebecca."

4

WHEN WE RETURNED to the mainland that night, Diggs gave me a brief tour of his house-in-progress—a three-bedroom cape overlooking the ocean, with cedar shingles neatly stacked on the lawn, a 52-inch plasma TV, and no furniture to speak of. He had work to do at the paper, but he'd generously strayed from his usual diet of roots and berries and stocked the fridge with an approximation of actual, human food: free-range chicken dogs and homegrown tater tots, with an overwhelming supply of organic veggies to round things out. I even found Ben & Jerry's "Everything But The…" in the freezer.

God bless Diggs.

My bedroom was apparently the only room Diggs had seen fit to furnish; it came complete with a four-poster bed, mismatched bureaus, and even a dog bed in the corner for Einstein. I put away my things, then spent half an hour with Diggs' top-of-the-line shower massage drilling holes in my back before I felt ready to rejoin the land of the living. I toweled off, changed into sweats, and went in search of something to eat.

Sometime between getting home and emerging from the shower, dusk had given way to a very dark night outside. Inside wasn't much better, with only a dim lamp in the living room to light my way.

I called for Einstein. No response. Those little hairs at the back of my neck stood on end. A door opened and closed on the other side of the house.

"Diggs?"

Nothing.

I went for my cell phone with the events of the past twelve hours racing through my head: Joe Ashmont's threats, Noel Hammond's reticence, the bloodied lamb's head on the island. I was dialing Diggs when Einstein came racing toward me from down the hall, tail wagging, goofy terrier grin firmly in place.

He didn't seem traumatized, at least.

A moment later, I realized *why* he didn't seem traumatized.

Not far behind him, a tall, dark-haired stranger followed. He had the lean build of an athlete who trained hard and lived well, his jeans cut just right and his charcoal turtleneck setting off his dark eyes beautifully.

I blinked once or twice, just in case I was hallucinating. The stranger didn't disappear. My hand flew to my hair, by now drying in all the wrong ways.

"You must be Erin," he said. He nodded toward Einstein. "Sorry—he found his way to my room, and I didn't have the heart to turn him out."

He had one of those low, even voices designed for whispering sweet nothings, complete with a faint accent—possibly Cuban, maybe Mexican. Broad shoulders. Great eyes. I forced myself to focus.

"Your room?" I asked.

"Diggs didn't tell you?" He didn't look that surprised, all things considered. "I was supposed to be gone for a few days, but my plans changed at the last minute. I'm sure he just figured he'd have a week with you all to himself before I came back on the scene."

"Yeah, I'm sure." My brain was having an unusually hard time connecting the dots. "So... I'm sorry—you live here?"

"Just for the moment—Diggs is letting me crash in the other spare room while I take care of some family stuff." He took a step closer. The light did nothing to diminish his good looks—if anything, he looked better. My decision to go braless seemed like an epic miscalculation.

"You let your hair grow out," he noted. "It looks good—I always thought you'd look pretty with longer hair."

Surreal wasn't a strong enough word for the day I was having. I searched through the faces of old classmates I'd known in Littlehope, but somehow I couldn't imagine any of the redneck hooligans I'd matriculated with magically turning into this.

"You don't remember me," he said. I shook my head, too surprised to bother with tact. "I'm Jack Juarez—I used to spend summers out here. Matt Perkins' nephew?"

Matt Perkins: the local constable. Now I remembered him—an awkward, lanky boy a couple of years older than me, who used to cruise around town in Constable Perkins' police car all summer long.

"Wow. You got...taller," I said. And broader. And... gorgeous.

"Yeah, well—fifteen years will do that for a man, I guess. Anyway, I didn't mean to disturb you—I was just going to make some dinner. Have you eaten?"

I told him I had not.

He magically produced a bottle of merlot from his room, and took over the kitchen. I squelched a minor panic attack at the realization that a gorgeous man was making me dinner two weeks after my divorce had been finalized, in the home of the man who had been my mentor-slash-best friend-slash-...whatever else Diggs and I had been over the years, while the rest of my life was basically falling to pieces. I took a breath, got a grip, and went to find my bra.

While Jack cooked, I went to my room and tried on two skirts and three pairs of jeans before settling on slightly snug denim. Not that I expected anything to happen, of course... Still, a girl likes to look her best. When I emerged, the house smelled of sautéing garlic and vegetables. Jack had set the lopsided dining room table with mismatched plates and two very full glasses of wine.

The wine worked its magic after an awkward start; before long we were recounting experiences I hadn't even realized we had shared. We finished dinner and did the dishes together, and by the time we got around to the present I'd changed back into yoga pants and an old Wellesley sweatshirt. Jack was down to bare feet, jeans, and a t-shirt. We sat on the floor in front of Diggs' fireplace with Einstein snoring between us. It was nearly midnight.

"So, enough about the good old days," I said. "What do you do now? You said you live in D.C...?"

He nodded. He was stretched out on the floor, leaning back on his elbows. Shadows from the fire played across his features, light chasing dark.

"Yeah." He looked a little self-conscious. "I work for the FBI."

I couldn't tell whether or not he was kidding. "As in Federal Bureau of...?"

"The one and only. I'm taking some personal time right now, but I'll be going back once I have things figured out here." I waited for him to elaborate. "My uncle's not doing well—I came back to try and give him a hand."

"I'm sorry to hear that." Something about the way his eyes slid from mine suggested this might not be the whole truth. Interesting. "So… A Fed. You must have some great stories."

I curled up next to Einstein, laying my chin on his body so I could get a better look at the man across from me. It occurred to me that I was drunk. And recently single. And Diggs could be home any second now.

"A few," Jack said. "I'm mostly just a cop, though. A cop for the government—more red tape, better benefits."

"What division are you in?"

"Homicide."

I wasn't sure how to respond to that. The reporter in me came up with two dozen questions and at least three stories to pitch to editors I knew in the business. One-on-one with a bottle of wine and a gorgeous homicide agent—wasn't that how most Pulitzer prize-winning stories began?

Jack tipped his head back, checking the time on a wall clock behind us. "Diggs will be back soon—we should turn in. I'm sure you have a big day tomorrow."

I nodded. Closed my eyes. Stories and pitches and Pulitzer speeches faded. An image of Michael flashed through my mind. I wondered if my ex-husband was alone tonight. For the last two weeks before I left, though the divorce was final, we'd still lived together. Still slept together. I had still kissed him goodnight, and we'd made love for the last time less than twenty-four hours ago. My head spun, lying on the floor in Diggs' half-finished home with a man I'd spoken no more than two sentences to before tonight.

When I opened my eyes, Jack was closer. He studied me intently.

"Are you all right?"

"Just tired," I told him. "I'm gonna take Stein out one last time and hit the hay. See you in the morning?"

His eyes remained on mine. I didn't know much about him so far, but he didn't seem happy. Or maybe I was just projecting. For a second I thought he might kiss me, but the moment passed. He stood. Extended his hand and helped me to my feet, where I swayed with his hand still in mine.

"Thank you for the company," he said.

Things went still for a moment. "My pleasure."

He stepped back. "Sleep well, Erin. See you tomorrow."

He went his way. I walked the dog.

5

ONCE EINSTEIN HAD BEEN WALKED and we were curled up together in my new bed, sleep proved more elusive than I'd expected. I went over the events of the day ad nauseam. The interview with Noel Hammond had been less than rewarding. I don't know what I'd been hoping for, but it was something along the lines of, 'Sorry I held out on you all these years—Colonel Mustard did it in the chapel with a tiki torch and a bottle of lighter fluid. And, oh yeah, here's why.'

Clearly, that wasn't going to happen. The Payson house seemed like a bigger project than I could realistically handle, and the fact that I was now proud owner of an island and all its ghosts was not comforting. I got out of bed. Paced the floor. Got dressed again, snapped the leash to Einstein's collar, and headed out.

It was one-thirty in the morning, and Diggs wasn't home yet.

Once I was outside, there was no question where I was headed—the place that had been my refuge in Littlehope even as a teen: the *Trib*. My breath came in puffs of cold white air in the darkness. The unpaved road leading into

Diggs' place was at least half a mile long, with no neighbors along the way. He'd purchased the land cheap from an old neighbor of his father's a couple of years before—driven into seclusion, I suspected, because his third marriage had gone sour and this was Diggs' version of a new, monastic leaf.

Evergreens stood in black silhouette against a deep blue night sky, the moon and a thousand stars lighting my way into town. Coyotes howled in the distance. Einstein growled but stuck close. A steady chorus of frogs trilled froggily; a dog barked somewhere nearby. Einstein stopped moving and growled again.

"No fair freaking out the city girl, Stein," I said.

He looked at me and thumped his tail. We resumed our trek.

Michael had never visited Littlehope. I always told him he would hate it, and he took me at my word. Raised in Brooklyn by a widowed mother with an overactive social conscience, Michael hummed the dueling banjos bit from "Deliverance" every time we headed to the Hamptons for the weekend. No, my ex-husband would not be a fan of Littlehope.

Behind me, Diggs' motion-sensitive porch light had gone out some time ago. There was no sign of lights up ahead, either; I was starting to question the wisdom of a midnight stroll, even in the relative safety of Littlehope. The coyotes took up their call once more—one would begin, another would join in, a third would answer. Einstein stopped moving, his tail low, his body tensed. When he growled this time, it came from deep in his chest.

Something moved in the underbrush to our left. Einstein lunged, coming up short at the end of his leash.

"Okay, this is less fun now." I dragged the dog along

until he was forced to walk beside me, took the cell phone from my pocket, and hit the first number on speed dial.

"You should be sleeping," Diggs said, without so much as a howdy do.

"Ditto. I'm not tired." I kept my eyes straight ahead and upped our pace to just shy of a jog, though I'd be damned if I'd let Diggs know what a pansy I'd become since moving to the big city. "I thought I'd stop by the office and try to get some work done, since your house is a little crowded."

There was a pause on the line. "Shit. I'm sorry about that—he was supposed to be out of town for a couple of weeks."

"Don't worry about it. We had dinner—it was kind of nice."

"Was it, now?"

"Don't start. I was wondering how your contacts are around here."

A branch snapped about ten yards behind me. Einstein stopped again. Diggs was talking, but my heart was thumping too loudly to hear him; I had to ask him to repeat himself.

"Where are you?" he asked.

"On your road, I think—it's hard to tell without a smoggy skyline to light the way. Einstein's a little freaked out."

"You're walking?"

"You're the one who said I should get back in shape."

He called me a pain in the ass and said he would come pick me up. Out of obligation, I argued the point for ten seconds before I agreed that a late-night drive might not be such a bad idea. By the time I hung up, I felt better for having called, but much, much worse for the time I would have to wait until he arrived.

Another branch snapped, this one closer.

Einstein was on high alert now. All the night sounds had gone silent—no more frogs, no more crickets, no more coyotes. Nothing but Einstein's growls and my hastened breathing. And then, so quiet it was almost undetectable, I heard it: the whisper of a body crouching low to the ground, pushing through dense brush.

The leash went taut as Einstein strained forward. My heart was pounding, blood rushing in my ears. Somehow in the midst of everything I got turned around; when the figure lurking in the shadows finally appeared, he came in from the right. For a split second I just stood there stupidly, waiting for someone to come from the direction I'd been expecting.

I didn't recognize him at first. Matt Perkins had been fifteen years younger when I'd seen him last, and since that time he had aged a lifetime. The former Littlehope constable had always been an athletic man—it was a surprisingly physical job, and he had taken the role seriously. Now, he was wiry and much thinner than I remembered him, his stride hindered by an obvious limp. Despite any physical infirmity, he came up on us fast and stood too close, his eyes searching mine in the darkness. Einstein growled furiously while I held tight to his leash.

"I dreamed you," Perkins said to me. I shined my flashlight at him. He blinked in the glare. His hair was white and his pupils were too large, his face slack on one side as though he had suffered a stroke in recent years.

I took a step back. "Constable Perkins?"

"I dreamed you. I dream people, and they arrive. I dreamed you, and wished that I hadn't. No one invited you back."

He closed the distance and kept coming, ignoring Einstein, until we were standing close enough to touch.

"I need you to take a step back—you're upsetting my dog."

"Your dog will die like a dog," he said. He laughed. There was a manic light in his eyes that scared the holy hell out of me, a tiny trail of spittle down the right side of his mouth. I stepped back again, pulling Einstein with me. Off in the distance, I could hear a car engine coming closer.

"I dreamed you. I dreamed them all—I watched the fires burn and I'll watch you die with a bullet in your skull. Just like him." The light went out in his eyes, suddenly. A single tear fell down his cheek.

"You shouldn't have come," he said again. "I'm sorry for that dream."

He turned around and disappeared back into the woods just as Diggs topped the hill. I'd wrapped Einstein's leash around my hand one too many times and it had cut off my circulation; I unwound the line to give Einstein more lead, but he didn't seem anxious to take it. Diggs pulled up alongside us in his Jeep.

"Hop in."

"Did you see him?"

He looked at me blankly.

"Matt Perkins—the constable. He was here."

For a second, Diggs looked doubtful. When he realized it was unlikely I'd make up the story, he got serious.

"Get in, we'll head back to the house. We'll have to let Jack know he's gone off the reservation again."

"Again?"

Diggs nodded. He looked tired, and not all that interested in telling stories. "The last year or so he hasn't been doing great. He's been staying at a residential place that Edie Woolwich runs, but he likes midnight strolls."

"He scared the shit out of me."

This earned another nod. He drove slowly, both of us looking along the side of the road for any trace of the old man.

"Yeah. He does that." He glanced at me, shifting gears—both literal and metaphoric. "Listen, I gave the State Fire Marshal a call today."

"Yeah?"

"He said he'd talk to you if you want to swing by tomorrow morning. I told him a little about the story, and he said you can have access to whatever you want—check out the archives, talk to anyone who might have worked the case back in the day, whatever."

"He remembered the fire?"

"Uh, yeah—he had a vague recollection of one of the biggest fatal fires in Maine history."

"What time?"

"He said ten, if it works for you. I have to work, but I figured you'd be okay on your own."

"Yeah, of course. Thanks."

When we pulled up in front of the house, Diggs wrapped his hand around my wrist as I was getting out of the Jeep.

"Hang on—can I talk to you for a second?"

I got back in and shut the door as quietly as I could. Einstein whimpered, then circled the backseat a couple of times before he lay back down. The porch light had come on when we rolled up but now it went off again, leaving us in darkness once more.

"What?"

"I'm sorry Jack's here—I really did think he'd be gone for a while. It's bad timing, I know." I waited for him to say what was really on his mind. Finally, he sighed. "Listen,

Solomon, I've been where you are right now."

I glanced around to indicate that I had no clue what he was talking about, though of course I knew full well.

"You're just getting your feet back under you after…you know, everything. Things might be a little raw for a while."

I raised an eyebrow, but remained silent while I waited for him to get to the point.

"I'm just saying, you might not be making the best decisions right now. So jumping into something with somebody new, while it might seem like a good idea now, can lead to complications you may want to avoid."

"Jesus, Diggs—I told you, nothing happened. We had dinner. We talked. He went to bed; I had a close encounter with his crazy uncle, and called you."

His hand was still on my wrist, warm against my cool skin. Our eyes held, his frustration clear.

"I'm not just talking about Juarez," he said. "The last time I saw you, you were—"

I pulled away. "I'm fine, Diggs. And if you'd stop hovering and just let me do what I came here to do, I'd be that much better."

His jaw tensed, but he didn't say anything further. I let Einstein out the back and went inside. Diggs didn't follow me. When I looked back at him from the front door, he was still sitting in the driver's seat, hands on the wheel, watching me with frustration and worry and that tangle of emotions that had been tripping us both up for years now.

I turned my back on him and went inside alone.

6

IT WAS JUST AFTER EIGHT when I woke up the next morning, and Diggs and Juarez were both long gone. I showered and dressed and tried not to think about my fight with Diggs the night before, or the fact that he seemed to be sleeping even less than I was, or how justified he was in being pissed at me. Which meant, of course, that I just thought about it more.

I'd been visiting Maine the last time I saw Diggs, ostensibly covering a story on one of the neighboring islands in Penobscot Bay. I was three months pregnant at the time—though I hadn't shared that with Diggs. Or my husband, for that matter. I had also neglected to tell anyone about the unexpected windfall that resulted from Malcolm Payson's death. I didn't mention inheriting Payson Isle, or the discovery of the photos Noel Hammond had taken. I wasn't sleeping, I wasn't eating, and I sure as hell wasn't talking.

An OBGYN would probably have caught the fact that the pregnancy was ectopic weeks earlier; that diagnosis was complicated by the fact that I never actually *saw* an OBGYN, however. Diggs got a call from Michael after my fallopian tube burst, telling him they weren't sure I'd make it. He drove down to Boston that night. I was unconscious when he got there, and just coming around when he left forty-eight hours later.

So… In all fairness, Diggs' concern wasn't completely unjustified. I just wished he'd stop worrying and leave me be. I'd survived the miscarriage and my subsequent divorce, and now for the first time, there was nothing stopping me from learning the truth behind the Payson fire. I could dig as deeply as I wanted, work as long and as hard as I liked, and answer to no one while I was doing it. Unless, of course, Diggs kept up his self-appointed role as my Great Protector.

By the time I got to Augusta that morning, I'd convinced myself that whatever it took to get the information I needed was worth it. If that meant I had to shut Diggs out of the investigation, so be it. I parked outside the Maine State Sheriff's Barracks, locked my car, and went inside with renewed focus.

Sergeant Bill Flint had the square jaw and the piercing blue eyes of a Hollywood action hero. We met in his office, a concrete enclave in the back corner of a larger concrete enclave that housed the Sheriff's Barracks. Five minutes after he showed me in and mysteriously vanished, he returned with two cans of Coke and a box of files. He set the box on a card table in the corner of the room, where I'd already seated myself.

"Sorry," he said, indicating the soda. "I'm trying to quit, but we got called in at midnight for a house fire in Lewiston. All-nighters don't come as easy as they used to."

Laugh lines and graying at his temples suggested the sergeant was in his fifties. The hint of shadow under his eyes and the faintest hint of stubble nudged the action hero mythos a shade closer to icon status. Between Diggs, Juarez, and Captain America here, it was getting damned difficult to stay focused.

"No need to apologize—I just appreciate you meeting with me. These are the files?"

"You lucked out. We had an intern here yesterday, so I had him photocopy what you'll need. We won't have time to go through all of it, I'm sure, but you can take the copies back with you. The ME will have the autopsy reports over in the crime lab archives—I've already put in a call. They're expecting you."

Working as a reporter in Boston, I'd gotten used to being stonewalled at every turn. This new spirit of cooperation was unnerving.

"Thank you. I was hoping to ask a few questions, too. Diggs told me you were on the scene—I know it was a while ago, but I was hoping you might remember a few details."

He looked amused.

"That's funny?" I asked.

"Sorry," he said quickly. "Diggs told me your connection to the fire—believe me, I don't think it's funny at all. It's just that we've all gone over the case so many times that I think even our newbies could walk you through it, point by point. Everyone here's been trained on the details, using it as an example of what *not* to do in an emergency."

I assumed my poker face, sensing a lead. "There were problems that night?"

"Not from this office," he assured me. "The Fire Marshal and the other agencies did a great job of handling the investigation and the inevitable fallout, considering it was a situation no one had been remotely prepared for."

I didn't say anything. I was crossing into dangerous territory—even twenty years after the fact, any government agency would do its best to protect its own. Flint seemed to sense my skepticism, however. He leaned forward.

"I spoke with Fire Marshal Cooper this morning, before meeting with you. He was clear on one thing: he wants you to have access to whatever you need in your investigation. We did a good job on that case—or as good as we could, considering what was handed to us. You can ask me anything, Ms. Solomon, and I'll do my best to give you whatever answers I have. I'm confident that any issues you might find with the way the investigation was conducted, the fault won't lie with this department."

"So where do you think the fault *should* lie?"

He grinned—a broad, boyish smile that made me like him that much more. "I guess that's the question, isn't it? But if you're looking to lay blame, you don't need to look much farther than your hometown."

"Littlehope?"

"They were first on the scene. And while I know small-town fire departments are sometimes lacking in training and equipment, that doesn't really explain what we found when we got out to the island."

I slipped a digital recorder from my bag and set it in the center of the table. Flint stood and closed the door, then returned to his seat. I waited until he'd taken a long pull from his Coke, and switched on the recorder.

"Would you mind walking me through what you found when you first arrived on the scene?" I asked.

He nodded.

I leaned back, giving him space, and he began.

"Because it'd been a dry summer that year, everyone was pretty maxed out by the time August rolled around—lots of brush fires, that kind of thing. I was new in the department. I'd trained as a fireman, then went through the Academy and got a degree in criminal science before I wound up here. Still, there's not a lot of training short of the battlefield that can prepare you for something like the Payson fire.

"The first we heard of it was the afternoon of Wednesday, August 22nd. The reports were conflicting—somebody from the volunteer fire department in the next town said there was a fire out on one of the islands, but then we got another call from the Littlehope fire chief saying that everything was under control."

"What time did you get that call?" I asked.

Flint checked his notes. "That came in early that afternoon—around noon."

"And Joe Ashmont was the fire chief then, right?"

He nodded grimly.

"And he told you that the Fire Marshal wouldn't be needed for the Payson fire? That would mean he told you there were no casualties out on the island, wouldn't it?"

This earned another nod. "We're charged with investigating any fire that results in a death, whether accidental or otherwise. So, yes—if Ashmont told us we wouldn't be needed, he was basically saying the fire was harmless. Everyone was okay. He made it out to sound like a brush fire that had gotten a little out of hand."

"What time did you finally get the call saying you *would* be needed out there?"

"At four o'clock that afternoon, we got a call from a volunteer fireman summering in Littlehope."

"Noel Hammond," I said.

"That's right. Hammond put in the call, and because we'd already been getting conflicting information all day, we had an idea that something was up. Until we heard from him, we had no idea what a large-scale investigation would be required. And no clue of the number of fatalities, of course."

"So, how long did it take you to get to the island?"

"There were a number of different agencies involved—the ME's office, State police, criminal investigations, the Fire Marshal... To get everyone out there, we had to pull in Marine Patrol. It took all night and part of the next day before everybody was on the same page and we were all headed out to Payson Isle."

"So, early afternoon on the 23rd?" I asked.

"Around eleven o'clock."

"And what did you find when you got out there?"

He scratched his chin. Eased back in his seat, something distant in his blue eyes. I had the sense that he was no longer seeing me; was no longer rooted in the safety of the barracks.

"The fire was out by then, of course. A few people had stayed on the island overnight to make sure no new fires sprung up—that can happen sometimes. You'll think a fire's dead, but it's just waiting for a little breathing room before it comes back to life. So, there were a few people on watch."

"Do you remember who?"

He checked his notes again. "Ashmont, of course. The town constable—Matt Perkins. Hammond was there. And there was a doctor there, too—Katherine Everett."

My mother. I tried not to show my surprise.

"And the scene itself? What did you see when you got there? What was your initial reaction?"

"Horror. I can't even begin to describe..." He stopped suddenly, his eyes on me. "But I don't really need to tell you that, do I?" he asked, his tone softer now. When I didn't respond, he continued. "It was the kind of thing you hope you never see. Everything burned to the ground. Bodies and rubble swept up and cast to the side."

The description triggered something in me—a memory

buried so deep that I'd thought it would never surface again. Crawling through soaked grass, inching closer to the fire. Blackened bodies. A hand with fingers curled as though beckoning me.

"Ms. Solomon?"

"I'm sorry—I was just…" I shook my head. "Sorry. You said the bodies were swept to the side. That's not the way they would have fallen though, would they?"

He smiled, just slightly. "Diggs said you were good. No—they wouldn't have fallen that way. They *hadn't* fallen that way. Sometime between when the fire was put out and the time we got there, Ashmont took it upon himself to clean things up a little."

"He moved the bodies?" The image sent a chill straight through me.

"He *stacked* the bodies, raked the debris, and didn't take so much as a Polaroid to give to the investigative team."

"How could he get away with that? He calls and blatantly lies to dispatch saying the Fire Marshal wouldn't be needed on the scene, breaks protocol, destroys evidence… How did he not get in trouble for any of this?"

"He did get in some—they forced his resignation, from what I recall. But it was hard to prove intent… He said he'd just been confused when he put that first call in and hadn't realized how bad things were, and then things got too chaotic to follow up."

"And the others who were there—Hammond and Perkins, Dr. Everett… They all corroborated his story?"

"That was the major reason we never prosecuted. Between you and me, it was a bullshit story and everybody knew it, but you've got four respected members of the community insisting that's what happened. Short of an eyewitness to say otherwise, there wasn't much anybody could do."

We spoke for another half-hour before Flint had given me all the details he could remember, and I was ready to end the interview. Beyond his description of those first impressions of the scene, there weren't a lot of surprises. The investigative team had set up camp on the island for several days, which I had known, with the ME conducting cursory exams of the bodies on site before the remains were returned to the mainland.

Before I said goodbye and prepared for an afternoon with the ME to follow up on their findings, I stood at the door with Flint and asked a final question.

"You said nothing could ever be proven, but you seem pretty clear on the fact that Ashmont and the others were hiding something. Do you think there's any chance he or one of the others started that fire?"

Flint shook his head without hesitation. "No—we know what happened, Ms. Solomon. Ashmont was hiding something, no question. They all were, but I'd say that had more to do with covering their own asses after making such a mess of things. The toxins in the victims' blood, the isolation of the community, the fact that there were almost no survivors…" He hesitated, and I could tell he was thinking of my father. "Isaac Payson set that fire, as far as the Maine State Fire Marshal and the law is concerned. That's why the case was closed. There were no questions left to answer."

I thought of the secret stash of photos Noel Hammond had kept hidden all those years. The false alibi I had provided for my father. The padlock on the door. The cloaked man chasing us through the woods.

If he'd known the truth, I was sure that Sergeant Flint would find there were, in fact, no shortage of questions left to answer.

7

NOTHING NEW CAME UP AT MY NEXT STOP, meeting with the Maine State Medical Examiner. Because of the extensive damage to the remains and the way the crime scene had been corrupted by Ashmont and his cohorts—my mother included—there was some question as to who, exactly, the investigative team had unearthed after the fire. Identification of the bodies had been slow, and because so many of the members of the Payson Church had little in the way of medical records, there had been a lot of guesswork that went into the process. Thirty-four bodies were recovered, but only thirty had been identified conclusively. The remaining four—two women and two children—were anyone's guess.

While this was less than confidence inspiring, I wasn't surprised. Dr. Pratt, the Chief Medical Examiner, let me take copies of all the files she had, but based on what I'd learned so far, I didn't expect them to reveal anything earth shattering. A dead body is a dead body is a dead body… Or so I thought at the time.

It was after four by the time I got back from Augusta. I debated going out to the island, but decided instead to set up shop at the *Trib* and start going through the box of files and photocopies I'd gotten from the Fire Marshal's office. An uncharacteristically quiet Diggs set me up in a closet-sized office with Internet access and a boxy little window overlooking the harbor, and I went to work.

Since I'd already seen most of the official paperwork before, I focused on the investigators' notes. There wasn't that much to go on—they'd followed protocol, just as Flint had said. My father was a suspect early on, that much was clear, but the police apparently ruled him out thanks in large part to the alibi I'd provided.

Or maybe not. At the bottom of a file marked "Witness Statements," I found a copy of handwritten notes dated August 28, 1990. My mother's name was in the upper left corner, with mine written beneath it.

One word was written directly underneath, underlined twice:

Lying??

I stared at the page. The file belonged to Jim Abbott, a police detective whose name had come up before when I was researching the investigation. The notes were paper clipped to my mother's official statement.

I called Sergeant Flint. Ten minutes on hold and a transfer to records later, and I had the phone number for Jim Abbott in my hot little hand. I could get used to this whole cooperating-with-the-press thing.

For the next several hours, I sat in my office and read reports and notes, looked at photographs, wrote down names. I borrowed Scotch tape from Diggs and began putting photos up on the walls: the barn before the fire, the barn after. The padlocked door. I taped the only photos I had of my father, Isaac, and several members of the church just below the crime scene shots. I wrote down what I knew so far. It wasn't much.

May, 1976—Isaac starts the Payson Church of Tomorrow
December, 1978—Dad joins the church
August, 1990—Payson Church burns

Of course, I knew plenty beyond that, but no matter what I tried, I couldn't make what I knew add up to the fire. I'd studied other cult suicides over the years: Jonestown, the Solar Temple, Heaven's Gate... In each instance, there was always something in the dogma that gave a good idea of what the congregation had been thinking would happen when their numbers were up.

The Payson Church was a fundamentalist, Christian church. As such, they had a very clear view on suicide. Essentially: you do it, and you never make it to the pearly gates. I remembered the Paysons. They were all about those pearly gates.

I added another note to my timeline:

October, 1989—I leave Payson Isle.

I stared at the entry for a few seconds, then added one more word:

Why?

I tossed that question around without any major revelations until one o'clock that morning, when Diggs knocked on my door.

"Come on—we're going home."

"I'll be there in a while. Go on without me."

He didn't budge. I looked up to find him standing with his arms crossed over his chest, leaning against the wall. My back and neck were tight, and my eyes stung from staring at a computer screen for far too long. Einstein was still peeved at having been left at home during my trek to Augusta earlier that day; being imprisoned in my tiny office for the remainder of the day hadn't done much to get me back in his good graces.

I stretched, yawned, and closed my laptop.

"Did you have dinner?" I asked.

"We'll make something when we get home," he said, showing the first trace of a smile I'd seen since the night before. "Come on. Play your cards right, and you can have beer and chocolate for dessert."

Diggs has always known the way to my heart.

●

Juarez's car wasn't in the driveway when we pulled in that night.

"Matt took a turn for the worst this morning," Diggs told me. "Jack said they were taking him back to Togus for a while." The Maine veteran's hospital. "Juarez'll probably stay there tonight."

I thought of how Old Man Perkins had looked in the woods the night before, stalking me and muttering psychotic epithets. Juarez might only be there overnight, but I was hoping they'd keep the constable under lock and key for a while.

"So we've got the house to ourselves?"

He nodded. "You want a burger?"

"A burger burger, or a veggie burger?"

"I've got cow, I've got chicken, I've got eggplant."

I went to the cupboard and got a couple of plates for the table. "Cow, please. You should have some, too. You look pale."

"Thanks. I'm pale because I never see daylight anymore,

not because I don't eat cows. One of the dangers of working the desk."

Once the food was cooking, he opened a beer for me and a sparkling water for himself, and leaned against the counter. Einstein sat at attention, veggie and cow burgers sizzling in separate fry pans on the stove.

"Sergeant Flint was great today—thanks for setting that up. He did everything but write the story."

"Did you get an honorary pin?" he asked.

"How'd you know?"

"It's because you're cute. I never get a pin."

"You're cute," I said.

"I'm pretty sure I'm not Flint's type."

"Fair enough. I got notes from the original investigation. All the old files. Photos."

"Any leads?"

"Can't tell yet."

We talked while he cooked, careful to keep things light. Once the food was done, we sat and ate in what was becoming an increasingly uncomfortable silence. The day was catching up to both of us. Halfway through the meal, I found it hard to keep my eyes open. I caught Diggs looking at me and sat up straighter.

"I'm more tired than I thought."

"I noticed." He hesitated. I had the feeling there was something he wanted to bring up, but wasn't. I waited him out.

"I was thinking about the people you want to talk to— the families of the victims. I think that's a good approach."

"Thanks." I took a bite of burger and wiped my mouth. And waited some more.

"It would probably be good to talk to somebody else,

though. Someone who was actually, I don't know, there. Someone who knew Isaac Payson and your father fairly well."

"I'm not calling her, Diggs."

"Why the hell not? She was there, Sol. She might not have talked to you about it before, but it's been a long time."

The clock on the microwave read quarter past two. I got up and took my plate to the sink, drinking the last of my beer on the way. Diggs followed.

"You don't have to do it as her daughter—do it as a reporter. Any other story and this would be your lead interview."

"My mother won't be able to make the distinction, trust me. I'm not calling her. She wouldn't answer my questions when I was a teenager, she wouldn't say a word about any of it after Dad died, and now that she knows I'm writing a book on the subject, I'm pretty sure her response will be exactly the same: 'No comment.' "

"What if you told her what you've found out? Tell her about the pictures you found. For Christ's sake, tell her what you told me about the morning of the fire with Adam. Then maybe she'll understand what you've been so obse—"

I stared at him for a long few seconds of silence. "You can say the word. It's not like I haven't heard it before."

"Obsessed." He said it quietly, without accusation. I was standing at the sink, Diggs' body close enough that I could feel his heat. Diggs is tall—I forget how tall sometimes, but standing there in my bare feet in his kitchen, he seemed very big. And very male. He has broad shoulders and a mean right hook and I remembered, suddenly, what it was like to kiss him all those years ago. Our eyes held for a breath, maybe two.

"You should get to bed. I'll clean up here," he said.

"You're sure?"

He nodded, but he didn't look all that sure to me. "Yeah. Go on—I'll see you in the morning."

I left him to his cleaning and retired to my room alone. Again.

8

I WAS AT THE OFFICE BY TEN THE NEXT DAY with Einstein in tow, ready to tackle the list of contacts Diggs had given me the day before. The first half-dozen calls I made went straight to voicemail. I left a message, though it was unlikely that anyone in their right mind would call back, and contented myself with the knowledge that at least that first contact had been made.

The eighth call was to a man named Jed Colby, whose sister-in-law Cynthia had been a member of the Payson Church. She'd been quiet, self-contained, but I remembered her laugh and her smile; remembered that she'd worked with my father and me in the greenhouse. She'd had a son a little older than me—Will. I hated to think ill of the dead, but I remembered Will Colby as a mean little prick who'd taunted me and the rest of the kids on the island relentlessly while I was there.

Cynthia had been nice, though.

Jed answered on the second ring, with "Colby's Garage."

"Mr. Colby, my name is Erin Solomon. I'm doing a—"

"I know who you are," he interrupted. "You wanna talk about the fire." His voice was hard, his Maine accent thick even by Littlehope standards.

"Partially, yes—I actually have some questions about the last few weeks leading up to the fire. I know it might be tough to talk about, but it would be a big help."

"Come on over," he said, much to my surprise. "Gracie's making sandwiches at eleven-thirty. You can come for lunch. You know where we are?"

I got directions, then spent the rest of the morning taking notes and making more calls. At eleven, I popped my head in to ask Diggs to keep an eye on Einstein while I was gone, left my car in the lot, and struck out on foot for Colby's Garage.

It was a foggy day, the landscape painted in muted shades of gray. Half a dozen lobster boats were still moored in the harbor. The rest were hard at work, the drone of diesel engines an undercurrent to my thoughts as I walked. It was a half-mile along East Shore Ave—a ribbon of a road skirting the coastline—to get to Jed Colby's place. The tulips were in bloom. New leaves were coming in on the elms and maples, crabapples and birches that lined the way. It was my first spring in Littlehope since I was a teenager, but walking the road that day it felt as though I'd never left.

Colby's Garage was painted bright red, set back from an overgrown lawn with several cars parked on the grass and three pickups and a tow truck in the driveway. The cars on the lawn had seen better days, sporting mashed-in bumpers and missing doors, tireless rims and popped hoods with no engines to speak of.

A man was buried under the hood of one of the pickups, a greasy baseball cap tucked in the back pocket of his overalls. The Kinks were singing out L-O-L-A on the tinny speakers of an old boom box sitting beside the left tire, the man's foot tapping in time to the music. A Basset hound lifted its head to blink red-rimmed eyes at me from his perch by the garage steps, but didn't bother to move or even offer a halfhearted 'woof.'

"Excuse me."

The man eased himself out from under the hood like he'd known I was there all along. "Erin Solomon?"

"That's right."

"I'm Jed. Nice to meet you." He wiped his hands on a soiled rag hanging over the side of the truck and shook my hand. "You hungry? Gracie's got egg salad and fresh coffee inside. Come on in."

The house was a single-story modular set back even farther on the lot, away from the garage. The lawn around the house was well-manicured, flowers just coming up along the front walk. The Basset got up on its short legs and waddled after us. Jed pulled a tricycle out of the driveway and set it up on the lawn, then kicked a couple of toy cars out of the way.

"I'm always telling them to keep their junk out of the way. Last week I run over my youngest's favorite stuffed dog—she cried for two days. You'd think they'd learn, but half them Matchboxes are hers."

I did some quick math. Jed had dark hair and a closely trimmed beard, with wrinkles at his pretty brown eyes. I knew Cynthia had been young when she had Will, but if she'd survived, she still would have been in her fifties Jed smiled at me once we were at the front door, as though reading my mind.

"My brother—Cindy's husband—was older than me by about fifteen years. I kinda caught my folks by surprise."

He opened the door for me and stood by politely when I entered the house. The Basset ambled in after me. The house had that neatly-lived-in feel that comes with stay-at-home moms and a lot of home cooking. We walked through the living room into a sunny kitchen, where a slim blonde woman was setting out plates.

"This is Erin, Gracie."

The woman turned. She looked familiar, though it took a minute to place her. She wiped her hands on her jeans, then reached over and shook my hand.

"Grace Colby—used to be Simmons. I was a year behind you in school. We had Spanish together."

My memory wasn't as specific as that, but I did remember her—a quiet girl who kept to herself, not popular, not unpopular. A ghost, like so many of us back in high school. She nodded toward a chair.

"Have a seat. You want coffee?"

Once coffee and sandwiches were on the table, the three of us sat down. We exchanged pleasantries, talked about the town and what I'd been up to and what Diggs—apparently mutual friend to everyone in Littlehope—was up to, before I finally got down to business. I got my notes out and explained what I was looking for. Things had been going smoothly up until then, but they looked like natives confronted with demon technology the second the red light on my recorder came on.

"No one will hear this tape but me. I just like to use these things so I know I got the story right," I explained. "If you think of something later, or there's something you'd rather not include, you can always let me know."

Jed scratched his neck, eyeing the recorder uneasily. "There's not all that much to tell. Cindy didn't have no family of her own, and I never knew her all that well. My folks would've been better to talk to, but they passed on a couple years back. I have another sister—she was closer to Cindy than me. She moved out to South Carolina last winter, but I can get you her number."

"That would be great," I said. "In the meantime, maybe I could just ask a couple of questions, see if it jogs any memories."

He nodded, but before I could ask anything, he stood and walked over to a wall of photos in the living room.

"You remember them?" he asked. I had the feeling he'd been waiting a while to ask that question.

"I do," I said. I joined him in the other room. There were a series of framed photos of Cynthia and Will with a man I didn't recognize, most of them studio portraits like the ones people used to have done at Sears.

"Your brother died?" I asked.

"Urchin diving," Jed said. "Will and Cindy were never the same after that. Will was eight when it happened—he took it hard. Cindy took it worse. She sold the house, sold the boat." He looked at me, but I couldn't tell what he was thinking. "Isaac Payson started sniffing around not long after. He'd come to the mainland, bring them stuff. I don't think Will ever liked the guy much, but Cindy…" He shook his head.

"So, you met Isaac?"

"What did you think of him?" he asked me, before I could ask him the same question.

"I didn't hate him," I said, after a little consideration. "And my father loved him. He never…" I searched for the words. "…Scared me, I guess, the way you might think somebody like that would. Being out there, part of the church, was never as horrible as people made it out to be afterward."

Jed nodded after a while. His eyes looked wet, though no tears fell. "That's what Cindy always said—well, mostly what she said. Will was a tough case, hard to reach—something was wrong there, even before his dad died. But I think Cindy felt like Payson was making an effort."

"You said, 'mostly what she said,'" I prompted. "When did she say otherwise?"

He thought about it for a few seconds. "It was about two weeks before the fire." He took a deep breath. I had the sense that whatever he was about to tell me had weighed on his mind for a long time. "Her and Will came back to Littlehope on a Friday afternoon. We had a picnic out to the lighthouse."

"And she said something changed?"

"She didn't say anything—that was the thing. I said something about how maybe I'd been wrong, maybe her being out there with Will was a good thing after all. Maybe Payson wasn't such a bad guy."

"And she said…"

"Not a damned thing. All she could talk about was something about a doll, some puppet that Will didn't get. Or Payson took."

I looked at him. "An angel?"

"Yeah. I don't know what the problem was. Something happened, though. Isaac took his doll back. The kid was twelve years old, I don't know what in hell he was doing playing with dolls, anyway."

"It was a marionette," I explained. "The Paysons made marionettes and sold them on the mainland."

"I've seen them," Gracie said. "They did a spread on them one time in *Down East*."

"Yeah—that's right," I said. "There were actually two

different kinds of angels, though. The ones they sold had black eyes. But every kid who was part of the church had their own angel—Isaac painted them himself. Those angels had blue eyes."

"And he took Will's angel?" Jed asked.

"I don't know anything about it," I said. "My father never mentioned it to me, but…" I didn't want to say anything against Will, but my mind was already spinning. So much of my time on the island was a blur, but I remembered vaguely that Isaac hadn't had the most patience when it came to the kids. Even Jed admitted that Will was a pain in the ass. Still, I couldn't remember the preacher ever taking one of his precious Payson Angels back.

"Well, whatever happened, Cindy wasn't happy about it," Jed said. "I should've seen it then. For the four years she'd been there before that, all she did was sing this guy's praises. She couldn't say enough about what he did for the congregation—what a friggin' Eden that island was, how much she loved everybody out there… Then, all of a sudden when I'm finally ready to admit that maybe she's got a point, she changes her tune."

He shook his head. Grace came over and took his hand, leading him back to the table. I followed suit. Jed sat back down and picked up his sandwich before he finished his thought.

"Two weeks later, they were both dead."

"You couldn't have known," I said. "Nobody could have."

"I wish to god I'd gotten her off that island then and there. You don't know how many times I've gone over that day, thought about how I should've done something."

I didn't know what to say to that. He studied me, his head tilted to one side, then offered a sad smile.

"She loved your dad, you know." I looked at him in surprise. "Not in *that* way, of course," he said quickly. "But she talked about him a lot. The things he taught her out in the garden, the time she spent with you out there. I know my nephew was a prick from the word go, but all you had to do was whisper the name Erin Solomon in his ear and he'd blush like a fool."

He looked down at his coffee cup. I couldn't tell if it was because he was trying to keep his own emotions in check, or just giving me a minute to do the same.

"I'm sorry about what happened to your dad," he said. "He was a good man. He didn't deserve that. Neither of you did."

"None of us did," I said. I stood before things got completely maudlin. "I should get going, let you finish your meal. But this has been good… Helpful, I mean."

Jed shook my hand. "I'll be curious to read what you finally find out about all this. It's been a sore spot for me—for this family, for a lot of years. It would mean a lot to understand how they wound up like that in the end."

"For me, too," I agreed.

We said our goodbyes. Just before I left, Grace gave me an impulsive hug—this quiet girl I couldn't really remember, from an adolescence I'd just as soon forget. I returned the embrace, then got out the door as fast as I could, already turning over this new piece of the Payson puzzle.

JULY 26, 1990

HER SON HAS A SMILE NOW that Rebecca hasn't seen since he was a toddler. He stands tall in front of the congregation, his shoulders back, his dark eyes staring straight ahead. Others in the church have commented on the startling resemblance between mother and child. His hair is thick, raven's-wing-black, and his complexion is smooth and dark—a clear indication of the Passamaquoddy tribe that runs strong in her blood. In almost every way, physically Zion is a replica of his mother. She imagines, sometimes, that there was no father at all… An immaculate conception, though she is certainly no virgin.

It is an evening service. The chapel is stuffy and close, the air heavy enough to feel as moisture-soaked breath at the back of her neck. There are no windows; Isaac had them boarded, saying they distracted from the glory of the Lord and the purity of their worship. The smell of the congregation triggers an almost orgiastic anticipation in Rebecca as she waits for the Reverend to begin.

They've been on the island for one week, and in that time Zion has given himself completely to the Reverend.

Isaac, in turn, has fostered that devotion; her son is at his right hand constantly. The other children help with chores, go to bed early, rarely attend evening services, but Zion is the exception. Rebecca hardly sees him now.

He stands with Isaac's hand on his shoulder, a peaceful half-smile on his lips. Rebecca thinks she understands, finally, what it is to be in love. There will never be another man who fills her, changes her, moves her, the way that Zion does. She glances around and sees admiration coming from the others, and knows she is not alone in her belief that there is something different about her son. Isaac has said it himself: *This boy will one day be a leader among men.*

Around her, the congregation is on their feet, singing to Adam's accompaniment on the old piano in the corner. Beside Rebecca, a woman's hands go up in the air, her lips fluttering "Praise Jesus" in hysterical gasps, tears streaming down her face. For the first time, Zion looks uneasy at the rage of passions coming to the fore in the crowded space. Rebecca feels a familiar tightening in her stomach, as though the cord that once joined them is still there, invisible but no less powerful. She prepares to intervene.

As it turns out, she is not needed. Isaac leans into Zion's ear, his hand still on the small, sturdy shoulder, his lips just inches from the boy. Rebecca watches the older man's mouth move. She feels a twinge of jealousy, but couldn't say which of the two she's jealous of. In response to Isaac's words, Zion looks puzzled for a moment before he shakes his head, holding the angel Isaac just presented to him tightly in one hand.

Isaac asks him something else, and this time receives a nod of affirmation. Zion's eyes are shining, black as midnight rain. In response to the nod, Isaac leans away from him and holds his hands in the air. Instantly, mid-verse, the church falls silent.

"This boy—this quiet, unsettled boy who stands before you today—has seen many things in his young life. You all know that he and his mother have risked their comfort, their livelihoods—their very lives—to join us here."

Individuals in the congregation turn toward Rebecca, flashing kind smiles before they return to Isaac.

"In speaking to this boy just now, I've learned that through all the trials of his life, he hasn't had a true opportunity…" Isaac pauses on the word, letting the silence close in around it and then open up again before he continues. "…to ask the Lord Jesus Christ into his heart."

A low murmur of incredulity rises like warm air. Zion looks from Isaac to Rebecca. She smiles encouragingly, nodding through tears she can no longer contain.

"Zion." Isaac keeps his voice up so everyone can hear, though he addresses only the boy. Zion nods. "Son, would you like to ask the Lord into your heart today? Are you ready to turn your back on the eternal fire of Satan, and let yourself curl up in the arms of the Lamb of God?"

Zion waits a moment, as though unsure whether or not the Reverend has finished, before he nods. "Yes, sir."

Isaac pushes the child to his knees. In the dim light of flickering candles, Rebecca is drawn from the picture before her to the dance of two shadows behind the pulpit. Isaac's is long, thin, climbing nearly to the ceiling and beyond, while Zion's shadow seems to shrink into itself before gradually merging into the larger of the two.

The Reverend is a big man who looks more like a fisherman than a preacher, and he has a voice that could carry far past the walls of the chapel if necessary. He rarely needs to use that voice, however—his power is conveyed with a single glance. It comes through in the strength of his smile, the weight of his eyes, and—most of all—through his hands.

Isaac's hands are long and fine. They don't fit the rest of his body. Every time he touches her with those hands, late at night while the rest of the church sleeps, Rebecca can feel God. There is a confidence in his touch that rushes through her in waves of white light. When he says he is chosen, she never even considers questioning him.

Now, standing with the rest of the congregation, Rebecca can't take her eyes from the image of the child she loves melding with the man she craves. She understands pictures better than words, interprets dreams the way she was taught by her tribe long ago, but this shadow written on the wall before her is a story she cannot read. She's not even sure she cares to try.

A steady stream of Hallelujahs issue from one woman, started as a single word and changing to a song that rises, clean and sweet, over Isaac's prayer for Zion. Both of the Reverend's hands are tight on the boy's head, Zion still kneeling as Isaac welcomes him into the fold. When the prayer is done, Zion stands and his eyes meet his mother's. In that instant, a cool breeze blows through the congregation. The candles flare before going out completely, and the shadows at last fall silent.

9

AFTER MY INTERVIEW with the Colbys, I got back to the paper shortly after noon. During the walk back, Jim Abbott—the lead detective from the original Payson investigation—returned my call to say he could meet with me in Portland the next day. I thought about making more calls once I was back in the office, but my lunch with Jed and Grace was still too fresh; I didn't want to talk to anyone else. Not yet, anyway.

Diggs was on the phone when I retrieved Einstein. I told him I'd be gone for the afternoon, dodged his questions about where I was going, and headed for the town landing. The fog had burned off by this time—the sun was bright, the water clear and calm. My outboard started on the first pull, and Einstein's tail was wagging as I navigated us out of the harbor. I set my sights on Payson Isle.

The island looked less formidable the second time around. Walking the same trail Diggs and I had traveled two days before, I was able to set my own pace and take in the world around me. I was still trying to get my head around the idea that this place was mine now: just over one square mile of granite and outbuildings, history and heartache. My father would have done great things with the place— farmed the land, added livestock, housed orphans or rescued puppies or... something.

I, on the other hand, didn't know what the hell to do with it.

I surveyed any damage that had been done over the years. Trees had come down in storms, paths were overgrown, and buoys and trash had washed up along the shoreline. Otherwise, the island really didn't look that bad.

The cottages where the families of the Payson Church had once lived were on the other side of the island. As a kid, I'd traveled the path from the boarding house to those cottages on a daily basis. One of my best friends lived there, as had some of my father's cohorts on the maintenance crew. I remembered Isaac Payson himself pulling me aside at the boarding house, handing me notes that he would tuck in my small hand.

Run and give this to Sister Wendy, he'd say, or *Brother Patrick was asking for this.* And I'd fly through the forest on an angel's mission, chosen by the Chosen One. When I arrived at the cottages, I'd be out of breath and filled with self-importance, while whomever I'd been running to would read my message and repay me with homemade bread or a game of checkers.

Diggs was convinced I'd spent my formative years with a lecherous preacher and a bunch of deranged minions, but my admittedly vague memories were closer to *Little House on the Prairie* than *Children of the Corn.* Of course, no one— including my mother and the long line of shrinks she hired for me after the fire—ever believed me when I told them that.

I decided I still wasn't quite ready to dive into Payson Village, where I knew my dad had spent his final years slowly going stark raving mad. Instead, I retraced my steps to the boarding house. I stopped at the fence and spent about fifteen minutes pushing and pulling the rusted iron gate out of the mud so I could get through without squishing my parts anymore than necessary. Once I reached the house, I pushed my way inside with only a fraction of the anxiety I'd felt on my first visit.

I started a fire in the fireplace, then decided to put my iron to the test. Armed with Einstein, a broom, and a hammer—the only blunt instrument I could find to defend myself against hobgoblins—I headed up the stairs to the bedrooms on the second floor.

Since Diggs and I hadn't taken any plywood off the windows above the ground floor, everything was cloaked in darkness. I shined my flashlight along the corridor at the top of the stairs. All the bedroom doors were closed. Wallpaper was peeling in strips; dust hung in curtains along the walls. A couple of paintings had fallen down, splinters of glass and wood scattered in all directions. I swept them up so Einstein wouldn't cut his paws, then continued.

There were three bedrooms on the right hand side of the hallway. Those had been for the single women in the congregation. Their kids stayed in bedrooms across the hall. I hesitated for a second or two before I chose the first room to my left. I pushed the door open and peered inside while Einstein sat at the threshold and whined.

"I know it's creepy. But we're reporters, Stein. This is what we do." He didn't budge. I went in without him.

Part of the plywood boarding the bedroom window had been damaged, allowing partial light to get through. I ran my flashlight through the room. Three sets of bunk beds were lined up against one wall, opposite a bank of built-in dresser drawers. The beds were all made.

Centered above the dressers, a homemade sign—water stained and torn almost all the way through the center—read, "God is Good."

Names were written in crayon on brittle, yellowed paper at the head of each bed. I ran the flashlight over each of them: *Julie, Andrea, Sara, Laura.* I stopped at the third bed. The name on the bottom bunk was written in faded pink, bubble letters: *Allie.* The top bunk was the only one with no bedding, but the name remained at the head of the bed: *Erin,* written in my father's fine script and decorated with glitter. Though I'd been gone nearly a year before the fire, no one had taken my spot.

Three of the girls still had blue-eyed angels hanging by their bedsides. Framed photos of the children with their mothers and other members of the church lined the walls. I went to the dresser drawers and opened one. Mice had nested in the clothing, tufts of fur mixed in with torn dresses and t-shirts, skirts and blue jeans.

I closed the drawers with my skin crawling, and left the room the way I'd found it.

A massive set of double doors stood at the end of the hallway, leading into a suite that had once belonged to my family; the place where my mother and father lived during their brief stint as blissful marrieds. Directly to the right of those doors was a second stairwell leading to the third floor. Everything good, everything safe, everything remotely childlike about my childhood, had happened behind those double doors. I thought of curling up beside my dad while he read to me; of coloring pictures and sharing secrets and the songs he used to sing when I was sick.

I turned away from the doors and opted for the stairwell instead.

The steps leading up to the Payson family sanctuary were narrower than I remembered. The stairs were steep and the ceiling was low and claustrophobia kicked in about halfway up. Einstein stayed in the hallway below, whining as I reached a door with peeling paint and a gold cross at the center.

"Just go on—nobody's here. They won't even know."

"Father Isaac says we're not supposed to come up here. It's just for his family."

Allie Tate stares back at me, her brown eyes enormous behind thick-lensed glasses. She has dark hair and pale skin and walks with a limp, but only I know why.

"Daddy says the island belongs to all of us. We can go wherever we want," I tell her. This is a lie—or at least it's not quite the truth—but right now I don't care. I've been dying to get into Father Isaac's secret lair for as long as I can remember, and I finally have the chance.

"That's not what my mom says," Allie insists. "We're not supposed to cross Father Isaac."

I push past her on the stairs, so impatient that I catch her off balance and she has to grip the railing to keep from falling.

"We're not supposed to have secrets," I say. "That's worse than crossing Isaac."

At nine years old, my father says I have my mother's will. I know that it's not meant as a compliment. I'm more curious than I used to be about this woman I have yet to meet; this woman who lives somewhere on the mainland and who chose to spend my childhood studying to be a doctor instead of raising me and caring for my father. I've heard that Isaac keeps information about everyone locked away in his rooms at the top of the stairs. If that's true, I'm convinced I can learn everything I want to know about my mother—all the questions my father refuses to answer.

"Don't turn back now," I tell Allie, who is slowly creeping back down the stairs. I've hurt her feelings, but I can't bring myself to stop. "We're almost there."

"They'll be back soon."

"Services are another hour. They won't come back."

Even as I say this, we hear the front door open on the first floor. Allie's eyes get wide and terrified, and I feel a jolt of electricity in my belly. It's not a bad feeling, necessarily. Allie rushes down the stairs, but I keep going. Two more steps.

"What if it's Father Isaac?" she whispers to me.

"It won't be. Just go talk to them. I'll just be a minute."

My heart is pounding now, the doorknob cool under my hand. Whoever is here, their footsteps are getting closer. Before I can turn the knob, I hear my father's voice.

"Erin? Are you up here, baby?"

I'm forced to turn back. It doesn't matter, though—within two weeks, I have all the answers I need about the mysterious woman who is my mother. And within a month, she has whisked me to the mainland before I ever have the chance to set foot inside Isaac Payson's inner sanctum.

I shook off the memory. I was an adult now, and Isaac Payson was long dead. I turned the knob.

It didn't budge.

Isaac's brother had left me a key ring with enough keys to unlock most of the mysteries of life, but it turned out that not one of those keys fit Isaac Payson's door. As I saw it, I had three choices: pick the lock, break down the door, or admit defeat and head back downstairs. Picking the lock turned out to be impossible—at least, it was for me. After a couple of halfhearted shoves at the aged wood with my shoulder, I decided that force wasn't going to do the job, either. Einstein stared up at me with limpid brown eyes.

The stairwell was dark. I imagined that Payson's room would be even darker. Truth be told, I wasn't that keen to explore the place alone, anyway. I started down the steps. About halfway down, Einstein started to bark.

"I'm coming, Stein—just chill." So far, he was proving to be less than helpful. Einstein was a great dog, but he could have taken some lessons from Lassie.

He started up the stairs, his barks sharpening in pitch, his body rigid. Something creaked behind me. The dog raced up three steps as I turned and shined my flashlight into the dim stairwell. My heart was thudding so hard against my breastbone I thought it might crack something.

There was nothing there.

I closed my eyes. "That's it. No more detecting tonight."

If something was up there, I wasn't prepared to find it tonight. Common sense told me it was probably just a raccoon or squirrel that had somehow gotten in the room, and Stein just heard it through the door. I'd seen too many horror flicks over the course of my lifetime to just dismiss it outright, though.

Instead, I gathered Einstein and our things and we headed for the dock. As I walked through the woods, the sky darkening with every step, I couldn't shake the feeling that someone was just behind me, watching my retreat.

10

DIGGS STAYED AT THE OFFICE THAT NIGHT, and was nowhere on the premises when I got up the next day. I had no doubt that he had work to do, but he was also clearly avoiding me. Understandable, since our last two heartfelt chats had ended with me jumping down his throat. I would have avoided me, too.

I wasn't meeting Jim Abbott in Portland until three, so I had the morning to pull myself together and figure out a plan of attack. I took advantage of the brisk, clear weather with a run into town. Einstein held up well. I, on the other hand, needed my left lung reinflated by mile two.

Around mile three, a car slowed down behind me. I yanked Einstein over to the shoulder, but the idiot in my wake still didn't pass us. I turned to shoot a glare at whoever was shadowing me.

Jack Juarez smiled at me from the driver's seat.

He rolled his window down and slowed the car to match my pace. Since actually speaking and running at the same time were beyond me, however, I pulled up short. As did Juarez. The road was empty, the sky was clear, and Juarez looked tastier than any mortal man had a right, particularly given the stress he'd presumably been under dealing with Uncle Crazy.

"I didn't know you were a runner," he said. There was just a hint of a smirk.

In between gasping for breath and nursing the stitch in my side, I pulled a pack of Camels from my jacket pocket. Juarez gave me the eye.

"I'm quitting."

"I didn't say anything."

"But you were thinking it."

The smirk transformed into a slow, easy grin. He eyed me up and down, his gaze lingering at the cigarette now between my lips. "That's not what I was thinking."

My heart sped up just a shade, though this time I couldn't lay the blame on exertion.

"Do you want a ride?"

I had another mile or so to get back to Diggs' place. My right calf was cramping, I was getting a blister on my left heel, and my sports bra didn't fit nearly as well as it had in the store. I glanced at Einstein, who didn't even have the decency to pant.

"Sure—I think Stein's tired."

Juarez just kept grinning.

●

When Juarez found out I was going to Portland, he managed to finagle an invite without too much actual finagling. He waited while I showered and changed, I did the unforgiveable and dumped Einstein on Diggs for the afternoon, and we were on the road by eleven.

The first forty-five minutes of the drive was awkward,

filled with stilted conversation and some of the most God-awful music I'd ever heard. Juarez was freshly shaven and appropriately casual in jeans and a black t-shirt that did obscene things for his arms. We took his car—a zippy little five-speed Honda Civic that didn't mesh with my image of an FBI man in the least. In fact, nothing about Jack Juarez meshed with my image of an FBI man. Didn't FBI men drive SUVs and believe in wire tapping, necessary force, and the innate beauty of the good old U.S. of A.?

Juarez talked about swimming with porpoises in Miami, appeared to know all the words to every Taylor Swift song ever penned, and drove five miles under the speed limit for the duration of the drive. Every so often, he would look at me with those dark, dark eyes, and a shiver would run from my kneecaps to my navel. Physically, everything about him whispered an implication of the erotic—he looked like the kind of man who could recite Yeats to you in one breath and tie you to the bedpost in the next. But, he drove like my grandfather and had the musical tastes of a prepubescent girl.

I couldn't get a read on him for the life of me.

We followed Route 17 into Augusta again because Juarez wanted to drop off a couple of things for Matt. Traffic was light and the sun was shining. Once we got to the veteran's hospital, I waited in the car while Jack went in.

Togus is the oldest VA hospital in the country, set up in 1866 by Abe Lincoln himself during the Civil War. The hospital itself is immense and old and brick, the grounds well-kept and quiet. I fiddled with the radio and tried not to feel guilty for dumping Einstein on Diggs for an afternoon in the city with another man, and ultimately ended up getting pissed off that I had to feel guilty in the first place when

Diggs had made it perfectly clear that any romantic interest he might have had in me once upon a time was long dead.

By the time Juarez returned, I was still feeling guilty but now I was feeling pissed off and guilty. Awesome. I pushed all of that aside, however, when I caught a glimpse of Juarez's face; clearly, the visit hadn't gone well. He got into the car and started the engine without looking at me. We were on 295 headed to Portland before he said a word.

"Sorry it took so long."

"Is he okay?"

"He's not doing as well as I'd hoped. The other night when he saw you, what did he say? He's been strange ever since—I'm trying to figure out if it might have triggered something."

I thought about it. "He said he dreamed I was coming. Or dreamed me. I got the sense it wasn't a good dream, in either case." He waited for me to continue, while I debated the wisdom of giving him the whole truth. Based on his demeanor, it seemed like the kindest option. "He said, 'Your dog will die like a dog... I watched the fires burn and I'll watch you die with a bullet in your skull. Just like him.'"

Working as a reporter from the time you're fifteen has its benefits; I can quote entire conversations verbatim should the need arise. It used to drive Michael nuts.

Juarez drove in silence for a while, staring straight ahead. Finally, he met my eye for an instant before he returned his attention to traffic.

"I really am sorry. I don't know what that meant... What he was thinking."

"He never liked me much. Apparently, the years haven't done anything to change his opinion."

I waited for him to argue the point. He did not.

"I'm assuming he was in Vietnam?" I asked.

"Three tours. Shrapnel in his knees and terrible stories he'd tell me when I was a kid. He and Joe signed up together."

That stopped me. "The old fire chief? I didn't know they even knew each other back then—it always seemed like your uncle and Joe Ashmont didn't get along."

Juarez shrugged. He passed a couple of pickups and slid back into the right lane without using his blinker, which was tantamount to vehicular madness compared to the way he'd been driving before. The Fed was loosening up.

"They had a fight at some point—over a woman, I think. But they grew up together in an orphanage in Westbrook. Neither of them had the best childhoods."

I saw an opening and took full advantage. "Did Matt ever talk to you about the fire when you were a kid? He and Joe were the first ones out there—them and my mother, anyway. I was hoping I'd get a chance to talk to Matt directly about the whole thing, but I don't know if that's the best idea given the circumstances."

He shot me a wry smile. "I think that's a safe bet. He never said very much about that day, though. Matt never liked to talk about work."

He was lying. I could tell by the way his hands tightened on the steering wheel as he risked a glance my way. His jaw tensed. Juarez had half a dozen tells, but the fact that he was a bad liar did nothing to ease my mind.

"That's weird—most cops I know love to relive their glory days."

"Thirty-four people died. He knew a lot of them. I don't think he thought of that as a glory day."

Right. Things got quiet again. I almost reached for the radio, but the thought that I might have to live through another Christina Aguilera/Kelly Clarkson medley stopped me cold.

"Do you remember the island?" he asked me after a few minutes. "You lived out there as a child, didn't you? You must remember what it was like out there."

"I remember a lot of it."

"The people?"

"It was a small community—we knew each other pretty well." Before he could continue with his questions, I countered with one of my own.

"What about you? You grew up in Miami—you must have some stories."

"A lot different than life in Maine, that's for sure. I went to a parochial high school. Joined the Marines not long after."

"And before that? You didn't start spending summers in Maine until you were a teenager, right? Where did little Jack Juarez spend his formative years?"

I'd been a reporter long enough to recognize the silence that followed: he was trying to decide how much of his story he was willing to tell. I kept my mouth shut and let him figure it out for himself.

"I don't remember," he finally said.

"You don't remember meaning, 'I don't want to talk about it'?"

" 'I don't remember' as in, I don't remember. I have no memories before I was a teenager."

That certainly stopped me. I stared at him. "No memories at all? Until when?"

"Thirteen," he said without hesitation. "I remember everything after that."

"But nothing before," I said. "Bike accidents, family pets, childhood illnesses?"

"No. What about you?"

"I remember all of them—I'm not the issue here. Don't you have family photos? What about stories your parents tell you?"

"My parents are dead. I don't remember them. I was raised by nuns in a convent just outside the city."

Logic was starting to stymie me. "Wait… Matt Perkins was an orphan."

He looked like he didn't get the connection.

"How did he find out he was your uncle? And why didn't he… I don't know, adopt you, instead of just having you up for the summers?"

Once the light bulb clicked, Juarez shook his head. "He's not really my uncle. He was in Miami one winter and ended up doing some maintenance work at the convent. We hit it off."

"And these nuns had no problem sending you a thousand miles away every summer to live with a strange bachelor who liked to give you presents and call you his nephew?"

That earned a smile. "They were very trusting women."

"Apparently."

We were in Portland by this time. Jack took the Forest Ave exit without directions from me and we merged with traffic heading past the University of Southern Maine, nestled in a neighborhood in the city's East End.

"Have you tried hypnosis?" I asked.

"Gee, I hadn't thought of that."

I gave him a look, which he returned.

"You said it's on Baxter?"

It took a second before I realized that he was talking about Jim Abbott's place. "Yeah—he's got a duplex." I gave him the address.

My experience with Portland in recent years was limited

to the downtown area, but Juarez navigated the quiet, tree-lined streets as though he'd spent some time there. Yet another topic to pursue when conversation lagged. For now, though, I had to get to work. He pulled into a rutted driveway badly in need of fresh paving, beside a faded gray duplex badly in need of fresh paint.

"I could come with you if you'd like," he offered.

"I think I've got it. Thanks, though. I probably won't be more than an hour, tops—I'll give you a call when I'm done?"

"Sounds good. I'll see you soon."

His hand brushed mine and our eyes caught. I forgot about his slow driving and terrible taste in music.

"Will you have dinner with me tonight?" he asked. "My treat. There's a nice little Eritrean place on the other side of town."

So, Juarez was familiar enough with Portland to know out-of-the-way ethnic places on the wrong side of the tracks. So many mysteries, so little time.

I nodded. "You're on. I'll talk to you soon."

The way things were going, we could spend another half an hour in the car discussing our plans for the evening, so I climbed out before I completely lost track of why I was there. He waited with the engine idling until I got to Jim Abbott's door, then drove off five miles under the speed limit once Abbott opened up and ushered me inside.

11

JIM ABBOTT WAS BUILT like a very tall stick figure with the posture of a yogi and a tangle of graying curls atop his narrow head. Two greyhounds, one flanking him on either side, completed what was a distinctly Seussian picture. Neither of the dogs barked, but they both sniffed at me politely before trotting off on slender legs to curl up side by side on a floral sofa pushed up against the far wall.

The apartment had old-fashioned wallpaper decorated with tiny pink roses, and a hardwood floor that needed buffing. Newspapers and boxes were piled high in every corner. A modular television the size of a bureau was tuned to a news program with the sound off.

Abbott motioned me through an archway to the kitchen, where the wallpaper had daisies and the appliances hadn't been updated since the '50s. We sat at a faded red kitchen table with matching vinyl chairs.

"It was my mother's place," Abbott explained. "She died six months ago—I'm still trying to clear everything out."

"I'm sorry. Don't worry about it, though—it's very Donna Reed."

He laughed. The sound triggered something—a flash of the past that was there and gone so quickly that it was hard to hang onto. Another kitchen table, long thin fingers clasped together. The same laugh, as my mother scolded me for… what?

"We've met before," I said. It was a revelation to me, and sounded it.

He nodded. His eyes were blue-gray and clear, giving the impression that he was younger than I suspected he must be.

"I wasn't sure you'd remember. It was a tough time, I know."

I tried to call up other memories, unsuccessfully. I felt like a swimmer navigating murky waters, the pictures around me too hazy to see clearly. Over the stove in Jim Abbott's kitchen, there was a black and white, plastic clock shaped like a cat's head. With each passing second, the bulging eyes moved from side to side. The time was quarter past two.

I handed him the photos I'd found in Malcolm Payson's things, uncertain how else to begin.

Abbott took them and shuffled through. "Son of a bitch," he said softly, when he got to the shot of the padlocked door. He looked annoyed, but not particularly surprised. "Where did you get these?"

"Isaac Payson's brother died—he left me the island, actually. These photos were in with a box of his things."

He shook his head and continued looking.

"I found the notes you took after you questioned my mother and me."

His eyes remained on the photos in his hands. I could tell by the slight tensing of his thin shoulders that I had his attention.

"You thought I was lying to you."

Abbott considered the statement long enough for the cat clock to roll its eyes a couple dozen times. He carefully put the photos back in order and set them on the table.

"Have you shown these to your mother?"

"Kat?" It wasn't the question I'd expected. "No—I've only told a couple of people about them. My mother and I don't really…"

He nodded without waiting for me to finish the sentence. "I'd be interested to hear what she has to say about them."

"Why?"

He knotted and unknotted his long fingers. Cracked the thumb knuckle of his left hand. The murky waters settled, for just a second.

"She's a child—she doesn't have to tell you a damned thing. She didn't see anything. She told Constable Perkins what she knows."

My mother is angry. I sit at the kitchen table in a chair too big for my child-sized legs to reach the floor, Jim Abbott seated across from me.

"You don't have to be afraid, Erin. I'm not here to hurt your Dad."

"Get out." My mother pulls the policeman from his chair, and I worry that he will shoot her. Arrest her. She's all I have left.

"I don't want to talk anymore." I start to cry.

The tall policeman goes away.

I couldn't remember him coming back.

"You think my mother had something to do with a cover-up?" I asked.

"I do," he said without hesitation. "She was one of the first ones out there. I think she was protecting your father."

"My father was with me."

He smiled, just a little. Kept his eyes steady on mine. "So you said."

I broke the stare first. I traced a crack in the Formica tabletop with my index finger. "My father died, you know."

"I heard that. I'm sorry."

"If something else happened that morning—something other than the story I gave police then…"

"You were ten years old, Erin. You're not culpable for anything. That case was closed a long time ago."

"What if I told you there was someone else on the island that morning? With that and these pictures, do you think they'd reopen the investigation?"

"What do you mean, there was someone else on the island?" he asked sharply. "When?"

"The day of the fire—my father and I went out there. There was a man in a black cloak… He chased me through the woods." I stopped. For the first time, I thought I understood why Kat had been so hell- bent on me keeping quiet; the whole story really did sound insane.

Abbott clearly thought so, too, though he was kind enough to play along. "You think that's the person who started the fire?"

I met his eye. "You were right—my father wasn't with me that morning. Something happened, but I don't know what. I don't know where he went. You talked to my mother, you talked to me. Did you…" I hesitated. "Did you interview my father?"

"I did." His voice was soft. "We spoke a few times. But he wasn't exactly… The fire took a toll on him."

"Meaning he went nuts," I interpreted. I tried to keep my voice matter of fact, but there was a ragged edge that I couldn't seem to control. "I know. He was never the same after that."

"He asked you to lie for him that day?"

I hesitated before I finally gave in. "That morning. We were staying in a motel on the mainland. He left while it was still dark out, and didn't get back until almost eleven. Before he left, he said I couldn't tell anyone he'd left me in the room alone or he'd get in trouble."

I thought of the giant motel beds, of scrounging for loose change in his pants pocket that morning so I could raid the hallway vending machine for breakfast. There was nothing usual about that morning.

"What was he like when he came back?" Abbott asked.

"That morning?" I thought about the question, phrasing my response carefully. "Distracted."

"That's it? Not upset?"

"We've gotta go, Erin—you don't have time to get your clothes. We'll get them later." My father is crying when he comes through the door. He grabs me by the arm and drags me outside. He won't answer my questions, and he drives too fast through Rockland traffic to get back to Littlehope.

"We're gonna get arrested, Dad—slow down."

He doesn't answer. He is too white, and his clothes are drenched. Rain is coming down hard. During the car ride, he prays softly and keeps his fingers tight around the steering wheel.

"Yeah. He might have been a little upset."

"What did he say? Did he tell you where he'd been?"

I shook my head—that much was true. "He didn't say anything. Just that we had to get to the island, but I had to stay in the boat."

"And when did you tell Katherine about this?"

"About what?"

"The lie. I mean… She knew, obviously. Did you tell her, or did Adam?"

"Nobody told her anything. She never knew."

Abbott scratched his pointed chin. "Listen, you don't need to protect her. It happened a long time ago… I'm just trying to get to the truth."

"And so am I," I insisted. "I'm not protecting her—I'm telling you, she never knew. I never told her, and my father sure as hell didn't. She was the whole reason he told me to lie in the first place."

I thought back to those days after the fire, trying to call up conversations I'd had with my mother. Had she asked me what happened? Pushed me to tell her the truth? I could remember little about that time, but I had a funny feeling that the reason I didn't remember that particular conversation was because we'd never had it.

"I don't know what to think anymore," I confessed. "If this was your investigation, where would you go next?"

"This *was* my investigation." He smiled dryly. "What about the other guy who was there—the one I'm assuming shot these pictures. Noel Hammond? He was there when the investigators arrived, if memory serves. And with the history between him and your mother, I always got the—"

"I'm sorry," I interrupted. "What history are you talking about, exactly?"

Abbott's eyebrows shot up toward his hairline. He bit his lip. "You didn't know about the, uh…"

" 'The uh' what? Noel Hammond was married."

"It was never confirmed—it was just a hunch I had. I could've been off base."

And pigs could fly. "Did my mother know about this theory of yours?"

"She denied it, as did Detective Hammond. No surprise there, of course."

"But you didn't believe them."

"I had my doubts."

He didn't come right out and say he knew my mother had been lying through her pearly white teeth, but it came through loud and clear anyway. My chair scraped across the linoleum as I stood. "Thank you for taking the time to speak with me—I really appreciate it. I should get going."

"Listen, I might have been wrong. I shouldn't have said anything."

"I'm sure you were right, actually. Don't worry about it. Things are making a little more sense now—thank you for being honest with me. If it's all right, could I call you with any further questions?"

He looked uncomfortable. Sorry for what he'd said, and even more sorry for me. I'd always loved being a reporter, but I'd never known what it was like to actually *be* the story.

It wasn't a good feeling.

"Of course," he agreed. "Call me anytime, I'll be happy to help any way that I can."

We shook hands and I was on my way. The prospect of a romantic dinner with Jack Juarez was suddenly the very last thing on my mind.

12

"NOEL FUCKING HAMMOND. Can you believe that?"

It was just after one a.m. I'd been waiting three hours for Diggs to get home from work; Juarez had given up and turned in at a little after ten. Our dinner together had been fine, but I was distracted and he was distracted, and neither one of us seemed eager to share the reasons for our distraction. Conversation was stilted, and we hurried through our Eritrean veggie platter and were back on the road by five. I'd had too much honey wine and ended up falling asleep in the car. I woke up as we were pulling into the driveway, glad to have the day come to an end.

And now, I was back in the kitchen with Diggs. We were both in sweats and slippers, munching on leftovers and talking quietly so we wouldn't wake Juarez. The fact that I'd never quite achieved this level of comfort with my ex-husband was not lost on me.

Diggs shook his head in response to my question. "It does seem a little coincidental. Noel Fucking Hammond." He was making fun of me, but that was fine. I knew I was onto something.

"She slept with him. Do you know how many times he

could have mentioned something about sleeping with my mother?"

"Several?"

"At least a few. You know how many times he *did* mention bumping uglies with my mom?"

"None?"

"None." I kicked back the last of my beer, my second of the night. "What the hell were they thinking? I mean, obviously something was going on. Do you think she slept with him to keep him quiet?"

Einstein sat up and rested his fuzzy chin on my thigh, ever hopeful. I gave him a piece of the leftover *injara* I'd brought home for Diggs. The dog gobbled it up, then resumed his position at my feet in hopes of more of the same.

Diggs got a glass of water from the fridge for himself, and I nodded gratefully when he tipped the pitcher my way. A headache was starting somewhere behind my eyes; more water and less beer was a good place to start. He sat back down, close enough that I could smell the chocolate on his breath from the hot cocoa he'd just finished.

"I don't have a clue why your mother would sleep with the guy," he finally answered. "Hey, you know who you could ask who probably *would* know?"

"Forget it," I returned. "I'm not calling my mother. I'm asking Hammond. And you better believe he's gonna tell me."

"Hammond won't even take your calls. Your mother, on the other hand…"

"Diggs."

"Solomon," he countered, the water at his lips.

Things got quiet for a few seconds. I kneaded the back of my neck, trying to ease the tension there. "Can we talk about something else, please?"

"Yeah, no problem." He studied me in that way he's been doing since I was fifteen—like I'm one of those translucent frogs you find somewhere in South America, all my twisted innards forever exposed to him. "I got a call today," he said. He let the silence stretch between us.

"Am I supposed to guess from whom? Because I'm a little tired for games."

"Michael."

"Michael my husband?"

"Ex-husband, isn't it?" I didn't say anything. He scratched his chin. "He said he's left a couple of messages but you're not returning his calls. He's worried—wanted to know if you saw your doctor before you left town."

I lay my head on the table, resting my cheek on the cool pine. I closed my eyes when Diggs brushed the hair from my forehead.

"You could've told me you were pregnant, you know," he said.

"I know that." His fingers remained in my hair, a ghost of a caress that brought back memories I wasn't prepared to revisit.

"How many times did we see each other? Hell, I saw you the weekend before the—"

"I didn't tell Michael, either."

He didn't say anything for so long that I looked up. "I don't want another call like that in the middle of the night— especially not from him."

Diggs had never made a secret of his disdain for Michael, but now there was pure bile in his tone. I got up and dumped the rest of my water down the drain. Diggs followed me over, but I noticed that he was careful not to stand too close when I turned to face him.

"So, this whole thing is…what? A pissing contest between you and my ex-husband because he was there to pick up the pieces when I almost bled to death on our bathroom floor, and you weren't? You're not my fucking guardian angel, Diggs. There was nothing you could've done."

His eyes flashed with that undercurrent of fury he always tries so hard to keep hidden. He closed the distance between us. I stood with my back to the sink, Diggs close enough that I could smell his aftershave and feel his heat, his gaze locked on mine.

"I should have known," he said. The anger was gone suddenly, replaced with a guilt so deep it almost hurt to look at him. "That weekend—I knew there was something wrong. You looked like hell, you weren't eating, didn't sleep… I've known you almost twenty years now. I should've known something was wrong."

I could have handled a fight—hell, I can always handle a fight. It's all those other, messier emotions that make me crazy.

"I didn't want you to know," I said. "Not yet. I needed to figure everything out first." I didn't go into the details, all the stupid scandalous crap with my philandering ex-husband and a baby I couldn't handle and the envelope from Malcolm Payson that had effectively upended my universe. I didn't really need to, though; Diggs always got that kind of thing.

We stood there in the kitchen in relative darkness for a few seconds, close but not quite touching. I fisted my hand in the front of his t-shirt. He didn't move. I took a step forward—enough that our bodies were flush, neither of us breathing. He tucked a tendril of hair behind my ear.

"Erin," he said. A whisper, so soft that it sounded part-plea.

I leaned up on my toes, my hands at his sides. He met me halfway, his lips softer than Michael's, his body familiar and tantalizing and terrifying against mine. For a few seconds, the kiss was the only thing that existed, his mouth warm and bruising, his hand tangled in my hair.

There was a battle he was fighting—I could feel it in the kiss, in the tension his body still held, in the way he never quite gave himself over to the moment. His left hand fell to my arm, squeezing gently as he started to pull away. Before he could disentangle himself entirely, there was the sound of movement at the kitchen door.

We sprang apart like a Roman candle had gone off between us.

Juarez stood at the door with an empty glass in his hand. "I was just—sorry, I couldn't sleep. I was getting some water. I'll—I can get it from the bathroom. Sorry," he repeated.

I couldn't look at Diggs. My face was burning, my body still charged with the kiss and the thought of where it might have led. I grabbed Einstein and hurried away, brushing past Juarez.

"Don't worry about it. I was just going to bed."

"Erin," Diggs called after me, but I was already halfway down the hall. I didn't turn back.

I tossed and turned for most of the night after that. About twenty minutes after I'd locked myself in my room like an angsty teen, I heard footsteps outside the door. If I'd expected Diggs to barge in, I was disappointed; he didn't even knock. I imagined him in the hallway wrestling with his conscience, already condemning himself for his moment of weakness. I told myself I was glad he didn't force the issue by making us talk it out then and there, and I almost believed it.

The next morning, I was up and out before dawn. I had been hoping to get Diggs to help me unlock Payson's mysterious suite that day, but I decided to go it alone. It wasn't like he'd been trained in lock picking anymore than I had. Besides which, it felt like I'd started to rely a little too much on the men in my life these days; it would do me good to stand on my own.

By the time I got to the island and made the trek up to the house, morning had broken. A cool, damp fog hung over the water and wrapped around the shore, and a light rain had dampened my hair and my spirits. My nose and fingers were ice cold. I could hear the low diesel hum of fishing boats in the harbor, but all else was silence. Apparently, the birds were sleeping in.

The wrought-iron gate I'd wrestled with the last time I was there had blown shut again, though I had thought I'd propped it open securely enough to stay that way. A niggling voice that sounded a lot like Diggs whispered warnings that I chose not to heed.

I checked my cell phone. There was a weak signal that might do the trick if I needed to make a call. Not that reassuring.

"It's my friggin' island," I said, after a few seconds of immobility. Einstein looked at me and whimpered, but he didn't argue.

I pulled the gate back open as wide as it would go, grabbed another branch from the forest floor, and wedged it in place. After a couple of times hauling on it, I convinced myself it wasn't moving again.

Einstein and I resumed our hike.

There was nothing strange about the house when I got there. Not that there would have been, necessarily, but I'd seen enough horror movies over the years that a ghostly face in the window or a slamming door wouldn't have been that surprising. Terrifying, yes; surprising, no. Once we were inside, though, there was nothing but the same old darkness and mildew and oppressive silence. Einstein growled at the meeting room entry, but after a few seconds waiting to see if the sky would fall, I convinced myself that he was just being paranoid. He's watched most of the same movies I have, after all.

The rain began to fall harder outside, beating down on the old roof and slashing against the windowpanes. I lit a couple of battery powered lanterns I'd brought over earlier in the week, and started a fire in the fireplace.

Einstein paced at the bottom of the stairs. He started up the steps a couple of times, whined, and returned to my side. I thought of the lamb's head we'd found the other day, then of the gate I had been almost positive I'd propped open securely before.

"We could call Diggs," I said.

Once the suggestion was out there, it sounded lame— especially given the incident the night before.

"Or not."

I got up from my spot by the fire, grabbed a flashlight and my trusty hammer, and headed up the stairs.

I opened the bedroom doors on the second floor in an effort to start airing the place out—which thrilled Einstein, who took advantage of the opportunity to explore a whole mausoleum's worth of new nooks and crannies. We were about halfway down the hall when he lost interest in the game and began to growl, then raced ahead of me, the fur raised along his spine and his tail held high. He stopped short at the double doors leading to my father's old room.

His nose was glued to the bottom of the door, his lips pulled back to reveal some very sharp canine teeth and a snarl I'd never seen before.

I went to the door and dragged him back by the collar. The growling gave way to a desperate whine as he tried to get away. He glanced at me, brown eyes anxious, then back at the door.

Shit.

I stood there for a moment of indecision. I could call someone. I *should* call someone. Especially if some lunatic had been out on the island screwing around with the gate—presumably the same lunatic with a penchant for decapitating farm animals.

Instead, I knocked on the bedroom door.

"Anybody in there? Ghosts, psychotic killers, mutants of the underworld?"

No answer.

I took a breath, since I'd forgotten to do so for a while. My hand fell to the doorknob.

I opened the door, the hammer held aloft.

Einstein tried to scoot past me, but I blocked his way. We stood in the doorway, the dog whining as my eyes adjusted to the darkness.

The smell was unmistakable. Something long dead lay in the center of the old wood floor, beside a double bed that had once belonged to my mother and father.

"So, I guess we found the rest of that lamb," I said.

I ordered Einstein to sit just outside the threshold, which he did grudgingly. Sure enough, by the light of my flashlight I traced the body of a decapitated lamb, the wool and part of the flesh well-rotted by now. Someone must have been holding onto this for a while—when we were here just two days ago, Einstein hadn't shown any signs of smelling it, so I couldn't imagine it had been in the house long.

Which meant someone had been here. Recently. The realization blindsided me: I wasn't overreacting. This wasn't my imagination, or just some redneck playing a prank. Someone had been here, and whoever that someone was, they had access to the house and an obvious axe to grind. I returned to the hallway and closed the bedroom door, then started to call Diggs before I reconsidered and called Juarez instead.

The call went straight to voicemail. I left a message and hung up. Once Einstein realized he wouldn't be having lamb for lunch, he abandoned me and headed back downstairs to chase wayward field mice around the house. I waited for Juarez to return my call and tried to sort through everything that had happened since I'd first gotten to town.

There were Joe Ashmont's threats on the first day, followed by the discovery of the lamb's head on the property and my bizarre run-in with Matt Perkins in the middle of the night. I was now convinced that it hadn't been the wind at all and someone had actually re-closed the gate to the property within the last day or so, but that was pretty minor compared to the beheaded corpse in my father's old bedroom. The fact that they'd chosen that particular room told me that whoever this was had some knowledge of the Payson boarding house—certainly more than they could have gotten from reading a few articles online.

I may be slow on the uptake, but I'm not a complete idiot—it was time to get the hell out of Dodge, at least until I had some backup. My mind made up, I headed for the stairwell before I realized I hadn't heard anything from Einstein in a few minutes. I called for him and heard a muffled 'woof' downstairs in response—as though he was barking behind a closed door.

My heart sped up and my mouth went dry. Einstein kept barking, his yips higher in pitch once he realized he couldn't get to me. I made for the stairs at just short of a run, the hammer clutched in my right hand. I was five steps away, maybe less, moving fast while the dog kept barking and the blood rushed in my ears and the darkness closed in, when I heard the clip of heavy footsteps coming toward me. I wheeled around an instant before he hit, tackling me with a lowered shoulder and the force of a freight train. The momentum carried us both a solid three feet before I slammed back against the wall with a faceless man's hands around my throat.

13

EVERYTHING AFTER THAT WAS A BLUR. I dropped my flashlight but managed to hang onto my precious hammer, slamming it hard into my attacker's side. He yelped and dropped his hands from around my throat, but he was on me again before I could get free. He pulled the hammer from my hand and it dropped to the floor. I struck out blindly, and managed to get a solid left hook in before he countered with a blow to my right cheek that nearly dropped me where I stood.

I kicked out blindly, trying to recall the lessons I'd learned in self-defense classes back in Boston. Knees, nuts, eyeballs. The problem was, I couldn't see a damned thing. I landed a glancing blow to his leg before I struck upward and the heel of my hand caught his chin; I felt the bristle of a beard before he knocked my arm aside and a second blow landed dead on as his knuckles connected with my lip.

I landed on my back, hard, tasting the cold copper of blood in my mouth as I fought for breath. He was on me in an instant, a thick body with no fat, his movements fast and fluid as he grabbed my bangs, tearing them out at the roots.

His fingernails dug into my scalp and he pulled my head forward, then smashed my skull back into the floor.

The world exploded into fragments of light on impact.

I just lay there for a moment, too stunned to fight.

He didn't move, still straddling me. When I finally got my wits about me again, I writhed beneath him, bucking my body, trying to free my arms to strike out. It didn't work; he pinned my wrists over my head with one large hand, the other wrapped around my throat.

I could smell his breath, could feel it against my face as his lips found my ear.

"Stop looking," he whispered. His hand tightened around my throat until the blackness gave way to white light swimming behind my eyelids and I tensed, bucking harder as I fought for breath.

And then, the world went still.

I didn't move for a good five minutes after I finally came around again. Einstein was still yelping frantically, from somewhere that sounded very far away. I managed to get to my hands and knees before dizziness and terror and pain took hold, and I threw up on the hardwood floor.

When I felt like it wasn't too radical a move, I got up slowly, walking my hands up the side of the wall like a toddler just learning to stand. My throat was sore, my voice raw when I called out to Einstein, trying to soothe him before I finally staggered down the stairs and let him out of the pantry where he'd been trapped.

My cell phone rang while Stein was still trying to reassure himself that we were both all right. I flipped it open, glanced at the caller ID, and tried to steady myself before I answered.

"I'm on the island. Can you come?" My voice sounded

anything but steady.

"I'll be right there." Juarez hung up without asking for details. I sank to the floor and gathered Einstein in my arms, both of us still shaking.

We waited for the cavalry.

●

"You didn't see him at all?"

"It was dark. I couldn't—ow," I pulled away from Juarez's probing fingers when he touched my cheekbone, sending a lightning bolt of pain straight to my aching head.

"Sorry."

We were sitting at one of the old picnic tables in the meeting room. Einstein had been trying to climb inside me ever since I'd managed to free him. Now he was in my lap—all forty pounds of him—whining incessantly. When I flinched, the whine became a growl. Juarez dropped his hand.

"I don't think anything's broken, but we need to get you to the hospital. You could have a concussion."

"I'm not going to the hospital." I took his index finger and raised it until it was eye level, then moved his hand back and forth across my line of sight.

"See? No problem tracking the movement. I checked my pupils, too—equal and reactive, just like on TV. I spent enough time tagging along as a kid with my mother to know what I'm talking about. There's no concussion. I'm fine."

Juarez didn't look so sure about that. I knew I'd sounded shaken on the phone, but now I was back in control. Sort of. A little freaked out and very sore, but in control all the same.

And very, very pissed.

"I didn't get a look at him because it was so dark, but it was definitely a man. I think he had a beard."

Juarez nodded. Despite a blazing fire and feeling slightly better than I had an hour ago, I couldn't stop shivering.

"Did he say anything?"

I thought of his mouth at my ear, the smell of stale breath. "Just 'Stop looking.' Short and sweet."

"And you didn't recognize the voice?"

I shook my head.

"What about smells? Close your eyes."

I did, but re-opened them almost immediately when the images came back too fast. "Can we do this later?"

"Sorry." He sat down beside me. "This kind of thing happens and I go straight into cop mode. Are you sure you're all right? If you won't go to the hospital, at least come back to the mainland with me. You need to lie down for a while."

"I will—later. But first..." I stood, then reconsidered when gravity proved more formidable than usual. "How are you at petty crime?"

Whatever you might say about his driving or his horrific musical taste, Juarez had it all over Diggs when it came to breaking and entering. Since the stairwell up to Isaac Payson's apartment on the third floor was so narrow, I let Juarez lead the way. He took a couple of small tools from his wallet, fiddled with the door for a few seconds, and, *voila*, he was inside. He glanced back my way.

"You want me to...?"

"Yeah, go ahead. I'm right behind you." My heart hammered in time to the pounding in my temples; the last thing I wanted was to be the first one entering another dark, forbidding room.

If I'd been expecting mirrors on the ceiling or chains

on the walls, I was disappointed; Payson's lair was tidy and innocuous. There were more of the same kinds of creepy religious paraphernalia found around the rest of the house: crosses and paintings; moldy needlepoint with Bible verses; Christ with kids and lambs. The first bedroom in the apartment was small, with just enough room for a bureau, a four-poster bed, and a couple of nightstands. I searched for photos of Payson and his wife Mae, but found none.

Juarez opened a door at the far side of the room and looked to me for the okay before he went inside. I followed him into a long, narrow alcove with a low ceiling and three twin beds spaced evenly apart from one another. There were no windows, and just the one entrance. Juarez and I both bounced our flashlight beams over the walls, where we found children's drawings and more Bible verses tacked on peeling floral wallpaper.

The room was warm compared with the rest of the house; it was hard to get a full breath in the fetid air. I remembered playing a game as a kid, where I'd jump onto my bed from the furthest point possible so any monsters lurking beneath couldn't grab my ankles. Standing there beside Juarez, just inches from beds that had belonged to children whose laughter I could still remember, I felt the same fear of unnamed beasties and ghosts from beyond the grave.

"His children slept here?" Juarez asked.

I nodded. "Micah, Sarah, and Ezra."

"You knew them?"

I walked out of the little alcove abruptly, my breath coming harder. "I knew everybody."

I headed for the door, intent on leaving the Paysons behind. Just as I was reaching for the doorknob, my flashlight beam bounced off something beside the dresser. Juarez stood by as I went to investigate.

Half-buried in dust and grime, almost hidden from view behind the old bureau, was a rosary. The crucifix was made of cut glass, the beads carved from what I suspected was bone.

"Why would someone running a Pentecostal church have a Catholic rosary?" Juarez asked, looking over my shoulder

I examined the pendant carefully, then paused when my fingers stumbled over letters etched into the glass. I shined my flashlight on the area. "RW," I said, half to myself.

"Payson's wife's name was Mae, wasn't it?" Jaurez asked. I nodded.

"So, who was RW?" he pressed.

I shook my head. The motion made my headache worse, and the surroundings weren't doing much for my mood. The kicker, of course, was the dawning realization that someone had tried to kill me. Okay—maybe *kill* was too strong a word. If my attacker had really wanted me dead, he sure as hell wouldn't have gotten much resistance from me, based on how ineffectual I'd been at fighting him off. But he *had* wanted me to go home, and he'd clearly wanted me to take his recommendation seriously.

I didn't know who RW was. I thought of the lamb's body still in my father's old bedroom, and the puddle of vomit in the hallway that I had yet to clean up. It wasn't even noon yet, and the whole world had turned upside down.

Juarez touched my shoulder. "Erin?"

I nodded. Standing was a monumental act of will. "Yeah. I don't know—I don't have a clue who RW was. I don't have any more answers than you do, at this point."

His hand remained at my shoulder. It was warm and solid, and after a moment it migrated to the back of my neck and his thumb brushed against my nape, his fingers kneading the tense muscles there. I closed my eyes.

"Let's go back to the mainland," he said. "You should rest."

For once, I didn't argue.

●

It was still raining when Juarez and I got back home that afternoon, a very bedraggled Einstein following in our wake. Diggs was still at work, for which I was grateful. Juarez made lunch while I popped a few Tylenol and avoided every mirror in the house. The chicken was sautéing and I was at the table contemplating my mysterious rosary when Juarez sat down beside me. He inched his chair closer to mine.

"How's your head?"

"I'm all right."

He cupped my cheek in his hand. It was cool and callused. After a second's hesitation, I leaned into his touch.

"I'm glad you called me," he said.

"I'm glad you came out."

He dropped his hand, but didn't move any further away. "Of course. But I still think we need to tell someone—report what happened. You could have been killed. And whoever did this is still out there somewhere."

"Not yet—I don't want cops swarming the island. I probably just surprised some squatter. If he'd wanted to do more damage, he could have. I'm fine." I couldn't tell whether he bought the story or not.

"I think Diggs is right about this," he said. "You shouldn't be out there alone."

"He told you that?"

"We had a talk the other day. He's just worried about you." He stopped. We'd managed to go all this time with neither of us mentioning the kiss he'd walked in on the night before, or why I'd called him instead of Diggs this morning. I had a feeling that streak was about to end, though.

"There's nothing going on between us," I said.

"I know that."

Well, that was certainly easier than I'd expected.

"I spoke with Diggs this morning—he said the same thing," Juarez said.

"That there's nothing going on," I repeated. It was fine for me to say it, but I felt inexplicably annoyed that Diggs was singing the same tune.

"It's not my business," he said. "He's concerned—we can leave it at that." His gaze fell back to the rosary in my hand. Apparently, that conversation was over.

"May I see it?"

I handed him the rosary.

"It's well made," he noted. "And old, I suspect. Do you remember anyone in the church with those initials?"

"I'll have to go back over the roster of members."

"I would have thought you'd have it memorized by now. No one comes to mind? Rachel, Raymond, Randall. Rebecca?"

I looked at him. His proximity was suddenly anything but comforting, and the intensity in his eyes was downright unsettling. I eased my chair backward.

"My head's not quite where it should be," I said. "Otherwise, I'm sure I'd remember."

He got up to tend the chicken and laid the rosary back on the table. I stood.

"I'm sorry—it turns out I'm not feeling quite as well as I'd thought. I think I'm just gonna take a shower and try to get a little sleep."

I took Einstein—who wasn't at all keen on leaving the chicken behind—and we retired to our room. When I was safely inside, I realized that my heart was beating too fast yet again. Another adrenaline surge like the ones I'd experienced today and I was likely to go into overdrive. Or sink into catatonia. I locked my bedroom door, my fingers curled around the rosary—the latest piece in a puzzle I was beginning to doubt I'd even survive to solve.

AUGUST 10, 1990

THE SUN IS a distant white haze, the field around thick with blades of tall grass gone yellow from the drought. Rebecca revels in the silence. The buzz of bees at her ankles, the sweetness of pine and sea salt on the wind, the call of island birds basking in the warmth of their summer home.

There was never peace with her husband, but there was immeasurable peace without him. Early mornings after Joe would leave for the boat, before Zion awoke, Rebecca would be alone. She would check on her son first, watching his chest rise and fall. Then, she would go down to the water and listen to the surf break over the granite shoreline. The constant tension of a warring homefront made those reprieves more than cathartic—they were like a lungful of air before she was pulled under once more.

It is early afternoon, and Rebecca feels she has earned a few moments of solitude. Seated on a boulder in a thicket of pine and spruce, she hears the crack of a dead tree limb underfoot. She knows before he enters her hiding place exactly who it is. Whispering through the silence, Rebecca looks up to meet Matt's eye.

"You shouldn't be here," she says.

Despite the fact that he is now the constable of Littlehope, Matt Perkins looks the way he always has to her: too fragile, slightly off-center, his blue eyes watching the world with the suspicion and naked hope of a beaten dog.

"I could say the same. I came to get you."

She shakes her head. "I'm staying, Matt."

"The hell you are. Get Zion—I'll take you someplace safe."

"Will you, now?"

He takes another step toward her. Rebecca notes for the first time that he's wearing his uniform. She wonders if he is armed. This might be cause for concern in anyone else, but Matt isn't anyone else. He's no one. The boy she loved grown to the only man she trusts. It doesn't matter, though; she knows his limitations.

"He'll find us. You know that," she says.

"He'll find you here, too."

"Isaac can keep us safe." *The way you can't.* She doesn't say the words, but she knows he hears them nonetheless.

"It isn't good for Zion. You don't know anything about Isaac Payson."

"I know he wouldn't hurt my son, and I know that he wouldn't hurt me. I know that he's been chosen."

Matt steps in closer. She can tell that he hasn't been sleeping. The whites of his eyes shine like glass, splintered with red veins. She remembers the same look when he used to sneak into her room at the home late at night, shaking from the latest nightmare. Pleading to stay with her.

"I've been reading about this, Becca. Talking to experts. People die in these kinds of places."

He stops. An instant later, Rebecca hears the rustle of leaves behind them. She turns, following Matt's gaze, to find Adam approaching. It's plain by the way he smiles at them both that he's heard at least a portion of their conversation.

"Good morning, Rebecca. Matt."

Matt nods, immediately assuming his role. For a man as weak, as tremblingly fallible as Rebecca knows Matt Perkins to be, he is still one of the best actors she's ever known. He smiles, and it appears entirely sincere.

"Nice to see you, Adam."

The men study one another. The sun bears down on Rebecca's back until she feels a trickle of sweat between her shoulder blades.

"How's everything on the mainland?" Adam asks.

"Fine. Couple of bar fights over at the Shanty. Kat patched everybody up and they were laughing it up by the end of the night." He keeps his eye on Adam. "Your girl was with her. Doesn't seem like the best way to raise a little one—patching up bloody fishermen, Erin playing pinball till closing while her mum drinks her weight in whiskey and leaves with whoever's sober enough to get 'em home in one piece."

The words strike their mark, as intended. A flicker of pain crosses Adam's face; she sees Matt's satisfaction in the way his arms hang loose at his side, a smile that's very nearly a sneer at the corner of his lips. He is not a cruel man—not as cruel as Joe, at any rate. He can be mean, though. She has seen him take pleasure in another's suffering more than once, always surprised to see the trait in one who has only shown her kind words and a gentle hand.

"Katherine has her problems, but she loves our daughter," Adam says. "She's a good mother." He doesn't sound convinced.

"It's better than being out here, I guess. An island out in the middle of nowhere's no place to raise a child." Matt looks at Rebecca meaningfully. She holds his eye until he looks away, as though ashamed of his behavior.

"There's nowhere safer than here for most children. You should speak to some of the young people raised on the island, Constable. Self-assured, well-adjusted, healthy. At peace."

"And yet, you toss your little one to the wolves on the mainland. Why is that, Adam?"

Rebecca waits for his answer, having considered the question herself. The man looks lost for a moment. When he comes to, he nods up the path toward the house.

"Isaac is at the greenhouse, Constable, if you'd like to see him. I'm sure he'd be happy if you joined us for lunch."

Rebecca sees the annoyance on Matt's face before he can hide it. He clears his throat; looks over his shoulder.

"No, I should get back—I just came to see Becca. Just wanted to make sure everything's okay out here."

"Everything's fine," Adam says. His façade of peaceful self-assurance has been restored. "She and Zion fit in very well."

Despite his words, Matt makes no move to go. Adam likewise remains where he is. It's a staring contest between two little boys, but Adam doesn't seem shaken by the competition. The smile on his face is less the easy warmth of an apostle, more the sleeping fire of an archangel. He does not budge. Matt looks away first. For a moment, Rebecca feels her old friend's defeat as though it were her own, and is disappointed to find a tiny stone of hatred for Adam beginning to form somewhere deep.

She considers asking Adam to leave them, but the look on his face changes her mind. Though she knows he would never lay a hand on her physically, he is still the closest person to Isaac. She can't risk going against a man with the power to turn the Reverend from her. The realization that she is once again caught between warring men, each intent on deciding her future, makes the tiny, hateful stone inside begin to grow.

For his part, Adam seems content with the way the conversation has gone. He straightens, ignoring Matt for a moment to address Rebecca. "When you're through, Isaac would like to see you in the garden."

He nods casually at Matt, and finally leaves them. Matt turns to her once he's out of sight. The mask has vanished, fury and terror mixed in his bloodshot eyes.

"See that? They're watching you. You're not safe here—you have to make a choice."

She shakes her head, turning her back on him in favor of the path toward Isaac. "That's where you're wrong. You were always the one with the choices. I had Joe; now God has sent me Isaac. There is no choice for me—there never has been."

She leaves him behind. As she walks away, she feels each blade of dead grass strike with razor-sharp precision at her bare ankles. She takes one last, deep breath and lets the silence work its magic before she rejoins the church.

14

UNDERSTANDABLY ENOUGH, sleep didn't come easily after the attack. I dozed on and off, but otherwise stayed up writing for most of the day and a good part of the night. When Diggs knocked softly on my door at a little after one a.m., I chose the coward's way rather than facing him and pretended I was sleeping.

By the time I actually did fall asleep, night had given way to the soft edges of a gray dawn. I dreamed of masked men and burning buildings, my father at the center of everything, and when I woke two hours later, my nerves were strung tight. Diggs was already gone for the day, and Juarez was likewise not in attendance. My right eye was swollen and purple, my bottom lip looked like a Botox injection gone horribly awry, and my body felt like I'd been run over— twice –and then wrung out bone by bone.

Since 'pretty' wasn't an adjective I expected anyone would be using to describe me anytime soon, I decided to get on with my day with the lofty goal of not scaring the crap out of the neighborhood kids. I put on jeans and t-shirt, and stole an old Nick Cave sweatshirt and a black baseball hat from Diggs' closet. I pulled my hair into a ponytail and added the requisite sunglasses, made myself coffee and toast, and then paused when I found a note from Diggs on the fridge.

Thought you'd want to know: your buddy Noel Hammond's back in town. Can we talk? I've made time tonight if you will. Love, D

I groaned. While it wasn't likely I would have been able to hide from Diggs until the swelling had gone down and the bruises had faded, I'd been prepared to give it the old college try. The news about Hammond being back in town was encouraging, though. I decided to lay aside my wounded pride after the disastrous kiss-that-wasn't the other night, and headed for the door as I hit speed dial on my cell.

Diggs answered on the second ring.

"So you are speaking to me," he said.

"Looks like. Thanks for the heads up on Hammond—I'm headed over there now."

"And we can talk tonight?"

Outside Diggs' front door, the sun shined and the birds sang. I waited while Einstein christened a nearby rosebush.

"We can, but…Diggs, it's not a big deal."

"It is a big deal—I just wanted to say I was sorry."

"For kissing me."

There was a breath's length of a pause on the line. "Well… Yeah, for that."

"Except I was the one who kissed you. So—no harm, no foul. It was just a kiss, Diggs. Don't tell me all this time in the sticks has turned you into a blushing virgin."

He laughed, just barely. "No, not yet. Give it a little time, though. I just…" He sighed. "You're important to me, Sol. And I know how much you have going on right now. Something in your life should be uncomplicated, you know?"

"And you want to be that something," I said.

"No one else seems to be volunteering."

He didn't mention Juarez, but the implication was clear. "Maybe we could go out to dinner tonight?" I asked, since it didn't appear there was a way around it. "Just you and me. I need to run some things by you."

That would give me an entire day to figure out how to tell him I'd been beaten to a pulp by a phantom assailant, and had called a virtual stranger instead of him to come save my ass.

"Eight o'clock at the Shanty okay with you?"

The Shanty was a little lobster shack-slash-bar on the water. It was long on history, short on class, and used to make the best chili fries this side of heaven. It seemed a fitting place for Diggs and me to renew our vows of sporadic chastity and enduring friendship.

"I'll see you then."

I disconnected first, clipped Einstein's leash to his collar, and we were off once more.

I stopped at Wallace's General Store for gas, and cursed the lack of technology that meant I'd have to go inside and face the cruel world rather than revel in the anonymity of a quick-and-dirty debit card swipe. It was ten o'clock on a sunny Saturday morning, which meant the store was packed. I stood in line with my eyes focused on the wooden floorboards, hoping no one would notice that I looked like an embittered battered wife in a Lifetime Movie of the Week.

That hope was shot to hell when I heard someone clear their throat behind me. I was next up in line at the cash register, a twenty dollar bill already in hand. When I didn't respond to the sound, Joe Ashmont chuckled.

"Looks like somebody put you in your place, missy."

I turned around. He held a whiskey bottle in one hand, already opened and missing the first round. In the other, he clutched a pack of cigarettes and, oddly enough, a bag of tangerines. Cirrhosis or lung cancer might be a valid concern for old Joe, but at least scurvy wasn't in the cards.

"That happen out on the island?" he asked.

I took a step away from him. "It's none of your business."

He nodded amicably. His eyes remained hard, his mouth fixed in a fool's grin as he continued to appraise me. "Guess you're right about that. No business of mine when a pretty woman gets her clock cleaned." He paused. "Not unless I'm the one did the cleanin', that is."

My mouth went dry. I met his gaze for the first time, trying to ignore my trembling hands and the sudden clench in my stomach. He nodded toward the cashier.

"Go on ahead—I think they're ready for you."

I put my twenty on the counter without speaking, aware that Ashmont's eyes were still on me.

"It's the Jetta at pump three," I managed. I headed for the door before the girl behind the counter could respond. I was still pumping my gas when Ashmont came out and headed straight for me.

Einstein growled at sight of him, his teeth bared, his nose quivering at the window I'd left cracked in the backseat.

"I told you people don't want you here," Ashmont said when he was still a few feet away.

"I hadn't noticed." I replaced the nozzle in the pump, screwed the gas cap back on, and tried to hide the fact that my knees were knocking together like castanets.

"You must get that spine of yours from your mum—your daddy was a pussy from the word go. Anybody'd think twice before they'd mess with Kat, though. And now, we're all gonna pay for that—for the way she used people up, got 'em to go her way."

He stepped closer. Einstein started barking, doing his damnedest to squeeze through the narrow opening I'd left for him.

"I'll tell you a secret, though." I could smell him—salt and whiskey, cigarettes and lobster bait. He smiled at me. His eyes were as hard as black jade. "Your mum's not getting out of this one. You take anybody down, she'll be first to fall. You remember that, when you think about whether this story you're telling is worth it."

He turned and left before I could ask him what the hell he was talking about. I got back in the car still shaking, thinking once more about the attack the day before. Could it have been Ashmont? Juarez had asked me about size and smell—Ashmont might be the right size, but you could smell him coming from a mile away. I would have known if it was him. Wouldn't I?

I was feeling a whole lot less confident about that by the time I pulled into Noel Hammond's driveway a few minutes later.

Hammond opened the door before I had a chance to knock. He took one look at my face and the color drained from his own. He stepped aside and motioned me in.

"I guess Diggs must have mentioned I'd be stopping by," I said.

"He didn't mention you'd look like you just went three rounds with Mike Tyson when you did, though."

"Yeah, well... He wasn't trying to keep you out of the loop, he just doesn't know that part yet."

Hammond's house was small and tidy, with a potbelly stove in the corner of the living room, one plump cat curled up on the windowsill, and another on the sofa. I could smell homemade bread baking in the next room. The walls were covered with pictures of a younger Hammond and a pretty blonde woman I assumed was his wife, along with framed photos documenting the growth of a cute blonde girl who grew into a cute blonde woman with two cute blonde babies.

I motioned to one of the photos. "Your daughter?"

"Jasmine. Those are her kids—Winnie and Ephraim. Twins."

"Nice."

We stood there for a few seconds in silence, our eyes fixed on the same photo.

"How old is she?"

He hesitated. "Twenty-one."

Born after the fire. And the affair with my mother, one assumed.

"Can I get you anything? Tea, coffee? I think I have a beer in there somewhere." He motioned to a spot on the sofa.

"I'm fine." I took a seat, doing my best to avoid disturbing the cat as I did so. Hammond turned a rocking chair by the stove so that it was facing me and sat down.

"Diggs said you had a conversation with Jim Abbott."

"That I did."

The cat opened sleepy eyes and gazed at me from half-shut lids. He stretched double paws, arched his back, and flicked his tail at me as he hopped down and headed for Hammond's lap.

When I didn't volunteer any further information about my meeting with Abbott, Hammond shook his head.

"You're as stubborn as your mother."

I looked at him. His eyes remained level with mine, as though he knew exactly how big a can of worms he'd just opened with the statement.

"Abbott said he thought you two were having an affair, back when he was doing the investigation."

"We weren't."

I looked at him doubtfully. For the first time, his cool demeanor wavered.

"It wasn't an affair." He scratched his chin and stared at the floor. "It was an indiscretion, no more. Alice—my late wife—and I were having a hard time. I came here to get away for a while; she stayed in the city. I got the call to come out and help with the fire that day."

"Were you and Kat already together at that point?"

"I never met her before that day. I was one of the first firefighters out there—when I got there, Kat was having a knock-down, drag-out with Joe Ashmont and Matt Perkins."

"The fire chief and the constable," I said.

"Yeah. I wasn't clear on why your mother was even there—there obviously weren't any survivors. There wasn't anything she could have done."

"What were they fighting about?"

Hammond ran his knuckles along the cat's spine; I could hear purring from my seat across the room. The other cat—a long-haired, marmalade butterball—got up from his spot at the window and threaded itself between his legs.

"You should talk to your mother," Hammond finally said.

"I don't want to talk to my mother. I'm here—just tell me. I know her. Nothing you say could shock me, trust me."

He smiled at that, like I was a kid who'd said something

cute.

"She's a good woman. A hard person to know, it's true—but she loves you. And she loved your father. She was just doing what she could to protect you both."

"By sleeping with you."

He sat up straighter. He looked more tired than he had when we first met, though it had only been a few days ago. I seemed to have that effect on people lately.

"Yeah." He smiled faintly. "You look like her, you know. Your eyes." Another second of silence passed before he made up his mind. "I never found out exactly what the fight was about. It was early afternoon. The Fire Marshal and his team, along with the investigators and the ME, didn't get out there till the next day. We were supposed to keep watch over the place until everybody got there. Preserve the scene."

I nodded, recalling Sergeant Flint's account of the story. "So, this was after my father and I got there."

"Yeah. Long after. I don't know where Adam was by then. You were there, though." He looked at me with pity, like he was seeing the child I'd been instead of the woman I'd become. Or maybe seeing both.

"Ashmont looked like he'd had the snot kicked out of him, and Perkins just looked like…a beaten man. Like everything worth living for had just gone up with that church. Kat was the only one in control."

"That sounds like my mother."

"The fire died down, and most of the crew left. It was early evening by this time. The second they were gone, Kat started moving the bodies. She told Ashmont and Perkins to shovel the remains into a pile, everything together. I don't think she even realized I was still there."

"And so the padlock…"

He nodded. "Everything. Anything that made it look

like what it was—the position of the bodies, the locked door… It all got shoveled away. It was all a mess anyway, of course—soaked and destroyed. But she wasn't doing it to be helpful."

"And Ashmont and Perkins just went along with this?"

"I told you—they'd already checked out. You ask me, they were as invested in covering things up as she was. When they realized I'd gotten some photos of the scene, Ashmont threatened me. I managed to back him down, though."

I thought of the man who had accosted me at the general store—his sour breath and cruel smile, the violence he wore like a badge. "How'd you do that?"

"I think a couple of swings might have been exchanged."

"But Kat was more persuasive."

He stopped again. Looked at the floor. "It was the next night. I had a cabin out on West Shore Road for the summer. Your mother showed up with a bottle of tequila and two shot glasses. She'd been crying."

This was the least plausible thing Noel had said so far. He saw the doubt on my face and shook his head.

"She's not as hard as you think. It wasn't an act—trust me, nobody's that good. She might have come there to seduce me, but the tears were real. The fear."

"She thought Dad did it," I said suddenly. It shouldn't have been surprising, but it was—I'd just assumed somehow that I was the only one with doubts about my father. "Did he?" I prompted, when he didn't say anything.

He continued to stare at the floor. My eyes watered. When I wiped the tears away, I forgot about the bruises; the physical pain pushed the emotional crap away, and I was back in control.

"I didn't think so at the time," he said. "I don't know

what I think anymore. But your mother believed he did. We... Everything just kind of happened from there. Two days later, Alice called and told me she was pregnant."

"And Kat told you to keep your mouth shut or she'd call your wife and tell her all about your little...indiscretion. And you agreed. Said nothing, leaving the murders of thirty-four people unsolved."

"I didn't see it that way."

I tried to read him, figure out what it was he thought had happened out there. Then, suddenly, it hit me.

"The man who was out there—did you see him?"

He looked up, unable to hide his surprise. "What man?"

"There was a man—my father told me he wasn't real, that I imagined him. Kat told me the same thing. Made me promise never to mention him. But there was a man who chased my father and me once we got on the island."

"You're sure about that?"

I was, suddenly. For the first time in my life, I was positive. The man I'd seen on the island that day had been real, no matter what my parents might have said to the contrary. "Yeah. I'm sure."

He got up from his rocking chair so fast both cats skittered away, their tails twitching. He went into the other room without a word, then returned a minute or two later with a thick manila file folder. He opened it and selected three photos.

A blackened body half-covered in charred wood and debris, one hand raised as though in supplication. "It's a burned body. What else am I supposed to be seeing?"

"Look at the placement—it's a burned body on the other side of the wreckage. Not everyone was locked inside the church."

I wasn't following him.

"It was Isaac Payson," he said before I had to ask. "Our theory was that he'd drugged everyone, locked them in the chapel, and then sat outside the door and waited for the flames to take him, too."

"These are more pictures no one saw, I take it?"

"I took them that afternoon when I first showed up, before Kat and the others got to the bodies."

It was a good minute or more before I could say anything. In the meantime, I sat in shocked silence while the cats purred and Hammond waited for me to pull myself together.

"I'm sorry," he said.

"This isn't just some little white lie," I said finally. "She destroyed evidence. She obliterated it, for Christ's sake." I thought of Ashmont's words about my mother earlier that morning: *You take anybody down, she'll be the first to fall.* I had no idea what the penalty for this kind of thing might be, but I couldn't imagine it would be light.

I cast an accusing eye at Hammond. "You were a cop— how could you just *let* her do that? You had proof, and you just let the killer go. There was a mass murder and no one was ever held accountable for that. That man I saw on the island—"

"The man no one else ever saw—the one both your parents said you imagined? Listen, your mom gave a hell of a good argument for why burying the evidence was the best thing for everyone. I could've fought her on it, but thirty-four people were dead. Including Isaac Payson, who as far as I could see was the one who set the fire in the first place. Your mother was right about one thing: a big investigation would've led right to your father's front door."

I felt sick. Sick and tired, and the more answers I got, the less any of this made sense. "So you did all this for my father? You and my mother and Joe Ashmont and Matt Perkins all risked your careers to save my father—*that's* the story you expect me to believe?"

"I expect you to believe whatever the hell you want. I'm just telling you what I thought was the truth at the time."

"But you don't think it's the truth anymore?"

He actually laughed at that—a tired, disgusted laugh that made me think Noel Hammond had been wrestling with the real story behind this fire for as long as I had. "I don't know what the truth is anymore. I'm working on a theory, though."

"Involving the man who chased me on the island that day?"

He hedged. "I don't know." I had the feeling he was being honest. "Give me a couple of days, though, and I think I'll have some answers for you."

I tried to imagine my mother doing everything Hammond said she'd done: sleeping with a stranger, destroying evidence, blackmailing a man who just wanted to get on with his life. From the time I was a child, my mother had been a mystery to me—a driven, ambitious woman who rarely let anything get in the way of a surgical career that eclipsed everything else in her life. She loved me—I knew that, because I had seen her give up that career to stay in Littlehope when we both probably would have been better off somewhere else.

Would she have done those things?

There wasn't a question in my mind. If it meant protecting my father and me, she would have done them without hesitation. Without remorse.

I took out the rosary Juarez and I found on the island the night before, and handed it to Noel.

"Do you know anyone from the Payson Church who might have had a rosary with the initials 'RW' carved in it? There was only one RW that I can remember—Rick Wallace." I might not have been completely honest when I told Juarez I couldn't remember all the members of the church.

"And it couldn't have been him?" Hammond held the rosary in his beefy hand, his gaze fixed on the crucifix.

"Rick was two years younger than me, born on the island. Trust me, the Paysons weren't huge on Catholicism—no self-respecting member of the church would have kept this."

He nodded. After a second or two, he stood and returned the relic to me. "If you have half an hour, we can go talk to somebody who might have some answers."

He didn't wait for me to agree, already shrugging on his coat. He returned the photos to his manila file folder, put it back in the other room, and we walked out together.

15

THE LTTLEHOPE RESIDENTIAL HOME was a massive old Victorian at the end of Seaside Lane, not far from the town landing. When I was a kid, the house had been rumored to be haunted. A fresh coat of paint, new windows, and a wheelchair ramp had done little to change that impression.

When Hammond and I arrived, three men sat together on the porch smoking. Their shoulders were curled in, their bodies tucked against a chill I didn't feel in the bright sunshine. I apologized to Einstein for being the worst dog owner on the planet and once more relegated him to the car while I went inside.

Edie Woolrich was in the kitchen when we arrived. The place smelled of homemade chicken soup and hot yeast rolls. If this was where one went when insanity came calling, I sincerely hoped I'd be next on the list. She didn't look surprised to see us when she looked up from the stove—in fact, she acted like she'd been expecting us all along.

"Erin Solomon," she said, with a long, low whistle. Edie was maybe five feet tall, with a pink scalp visible through thinning gray curls and a penchant for saying whatever came into her head at any given time. At least, she'd had that penchant when I was a kid; I supposed she could have changed over the years.

"Now who would've thought a little moppet like you'd grow into a gorgeous thing like this. You look just like your mum." She shook her head, eyeing me with furrowed brow. "How is the old battilax, anyway?"

Of course, it was possible time hadn't changed Edie in the least. "She's good—still in Portland."

"Good place for her," Edie said, with a hint of a harrumph. Edie had been the first in a very long line of nurses who'd assisted my mother at her beloved clinic; clearly, there was no love lost between them. "Noel said you were coming by—you've got some questions?" She turned to Noel with the air of someone accustomed to being obeyed. "Take her on into the dining room, hon. I'll be right with you."

A few minutes later, I was sitting in the belly of the old house with Hammond across from me at a massive antique dining room table. Edie sat beside me. Through glass French doors leading into a stately living room, I could see the residents sitting down to watch an old television in the corner.

Edie took one look at the rosary before she nodded to Hammond, as though confirming a question I hadn't realized had been asked.

"Rebecca—I'd bet money on it. That would've been hers."

"You're sure?" Hammond pressed.

"Sure as I'm sitting here," Edie said.

"Rebecca who?"

"Rebecca Westlake," Edie said.

Hammond stood and took his coat from where he'd draped it behind his chair.

"Wait—where the hell do you think you're going?" I asked.

"I've got a couple errands to run," he said. "I'm just gonna walk back into town. Edie'll tell you the story."

"I think you should stay and fill in the blanks," I said. Hammond shook his head.

"She knows it better than I do. I'll give you a call later today and we can compare notes."

I thought about putting up a fuss, but Edie was watching me like I was a child on the brink of a tantrum. Based on Hammond's face, he was bracing himself for the same. I decided to go the high road.

"Okay—fine. Just don't go far. I'll give you a call when I'm done here, and we can meet up again later."

He didn't look thrilled at the prospect, but nodded his agreement regardless. Once he was gone, Edie brought in tea and cookies, and reclaimed her seat beside me.

"I really can't get over how much you look like Kat. Except for the hair, of course—the hair's all Adam. But otherwise, you sure are your mum's girl."

I attempted a smile. "People have said that before. I never really saw the resemblance."

"No, I s'pose not." She eyed my bruises—the split lip and swollen eye that she had, as yet, not mentioned. "Being Kat's girl, I don't guess you had anybody take a look at you. Those are some pretty mean bruises. Your mum's clinic's still right where she left it—they do good work there. I'm sure they could fit you in."

"No need. I know the signs for a concussion. There were no broken bones. Nothing deep enough for stitches. They have better things to do at the clinic, I'm sure."

She didn't argue. All the same, I didn't care for the way she was looking at me—another person from my past who saw me only as the little outcast I'd once been in this town.

"You said you could tell me something about the rosary?" I pressed.

Her eyes lingered on mine, more intelligent than I suspected people gave her credit for. She nodded.

"Of course. The story Noel's been so keen on."

This got my attention. "Why?"

"You got me. There are dozens of sad stories that came out of that island. Becca's wasn't any better or worse than anybody else's."

"Rebecca Westlake, you said?" She nodded. "I didn't know her on the island—I've never even heard that name. It wasn't in any of the autopsy files."

"Well… First off, it was Becca Ashmont by the time she joined Isaac's church. And besides that, she didn't join up till you were back here with Kat. I don't know exact dates, but I'm pretty sure she took their boy and left Joe sometime that summer."

"Joe Ashmont?" The name was coming up too often to be mere coincidence. "She was his wife?"

"They'd been together since they were kids—her and Joe and Matt were joined at the hip from the time they moved here. Never saw the three of 'em apart in those early years."

Joe Ashmont had been married. I recalled the story Juarez had told on our trek to Portland the other day.

"Joe and Matt Perkins grew up in an orphanage together, didn't they?"

"Up in Westbrook, yeah. Becca was there, too. She was a beautiful girl—from one of the tribes up in northern Maine, I think. Or her daddy was, anyway. Something happened, though, and she ended up with the State. In and out of foster homes. She had…" Edie stopped.

I remained silent, waiting. Edie looked at me apologetically.

"Nothing was ever diagnosed, but she had problems. Depression. Maybe something more."

"And she joined up with the Paysons when?"

"I'm not positive, like I said. Summer, though. Joe came to shore and railed about it for a couple of days—went on one hell of a bender. Things went bad between them a long time before that, though."

"And you said they had a son?"

"Zion. Joe wouldn't let them come out to the mainland after a while—they all stayed out to Sheep Island, in that rattletrap shack he's got. But I went out there a few times when they needed me."

Yet another piece of the puzzle that made no sense. I tried to remember conversations with my father. Had he ever mentioned any of this? But then, there wouldn't have been any real reason to say anything. If there were problems, there wasn't a lot a nine-year-old could have done about them.

"And Hammond... He's been asking about this?"

"He's been real keen to hear her story, yeah. I sent him to talk to Reverend Diggins last night, and I think that answered a few of his questions."

Reverend Diggins. Diggs' father—the preacher at the town's Episcopal Church for as far back as I could remember. I had the feeling suddenly that I'd be trailing three steps behind Noel Hammond for this entire investigation.

"Why the Reverend?"

"Becca used to be a member of that church, not too long before she had Zion. She and the Reverend were..." her eyes slipped to the floor. "Close."

"As in...?" I prompted.

"I'd rather not say anymore, if you don't mind. It was just a rumor—you know these small towns."

Apparently, not as well as I'd thought I did.

"I just want to make sure I've got this," I pressed. "Rebecca Westlake grew up in an orphanage with Joe Ashmont and Matt Perkins. They all moved to Littlehope, and she married Joe. Somewhere along the lines things went sour, and she joined Daddy Diggs' congregation. Among other things."

Edie winced at the insinuation, but remained silent. I continued.

"Ashmont pulls her out of that church and kept her and her son locked away on Sheep Island until the summer of 1990, when they escaped?" I looked to Edie for confirmation. She nodded.

"So, she and her boy go into hiding on Payson Isle. And a month or so later, with no apparent warning, the Payson Church and all its members go up in flames."

"I think you have the gist of it," Edie said.

I looked in the next room. I could see a glimpse of *Who Wants to Be a Millionaire* playing on the TV, the same three men from the porch now crowded together on the sofa.

I stood.

"You're going to see Reverend Diggins now?" Edie asked.

"It's the most logical step, wouldn't you say? At least, Noel thought it was."

"Please don't tell Diggs what I said, whatever you might find out. He and his daddy never got on too well, and I don't see how this could help matters."

Saying Diggs and the Reverend didn't "get on" was like saying the Yankees and the Red Sox had some minor artistic differences. Still, I promised Edie that I would keep her revelations to myself. I climbed back in the car with Rebecca Westlake's rosary clutched in my left hand, and prepared myself to take on Daddy Diggs.

16

THE CHURCH REVEREND DIGGINS ran was across the road from Wallace's General Store. Ironically enough for a woman who'd run off to join a religious commune as a teenager, my mother was possibly the least God-fearing woman on the Maine coast, so growing up I'd had few run-ins with the good Reverend and his congregation. The few I did have, however, were memorable—and not in a good way. I didn't like the man then, primarily because of the way he treated Diggs, and I sincerely doubted that was about to change.

I got out of the car and lit a cigarette, leaning up against the door while I smoked. The sun had vanished once again and there was a light rain falling. I kept my sunglasses on despite the gloom, but I knew I wasn't fooling anyone. My back ached and my stomach was queasy and it felt like evil trolls were playing a snare drum inside my head.

And I really didn't want to talk to the Reverend.

When he was twelve years old, Diggs and his younger brother Josh skipped school to go swimming in the local quarry. Diggs' idea, of course. He'd been warned against it, and Josh—a blond, blue-eyed Hummel replica of a child who, by all accounts, was the twentieth-century equivalent to Christ himself—didn't really want to go. But Diggs needled and cajoled as big brothers will, and eventually Josh—ten years old at the time—agreed.

It was an unusually hot day in June, but that particular afternoon the Diggins boys were the only ones at the quarry. They biked up to the highest ledge. Diggs took the first dive, barely making a ripple as he sliced into the still waters below.

For all his extraordinary qualities, Josh was never the athlete his brother was. He stumbled when he was pushing off the ledge, failing to get the momentum or height he needed to clear the rocks.

At ten years old, Josh Diggins fell head-first into the Calderwood quarry, and hit the rocks below with a crunch of bones and flesh that Diggs wrote, many years later, still echoed in his sleep.

Diggs tried to revive him. When he couldn't do that, he biked two miles with his dead brother on his handlebars, to the nearest house he could find for help.

It took years before Diggs let me read the story he'd written about that afternoon. I'd known about his brother, of course—no secrets in a small town and all that. But it was an unspoken pact between us, particularly in those tenuous early years when he was the mentor and I his adoring student, that we both shoulder our dark burdens in silence. Somehow, just knowing life had kicked the crap out of both of us early on was enough for me; I didn't need the details.

After that day, the Reverend and Mama Diggins never got over the loss of their youngest son, and they never let Diggs forget the part he'd played in that loss. Though he graduated at the top of his class and set records in every sport Littlehope had to offer, he was always a wild child—bedding the towns' fairest daughters, drinking every keg dry, and smoking whatever happened to be available.

All the same, when Diggs got the call from his mother ten years later saying that she was dying and would he please come home, he dropped out of Columbia three months shy of a Master's in Journalism, and returned to his hometown.

That was when we met. He stayed while his mother fought a two-year battle with cancer that she ultimately lost and then, despite the undeniable tension between father and son, he stuck around town reporting for the *Trib* for another year after that. He left three days after I did, confirming my suspicion that he'd only remained in Littlehope to make sure I survived those last, lonely days of high school and was safely settled at Wellesley before he got on with his own life.

A shout from across the street jolted me back to the present. I looked up to find Jed Colby, the man I'd interviewed earlier in the week, smiling at me. He waved as he climbed into his pickup, then drove across the intersection and pulled up beside me.

"You look like you're thinking some pretty deep thoughts there," he said.

"Just pondering the little mysteries," I said. "Why are we here; where do we go when we die; am I really the only one who believes the Kardashians are a clear sign of the end times?"

He chuckled, but his face had darkened once he'd gotten close enough to see my bruises. "Well, when you find the answers, will you clue me in? Though you're definitely not alone on that last one. I just wanted to stop by to let you know Gracie wants you and Diggs to come over for dinner some night. It'd be nice to get a chance to visit. And to be honest, I'd like to talk to you some more, if you don't mind. After you left the other day, I thought of a half-dozen questions I never thought I'd get the chance to ask."

The invitation caught me off guard, but I nodded gamely. "That would be nice, actually. I'll tell Diggs. You guys pick the night, and I'll drag him out of his office if I need to."

"Good. Gracie'll be glad to hear it." He hesitated. "I don't want to pry, but are you all right?"

"Yeah, I am. I just…" Rather than downplaying what had happened, I had a sudden inspiration. "I know me being back here isn't the most popular thing in the world, but somebody got the best of me out on the island yesterday." I took off my sunglasses to give him the full effect. "You wouldn't happen to know who that might have been, would you?"

His jaw tensed a little while he took in the sight, but he shook his head. "If I did, they'd be walking funny about now. If they got up at all. We might talk tough, but any man who raises his hand to a woman isn't looked at too fondly around here."

"Even Joe Ashmont?"

"Especially Joe. Why? You think it could have been him?"

The look in his eye suggested vigilante justice wasn't out of the question and, if called upon, would be swift. I shook my head quickly.

"I don't think so, I was just asking. It's all right—it looks worse than it is. I just wanted to see if you might have any ideas."

"Sorry, no. But let me know if you find out who it was, though. I'd love to be there about the time old Diggs gets hold of him."

I laughed. Replaced my sunglasses as Jed drove away, tossed my cigarette butt in a trash can just outside the church's front door, took a deep breath, and went inside.

The Reverend was in his office when I arrived, downstairs in a dim and very chilly carpeted basement. His door was slightly ajar, so I knocked but didn't wait for him to invite me in.

He'd aged since I had seen him last. For some reason, Ethan Diggins' thinning hair and glacial smile seemed timeless all those years ago. Of all the people I'd encountered in my re-immersion in the old hometown, Daddy Diggs was the only one I had expected to find unchanged.

But, of course, everything changes.

His once-blond hair had faded to white, and was sparse around his mostly bald head, his shoulders hunched and his body smaller than I remembered it. He sat behind a massive oak desk that only served to emphasize his deterioration.

"Erin Solomon," he said, when I stepped into his office.

"Reverend Diggins," I said.

The office belonged to a scholar, not a zealot. One wall was filled with shelves of volumes on theology and philosophy, art, music, literature. It was a big space, and I suspected it had been his personal refuge for a long while now.

He stood behind the desk, gesturing me into an overstuffed leather chair.

"I've been expecting you," he said.

He wore glasses perched at the tip of his nose, and he didn't look nearly as forbidding as I'd once thought him to be.

"Have you?"

"Detective Hammond suggested I might see you soon."

"Did he tell you why I'd be coming?"

"Of course. Rebecca Ashmont, I presume. He seemed to think she might have been the key to some of the mysteries you are pursuing on Payson Isle."

I found myself at a disadvantage—apparently Daddy Diggs had been waiting for me, while I'd only found out I was headed this way twenty minutes ago. My gaze fell to an oversized crucifix mounted behind the Reverend's desk, complete with crown of thorns and a bloodied and very realistic looking Christ.

I looked away.

"Rebecca was part of this congregation?" I asked.

"She was."

"I heard that you two were close," I said, choosing the word Edie had used.

The Reverend smiled. He met my eye. "Is that pertinent to this investigation?"

"It could be—especially if she confided in you before she moved in with the Paysons. If you have an idea what happened when Isaac helped her escape from her husband… At this point, anything you could tell me about Rebecca and her son might be pertinent."

He leaned back in his chair, removed his glasses, and rubbed the bridge of his nose. The gesture reminded me of something, but it took a minute before I could place it. He replaced his glasses, tented his fingertips, and peered at me with a sour expression. That's when it hit me: Mr. Burns. Diggs' dad was straight out of the Simpsons. I forced back a bubble of hysterical laughter and wondered if I'd had some kind of psychotic break.

I struggled to refocus on what the Reverend was saying.

"I'm sorry, but as I told Detective Hammond," he said,

"I don't recall that much. She was a devout member of the congregation, and even taught Sunday School here for a time. But her attendance became sporadic, and we were unable to keep her on. She left the church shortly thereafter. There was a long interim before she joined Isaac, during which I don't believe she left the island very often. Isaac used to visit the more isolated residents to minister to those who might otherwise be excluded from organized religion; I suspect he met Rebecca that way."

"Do you know when she actually joined the Payson Church? I haven't been able to get an exact date yet."

"She was there barely a month—that's what was so tragic about it, why I remember the details so well. We'd just realized she was out there. We were taking steps to bring her back when we received word of the fire."

This got my attention. "Who was taking steps to bring her back? You? Joe? Did Isaac know you were coming for her?"

Too late, I realized that I was pressing too hard. The Reverend stood and nodded toward the door. "I'm sorry—I told Mr. Hammond, there are aspects of this case that I'm not comfortable discussing. The investigation has been closed for many years." He stared pointedly at my battered face. "Perhaps it would be better—safer—if you simply let the matter lie. Rebecca Ashmont was a troubled woman, with a painful history and an unpleasant home life. She sought refuge wherever she could; Isaac Payson happened to be the last port in her storm, but I assure you he was not the first."

"Something I've heard you can attest to firsthand, Reverend. Were you her port in the storm when she was a member of this church?"

His shoulders stiffened. "You and my son may have a

relationship that eschews the boundaries of etiquette and good taste, but I won't tolerate that kind of implication in a house of the Lord."

I stood, but made no move for the door. "Do you know why the Payson fire never made sense to me, Reverend?"

He shook his head, glancing down at the desk in a failed attempt to regain his composure. "Why is that, Ms. Solomon?"

"Because I could never find a motive. No trigger. In Waco, the pressure from the government was the final straw; a visit from Senate investigators set Jonestown into motion. The Solar Temple had been preaching the same dogma since their inception—everyone knew what to expect. It's the law of cause and effect, Reverend Diggins: nothing just happens. And I'm not the first one to notice this. Read any articles written on the Paysons, and you'll find more questions than answers. No one could ever give any reason for why this fire would have been set, out of the blue, when Isaac Payson never preached a message involving the kind of violent end his congregation met."

I took a step closer. More people were arriving upstairs—I heard hushed voices, occasional laughter. The Reverend waited for me to finish. For a moment, I thought I saw fear in his eyes.

"Were you planning to go in there to get Rebecca, Reverend? You and Joe Ashmont?"

"You believe that if Isaac thought someone was threatening to take one of his members away, it may have spurred him to take that kind of drastic action?"

I thought of the photo Hammond had shown me that morning: an unidentified figure that may or may not have been Isaac Payson, burned separately from the rest of his congregation. Had he panicked, locking his followers away from the world before anyone could take them from him? I shook my head again. Perpetual bafflement was fast losing its charm.

"I don't know," I admitted. "It's possible. Something obviously happened, and I'm getting a funny feeling that Rebecca Ashmont was at the center of it all."

He came out from behind his desk and leaned back against the edge, not far from me.

"Why are you doing this?" he asked. "Unearthing demons long since buried, in a town that still hasn't recovered? I fail to see how this investigation could help anyone. Yet, you persist."

"The story the public was given about that fire was a lie. I can't let that stand."

"*Now*, you can't let that stand? Where were you twenty-two years ago? As I recall, the alibi you provided for your father played a crucial role in the perpetuation of that lie."

I looked up sharply. "What do you know about that?"

A door opened and closed somewhere down the hall. The Reverend glanced at an old clock behind him, then back at me.

"I know Adam was not in that hotel room when you said he was."

"And how do you know that?"

He smiled, his eyes never leaving mine. "Because he called and asked me to meet him here."

Everything slowed. The Reverend could be lying, of course, but what would be the point?

"Why would he do that?" I asked. "What did he want?"

"I couldn't tell you—he never arrived. When he called me, it wasn't quite four a.m. He said he was on his way... I didn't hear from him again."

I remembered the phone ringing that night. My father had shouted at whoever was calling—it made an impression because I'd never heard him shout before. He hung up and made a call of his own. I never knew who he was calling, though. Had it been Reverend Diggins?

"Maybe he made the call, then decided he couldn't leave me alone. You can't know he wasn't with me," I said.

"Perhaps you should talk to your mother about this. You have so many questions—it's a shame that the people best equipped to address them are your own parents, and yet the answers have continued to elude you all these years. If I didn't know better, I would say you didn't actually want to learn the truth at all."

He stood and gestured to the door. "I can't tell you anymore, I'm sorry. Now, if you'll excuse me, there are people expecting me."

I opened my mouth to ask another question, but it was clear Daddy Diggs was done talking. I went out the back way, then circled around to get back to my car. Rebecca Ashmont was the key. Rebecca and Joe.

And my mother.

I stopped short when I reached the parking lot, looking for the first available escape route.

"You can't run—I've already spotted you," Diggs said.

He was sitting on my bumper, his hair and shoulders damp from the drizzling rain. He held a cigarette in his left hand, and he didn't look pleased. When he saw my face, he looked even less so. Juarez was sitting in the driver's seat of his Civic, parked next to my Jetta. He looked miserable. I shot a glare his way, but Diggs intercepted my gaze.

"Don't blame him—he didn't say a thing. Jed called. He

said Gracie'd love to have us over Tuesday night, if we're free. And, oh yeah, did I need any help with the manhunt to find the scum sucker who kicked the crap out of you?"

"I'm fine."

"Yeah, Solomon, I know—you're always fine. It'll be on your tombstone: 'Here lies Erin Rae Solomon: She was fine.' Jesus Christ."

He met me halfway, his eyes softening once he got a glimpse at the damage. He tipped my chin up and tilted my face to get a better look at my bruises.

"You think Ashmont did this?"

"No," I said, only just realizing it was the truth. "I would have known if it was him." I nodded toward the cigarette he held. "You're smoking."

"Yeah, I know. It was either that or strangle someone."

"Someone meaning me?"

He glanced at Juarez, who sank lower in his seat. "Not necessarily. Or at least you're not the only candidate. Come on—give me a ride back to the *Trib*. We'll get some food, and you can tell me what my old man has to do with this unfolding disaster."

Sometime between meeting with the Reverend and finding Diggs on the hood of my car, my headache had returned. I was tired—more tired than I could remember being in a very long time, and my fatigue was making it damned near impossible to form a coherent thought.

I nodded my agreement and gave him my keys, then went over to Juarez and waited as he rolled down the window.

"I'm sorry—I shouldn't have dragged you into this," I said.

"He's just worried. I can understand that." My hand was on his window, fingers curled at the edge of the glass. He put his hand over them, studying me with black, depthless eyes. "You look tired, Erin. Go home. Try to sleep this afternoon. I'll meet you at the house—we can talk then."

He squeezed my hand and let go, then waited until I was settled beside Diggs in the Jetta before he drove away.

As soon as I had my seatbelt on, Diggs put the car in gear and peeled out of the parking lot without a word.

17

PART OF THE REASON FOR DIGGS' SILENCE became clear when we arrived at the *Trib*. The county sheriff's cruiser was parked out front, a man I assumed was the sheriff seated behind the steering wheel. He smiled at sight of us, got out of the car, and approached Diggs and me.

"I don't want the police involved, Diggs," I whispered.

He cast an innocent eye at me, shrugged like he didn't know what the hell I was talking about, and turned his attention to the cop at his window.

"Hey, Chris. Fancy meeting you here."

"Just stopped in town for a little lunch," the man said, smiling. Playing along. He leaned down to peer into the car and tipped his hat at me. "You don't remember me, I guess—Chris Finnegan. I was a couple years ahead of you in school."

He was a big man, tall and broad-shouldered, with glasses and a casual way about him that I imagined was supposed to set people at ease. It wasn't working.

"I heard somebody had a couple pizzas delivered here," Diggs said. "Hey, here's an idea just off the top of my head." I glared at him, but he ignored me. "Why don't you join us, Chris? The more the merrier."

Indeed.

●

"You don't have to file a report, of course," Sheriff Finnegan informed me. We were packed in Diggs' office, Einstein finally liberated from the car and now poised to attack the first stray piece of pepperoni or hamburg that fell to the floor. The evil trolls drumming inside my head had gotten louder and more unruly, and my mood was not improving.

"I don't need to file a report, thanks. I told you—I ran into a door."

Finnegan smiled. He had a slice of Wallace's loaded, extra cheese pizza in one hand, a can of Coke in the other. He took no notes.

"A door that tagged you in the noggin twice and, based on the way you're holding yourself, probably got in a couple of serious body blows to boot." He finished chewing and looked at me thoughtfully. "You don't mind me saying, that's one mean son of a bitch of a door."

I attempted a smile. I felt bad for lying, and worse because Finnegan was obviously just trying to do Diggs a favor. He looked at Diggs, who looked at me.

"Can I talk to you for a minute?"

I closed my eyes. The trolls were doing the conga now, moving to some primal rhythm that was fast making my stomach roll to the beat.

"Maybe later."

He stood, nodding toward the doorway. "Just for a minute."

As soon as we were out the door and down the hall, he turned on me.

"What the hell are you doing? You're acting like some fucking battered wife—you got hit by a door? What is that?"

I could feel the blood in my cheeks as a week's worth of impotent rage reached its boiling point. I advanced on him so fast that he took a step back.

"It's my story, Diggs—*mine.* It's my book, it's my family, it's my fucking body. Back off. If I file a report, cops will be swarming the island. Whatever is going on, whoever it is will get spooked—"

"Or *caught*—"

I glared at him. "I mean it, Diggs. I'm not filing a report. I'm not making a statement. And if you don't back the fuck off, I'll find someplace else to hang my hat until I'm done here."

Diggs shook his head. I'd never seen him angrier.

"Fine. Screw it—you want to kill yourself, go ahead. But if you go out there alone again—"

"I'm not going to."

He caught the front of my shirt in his hand and pulled me closer. My heart was beating too fast. Diggs chest rose and fell and his breath came hard. Five seconds came and went while he tried to get himself back under control.

"I'm serious, Solomon," he said, quieter now. "You see this face? This is the face of a terrified man. And doubly so because you aren't taking this shit seriously."

The rage left as quickly as it had come, leaving exhaustion in its place. I leaned into him, resting the top of my head against his chest—a move that was half embrace, half defense tackle.

"I'm taking it seriously," I mumbled.

He smoothed back my hair. "If you go out to the island again, you'll take me or Juarez? I don't know how much help I'd be, but Juarez has a gun and James Bond hair, so I'm pretty sure he could do some damage. And when push comes to shove, I can scream like a banshee."

I'd seen Diggs do a hell of a lot more than scream when we were in trouble before, but I let it go. "I won't go out to the island alone again."

He wrapped his arms around me and held me close. "You're really okay?"

My eyes stung. If I could have stayed that way—Diggs' voice in my ear, my body enveloped in his—for another five years, I would have been seriously tempted to do so.

"I'm fine, Diggs."

He laughed. Shook his head. "Liar," he whispered.

Once Sheriff Finnegan realized I wouldn't be making any revelations about the attack, he excused himself to hit the mean streets of Midcoast Maine once more. I bowed out shortly thereafter, intent on only one thing:

Bed.

I drove past the town landing on my way back to Diggs' place and noted that Hammond's boat wasn't at its mooring. I tried his cell phone, but it went straight to voicemail. The bastard was ignoring me—probably out solving the case, for all I knew. I was so tired I honestly couldn't work up the energy to care. It was only four in the afternoon, but I'd been running on fumes for so long I was about twenty-four hours past empty.

Back at Diggs' place, Einstein settled on the bathmat while I soaked in the tub with half a dozen scented candles and a bottle of wine at my fingertips. I'd closed the curtains, popped two pain pills Edie Woolrich had given me, and was just beginning to feel the tension start to ease.

The conversations I'd had over the past week replayed in my head. I did a cast call of the major players in my unfolding drama:

Joe Ashmont, Matt Perkins, Noel Hammond. My mother and father. Rebecca Ashmont. Reverend Diggins. Isaac Payson.

Christ. Had the whole town been involved in this?

I now knew that Matt, Joe, and Rebecca grew up together. Rebecca married Joe, then apparently had an affair with Reverend Diggins when she was still part of his congregation, if the stories were to be believed. Joe moved her out to his island, where she had a son.

Somewhere during those years alone on the island with her boy, Isaac Payson made contact with her. I went over what I knew about the founder of the Payson Church and realized it was precious little, gleaned mostly from articles I'd read by others even less informed than myself. Raised in Maine by a good, God-fearing family before he slipped the draft by disappearing to parts unknown during Vietnam; started a church in Mexico sometime in the mid-'70s; returned to Maine in 1976 with a small troupe of followers who settled with him on Payson Isle. As far as I could tell, he'd never been in trouble with the law, and the work he did out on the island and up and down the Midcoast kept him in good standing with the community.

I could remember other women from abusive situations taking refuge with the Paysons; it would hardly have been unprecedented for Isaac to help Rebecca and Zion escape Ashmont's iron rule.

That brought me to the summer of 1990, and whatever events might have led to the fire.

My father got a phone call early that morning. He in

turn called Reverend Diggins for some ungodly reason, and told him he was on his way to the church. He left me at the hotel, but for some reason he never followed through on that meeting with the Reverend.

Then there was my mother, and the story Hammond had given me about her: stacking all the bodies, destroying the evidence, seducing Hammond to ensure his silence. All of this done with the knowledge of Joe Ashmont and Matt Perkins.

I got out of the tub and toweled myself off. The drizzle outside hadn't gotten any worse, but it hadn't gotten any better, either. The sky was boiled gray outside my bedroom window, heavy clouds hanging low overhead. It felt much later than early evening.

The Reverend's words were bothering me: *If I didn't know better, I would say you didn't actually want to learn the truth at all.*

I could concede that that may have been true at one time. Hell, most of my teen years I'd been terrified of what my father might have been doing while he wasn't with me the morning of the fire. Even then, I'd known that whether or not my father actually started the fire, he clearly knew more than he was saying. The question was, how much more? Maybe I hadn't wanted the truth then, but I didn't want to live this way anymore—plagued by guilt over what my father may or may not have done, the lies that he told and the lives that were lost. I wanted the truth.

"So, why haven't I called my mother?" I asked Einstein.

I sat at the edge of the bed, Einstein at my feet. He perked up when he realized I was talking to him. What had the Reverend said? The people best equipped to answer my questions were my own parents.

He hadn't said the *person* best equipped, I realized.

The people. My parents. Plural.

I still hadn't been to the cabin where my father lived out his final days. There was no good reason for that—I just didn't want to go. Didn't want to see what his life had been, how the man I'd worshiped had unraveled over the years. After his death, my mother had asked if I wanted any keepsakes to remember him by. I'd said no. As far as I knew, she hadn't gone through his belongings. And if she hadn't, chances were good that no one had.

After all these years, did my father still have the answers I needed?

I put on jeans and a sweatshirt and powered through the heady combo of muscle relaxants, wine, and fatigue. I grabbed my cell phone and hit speed dial.

"I thought you were napping," Diggs said.

"I got my second wind. You're probably not free tonight, are you?"

"Seriously, woman? Don't you ever rest?"

"I did rest," I said. "I thought of something I want to check out. So...do you have plans?"

He hesitated—wrestling, I knew, with deadlines he couldn't miss.

"Don't worry about it," I interrupted before he tied himself in a knot. "What about your Cuban comrade-in-arms. Is he around?"

"Yeah," Diggs said. "He just swung by, actually. I think he's headed your way. You're going out to the island?"

"I just want to check something out," I said before he could lecture me on all the sleep I wasn't getting and all the ways it was bound to kill me. "I'll make sure he brings his gun and his Bond 'do, don't worry. I'll be okay."

"So I'm guessing our late dinner at the Shanty is out, then."

"Shit. I forgot." My ill-advised lip lock with Diggs seemed like a lifetime ago, the big talk we'd planned downright silly compared with everything else going on. "I'm sorry. Raincheck?"

"Yeah, of course. Don't worry about it. Give Juarez my regards—and, Solomon?"

"I know, Diggs—be careful."

"Very careful. Careful to the power of ten. Squared."

Though the math was beyond me, I made the promise all the same. After I hung up, I tried Hammond's cell phone again. It went straight to voicemail. Again. He wasn't picking up at home, either—avoiding me, or was he still out on his boat?

I took Einstein out for a quick pee and left him to keep the home fires burning at Diggs' place. Juarez was just driving in when I intercepted him.

"Do you have any plans for the afternoon?"

"As far as I know, all my plans involve tailing you, unless I want Diggs to castrate me by nightfall." He tried for a smile, but he didn't look that amused.

"You don't need to tail me—I think I popped one pain pill too many. You mind driving?"

"Where to?"

"Noel Hammond's place first. Then, how about a nice evening jaunt across the bay?"

I braced myself for a lecture that, refreshingly enough, didn't come.

"You're the boss. I'm just here to make sure you get home in one piece."

He opened his passenger's side door for me. I hip-checked him as I climbed in, giving him what I hoped was a sexy grin—though given the painkillers, bruises, and swelling, I may have come up short. "And to look pretty—don't forget that, Jack. You make great arm candy."

He laughed and shook his head, but I could tell that he was pleased. Men. A little flattery really will get you anything.

18

HAMMOND'S TRUCK WASN'T in his driveway when we got there. I pounded on his front door anyway, but predictably got no answer. The way I figured it, he was still at least one step ahead of me, maybe more. With that in mind, there was really only one logical place he could have gone. Payson Isle.

"Son of a bitch," I said as soon as the realization struck.

Juarez was waiting in the car. I glanced his way, then tried the front door. It was locked. I went around to the side and peered in the kitchen window.

A car door slammed. A moment later, Juarez joined me.

"You think you could jimmy the lock on the front door?" I asked.

"Not unless I have a damned good reason to, no."

I trailed behind as he walked around to the back. A low deck with a barbecue grill and two lawn chairs, a glass-topped table with an ashtray half-filled with cigarette butts…and a sliding glass door that led into the kitchen. Juarez opened it easily and stood aside.

"No breaking, just entering," he said.

"A man after my own heart. I just want to leave a note, let him know I was here."

"Sure you do."

Juarez stayed on the deck while I went in.

"Noel?" I called. I wasn't sure whether I wanted him to answer or not.

The house remained quiet. The black and white cat materialized, threading his way between my legs. Juarez finally gave in and followed me inside.

"I'm just looking for some paper—to leave that note," I said.

He found a notepad and pen by the phone and tried to push them into my hand, but I ignored him. Instead, I went into the room where I'd seen Hammond get his files earlier that day, and found a cramped study with shelves of books lining the walls. Many of the titles were familiar—books on Jim Jones and David Karesh, Heaven's Gate, Amityville, and two thin volumes on the Paysons that I'd practically memorized.

Two oversized scrapbooks were lying on Hammond's desk. I opened the first and several yellowed newspaper clippings fell to the floor.

"Erin," Juarez said, standing at the threshold to the room, "you should put those back."

"I will—just give me a second."

I knelt in the dim, crowded room, scanning articles Hammond had been hanging onto for years now. Most were from the days following the fire—some from the *Trib*, some from larger newspapers around the state, and one lengthy article I knew well from the *Boston Globe.* There was a profile piece I'd read before on my father, done by the *Portland Press Herald* on the tenth anniversary of the fire—not long before Dad's death. I studied the picture.

I had few photos of my father. He always used to say

he wasn't good looking enough to waste film on, though this was hardly true. The photo had been taken before he'd lost everything in the fire, but looking back I realized there had always been something a little haunted about Dad. In the picture, he was working on the island. He wore a t-shirt, his hand up to shield his eyes, squinting in the glare of the afternoon sun. He didn't look thrilled at whoever had snapped the shot.

"Erin," Juarez said again. He crouched beside me and helped pick up the scraps scattered at my feet. "We need to go."

"In a minute," I said. I leafed through the rest of the book. There were also clippings from other mass suicides—mostly Jonestown. Some of the text was highlighted, with scrawled notes in the margins.

Juarez took my arm. "Dammit, Erin—you can't just come into someone's home and start prowling around."

I pulled away. "Keep your knickers on, would you? I just want to look—he's been doing the same investigation I have, probably for a hell of a lot longer."

He didn't answer me. When I looked up, he'd straightened and was staring at the notepad he'd taken from the phone stand in the other room.

"I think you should take a look at this."

I set the scrapbook down carefully and stood. Juarez bit his lip and handed me the paper.

There was a telephone number written in red ink, with a *206* prefix—Washington state, if I remembered correctly.

Above it, written in Hammond's sloping scrawl, was a name.

Adam S.

I went straight to his telephone, picked up the receiver,

and dialed the number.

My hands were shaking.

"That could be anyone—could mean anything," Juarez said. He was watching me like I might burst into flames any second now. I didn't blame him; at this point, I wasn't willing to discount anything.

On the other end of the line, a phone rang. Five, ten, fifteen times. No answering machine, no voicemail. Juarez didn't say anything. Just stood there, waiting with me.

Twenty-two rings, and then a voice.

"Dammit, Noel—I told you not to call me again."

I nearly choked on the sound. My eyes flooded; the world tilted sideways.

"Dad?" I barely recognized my own voice. A few seconds of silence passed between us—no one speaking, no one breathing.

The line went dead.

AUGUST 14, 1990

ON A FRIDAY AFTERNOON, the wet heat of July having given way to the golden swelter of August, there is a fight on the compound. Rebecca watches it unfold from a distance: Zion and Will Colby, another boy from the church. It's not so much a fight as an attack, really, because Zion does nothing to defend himself. Rebecca has seen this boy watching her son. She's seen the envy, the hatred, in young eyes spoiled not by experience but by a soul that Rebecca imagines has always been rotten.

The boy is wiry, quick and lean, a head taller than Zion and perhaps two years older. Though most of the children in the church are quiet and well behaved, Will is argumentative, lazy, always looking for a way out of daily chores or evening services. He hates Zion. Rebecca sees it in the way he fixates on her son, the way he slows to whisper remarks to him— remarks that Rebecca cannot hear but can nevertheless imagine, by the snakelike twist of the boy's mouth, his fists clenched as though he's just delivered a physical blow.

Zion never responds.

On this day, however, the boy has apparently had enough

of her son's passivity.

Rebecca watches Will lean in to whisper something. She stands at the open entrance to the greenhouse, the doors open to allow a breeze through the stifling space. The boys are across the field, alone, the other children having already returned to the house for lunch. Zion turns and walks away. Will chases after him and shoves him, hard, in the back. Zion stumbles two or three steps but does not fall. He pauses, rights himself, and continues to walk away.

Will races out in front of him, and Rebecca remembers similar fights between Matt and Joe when they were boys. Joe—teeth and hands clenched, his entire body tensed like a fist ready to strike. She feels the blow Will delivers before Zion does. It is not a practiced swing like one Joe might have thrown, but it does the job. Zion falls backward and lands in the tall grass. Rebecca can just see his head as he shakes it slowly, clearing it of the pain. He does not rise, though Rebecca can hear the other boy shouting for him to do so.

There is a moment when she considers going to defend her son herself. Thinks of what it must have been like for Mary to watch her child take the lashes, unable to intervene. Like Mary, however, Rebecca knows it is not her place. She stands silent in the distance and watches, motionless.

Zion grunts as the larger boy attacks him, but it is the only sound she hears from him. A few seconds into the fight, there are footsteps behind her. She does not turn, sensing Isaac's presence more than seeing it.

"He is being tested," she whispers to Isaac.

When she looks at him, there is unmistakable fury in the Reverend's eyes. "No," Isaac whispers back, before leaving the greenhouse and running toward the boys. "He is being beaten, you fool."

He reaches the two boys and pulls Will—struggling, grunting, pink and angry and futile—from Zion. Rebecca goes to them as Zion stands with some difficulty. He is bloodied, his left eye cut and already beginning to swell. She feels sick, dizzy. Confused. This is her role? To stand idly by and let her son pay with his own blood, for a destiny he did not choose? Was Mary a pacifist, or merely a victim?

At that evening's service, Isaac orders Will to stand alone at the pulpit. The candlelight flickers over his features; Rebecca believes that she glimpses the demons living in his young soul. The boy's mother, Cynthia, stands with averted eyes while Isaac circles her son.

"Cruelty is not a godly trait," Isaac begins. "Violence is a vice borne of man. It is not God's will that we inflict pain upon others, merely to lessen the pain within ourselves."

He turns to Will, the boy now standing with arms slack at his side, face blank and eyes downcast. Zion stands beside Rebecca, his eyes also on the ground. He said nothing while she washed his cuts, tended his bruises. He says nothing still, as Isaac continues to circle.

"Son," Isaac addresses the boy at the pulpit. "I know that you feel pain and shame for what you have done. But I believe that Satan has buried that pain so deeply beneath hatred and envy that you don't understand the turmoil that resides in your soul."

The congregation is silent. Will still stands with his eyes averted, the faintest tremor visible in hands that are now bruised from the earlier attack.

"But I believe the only way for you to truly reconcile the torment and hate that has seduced you is to confront it. Here and now."

Isaac stands in front of the boy, his back to the

congregation, completely obscuring the smaller figure before him. "It is time for you to kneel before this church and beg forgiveness for the violence you have brought to this tranquil place."

He puts a hand on the boy's shoulder, pushing him down. There is no air, no sound, in the chapel. The boy resists. Isaac's other hand goes to Will's opposite shoulder, forcing him to his knees. Zion is watching now, his good eye open wide.

"Have you never heard, boy, that violence begets violence? When the Romans doled out lashes to Christ until his body was broken, did he strike back? Wish them ill?"

Isaac's voice lifts, echoing in the too-warm room. He moves so that the congregation can see the kneeling boy, tears now running down the child's pink cheeks.

"No, sir," the boy replies, his voice barely a whisper in the stillness.

"And the passivity demonstrated by Zion this afternoon—do you believe that in his place, you would have the restraint—the courage—to lie still and silent in the face of such violence?"

There is a moment's pause before the boy shakes his head. Isaac turns to the congregation, locking eyes with Zion.

"Son. Come here."

Zion does as he is told, avoiding eye contact with his assailant.

"Would you take up arms against your oppressor?"

Zion does not hesitate. "No, sir."

"But what about an eye for an eye, son?" Isaac's voice is low, tempting; he is suddenly Lucifer promising the forbidden fruit. "You deserve to be safe in your own home, do you not?"

There is silence as Zion puzzles this out before he finally speaks. "My soul is what matters. My soul is safe."

Rebecca sees the smile of admiration on the Reverend's lips before he can hide it. He nods approvingly. "Yes. Your soul is indeed safe."

The tears have dried on Will's cheeks now. His eyes are hard, staring straight ahead, no longer paying heed to the faces fixed upon him.

"But what of *this* soul?" Isaac continues. Zion moves to return to his seat, but Isaac stops him with a hand on his shoulder. "This soul, my friends—do you not smell the decay that comes from this boy?"

Isaac takes Zion aside, whispering to him. Zion shakes his head—slowly at first, then with more vehemence. Pleading. The congregation looks on, silent, the air filled with the low tremor of blood. Rebecca remembers the Romans in Isaac's paintings, and feels that she now understands their fire-filled eyes.

"Zion." Isaac's voice is firm, uncompromising, as he leads her son to the kneeling boy. "For the good of another's soul, for the sake of this child's redemption, I command it."

Isaac presents Zion with a whip, long and black as a serpent, the end trailing to the floor.

The first blow Zion delivers is weak; there is a small slap as leather connects with flesh, and Will rocks slightly in his place before a sneer touches his lips.

"Again!" Isaac shouts.

The congregation is on their feet. Zion is weeping, the tears clean and bright, when he strikes the second time. Harder now. Will falls slightly to the left, his smile faltering before he rights himself.

"Do you fear the path of your soul, William?" Isaac's

voice tears through the chapel; Rebecca trembles at the sound.

The boy does not reply. Isaac says nothing, looking to Zion. Zion's jaw tightens. He closes his eyes for a moment. When he opens them, his tears have dried. When he strikes this time, it is with all the strength in his small body. The whip cracks across pale, lean shoulder blades. Will falls. His fists clench, and he starts to rise. Isaac keeps him down with a hand on his shoulder, until the boy obediently kneels once more.

"Do you feel the rage, son? The hate? Do you feel Satan undermining Christ's love, twisting your soul to tar?"

There is a madness in Will's eyes, a hatred so pure its only equal could be love. Rebecca stands by and waits, whispering her son's name, understanding now that Zion is the only one who can save this lost boy. She doesn't flinch, and neither does Zion, when he delivers the next blow.

19

"YOU CAN DO a reverse address search, right?"

I'd wiped my eyes half a dozen times, but I couldn't get the tears to stop. I was shaking, seated on Hammond's couch with his cats eyeing me warily. Juarez looked pretty wary himself.

"You're sure it was your father?"

"I haven't heard his voice in twenty years and I have every reason to believe he's dead, so... No, Jack, I'm not sure it was him. But if it's all the same to you, I'd still like to follow up."

He didn't ask any other questions. I listened as he made the request to an anonymous voice on the other end of the line, and we waited in silence until he motioned for the notepad and paper. He wrote down an address and a name, thanked the person on the other end of the line, and hung up.

"It's registered to a Jane Bellows," he said. "1162 Highgate Lane. Olympia, Washington."

"Jane Bellows."

"Does the name mean anything to you?"

I shook my head. When I finally had my wits about me enough to move again, I gathered the scrapbooks and the notepad and headed for the door. Juarez cleared his throat, blocking my path with clear intent.

"What are you doing?" he asked.

"I'm taking these. I need to know what Hammond knows—he's too far ahead in this, and I'm completely fucking lost."

"Erin, I work for the government—I took an oath to uphold the law. I can't just stand by while you steal someone's stuff."

"Seriously?" The look on his face made it clear that, yes, he was indeed serious. "You've gotta be kidding me. Imagine if this was you, okay? This is you, and you finally have a lead on your family and that whole thirteen-year blank slate you've been lugging around. It's all locked away in these two volumes. You're telling me you wouldn't take them?"

He crossed his arms over his chest. "I'm beginning to understand why Diggs is always saying you're a pain in the ass."

"I'm just focused. Dedicated."

"Or obsessive and completely lacking in conscience." He smiled when he said it, but he still didn't move out of my way. "I'm going back to the car. Leave things as you found them when we came in. If you don't, of course," he looked at me significantly, "I will have no way of knowing that."

He squeezed my shoulder on the way out. I waited until he was out of sight, then tossed the two scrapbooks and the notepad with the Washington phone number into my bag. I turned off the lights, slid the door shut, and went to the car. I'd made no attempt to hide my presence from Hammond, and didn't plan to. He would know exactly who had taken his research, which meant he would have no alternative but to return my calls.

And, finally, tell me what the hell was going on.

Hammond's truck was in the parking lot at the town landing when we got there, his boat nowhere to be seen. I tried to keep an eye out on our way to Payson Isle, but between approaching nightfall and the low-lying fog, we might as well have been looking for a ghost ship. When we reached Payson Isle, though, it was clear that he—or *someone*—had been there. I'd expected the trail to my father's cabin to be nearly impenetrable; instead, freshly broken branches and clear footprints marked the way.

"I don't suppose you were an Indian guide in a former life?" I asked Juarez.

"Do you need me to send up a smoke signal?"

I shook my head and knelt at one of the most sharply defined prints. "That's a big shoe, wouldn't you say?"

He set his own beside it, clad in a very-slightly-scuffed LL Bean boot. Juarez's were maybe half a size larger.

"It's not so big."

"Show off." I waited for him to make the tired joke about men with big shoes. To his credit, he did not.

"They're big enough to be Noel Hammond's though, right?"

"You think he was out here?"

"I'd bet money on it."

There were seven cabins in the little Payson village on the other side of the island. All of them were obscured by years of overgrowth, and all of them were smaller than I remembered.

"You've been here before? Since the fire, I mean." Juarez asked.

"A couple of times—I borrowed my mother's boat and came out."

We were a few feet from my father's cabin. Night had fallen, the sound of the ocean like some haunting lullaby in the distance.

"So you saw him then?" Juarez asked.

"Yeah." I took another step toward the cabin. "He just didn't see me."

It had been a gray night the first time I saw my father at the cabin—not quite raining, but damp enough that it might as well have been. When I reached the cabin, my father was outside. His hair was long, his beard had grown out, and he wore jeans that hung low on his bony hips. No shirt. He knelt beside a wood fire in front of the cabin, focused on the blaze. He could have been there an hour, or he could have been there the whole two years since I'd seen him last.

I'd stood there watching from the woods, shivering, but I couldn't bring myself to say anything. I left my father kneeling by the fire, staring into the flames. Even at fourteen, I'd known there was no way to get back the man I remembered—the one who told me stories and tucked me in at night, kept me safe and loved and protected for nine perfect years. He might as well have died in the fire with the rest of the Paysons. That night, not for the first time, I wished neither of us had survived.

Juarez and I faced each other on the path. He tucked a strand of hair behind my ear, waiting for me to tell my story.

It wasn't a story I cared to tell, though.

"You never came back here after he died?"

I shook my head wordlessly.

"And now you don't want to go in." His hand was still on my face. It was warm and I was cold, and his eyes had a strength to them that I hadn't noticed before.

"I do." I shrugged and blew out a lungful of air. "And

I don't. It doesn't matter, though. If this is where the story leads, this is where I go."

I headed for my father's front door.

I don't know what I expected from the cabin, but it definitely wasn't what I found when we crossed the threshold.

"Wow," Juarez said. He stood behind me, flashlight in hand.

I shined my own light over the opposite side of the room. I'd prepared myself for more of what I'd seen at the boarding house: mildew and mold, vermin and debris. We found anything but. The cabin was small, but immaculate— the windows clean, the twin bed made up neatly with what appeared to be fresh linens. A sturdy-looking homemade bookshelf stood beside the bed, a very thin layer of dust on the top.

I'd always known my father to be a fastidious housekeeper, but I somehow doubted that quality would extend twelve years beyond the grave. I thought again of the voice I'd heard on the phone earlier that day. That number might belong to someone in Washington, but that didn't necessarily mean Dad hadn't been back here. Had he been living here the entire time that I thought he was dead?

As I approached the bookshelf, Juarez ran his light up another wall, the beam a pale yellow wash over words grown barely legible with time.

"Do you remember that being there?" he asked.

I shook my head. "I never came inside. It could have been."

I set my flashlight aside. Juarez kept his light trained on the wall as I knelt at the base. With a gloved hand, I polished the rough boards until I could read what my father had written.

Know ye not that your body is the temple of the Holy Ghost which is in you, which ye have of God, and ye are not your own? 6/4/94

Another verse was scrawled beside it, dated three years earlier. I turned my attention to the floor. More words were written beneath me. Jack lit a lantern by the bedside and set it in the center of the tiny cabin. A soft glow, more shadow than light, slowly brought the details into focus.

Floor to ceiling, beneath Spartan furniture and faded curtains, I found Bible verse after Bible verse. The dates were in red marker faded to a pale pink, the verses in black, with the most prominent passages written on the floor in large block letters. On hands and knees, I used my shirtsleeves to clean the floorboards.

My God, my God, why hast thou forsaken me? Why art thou so far from helping me, and from the words of my roaring? 8/22/2000.

It was the most recent date I could find. Two weeks after that, my mother told the world that she'd found his body hanging in the greenhouse… It seemed beyond unbelievable to think she could have been lying about that all these years.

I sat on the floor. Juarez took a seat on the edge of the bed. I was cold and tired, and I couldn't shake those words: *Why hast thou forsaken me?* Was that how he'd felt? Abandoned by his God, doomed to live the rest of his years alone? Or had something changed that day?

I turned my attention back to the titles lined up neatly on the bookshelf: *Robinson Crusoe; 20,000 Leagues Under the Sea; Last of the Mohicans.* They were old and a little dusty, but still in remarkably good condition—and they sure as hell had been handled less than twelve years ago. There was one title that I didn't find there, though. I searched all three shelves, then stood and checked the nightstand on the other side of the bed. There was a circle free of dust where the lantern Juarez was using had been, and a small, plastic travel alarm clock stopped at 11:20.

"His Bible isn't here," I said.

"Could he have taken it with him, before he…?"

He left the question uncompleted, though I knew what he was asking. "Kat never mentioned finding anything with the body. I think she would have told me. It was a nice Bible—illustrated. Antique."

My heart was beating faster, a clear blue certainty settling in place of the loss I'd lived with for years.

"He's still alive," I said.

I waited for Juarez to argue. He didn't. "Who was the one who discovered his body?"

"My mother. She told me she came out to check on him—she'd been doing it for years. She'd bring supplies, medicine, whatever he needed."

"And you didn't see him at the burial?"

"She had him cremated before I could see the body. She said he'd been…" I swallowed. "She told me it had been a couple of weeks before she found him. With the high temps that summer, the body was pretty far gone."

"So, it may have been difficult to positively identify the body she found," he said.

"No. She would have known if it wasn't him."

"Why would she lie?"

I didn't know. But I was damned well going to find out—just as soon as I figured out what Noel Hammond knew that I didn't.

I left the cabin with Juarez on my heels. There was no moon, no stars, the night fully fallen and a darkness so complete that I felt newly blind, opening my eyes as wide as possible in a vain quest for light. I pulled out my cell phone. We were almost back to the dock before I got a signal.

My call to Hammond went straight to voicemail, yet again. I'd been angry before, but that began to ebb as worry took its place. I called Diggs instead.

"Everything okay?" he asked immediately.

"Have you seen Hammond anywhere?"

"Nope. Has he given you the slip again?"

"Yeah. Listen, can you find out whether his boat's back at the landing yet, and give me a call back?"

"Done. Give me a couple minutes."

Juarez had been silent since we'd left the cabin, guiding the way with his flashlight while he kept his thoughts to himself. After I hung up, he cleared his throat awkwardly.

"This woman—Rebecca Westlake, the one with the rosary. You think she had something to do with all this?"

With all the discoveries surrounding my father, I'd almost forgotten about Rebecca. I glanced behind me to get a glimpse of Juarez's face. Something about his voice bothered me. He was trying to be casual, I knew, but underneath it was a near-desperation that I recognized—I'd heard it in my own voice more than once over the past few months, as I probed deeper into the Payson mystery.

"I don't know," I told him. "I don't know anything about her—I'd never even heard of her until today." I turned around to look at him fully. "She was Matt's friend, though. Have you heard of her? Has he ever mentioned the name?"

He hesitated. "He's talked about a Becca before. Becca and Joe."

"For someone who's just a third party in all this, here to look after a man who isn't even a blood relative, you've taken a lot of interest in this story."

"I'm a cop; it's a mystery. And a damned good one. And I'll admit that the fact that it has something to do with why Matt—a man who was there for me more than anyone else in my life—is circling the drain right now, has a lot to do with it."

He took a step closer, his hand falling once more to my face. His knuckles brushed lightly across my bruised cheek.

"I'd like you to get the answers you're looking for, too," he said.

"Why?"

This time, I could see his eyes as they shifted from mine. "I don't know. I just… It seems like you deserve them. And maybe I know what it's like, not really understanding what you came from. Trying to sort through everyone else's stories to find the truth."

His hand slid to the back of my neck. I held onto the lapels of his jacket, our eyes locked now. He moved closer.

And my cell phone rang.

Neither of us moved.

"That'll be Diggs," I said.

"Good timing."

I managed a nervous laugh. "Probably so, actually." I stepped away and caught my breath as I pulled the phone from my pocket.

"His boat's back, but he's not answering his phone," Diggs said when I answered.

"Not even for you?"

"I know, right?" Diggs asked. "I can understand him not wanting to talk to you, but who the hell avoids *my* calls?"

"You don't happen to know whether—"

"Truck's in the driveway, kitchen light is on."

A boulder settled at the bottom of my stomach. "Did

someone knock on the door?"

"No, I just had a neighbor do a drive-by. Why?" His voice got serious. "You think something's wrong?"

I started down the old steps to the dock with the phone still at my ear. "Get your friend from the sheriff's department on the phone. I'll meet you at Hammond's as soon as we hit the mainland."

●

We'd only been on the water a few minutes, trying to navigate through the fog over rough seas, when my cell rang again. I let Juarez take the helm. Diggs' number was on the caller ID. Everything slowed. When I picked up, it took a few seconds of silence before he said anything.

"Diggs?" I finally prompted.

"You were right," he said. I felt shock settle in deep, mingling with cold sea spray and heavy fog and the ocean beneath. Diggs' voice sounded strange. People were shouting in the distance.

"Where are you?"

"I'm here—at Noel's house. About thirty seconds after I hung up with you, a call came into the fire station."

"You think he's inside?" I could barely hear him between the noise on my end and the chaos on his.

"They don't know yet. But I think so. Don't you? He would've gotten in touch with someone by now otherwise."

"Will you still be there when I get to the mainland?"

"Yeah. Fire crews are still getting here—it's a hell of a blaze. I'll be here a while."

I hung up. I stood beside Juarez, both of us at the wheel as he guided the boat home.

"They killed him," I said. I didn't even know who 'they' were, but I knew I was right.

Juarez put his arm around me and pulled me close. We rode the rest of the way back in silence.

20

WE WATCHED HAMMOND'S HOUSE BURN from the water. A blur of orange flames smudged into the fog, the colors muted like the pastels I used to use as a kid. I stopped off at Diggs' place on the way and stashed the scrapbooks I'd stolen from Noel. My father was alive, and someone had murdered Noel Hammond; it was clear that those two facts were intricately related, and I was sure that Hammond's notes would reveal something about both of them.

When the scrapbooks were secure and Einstein was happily oblivious at my heels once more, Juarez drove us to Hammond's place. The sirens could be heard all over town. Whole sections of Littlehope had been cordoned off, cars lined up to the end of the little lane where Hammond lived. I was shivering, my stomach tight, my mind muddy. We parked at the end of the road, behind a long line of pickups carrying locals who had already arrived on the scene—either to help or, more likely, just to soak in the excitement on an otherwise dull Saturday night.

The red lights from the fire trucks illuminated the trees in waves of color. A trooper's car was parked vertically across the road to halt traffic; Sheriff Finnegan stood beside it talking to a cluster of neighbors, some still in bathrobes and slippers.

He spotted Juarez and me and gave me a kind smile. "Diggs is waiting for you. Go on through."

The house was engulfed in flames by the time we got there. The weight of the smoke, the strobe effect from the sirens, the knowledge of what had happened… All of it was surreal. I couldn't make sense of anything.

"We need to find Diggs," I finally said aloud.

"That's what I was thinking," Juarez agreed.

He scanned the crowd, though I knew it was more likely that Diggs would be closer to the action. The air changed the closer we got to the blaze, thickening into waves of heat and black smoke. My eyes stung and my lungs ached. Three fire trucks stood in front of the burning house, one from Littlehope and two from neighboring towns. Hammond's truck was in the driveway. The paint on the hood was bubbling from the high temps; my cheeks and forehead felt too hot, stretched tight across my bones.

Diggs was with the firefighters, who were posted at strategic intervals around the property. He had a fire helmet on and his camera out, doing his best to stay out of the way as the firemen focused on trying to get the flames under control. I thought of Hammond's cats; of the few conversations we'd shared; the mystery he'd been working to solve; the books that we had both read in an effort to understand that single, life-altering event over twenty years ago.

Juarez turned to speak to me, but I ignored him. The fire was loud: breathing, creaking, the timbers of the house hissing as they burned. I continued walking toward the fire, mesmerized by the flames, until Juarez caught my hand and pulled me back. He leaned in until his lips were at my ear.

"The truck. That's probably where he was last."

No one was paying much attention to the vehicle, the firemen too busy trying to control the blaze while the cops kept the locals at bay. Juarez was good at staying under everyone's radar, guiding me to the truck with his hand at my back.

Just as I was reaching for the door handle, he intercepted my hand. He took a handkerchief from his pocket and opened it himself.

"Heat, remember? And a possible crime scene," he said, once more at my ear.

I nodded, and felt like an idiot for not realizing that myself and like crap for having to realize it at all.

Hammond's truck smelled like cigarettes, but the interior—like his home—was clean and orderly. A blue chamois shirt covered in cat hair was on the passenger's seat, a cell phone and a bag of groceries resting on top.

"He wouldn't just leave these in the truck," I said.

I went around to the other side, the fire hot at the back of my neck. I opened the passenger's side door with my jacket sleeve, the heat from the metal burning my fingers even through the fabric. The keys dangled in the ignition. Juarez frowned.

"It's not exactly a crime Mecca here," I said. "People leave their keys in the car all the time."

"Not if they were city cops, they don't."

"So, whoever it was jumped him while he was in the truck?" I asked. I nodded toward the cell phone. "Should we...?"

Juarez looked over his shoulder to make sure no one was watching. He picked up the phone and flipped it open, still glancing over his shoulder occasionally. Something was happening in the house—firefighters motioned frantically, shouting just before a crash inside brought the blaze to life with renewed fury. A central beam in the house collapsed in a frenzy of sparks and thunder. I stood half-in, half-out of the truck, transfixed by the sight.

There was another crash, raising with it a series of shouts from the firefighters. Diggs had put his camera away and was gesturing toward the back of the house. While someone sprinted toward an ambulance parked on the road, another man took off running for the back door.

"I think they found something," I said. When I turned to Juarez he was looking at me strangely, Hammond's cell phone still in hand, as though something in the scene was out of place. "What is it?"

Sheriff Finnegan spotted us and came running over, while another trooper pushed people back so an ambulance could get closer to the house. When Finnegan reached us he headed immediately for Juarez, his face flushed.

"I'm sorry, Jack—I need you to take a step back. This is a crime scene."

Juarez apologized. He discreetly returned Hammond's phone to its place on the seat before he stepped away from the truck.

"Have they found Hammond?" I asked Finnegan.

He managed a pained smile. "We're not sure yet—things are too chaotic to know much of anything right now."

I was too busy watching the paramedics to respond. They disappeared behind the house with a backboard; when they returned, there was a body covered in blankets between them. The night was bathed in reds, oranges, and blues, as though I was watching the world through a colored lens.

The paramedics moved slowly. They didn't tend to the body they carried—they barely looked at it. Juarez looked away at the same time I did, and I knew we'd both reached the same conclusion.

"You two should get back," Finnegan said. "Behind the line, if you don't mind. Diggs will come find you when there's news, but you really can't be going through things over here."

Juarez nodded. "You're right—I'm sorry, just habit. You guys will let me know if there's anything I can do?"

"We will."

Juarez took my arm. He attempted a smile and failed miserably, looking once again toward the crowd. "Come on, there's nothing we can do here. We'll catch up with Diggs later."

Once we were out of earshot of the police, I turned to Juarez. "Did you get a chance to check out Hammond's phone?"

He nodded. "Yeah—I checked both ingoing and outgoing calls."

"And?"

"According to caller ID, the last call he made and the last he received were from the same person."

I waited. I had a bad feeling I knew where this was going. "Who?"

"Dr. Katherine Everett," he said, watching me closely.

I nodded. I reached for my cell phone, resigned at last to the one thing I'd been hoping to avoid since I'd started this whole thing.

I called my mother.

21

KAT ANSWERED ON THE SECOND RING. She was asleep when I called, but woke quickly—a skill perfected after years working in emergent care. When I told her about Hammond and the fire, there was a pause on the line before she said she'd drive up from Portland and be there shortly. No argument, no tears, no questions. I hung up feeling like we'd just sealed a not-terribly-significant business deal.

Juarez and I returned to his car, where I let Einstein out to water a few unsuspecting shrubs. The spectators had thinned as the fire died down, though the volunteer fire brigade had come *en force* and wouldn't be leaving any time soon; a long line of pickups with red lights on the dash were parked along the side of the road, with others still arriving as the night wore on.

Juarez walked with me, though we both remained silent. When his phone rang just as we were returning to the car, we both started. I took small comfort in the fact that at least I wasn't the only one running on pure adrenaline these days. He checked the caller ID and apologized to me before he turned his back and answered.

I was left to listen to the heavy, dull thud of wet timber falling as the fire crew brought down the last of Hammond's house. I surveyed the scene, stopping at sight of a man standing beside a decrepit red pickup. He wore an orange hunting cap pulled low over his eyes, but even from a distance I knew who it was: Joe Ashmont. He climbed back into his truck and drove away before I could do anything—not that I had a clue what the hell that might be. I couldn't shake the feeling that he'd wanted me to see him there.

Juarez returned with his boxers clearly in a bunch, forehead furrowed and jaw tensed. So far, I'd only seen one person who had that effect on him.

"Matt?" I asked.

He nodded. "He's not at Togus—they don't know when he left, or how he got out." He rubbed his stubbled chin. He looked as tired as I felt.

"You should go—try and help find him."

"I can give you a ride back to Diggs' place…"

"No, that's all right. I'll just wait for him to finish up, we'll be fine."

He still didn't move, though. I took a step closer. It seemed like a good idea at the time, but then all of a sudden I had my arms around him and my head on his chest. I've never been the hugging type. Juarez, on the other hand, returned the embrace without hesitation.

"I'll see you tomorrow," he said. "Try to get some rest tonight?"

"You're one to talk. Thanks for…everything. Really. You don't know me, yet you keep showing up to dig my ass out of some of the most god awful messes."

He leaned down and kissed me on the mouth, then pulled back so quickly I had no time to respond one way or the other.

"It's no trouble—it keeps me from dwelling on my own mess. I'll give you a call when I know what's going on with Matt. Stay safe." He squeezed my hand, climbed into his car, and drove away.

Einstein and I stood abandoned in the middle of the road for a couple of minutes while I tried to decide my next move. Kat was on her way, but it would take her at least a couple of hours to get to Littlehope from Portland. Hammond's house was just a hulking, blackened frame, the inside unrecognizable. I spotted Diggs standing beside the wreckage. He'd taken off the helmet the fire crew had loaned him; now, he stood there with blackened face and tired eyes, the cover boy for our most recent tragedy.

I tugged on Stein's leash, and the two of us met Diggs as he walked toward us.

"Are you okay?"

He looked like he might cry. Instead, he stepped closer and reached into my coat pocket, fishing around for something. He smelled like smoke and sweat and exhaustion. I wasn't sure what he was doing until he pulled my cigarettes from the pocket, extracted one, and lit it without ever taking a step back. One deep inhale and a shaky exhale, careful to blow the smoke away from me, and only then did he say a word.

"I'm okay," he said.

"I called Kat. She's on her way."

"I'm sorry."

I wasn't sure whether he was sorry for the fire or Hammond's death or the fact that my mother was coming. Probably all of the above. I managed what I hoped was a brave smile, and held his hand as we walked away from the shell of Hammond's home.

My mother showed up about an hour and a half later, as promised. Diggs and I were back at the *Trib,* Diggs writing up some late-night copy on the fire, Einstein and I curled up on an uncomfortably overstuffed sofa in his office. I'd just dozed off when I heard a door on the other side of the building open and slam closed.

"Shit," I said.

Diggs didn't even look up from his keyboard. "You'll be fine."

Easy for him to say. Another two minutes of suspense, and Kat found us.

"Sweet Jesus," she said as soon as she'd laid eyes on me. "What the hell happened to you?"

"I told you—there was a fire."

She came closer. "What'd they do, put it out with your face?"

In the chaos, I'd completely forgotten about the attack. Kat took my head in her hands, tilting my face this way and that, pressing none-too-gently on my bruised cheekbone. There would be no hugs, no tearful reunions, with my mother. Just the palpating of battered bones to prove she cared.

"Nothing's broken," she announced.

I pulled away. "Thanks. I know."

Kat's coal-black hair was pulled into a ponytail, a couple of curls hanging daintily at her ears. She wore jeans and a black cashmere sweater that set off her fair complexion well. The best Hollywood costume designer couldn't have chosen a more appropriate outfit for someone coming to see the wreckage of an old lover's home in the middle of the night.

"You look worse than she does," she said to Diggs. He looked up from the computer. He hadn't bothered to change after the fire, choosing instead to head straight to his computer to get the story up on the paper's online site, since he couldn't make the morning edition.

"I sincerely doubt that," Diggs said.

Kat looked back at me. "Yeah, you're right. Not even close. Come on—I'm taking you both wherever it is you're shacked up these days."

"I have to work," Diggs said. "You're welcome to stay at my place as long as you're in town, though. Erin knows the way."

Einstein's tail wagged ecstatically as he turned himself inside out at Kat's feet. She always had that effect on dogs—growing up, we always had at least a couple of rescued mutts who trailed her at the clinic and slept by her side at night. I always imagined she'd end up retiring to a big mansion with fifteen hounds and no contact with humanity save late nights in a chat room, thrilling the masses with her most gruesome surgeries.

She scratched Stein's ears and chin. "Einstein, right? He got bigger."

"He did," I said. "Puppies tend to do that when they grow into dogs."

"Come on, Einstein," she said. She turned and left with my turncoat of a hound on her heels, without bothering to say goodbye to Diggs. There was the implicit expectation that I would follow behind. I shot a last pleading look at Diggs.

"Come home soon," I said.

"Yeah, right. Between your mom and the Greatest Cuban-American Hero, I'm thinking of having a shower installed here." At the look on my face, he changed his tune. "I'll wrap up in an hour or so—you'll be fine. Very few mothers eat their young once they've hit maturity."

With that questionable reassurance, I grabbed my coat and Einstein's leash and headed for the door.

My mother drove a vintage cherry red VW Beetle convertible. Stein hopped in the back and settled down immediately. I took the front, directing Kat along roads we'd traveled together back sixteen or seventeen light years before.

"How's Maxwell?" she asked, shortly before we reached the turnoff to Diggs' place. I looked at her blankly.

"The professor."

"Michael," I corrected her. "He's fine. We got a divorce."

For a second, she looked thrown. "I didn't know. When?"

"Not long ago. You never liked him anyway."

"He was too old for you. And clearly sleeping with every willing coed in greater Boston."

Ah, the unbridled charm of Dr. Everett. Since I couldn't argue either of her points, however, I chose not to comment. "I want to talk to you about Noel Hammond," I said instead.

She drove too fast on Diggs' dirt road, sending the Beetle flying up over the final hill before his house came into sight. She didn't say anything until she'd stopped the car.

"Go inside and get cleaned up first. I'll make some tea. We'll talk then."

There was no point in arguing. Instead, I let her put her bag in my room and showed her to the kitchen.

The shower did little to reenergize me. In fact, it did the opposite; I found myself dozing with my forehead against the tiled wall halfway through, and ended up curled up naked on the shower floor while the pulsing spray rained down on my weary head. Kat knocked on the bathroom door.

"Are you still alive in there?"

I managed to revive myself enough to get out, towel myself dry, and put on semi-clean pajamas. Einstein had crashed out on his dog bed. He didn't even stir at the promise of tea and crumpets. I left the bedroom door open in case he changed his mind, and went to face my mother.

A cup of steaming chamomile tea was waiting for me, along with a toasted English muffin that I pushed aside without a thought. The tea was more bitter than I'd expected, but it was hot and the smell of chamomile was a nice alternative to the smoke that still lingered in my nostrils. I drank half of it without waiting for it to cool.

"You've lost weight—and not in a good way. You should eat something."

"I'm not hungry. Tell me about Noel, Kat."

"Why don't *you* tell me about Noel? You got pretty chummy with him toward the end."

The turnabout wasn't unexpected, but it still annoyed me. "You slept with him to keep him quiet after he saw you destroy evidence out on the island the day of the fire. You lied to police, blackmailed a detective…"

She looked bored. "It sounds like you have it all figured out. Is there some kind of confession you'd like me to sign?"

"I want you to tell me the truth for once in your life!" I heard Einstein stir at my tone, his toenails clacking on the hardwood floor before he appeared at the kitchen door. Actually, two dogs appeared at the kitchen door. Neither of them were in focus. I closed my eyes.

"Why did you lie?" I asked. My voice sounded small, that of a child instead of a thirty-three-year-old woman with degrees and awards and a recent divorce under her belt. My eyes were still closed, my head spinning.

"I think you should get some rest. You don't look well," she said.

I shook my head in an effort to clear it. Opened my eyes. My mother was closer now, peering interestedly at me.

"Shit. You…" My voice faded. "You drugged me."

"You're so dramatic. I'm a doctor, Erin—I medicate people, I don't drug them. You need to sleep. This should help."

She pulled me to my feet and led me down the hall. I'd already told her she could take my room, and I'd take Juarez's for the night. His bed was a mattress on the floor that seemed much lower than I suspected it would have if my mom hadn't slipped some kind of elephant tranquilizer in my tea. I crashed onto it like a tree felled in the forest. Kat pulled the blankets up around me. I couldn't remember her ever tucking me in like this as a child.

"Where's Dad?" I asked.

She looked sorry for just a moment—a flicker of regret that touched her pretty green eyes for an instant before it vanished.

"Your father's dead," she said. There was no emotion in her voice. "Go to sleep, Erin. We'll talk in the morning."

I was dimly aware of her leaving my side. Einstein's cold nose nuzzled my neck before he settled down beside me, his body warm against mine. The bed smelled like Juarez. It wasn't familiar per se, but it wasn't unpleasant, either. I closed my eyes.

And slept.

22

I WOKE AN INDETERMINATE NUMBER of hours later to blinding sunlight streaming into windows devoid of drapes or dressings. It took a few seconds to reorient myself to my surroundings: strange bed, cardboard boxes sealed with duct tape against one wall, a table lamp and a dog-eared copy of *One Hundred Years of Solitude* on the floor by my head.

Juarez's room.

Einstein was nowhere to be found. My cell phone was on the kitchen table and the house was spotless, dishes washed and stacked neatly in the strainer. There was no sign of Diggs, Juarez, or my mother. I dialed her cell while waiting for my coffee to brew, disoriented and pissed off. The clock on Diggs' microwave read 1:20.

Kat answered on the fourth ring, her voice clipped and professional.

"Where the hell are you?" I interrupted, before she could finish her greeting. "And please tell me you have my dog."

"He's spreading a little cheer—I thought he could use an outing, and you clearly weren't getting up anytime soon."

"Because you drugged me, you psychopath."

"And again with the drama. I'm at the clinic—I figured

since I was in town, I should make some time to check the place out, make sure they're still doing my name justice. I'll just be another hour or so. You can meet me here if you'd like."

I suppressed the urge to reach through the phone and strangle her. "No, that's all right. Just come by the *Trib* when you're done. An hour, right?"

I hung up and drank my coffee, no doubt in my mind that I wouldn't see Kat before four o'clock.

At the *Trib*, Diggs was still weeding through conflicting reports from the cops about Hammond's death. I retired to my office to sort through my own evidence, in a vain attempt to make sense of the latest bizarre developments in the story. My wall looked like one of those creepy serial killer shrines they have on all the primetime cop shows: charred bodies, medical reports and newspaper clippings, a sketchy timeline written in washable marker on the wall below.

As expected, there was still no sign of my mother when four o'clock rolled around. Diggs came in with coffee and a sandwich, and took his customary seat on the edge of my desk.

"So, what have we got here?"

I broke off a corner of his sandwich and popped it in my mouth, then grimaced when I realized it was some kind of that tofurkey crap he's always eating.

"That'll teach you to steal my food."

"Probably not." I considered his original question. "I think whoever attacked me had to be the one who killed Hammond."

"Makes sense. Any idea who that could be, though?"

I went through the list of suspects. Matt Perkins was

missing now, but as far as I knew he had been safely tucked away in a hospital bed during my attack. Joe Ashmont, on the other hand...

"You're sure it wasn't Ashmont who jumped you?" Diggs asked, reading my mind.

"I think so. I can't really explain why, but I just don't think it was him."

"'Cause he's too sweet?"

I laughed. He took a sip of my coffee without asking, and pushed the rest of his sandwich toward me. I picked at a scrap of crust.

"No, I just—I would have known if it was him. I saw him at Hammond's last night after the fire, and I just..." I stopped, trying to figure out how to verbalize what so far was nothing more than a gut feeling. "I feel like he wants to tell me something, but he can't. As much shit as he's given me, I'm not sure he'd actually hurt me."

Diggs didn't look convinced.

"What about you?" I asked. "What's the word so far on Hammond and the fire?"

"Officially? Undetermined. Unofficially—arson, and Noel was killed before the fire. It seems we have a killer with a conscience, though."

I looked at him curiously.

"The cats," he explained. "Whoever blew up the house took the time to get them out first—a neighbor found them prowling around the wreckage this morning."

"So, a killer who doesn't mind beating the crap out of girls or murdering an ex-cop with tow-headed grandbabies, but gets squeamish about torching the family feline. Bizarre."

"Very," agreed Diggs. "What did Kat have to say on the subject?"

"You mean before or after she slipped me a mickey and stole my dog? Precious little. She doesn't actually deny any of it, but she's definitely reticent about sharing her motives. As soon as she gets here, we're gonna have a conversation."

Since he had no response for this, I took the time to study my graffiti timeline. It was beginning to shape up in terms of names and dates, the ink still wet on the latest addition: *July, 1990—Rebecca Ashmont joins Payson Church.*

"I still think it goes back to Becca Ashmont," I said. "Which means Matt Perkins and my buddy Joe have to be in on this, one way or another."

Diggs was quiet for a second or two. "And my father? You think he has something to do with this, too?"

I thought of the conversation I'd had with the Reverend yesterday afternoon—something I still hadn't shared with Diggs. I'd known the question would come up eventually, of course. I just wished I had a better answer for him.

"There's a chance he was involved."

"With the fire, or with Rebecca Ashmont?"

I didn't say anything for a second too long. I'm not a bad liar in general, but I've never been able to pull one over on Diggs.

"So, Daddy Diggs was a philanderer in his day," he said. There was no real bitterness in his tone, but I knew better than to think that meant he was okay with the news. "The old man's full of surprises. And you think he might have had something to do with the fire?"

Now that the big secret was out, it was pointless to hold anything else back. I began, relieved that I could finally paint the whole picture for someone else, in the hopes that he might see something I hadn't. I told him about the call my father had received the night before the fire, and the subsequent call Adam had placed to Reverend Diggins before he dropped out of sight. I finished with my theory that the Reverend and Joe Ashmont had been headed out to the island to take Rebecca and her son away from the Paysons.

"And you think that kind of thing could have unsettled Payson enough that he might have lost it and killed the whole congregation? You knew this man, Sol—you honestly think he would have done that?"

I thought about it, flashing back to my own memories of Isaac Payson: a revival that ran late, with me stretched out on a homemade pew, my chin propped in my hands as I watched a woman writhe on the floor in the aisle, her skirt hiked high, tears streaming down reddened cheeks. Isaac's hands on my shoulders, pushing me under frigid ocean water with my father looking on, waiting until I came back up.

"You are baptized in the holy spirit, washed in the blood of the lamb," Isaac says to me. "Let it be known that him who goes against you goes against God, and he shall perish in the flames."

I hadn't been afraid.

But should I have been?

"I don't know," I finally said. I shook my head, the images coming back more quickly now, my head pounding once again. A man on his knees at the front of the church, his back bared; a woman with a cruel-looking switch in her hands, both of them crying. My father taking my hand.

"Come on, baby—let's go back to the house. This isn't for us." Isaac standing in the background with his hands in the air, his eyes cast to the ceiling. The preacher's voice, for us alone—"Stay." An order. "She needs to see what happens to

Satan when he dares walk among us."

"Erin?" Diggs had gotten up. He stood in front of me, clearly concerned. "You still with me?"

I managed a nod. "I have to go. I need to talk to Kat."

When I was a kid, the clinic was where I hung my hat more often than not. It was housed in a modular unit with a wheelchair ramp out front and limited off-street parking, just a few buildings down from the Diggins church. I wasn't ready for the sense of familiarity it sparked when I walked through the front doors. More than the island, more than the *Tribune,* more than anything else I'd encountered since crossing the Littlehope town line, this felt like home.

I hung my coat on a wooden peg just inside the door, then took in the lobby. A pregnant girl no more than fifteen years old sat in an orange plastic chair, thumbing through a back issue of *Cosmo.* The woman behind the counter looked vaguely familiar, but only because Littlehope is a small town—a limited gene pool means just about everyone looks vaguely familiar. She was in her early twenties at the most, way too young for me to have known her when Kat was running the place.

"Can you tell me if Dr. Everett is here?" I asked.

At the sound of my voice, Einstein came barreling out of one of the back rooms. The receptionist did not look amused.

"She's back there," she said flatly.

Kat was reorganizing the old storage room—which, to her credit, did actually look like it could use some reorganization. Or a blowtorch.

"Can you believe this shit?" she asked. She didn't even

look up when I came in the room. "I obviously need to come back here more often—have you met the teenager at the front desk? And the so-called doctors here are a joke. I know it's a full load, but there's no excuse for this kind of laziness."

I leaned against the doorsill, my arms crossed over my chest. Once it dawned on her that I wasn't speaking, she stopped working and looked at me.

"I know—I'm late," she said.

"Two hours late, actually, but who's counting?"

"Just let me finish up here, and I'll be right out. Another twenty minutes and I should have things wrapped up."

Rather than starting another pointless argument, I dove into the fray with her. I started at a wall a few feet from where my mother was working, stacked floor to ceiling with shelves of unlabeled supplies.

"You have a marker?" I asked.

She smiled—a genuine Kat smile, almost impossible to find in nature. I felt that little thrill of triumph I used to get when I'd made her happy, which only succeeded in pissing me off further. I took the black Sharpie she handed me and got to work.

"I want you to tell me about Noel Hammond—your relationship with him. What happened the day of the fire," I began, after we'd been working a while.

"It seems like you have it all figured out—that's what Noel said, anyway."

"You spoke with him?"

She met my eye. I tried to read her—to find a trace of remorse, some regret over the death of someone who, at the very least, had shared a bed with her once upon a time. True to form, she gave nothing away.

"He called me a few days ago to tell me I should call you

and explain some things."

"Why didn't you?"

"I didn't see you burning up the phone lines to get to me, either. I knew you'd call once you ran out of alternatives."

If the comment was meant to make me feel guilty, it didn't succeed. I pulled down another box, this one filled with sterile dressings, and counted, repacked, and labeled the contents.

"I just want to know what happened. The morning of the fire twenty years ago…" I prompted her.

"You mean when you and Adam were holed up in that hotel?"

There was no missing the challenge in her tone. She was standing on a stepstool, back to the wall, her eyes hard on mine. And like that, she was the adult and I was the child, caught in a lie I'd been keeping far too long.

"You knew he left me alone? How?"

"I saw him that day—early that morning. I got called in for an emergency at Ethan Diggins' church."

The church where my father had been heading that morning, according to Reverend Diggins.

"Who made the call?" I asked.

"The Reverend. Joe Ashmont had shown up on his doorstep—six sheets to the wind, beaten till he was half-dead in a bar fight. The Reverend called me to come patch him up."

"And you saw Dad drive in, just as you were getting there," I guessed.

"He saw me and took off before we could talk." She dropped her eyes for the first time. "I assumed he was going back to the hotel. If I'd known he wasn't, I would have gone to the hotel to get you."

"How did you find out he hadn't gone back for me?"

She didn't answer. This was the key—what I'd been looking for all this time. I sensed it, more from the way she wouldn't meet my eye and the thick tension that filled the room than anything else. I sat down on a cardboard box and waited for an answer my mother couldn't seem to give me.

"Did you see him go out to the island that morning?" I pressed.

She hesitated. The look on my face must have convinced her there was no putting the conversation off any longer, because she finally gave in. She sat on the stepstool, her legs crossed and her hands in her lap, the picture of composure.

"I didn't see him. The others did, though—Matt Perkins saw him leave the town landing that morning, headed for the island."

"*You* didn't see him, though? Only Perkins?"

"Joe said he'd known Adam was going out there. And the Reverend said the same thing—said he'd sounded strange, desperate, on the phone. There was enough circumstantial evidence. Thirty-four people died out there; there wouldn't have been an impartial jury, no due process. The press, the locals, anyone and everyone was ready to lynch the first likely suspect."

"So, you just...what? Went out there and destroyed anything you thought might look bad, and created some fantasy story—"

"I don't expect you to understand." Her voice was dangerously calm. "I did what I needed to do to keep your father safe. To keep you safe."

"Because Dad did it—" I choked on the words. The images came back again: Isaac shouting, a child crying, my father...where? When all of these things were happening on the island, when I was being dunked under frigid waters or watching Isaac dole out retribution to his congregation, why hadn't my father intervened?

"Is that what you're saying?" I continued, hating the weakness in my voice. "Daddy set the fire, killed all those people? *That's* what you were protecting? What about the man I told you I saw out there? The one you and Dad told me I was crazy for mentioning? Or what about Isaac, for Christ's sake? He was on the outside of the locked door, right? He could've done it."

She didn't say anything. Her eyes slid from mine to the floor, her hands twisting in her lap—the only sign that something might be breaking through that cool exterior. I stood so suddenly I knocked a pile of cardboard boxes to the floor. Einstein had been at my feet, but now he leapt up and skittered out of the stockroom like I'd made some physical threat.

"Finish up here," I said. I did my best to force some strength back into my voice. "We're going for a ride."

"Where?"

"I'm going to prove to you that my father didn't set that fire," I said. "I'm going to prove the ghoul that chased us in the woods that day was real, and you'll see for yourself exactly what you've been protecting all this time."

Tough words for someone who didn't actually have a clue what the hell she was talking about, but I didn't care. There was one man who I suspected might be able to answer at least a few of my questions, and I was damned well going to ask them before something happened to him, too.

Since it was likely I would kill either my mother or myself—or some combination thereof—before the day was out, I left Diggs with our furry love child and vague reassurances that everything was under control. Einstein stood at the office door with Diggs by his side as I was leaving; neither of them looked happy to see me go. I could understand their concern.

At the town landing, I paid no attention to Kat's protests as I took the helm of my trusty speedboat and we left Littlehope Harbor.

"I'm not high on Joe Ashmont's list of favorite people lately," she shouted to me above the boat's engine.

"We won't stay long."

"If he even lets us come ashore."

I shrugged. My mother wore jeans and an LL Bean jacket, her hair pulled back and her cheeks attractively flushed from the cold. Despite a few years of heavy drinking when I was a kid, good genes had paid off—at fifty-two, Kat had a toned, slender body that I imagined still turned men's heads.

I, on the other hand, wore jeans that hung loose at the waist and sagged at the ass, along with Diggs' too-large pea coat, since my own reeked of smoke. My tangled red hair was pulled back in a ponytail and topped with a baseball cap, and I still wore sunglasses to hide my bruises. I made sure my cell phone was on, just in case the producers of *Project Runway* were trying to reach me.

A relatively nice spring day had given way to a chilly evening, the sun low on the horizon, the wind rising from the east. I kept thinking of Ashmont at the fire the night before. He had wanted me to see him—I was sure of it. I couldn't shake the feeling that somewhere deep down, Joe Ashmont wanted to tell me his story. I just hoped the desire wasn't buried so deep he wouldn't recognize it until after he'd blown my boat out of the water.

I navigated us through an inlet where jagged hunks of black rock waited just below the water's surface, sharp enough to tear a hole in the hull and sink us both if I hit at the right angle. I eased back on the throttle as we approached the island Joe Ashmont had called home for as far back as I could remember.

Sheep Island was a tiny stretch of land marked by wind-battered evergreens and an unwelcoming shoreline of steep granite cliffs. I tied the boat off at a dock on the north side of the island, beside an old red skiff that I assumed belonged to Ashmont. Since Ashmont had seen fit to build his dock as far from his home as humanly possible, Kat and I were forced to climb steep ledges and fight knee-deep bayberry and juniper brambles to get there.

Ashmont's house was surprisingly colorful, with peeling pink shutters, aquamarine siding, and a tarpaper roof. Buoys and lobster traps littered the overgrown front yard. A dog barked inside the house. Gulls screamed overhead. I thought I saw movement in one of the windows, but no one appeared. My brilliant plan was looking less brilliant by the minute.

Just when I had almost worked up the courage to knock on the front door, an explosion shook the ground beneath my feet. Kat and I stood there for a split second before she grabbed my arm and we ducked into a grove of spruce and pine.

I saw the muzzle of a shotgun before I saw Ashmont. He stepped outside wearing coveralls and his hunting cap, set far back on his grizzled head.

"You shouldn't've brought her," he said.

Kat looked at me. "I'm sorry, Joe," she called out. "This was her idea."

"Not you, you ignorant bitch. You're not welcome here,"

he shouted back. He was coming toward us, fast, his gun thankfully pointed at the ground. "I told you before, I never want to lay eyes on you again. I'll talk to her—I won't talk to you."

Despite the big-ass gun Ashmont was holding, I couldn't help feel just a twinge of satisfaction. I signaled for Kat to remain where she was and stepped into the clearing alone, my hands raised.

"You haven't been all that keen on talking to me so far—I thought you might change your mind if she was here," I said.

He stepped closer, until we were only a few feet apart. He hadn't bathed since the fire—or possibly the Clinton administration—and his callused hands were black with grime, one curled around the handle of his shotgun while the other pushed his hat farther back on his head. He scratched at his ear for a few seconds before he fixed his gaze on me. His eyes were dark, the pupils way too large for someone remotely sober.

"You got questions she won't answer?" he asked me.

I shook my head. "I think she's told me what she knows."

"That she fucked Hammond?"

I nodded. This appeared to surprise him. I heard movement behind me; before I could warn her to stay back, Kat joined me. Ashmont's face darkened.

"I don't want to see you," he said.

"Well, you can't always get what you want, Joe. You know that better than anybody. She just wants to know what happened."

"You lied," he said to her, shifting his focus back to me. "That's what happened—she told every one of us a goddamn lie. She was the one who said to do it. Move the bodies, hide the evidence, make up the lie. Keep the secret."

"She wasn't the only one though, was she?" I asked. My voice was steadier than I'd expected. "You had your own reasons for burying the evidence. You called Reverend Diggins the morning of the fire. It was about Rebecca, right? Something happened—or something was going to happen. You were coming to get her. What changed your mind?"

I think I half-expected him to shoot me for asking the question. I'm not sure I would have cared. Instead of rage, though, Ashmont's face fell. His eyes went glassy, but he wiped the tears away with a filthy hand.

"It was your daddy's idea," he said. His voice was little more than a growl now, and I know the words were meant to hurt me. "It was all Adam's idea. You don't know what he was dealing with—how scared he was of Becca. She was threatening him with something. He wouldn't tell me what, but she'd turned his fuckin' Garden of Eden upside down."

"What the hell are you talking about?" Kat asked. "Rebecca...?"

"My wife," Ashmont said with a sneer. "You didn't ask. You were so busy thinking you had it all figured out, trying to hide the truth when you didn't even know what the truth was. You didn't know shit."

"Rebecca was on the island—I found her rosary," I interrupted, before the conversation devolved into my mother and Ashmont beating the crap out of each other. "She died in the fire."

Ashmont smiled at my mother—a greasy, trembling smile, but a smile all the same. "You got a regular Nancy Drew here, Doc. I was wondering why Becca ain't been around to cook dinner the past twenty-five years. Shit, I thought she was out to the mall. Guess that's one mystery solved."

I ignored his disdain and tried to soften my tone for my next words. "And your son was in the fire?"

My tone had the opposite effect. Ashmont turned on me like a snake ready to strike. I took a step back.

"If he was even mine. That bitch screwed any man with a cross and a reason to use it from here to the Waldo county line." He looked away, lost in the past. When he spoke again, resignation overrode the bitterness. "The goddamn kid never looked like me, anyway."

"You said my father wanted her off the island—why? What was she threatening him with? Why would he want her gone?"

"I told you," Ashmont said. "He wouldn't say what she had on him—all I know is, it all went to hell once she got there." His smile twisted cruelly at one corner. "Becca was a whore, but she knew what she liked. She'd spread her legs for any preacher she laid eyes on—only bitch I ever knew got wet during confession. Your daddy couldn't take seeing Preacher Payson's fall from grace.

"He was the one who called and told me she was out there—I never would've found her otherwise. So, Adam was gonna spend the day before with you," he looked at me. "Then, that night we'd go out to the island. Me and Matt, your daddy, and Reverend Diggins. And we'd haul her out of there, one way or the other."

"What happened to that plan? You were the one who called my father at the hotel that night, weren't you?" I asked, only realizing it as I was saying the words. "Something happened—someone got to you, changed your mind about what you were about to do."

"I changed my own mind," he said. His eyes slid from mine. "That night didn't have nothing to do with any of it—I just got to thinking, and then I called Adam and told him I didn't want to do it. Payson could have Becca and the boy, I didn't give a rat's ass anymore. And I guess from there your daddy just decided he'd best take things into his own hands."

"Bullshit," I said, advancing on him so fast that he stepped back instead of shooting me where I stood. "Something happened. If you'd gotten that far with the plan, you wouldn't have just changed your mind."

He recovered more quickly than I'd anticipated. Before I had a chance to react, he dropped the gun and let it lay where it landed. With a single stride, he had his hand around my neck, pushing me backward until he'd slammed my back against a tree. He held me there, his face close to mine, his breath a rancid mix of whiskey, stale cigarettes, and epically poor dental hygiene.

"Nothing happened. You hear me, you little bitch? I told you: I called your daddy, I told him it was off. I'd had a change of heart. He called Diggins, tried to get him to help change my mind. I knew he was on the way over, so I told the Reverend to call your mum. No way that pussy would show his face if the mighty Doctor Kat was there, no way he'd let on just how far things had gone. And I was right… She showed, he didn't. Matt saw him leave for the island, and two hours later everybody out there was dust. You do the math on that one, and tell me if it adds up to anything other than your daddy going out there and torching every last one of 'em."

His hand held me still, but it didn't tighten around my neck as he gauged my response—trying to figure out whether I believed the story, I knew. Before I could tell him I didn't buy a word of it, a blast split the stillness, so loud that it rattled my teeth and left my ears ringing. Ashmont dropped his hand from my neck, his eyes wide. I waited to see if one or the other of us was dead. Neither of us appeared to be. Kat held his shotgun tilted toward the sky, her eyes pure iron.

"Get away from her," she said.

Ashmont took a few steps, hands raised, sneer still in place. "Get off my land," he said.

"You forget who has the gun here," Kat said.

He walked toward her without hesitation and ripped the gun from her hand. The look on her face was one I'd never seen before—shame, I realized after a moment. Kat wasn't used to being weak.

"Don't play at games you can't finish, Kat—it doesn't suit you. Get off my land. I see you out here again, I won't think twice before I put you both in the ground."

Neither my mother nor I argued with him. We left in silence. My knees were knocking together during the hike back to the boat, and neither of us spoke until we were safely back at sea.

AUGUST 15, 1990

REBECCA SITS IN THE GREENHOUSE, the night thick with the slow broil of August, moisture forming at the small of her back and the nape of her neck. Tendrils of dark hair curl at her ears from the humidity. Tomatoes ripe on the vine sweeten the air so completely that she can almost taste them. She sits on a granite bench in the light of a full moon. When she first arrived, nearly an hour before, the stone was cool; now, it has warmed to her body temperature. She shifts, and the underside of her naked thigh sticks for a moment before peeling from the hard surface.

Isaac is late, but she is not concerned. Though he told her this morning that he would not come, that he can no longer see her this way, she doesn't worry. He says the same thing every time they meet: what they are doing is wrong. He has a wife, children, a congregation; their time together is a sin. Rebecca nods her head, tells him that she understands, but in truth she understands far better than he ever will: what they are doing—what *she* is doing—is exactly as God planned it.

The moon is high above when Isaac finally arrives.

Though he makes no sound, she knows he is there in a way that runs deeper than the five senses. When he stands at the entrance to the greenhouse, one hand on the doorsill, Rebecca's heart slows. Her breath becomes less weighted. It is always this way. When they are alone together, it is the only time Rebecca truly believes that God might walk among them.

"I can't stay," he begins.

She nods. When she stands, he realizes for the first time that she is naked—she can tell by his virtually inaudible intake of breath, a sound no one would hear but her. A breeze stirs the air and the fine, dark hairs on her arms stand on end. It isn't cold, but the breeze on her already-damp skin makes her shiver. Her nipples tighten, and she wonders if Isaac can tell in the scant light; wonders if he believes he is the cause. She hopes, for an instant, that he does.

"I told Mae I had to cover the plants in the garden—that there might be rain tonight."

There hasn't been rain in three weeks now. A passing drizzle here or there, but nothing significant enough to warrant a late-night trek to the gardens. Isaac knows this as well as Rebecca does. She imagines his wife, Mae, knows it quite well herself.

"So, go cover the plants." She says it with no challenge in her tone, still making no move to go to him. Isaac remains in the doorway. The moonlight casts him in a glow that Rebecca believes makes him look distinctly Christ-like.

"Zion was asleep when you left?"

She nods again. Isaac takes the first step inside, and she gestures toward the plants at her feet. "Adam should tend the tomatoes—they'll rot if we don't pick them soon."

He takes another few steps, under the guise of verifying

her words. She considers telling him now what she's recently learned of his sacred Adam—who, as it happens, is not Adam at all. Matt has been unable to find out the truth of his identity, but the Adam Solomon he claims to be died an infant in a Midwest hospital in 1954. The Adam Solomon Isaac considers his trusted confidante is nothing but a lie. She remains silent, however. All in good time.

Isaac kneels only a few inches from her, his back turned away, head bowed as though praying. Rebecca wonders what he would do if she reached for him now—let her hand fall to his head, allowed her fingers to curl in the soft thickness of his hair. It is an idle thought, though. She makes no move.

Still on his knees, Isaac turns until his head is even with her waist. She can feel his breath on her right hip when he exhales, warmer even than the night air. He reaches out and touches the back of her thigh with one hand, pulling her closer. They remain like this for a moment: the preacher and his whore, his face pressed to her sex, both hands at the backs of her thighs. His hands begin to move first, sliding up the backs of her legs. He straightens, his lips leaving a trail of wet kisses up the soft flesh of her stomach, to her breasts. When his teeth graze a nipple, she gasps; he bites down harder at the sound, his hands at her buttocks, and he finally stands before her. She can feel him now, hard inside his jeans, pressed against her naked stomach.

They remain that way only a moment before he turns her away from him—as he always does. It is unspoken, but understood: she will never lock eyes with him when he is this man. She reaches behind her, unable to stop touching him now that she's started, her hands lighting on the worn cotton of his t-shirt, the denim of his jeans. There is nothing in the world but this instant.

She hears his clothes fall to the soil beneath them. Isaac guides her to her knees, one hand at her shoulder, the other on her hip. Though everything she has ever been taught runs counter to the notion, she knows this is a holy moment. Isaac kneels behind her, naked now. His hand is at her back, guiding her forward; she complies until she is on hands and knees. A single pebble in the soil bites into the heel of her left hand. Isaac reaches between her legs and she knows that he finds her wet, ripe for this moment. He positions himself at her entrance with one hand, wrapping his other arm around her neck, his right hand braced on her left shoulder to keep her still. It is the closest to embracing her that he ever allows himself.

When he fills her, he does so completely. He makes no sound—does not speak her name, does not moan, barely breathes. Rebecca is also quiet, knowing the risk of someone finding them like this, but she is unable to match his absolute silence. With every whimper that escapes her lips, Isaac moves with a little more violence than before. She believes that in this moment, he sees them all: Eve, Jezebel, Delilah… She is the whore Magdalene beneath him, at once Christ's greatest weakness and his solitary comfort, during his trials on Earth.

Isaac's mouth is at her neck, but he does not kiss her. When her inner muscles contract around him, he bites into her shoulder, hard enough to pull her back from the pulse of white light running through her. Present once more, she pictures the scene as an onlooker would: She on hands and knees beneath him, their coupling increasingly frantic as Isaac buries himself deeper with every thrust. They are animals—a fact that Rebecca alone freely acknowledges in this place. Every day they eat, they sleep, they excrete, and then have the arrogance to ascribe a higher meaning to their lives than those of every other creature on the planet. But in this instant, the single instant when Isaac can no longer stop himself and his strangled cry breaks the stillness, the truth is undeniable:

They are animals.

Just as God intended.

23

THE BOAT RIDE back to Littlehope was notably silent. Kat stood starboard with her eyes on the horizon, and I didn't have a clue how to reach her. But then, I never really had. Night had fallen, dark and starless. The forecast called for heavy rain and high winds over the next few days, and I could feel it in the damp bite of the ocean breeze.

My mother's cell phone rang just before we docked back in Littlehope. I was grateful—the silence was getting old. There were still questions I needed answered, but the standoff between Kat and Ashmont had thrown everything off kilter. I could handle my mother drunk, raging, irreverent, in control, out of control... I just didn't know how to handle her when she was weak. I'd never had to.

The call was from the hospital. She stayed on the line while I docked the boat, and didn't hang up until a good ten minutes after I'd cut the engine and checked my watch pointedly a dozen times. Apparently, all she'd needed was the chance to play Dr. Everett again—once she was off the phone and out of the boat, Kat got behind the wheel of her Beetle without waiting for me, clearly back on top.

"His story doesn't change anything," she said, once I'd gotten in the passenger's seat.

"Excuse me?"

"That shit Joe just told us. So he and Matt had their own reasons for keeping things quiet—it's not like I thought they were keeping the secret to protect me all that time."

Kat is a sociopathically good liar, but this was one time when I could see right through her.

"I think that's exactly what you thought. All this time, you've been thinking you were part of this exclusive society of men who'd do anything to keep your secret. Jesus, Kat—your ego knows no bounds."

Her hands tightened on the steering wheel as she pulled in front of the *Trib*. I noticed that Sheriff Finnegan's patrol car was parked out front again. Kat put the car in park, but made no move to cut the engine.

"I should get back."

"What?"

"You heard me—I should get back. You have the answers you were looking for; I'm going back to Portland."

"You can't leave now. I still have questions—"

Before I could finish the sentence, someone rapped lightly on the window. Kat and I both jumped, which made me feel marginally better. She might put up a good front, but it was nice to know she wasn't completely unruffled by the events of the past twenty-four hours.

Finnegan leaned in after I rolled down the window.

"Sorry to startle you ladies. Erin, I wondered if I might have a word with you?" He leaned in a little further, giving my mother a polite smile. "You too, ma'am. Just a couple of routine questions."

Kat put up a perfunctory protest, but gave up when Sheriff Finnegan just arched an eyebrow and shot me a little twist of a smile. Clearly, he'd dealt with worse than she was prepared to dish out today.

"Do you need us to follow you to the station or something?" I asked.

He laughed. "No, no—that won't be necessary. I'm just trying to get a handle on the timeline for everything that happened yesterday, and I understand you both spoke with the victim before he died. Diggs said we could use his office."

Kat shot me a glare that suggested I was to blame for the whole mess we were in. I ignored her and we followed the sheriff inside.

Half a dozen newspaper folk looked up from their desks as we walked past, sensing a story. Finnegan spoke with me first. He shut the door to Diggs' office and offered a kind smile before he began. His questions were pretty basic: When had I spoken with Hammond last; what had the last conversation been about; had I noticed him acting strangely?

I sat in a folding chair in front of the desk while the sheriff made himself comfortable in Diggs' leather editor's chair. Just when he'd lulled me into thinking the interview was almost over, Finnegan surprised me with a follow-up question that went straight for the jugular.

"You know, I was thinking this morning about your run-in the other day with that ornery door that gave you so much trouble."

I froze. "Yes?"

"It's your business if you don't want to file a report—I'm not sure of your thinking, but you're clearly a smart woman. I imagine you've got your reasons. But now I have a problem, because I have a dead man—a former policeman, and you know how we cops stick together… There's gonna be a lot of people asking a lot of questions about this. If the…*incident* you had the other day does end up having something to do with Noel Hammond's murder, how do you think you'll feel about that? Especially if somebody else gets hurt because you wouldn't come forward?"

I didn't know what to say. He was right, of course. Whoever attacked me had to be the same person who killed Hammond—nothing else made sense. He'd been very clear with me: stop looking. Hammond had been one step ahead of me in the investigation. What had he found that got him killed?

"Erin," Finnegan said. His voice was gentle, but something in his eyes suggested that things could take a turn if needed. "If you want to change your story, now would be the time."

I hesitated. The phone number Hammond had written, the voice so hauntingly familiar on the other end of the line, the secret Ashmont said Rebecca had been threatening to expose about my father... I was so close. I didn't have a goddamn clue anymore *what* I was close to—but I was close. I couldn't show my hand yet. Not now.

"I'm sorry, Sheriff. I told you—I'm just clumsy."

"So you're telling me, here and now, on the record, that those bruises on your face, the injuries you sustained, had nothing to do with Detective Hammond's death."

Those formerly peaceable eyes had hardened. I held my ground.

"Not to my knowledge, Sheriff. They do not."

He looked genuinely disappointed in me. "All right, Erin. Take my card—give me a call anytime if you think of anything that might help. You can send your mom in now."

Kat went in without saying a word to me. She didn't look nervous so much as pissed off. I'd been on the receiving end of the look enough times to feel sorry for Finnegan. I sat down at an empty desk in the newsroom. MSNBC was still on the TV, the BBC World Report on the radio. A couple of the reporters gawked at me when they thought I wasn't paying attention, but no one said a word until Diggs came in and sat on the edge of the desk.

"Kat's in there now?"

"She is."

"Did you find anything out?"

I looked around at the mini-squadron of prying eyes. "I'll tell you later. Have you heard anything from Jack?"

"Perkins is still on the loose. Finnegan hasn't said anything, but I have a feeling our former constable is high on the list of suspects for Noel's death."

This was hardly surprising.

"So, what's the plan from here?" he asked.

"I just need to try and get a few final answers from Kat, but she's on her way out of town after that." I looked around at everyone typing madly at their desks. "I'm guessing tonight's another late one around here?"

"Between the fire and this whole Hammond's-been-murdered thing, we'll definitely have our work cut out for us." He eyed me guiltily. "Sorry. I wish I could be there for you a little more than I have been. This job…"

"Don't worry about it, I'd be doing the same thing in your shoes." I stood when Diggs' office door opened and Kat emerged. "I've gotta go. I'll give you a call later?"

He nodded.

Kat didn't give either of us so much as a glance before she swept out the door, and she was already in the driver's seat with the car in gear before I caught up to her. As it was, I had to stand in front of the car to get her to stop; if

I hadn't had Einstein with me, I'm pretty sure she would have just run me down. Instead, she waited with obvious impatience while I put the dog in the back and got in the passenger's seat yet again. I was barely buckled in before she was barreling down the road.

"What did you tell Finnegan?" I asked.

"The truth. Noel and I spoke a few times over the past few days, but I didn't see him and I sure as hell don't have a clue who killed him."

"Matt Perkins is still missing. You think it could have been him?"

She glanced at me. "Well, he's always been a few Froot Loops shy of a full bowl—it wouldn't surprise me. I don't know how he could have overpowered a man like Noel, though."

"Unless Matt got the drop on him when he wasn't expecting it," I said. She didn't look convinced; I didn't blame her. It didn't add up for me, either.

We were closing in on the road to Diggs' place, and I knew Kat wouldn't stick around once we were there. If I wanted answers, it was now or never.

"The secret Rebecca knew about Dad—what do you think it was?"

"I don't think there was a secret," she said, like she'd been expecting the question. "Based on Joe's description, she sounds like just another lunatic who allied herself with the Paysons—but this time, she may have been more nuts than even they could handle."

"Do you think Isaac was sleeping with her?"

"Wouldn't surprise me. He and Mae always seemed happy when I was out there, but things change."

I waited a couple of seconds before asking the question

that had been burning a hole in my brain for the past twenty-four hours.

"Is Dad really dead?"

She didn't look at me. She gripped the steering wheel more tightly, a flicker of something—regret, pain... guilt?—crossing her face before it was gone.

"Of course he's dead. For Christ's sake, Erin, you're not a kid—this is a conversation I might've expected when you were ten or eleven, but not now. He's gone. Stop wasting your time on something that will only bring more pain."

She pulled up in front of Diggs' place, threw the car in park, and got out without waiting for me. I let Einstein out and ran after her.

"You're lying—I talked to him. I heard his voice."

She stopped dead in her tracks and turned. I'd never seen Kat afraid before, but if I had I was willing to bet this was what it would have looked like.

"What are you talking about?"

"I found a number. Going through Noel's place, I found a bunch of paperwork and a telephone number with Dad's name on it. I called. He answered."

It took a few seconds before she schooled her expression back to its usually impassive mask. She shook her head.

"When was the last time you actually talked to your father? You were, what, twelve? We hear what we want to hear; we see what we want to see. Your father is dead." She turned on her heel and left me standing there.

"Why should I believe you now? Until I started digging up your old secrets, everything you ever told me about the fire was a lie. What makes this any different?"

She kept walking. It was dark, but Kat didn't bother to turn the lights on when we got inside, using some kind of half-human, half-doctor stealth radar to move from room to room without bumping into anything. The rain had started. The house was empty, but the sound of wind lashing against the windows and raindrops beating on the roof made it anything but silent. She wouldn't answer me.

I caught up to her in my bedroom and grabbed her arm. She wheeled. Her eyes were cold, hard in a way that I'd almost forgotten. I stepped back.

"Why did you take me from him?" I asked. It wasn't the question she'd expected. To be fair, I wasn't really expecting it myself—and I definitely wasn't expecting the tremor in my voice when I asked it. "We were happy out there. Why would you take me away, when you never wanted to be a mother in the first place?"

"You think you would have been better off on the island?" she asked. She was the ice queen now—not a trace of emotion to be found. Kat was bred to be a surgeon, but for all her healing ways, she never could stand personal weakness. There was no doubt in my mind that she'd rather have me bleeding from the eyeballs and fingernails than the emotional wreck I'd become. That certainly would have been my preference.

"This mythic childhood you created, this community of people who loved and cared for you, this perfect bond you had with your father? I think it's time you face the fact that most of that's a fantasy, a story you created to comfort yourself after the fire."

I thought of all the images that had been running through my head in the past few days: Isaac's need for control, the beatings I witnessed, the singular devotion he demanded from his followers.

"You weren't there," I said. "You left before I even knew

who you were. You don't have a clue what my childhood was like out there."

"I was there for a year before you came along—I knew Isaac Payson, Erin. Trust me, that church was no place for you. "

"And you thought you could do better? Leaving me alone while you screwed every man in town, dragging me out to your calls and then sitting me at the bar till closing to drink root beer and wait until you got your shit together enough to drag us both home? That's a better life than Dad could have given me?"

We were both shouting, inches away from each other. I knew exactly what would happen the second I pushed too hard—I'd seen it before. For the first time in my life, my own anger outshone even my mother's controlling hand.

Her eyes flashed. When she spoke again, her voice was quiet, her eyes cold and still.

"If I hadn't taken you, you both would have died along with everybody else. Believe me, I know that for most of your childhood with me, that's what you would have preferred. But has your life really been so shitty that now, twenty years later, you would've rather died at ten years old in a fire with a church of zealots?"

My eyes burned the way they used to when I'd stared too long into the woodstove, focused on the flames.

"Why did you take me?" I asked again.

"Because your father asked me to," she finally said. Everything slowed. She kept her eyes on mine as she delivered the killing blow. "He called me in Boston and told me he couldn't handle you anymore—he couldn't keep you safe. I would have left you there, let you grow up with Isaac and the rest of his shiny happy fucking cult."

When I didn't say anything, she sighed. I looked away from her, focused on the floor when she continued.

"Maybe I should have told you sooner. If I had, you might not have clung so hard to all these delusions about your life on that island. I came for you because I had no choice. Your father didn't want you, Erin."

24

AFTER KAT LEFT, I got a bottle of wine and started a fire in the fireplace, then sat in the dark with Einstein for a long time, thinking about what she'd said. Trying to remember more details of a shitty childhood that I'd apparently painted in shades of blue and gold—a fairytale I had told myself because the facts had been too much for me to handle.

So, what were those facts?

Someone set fire to the Payson Church. That was a fact. If Isaac really had been screwing Rebecca Ashmont, would he have gone over the edge if someone threatened to take her away? Would he have taken the lives of his entire congregation, just so no one else could get to them?

And what about my father? Kat may have tried to minimize what I'd heard on the phone, but her reaction just reinforced what I'd already known in my gut the second I heard his voice: my father was alive. Noel Hammond had known it. My mother knew it. The question was, why had they gone to such great lengths to convince me—and the world—that he was dead?

When I got nowhere with that line of thinking, I returned to the Payson fire. I thought of the body that had been found outside the church that day. The prevailing theory, at least according to Hammond, was that that had been Isaac. The preacher had locked the congregation inside the church, set the fire, and then waited there to die with them. There was no proof of that, though—Isaac's body had been recovered at the scene, but thanks to Kat there was no way of knowing if his was the body Hammond had photographed. And no one had even known Rebecca and Zion were out there, so their remains had never been identified.

I thought about that for a few minutes before another question popped into my head. What if the reason Joe Ashmont's wife and son weren't found with the other remains wasn't because no one was looking, but because they simply weren't there? And if they *hadn't* died in the fire, where the hell were they now?

And what about the man chasing me that day? What about this mysterious secret Rebecca had been holding over my father's head? What part had my father played in the whole thing?

"This is what we call a giant cluster fuck," I informed Einstein. He looked at me sagely and whined.

I sat there thinking that over, wine bottle still in hand, until Stein shattered the stillness with a bark that nearly sent me into orbit. He raced for the front door. Headlights shined through the living room window, coming to rest on the far wall. The engine went off; the light vanished. I waited by the fire.

Juarez came in a few minutes later and sat down on the floor beside me without turning on the overhead light or saying a word. I handed him my half-full bottle of merlot; he tipped it back and took a long pull. He had a full day's beard growth, shadows beneath his eyes, and his shirt was rumpled. His sleeves were rolled up, and a tie hung loose at his collar—silk, gray with a black diamond pattern. He removed it, and for a second I thought he might toss it into the fire.

Instead, he folded it carefully in half and set it aside.

He scrubbed his eyes with the heels of his hands.

"Diggs should really get some fuckin' furniture," he said. It was so unexpected that I laughed out loud.

"We should spring for some before we leave. Nothing fancy—just a deck chair or two, maybe."

"Or one of those free-standing porch swings," he said. "We could set it up in front of the fire."

We fell silent, meditating on that.

"So, I take it you've had no luck finding Matt?" I finally asked, when it became awkward not to.

He shook his head and took another pull from the wine bottle. "I looked in all the old spots—everywhere I could think of. Somebody said they saw him get in a red pickup when he left the hospital, but no one's seen a trace of him since."

I thought of Ashmont, and the conversation on his island. "Joe…" I began.

"I know," he said. "…Has a red pickup. I talked to him earlier. He said it wasn't him."

"And you believe him?"

"I don't know what to believe anymore," he said.

He looked at me. His eyes were rimmed with red, any trace of humor gone from his face. I thought of what he'd told me about his childhood, and tried to imagine having no memory of my past. My family was clearly fucked up, but those early days with my father—whatever they had or hadn't been—had shaped me, given me a sense of self that remained to this day. What would it be like not to have that to hold onto?

I put my hand on Juarez's denim-clad knee. It was cold and damp, like he'd been out in the rain for a while. I scratched lightly at the fabric, feeling the muscle and bone beneath, the power and tension of his body. His eyes were on me when his hand fell to mine, stilling the movement. I inched closer.

"Where's Diggs?" he asked.

"Work. With the fire and Hammond's death, he'll be late. If he makes it back at all."

He hadn't moved his hand from mine. He traced the lines on my palm with a fingertip, as attentive as a fortune teller.

"And your mom?"

"Came and went. We're not much for long visits."

More silence. Our fingers twined, his hands long and fine and masculine. When I looked up, I realized he was watching me—his eyes dark and sad, as though something heartbreaking was happening. I didn't know what that something might be until I noticed the tan line on his ring finger.

"You're married," I said.

He pulled his hand back, staring at it like he expected the ring to magically reappear.

"Not anymore," he said. "Not for a while."

He leaned in before I could ask any follow-up questions. Unlike with Diggs, there were no remonstrations when our lips met. No hesitation. Jack's hand moved to the back of my neck to pull me closer; the kiss deepened. He leaned back and pulled me with him until our bodies were flush.

Outside, the storm was getting worse—I could hear tree limbs creaking as the rain fell in torrents against the double-paned windows. His hands were on my face, in my hair, moving over me with a desperation that matched my own. For the first time in weeks, my father and the Payson fire weren't the first things on my mind.

After a few minutes of heavy petting, during which my bra mysteriously came undone and Juarez's jeans visibly tightened, I summoned enough self control to pull away.

"Do you want to take this someplace else?"

I held my breath, waiting for him to explain all the very valid reasons why sex right now wasn't a good idea. Instead, he stood. Our eyes caught. If we were going to have that whole horrible Should We Or Shouldn't We talk, now would be the time. He held out his hand.

I took it.

We went to his room—after the fight with Kat, my bedroom was the last place I wanted to be. Einstein must have sensed trouble afoot, because he made no move to follow us.

I shut the bedroom door and we stood in the dark for a few seconds—not quite touching, not quite moving. I found the hem of his shirt and ran my hand along his bare stomach, reveling in his intake of air, the coiling of muscle beneath my fingertips.

"We can go as slowly as you want," he said.

I had been chilled all day, but now my clothes felt too close, the air too warm, my skin hot enough to burn on contact. I pushed him backward until he was against the wall, and did my best to illustrate just how uninterested I was in going slow. I unbuttoned his shirt and already had my hands on the fly of his jeans while his lips were still nipping at my earlobe. He intercepted me just as my fingertips were inching past the waistband of his boxers.

"Erin," he said.

I looked up. It was dark in the room, but I found his eyes and felt myself quiet suddenly. He ran a hand down my cheek.

"It's been a while," he said, in the same tone a prospective lover might tell you he has VD or still lives with his mom. "I don't want to rush this."

I nodded. When we kissed again, it was different—not languorous, necessarily, but the intensity was less frantic. I was hardly a blushing virgin, but I hadn't been with anyone but Michael for a hell of a long time myself. The fact that Juarez might be in the same boat was unexpectedly comforting.

When we were on the mattress, he pulled my shirt up over my head and tossed it in a pile in the middle of the room with the rest of our clothes. Then, he just sat there—studying me. My hair was a mess and my heart was beating too fast and it was only by some miracle of fate that I was wearing Victoria's Secret instead of my sports bra and a pair of Diggs' boxer shorts.

"What?" I asked. I pulled the comforter up over my lap.

"You're beautiful, you know."

I rolled my eyes. "So are you."

He was, actually. He had the calves of a distance runner and the ass of a Roman god. His dark hair was rumpled, an errant lock across his forehead and a cowlick in the back. His stomach was flat and his boxers were tented. My blood felt like warm honey slipping through my veins as I dropped my hand to his ankle, tracing light patterns up his leg.

His breath caught at the contact. "Can I tell you

something that may come across as vaguely creepy?"

"You really want to keep talking?"

He grinned at me. "You don't like talking?"

I lay down, my body curled around him, but Juarez remained sitting. "Not as much as you, apparently," I said.

"I had a crush on you, the second summer I was here."

I kissed his ankle, in the spot where my hand had been a moment before. He tasted like salt and cedar—masculine and earthy, strong and sweet. His hand fell to my head, fingers twining in my hair while I continued my seduction.

"That is creepy. The second summer you were here, I was only…"

"Fifteen," he said.

I could feel the tension in his body coiling tighter when I kissed my way up his leg. I traded tongue for teeth behind his knee.

"Christ," he whispered. He shifted where he sat, but he didn't stop talking.

"And I was only seventeen, you forget—so not *so* creepy. Particularly considering the men you're typically attracted to."

I paused. His hand remained in my hair, stroking me like some cherished pet. I realized that he was waiting for me to make the decision: stop, or continue.

I nipped him again, harder this time. He lay back on the bed, but I made no move to go with him. I kissed my way up his inner thigh, my hand stroking higher up his leg.

"What do you know about the men I'm typically attracted to?" I asked, when it became apparent he wasn't going to explain himself.

This time, he did pull me up. I let my hand brush against the front of his boxers and smiled when he closed his eyes at the contact, whispering curses I hadn't heard him use before tonight. He turned onto his side before I could find a more comfortable position—preferably on top, and without that last pesky layer of clothes. We faced each other on the bed, eyes wide open.

"Diggs is what, ten years older than you?"

"Eight," I said. I wasn't crazy about where this was going. "And Diggs and I don't date."

"Right," he said. He didn't roll his eyes, but it was implicit. "You said your ex-husband had been your professor, didn't you?"

"Your idea of pillow talk could use some work."

His hand traveled down my side, his long fingers tracing patterns on my stomach. It made me think of Michael suddenly—of what we'd had, and what we'd lost. I moved Juarez's roaming digits to my ass, where my thoughts were considerably less sentimental.

"So, your ex was…?" He studied me. I tensed. "…twenty—no, maybe seventeen, eighteen years older than you?"

I backed away from him. He stopped me, his eyes holding me as surely as his hands.

"You like powerful men," he said. "Crave them, even. They're in control or you are—and if you are, you're not with them long." He bit his lip, his forehead furrowed like he was working a complex math problem. If two trains leave Boston at the same time and one is traveling at sixty miles an hour and the other at forty, the wind is coming from the west and x is equal to 42.6, what makes Erin Solomon tick?

"Am I wrong?" he asked.

"I've never really thought about it," I lied. My voice sounded colder than I'd intended.

I started to sit up, but Juarez wouldn't let me go. He pushed me onto my back and an instant later was on top of me, his body pinning me to the mattress. His eyes bore into mine, his hands loose at my wrists. A vision of the attack on the island flashed through my mind.

"Get off me," I said.

He didn't move. His eyes had taken on that darkness again, a hint of the sadness I'd seen earlier.

"Is this the kind of power you like?" he asked, his breath hot in my ear. "Someone who takes what he wants, keeps things simple?"

I tipped my head up, intending to bite or head butt or…something. He kissed me, his tongue pressing past my lips without invitation. I wanted to be offended, repulsed. Terrified. Instead, my legs came up and wrapped around his thighs, my feet at the backs of his knees. He rolled so that I was on top again, and pushed the hair back from my forehead as he kissed me more slowly.

"I don't like simple," he whispered.

I had no answer for that.

I was afraid he was about to start talking again, but instead he turned his attention to my shoulder, then lower. His teeth grazed a sweet spot on my collarbone while I tried to divest both of us of our underwear at the same time— not that successfully. Mine were tangled at my ankles and his had him bound at the knees, but neither of us seemed interested in parting long enough to finish disrobing.

And then, the phone rang.

"Shit," I said. "One minute—I just need one more minute." I made no effort to keep the desperation from my voice.

Juarez managed a strained laugh. "Trust me, we're gonna

need more than one minute. I'm sorry." He looked so sorry, in fact, that I thought he might cry. I thought I might join him.

I rolled off his body and pulled my underpants back up, while he went to retrieve his phone. He pulled on his boxers and answered with a hushed, "Juarez here."

He straightened when he heard whoever was on the other end of the line, then went to the other room with an apologetic glance my way, gathering the rest of his clothes under his arm. I gave him what I considered a respectful amount of privacy—maybe forty-five seconds—before I followed him with the sheet wrapped around me.

The storm hadn't let up while Juarez and I had been getting to know each other in the other room. The lights flickered as a gust of wind rocked the house and rain battered the windows. Einstein got up from his spot by the fire, whimpering now that I'd chosen to rejoin him. Jack stood at the fireplace with his shirt off and his jeans unbuttoned, his hand running distractedly through his hair as he listened to the caller.

"Listen to me," he said. His voice was even, but there was no mistaking his anxiety. "You need to calm down. It doesn't matter what happened—it doesn't matter what you did. We can handle this."

I touched his side. His arm came around me with an ease I found disconcerting.

"Matt?" I mouthed.

He nodded. "Just tell me where you are and I'll come get you."

Matt's voice rose, loud enough for me to hear him shouting, though not clear enough to make out the words. Jack turned his back to me.

"Nothing will happen—everybody's safe. I'm safe, Matt. You don't need to protect anyone anymore. You just need to tell me where you are."

The call went on like that for another ten minutes, Juarez alternately soothing and pleading, before he finally stopped talking mid-sentence and the call disconnected. For a few seconds, he didn't say anything—just stood at the fireplace, still half-dressed.

"Where is he?"

"He wouldn't say." He ran a hand through his hair, his eyes wide and weary. "He didn't sound good, though."

"Do you think he's dangerous?"

"To himself—absolutely. To others… I don't know anymore. Maybe." He took a step back. I handed him his jacket, already aware of what came next.

"You should go," I said. "I can give Finnegan a call over at the sheriff's office if you want, let him know you talked to Matt. That you're still looking for him. But if you have any idea where he might be…"

He nodded. I expected distance from him—that inevitable, mumbled apology and the awkward after-kiss before we parted ways. Instead, we walked to the doorway of Diggs' house with the rain pouring down, me still clad in only a sheet, Juarez exhausted and disheveled and surprisingly sweet, by my side.

"I'll call you as soon as I find out anything," he said.

He kissed me again. Whispered 'thank you' in my ear—presumably for all the sex we hadn't had—and left. Einstein and I remained in the doorway, watching his taillights disappear into the night.

25

IT WAS THREE A.M. when Juarez left and I couldn't sleep. I considered calling Diggs but refrained, afraid he might be trying to get some rest himself. I flipped the light switch in my bedroom. The bed was neatly made, everything on my nightstand at perfect right angles. I went over the events of the past forty-eight hours, lingering on the things I'd discovered at Noel Hammond's house and then out on the island.

It may not have been my father who'd been living in his old cabin, but someone had clearly been there recently. The same someone who had attacked me and killed Hammond? If it was, then it stood to reason that Hammond had figured out who that someone was—which was why he was dead. The fact that I was still clueless about who the bad guys were in this unfolding drama had presumably saved me up to this point.

For the first time since Hammond's death, I remembered the notes and clippings I'd taken from his house. I went to the closet and felt blindly along the top shelf for the shoebox I'd hidden Hammond's research in.

It wasn't there.

I'd been rushed and in a panic when I'd returned from the island with Juarez the night of the fire. Despite that, I'd still taken the time to hide Hammond's research, aware of how critical what I might find in those faded notes might be. Shoe box, top shelf. There was no question in my mind.

I did a perfunctory search of the rest of the bedroom anyway, though I knew I wouldn't find what I was looking for. When that was done, I retrieved my cell phone from Juarez's bedroom floor. Dawn was still hours away—anyone in their right mind would be sound asleep at this hour—including the woman who, I was sure, had taken the shoebox filled with Hammond's research with her when she high-tailed it out of Littlehope just a few hours before.

Frankly, I wasn't at all concerned about interrupting my mother's beauty sleep.

Kat's cell phone went straight to voicemail. I tried her house phone, and got the same result after six rings. An answering service picked up when I called her office. I left messages of varying degrees of urgency at each number. I considered getting in the car and driving to Portland. I'd track her down, give her holy hell for going through my room, and force her to give me back my stuff. And then, I'd demand to know why the hell she'd taken it in the first place.

Portland was two hours away, though. There was a typhoon raging outside, and I didn't want to go anywhere until I'd heard back from Juarez. There wasn't a lot I could do for him, I knew, but I still wanted to at least be there to find out how things with Matt resolved themselves.

Matt. I thought again of the most plausible scenario I'd come up with so far, given everything I knew about the Paysons now: Matt and Ashmont, about to kidnap Rebecca and take her away from the island. When Isaac found out, he... what? Decided to make a clean break from the church by killing everyone in the congregation, so he could be with Rebecca? That made no sense.

But then, there wasn't a whole lot about this that did make sense. Who was the man who chased Dad and me on the island that day? What was the secret Rebecca had been holding over my father's head? And why was her rosary in Isaac Payson's bedroom twenty-two years after the fire that had killed them both? I thought again of everything I'd learned about Rebecca and Zion Ashmont, including Rebecca's apparent compulsion to sleep with every man of the cloth who crossed her path. Their remains had never been found.

Joe Ashmont had known they were out there; Reverend Diggins had known they were out there. Edie Woolrich had told me she'd gone out to the island to tend to Rebecca and Zion over the years, presumably providing medical care of some kind. Which meant they must have had some kind of medical documentation, right?

If it was general knowledge that they were out there, and medical records had been available, why hadn't anyone been able to identify their bodies with the rest of the victims in the Payson fire?

I thought about Zion Ashmont for a minute.

Rebecca had been Native American, Edie had said. Dark-skinned. Zion was born in '77.

"I was only seventeen—two years older than you..." Juarez had said.

Jack Juarez, a teenager with no memories of his childhood, whose life changed abruptly when a stranger from Maine showed up and became his mentor. His friend. Uncle Matt.

I went to Juarez's room with my heart hammering so hard my teeth rattled. The cardboard boxes I'd noticed the day before were still there, pushed up against the wall and sealed with duct tape. I used my fingernails to open them, too impatient to look for a knife. Someone else might have felt guilty, may have had some stab of conscience at such a blatant violation of personal space. I had none.

The first box was filled with books, DVDs, and a few CDs that made me wince. I expected they were things Matt had been hanging onto for Juarez for a while. Einstein eyed me accusingly from Juarez's bed, where he'd hunkered down among blankets still tangled from Jack's and my thwarted tryst. I ignored him and went for the second box.

A handmade afghan was on top, with a couple of cracked knickknacks beneath—salt and pepper shaker policemen that I was sure must have belonged to Matt; a crudely carved dolphin with *JJ* and the year—1993—on the tail. There was a small stack of letters that I looked at but didn't read, all of them addressed to Matt. Jack's name and a Miami address were in the upper left corner. I was just starting to feel guilty for the breach of trust when I caught a glimpse of what looked like a feather, half-hidden in an old tapestry I hadn't bothered to take out.

I moved the fabric aside.

Everything stopped.

One feather became several, stitched together to form one of two delicate wings. Placed carefully in the tapestry to keep it safe, a Payson angel stared up at me with piercing, china-blue eyes.

The rain was still falling and the wind was still blowing when I left the house that morning. Einstein stayed out just long enough to do his thing before he leapt into the car, settling in the backseat without complaint. It was six a.m. Kat had probably been asleep when I'd called before, but I had no doubt she'd be up now. I tried every contact I had for her, yet again. Yet again, I had no luck.

Reverend Diggins had always been an early riser—I was thrilled to see that that hadn't changed over the years. When I pulled in front of the church, his PT Cruiser was the only vehicle in the lot. Across the street, the general store was already in full swing. Pickups were packed in tight, fishermen in yellow slickers loitering outside with cigarettes and hot coffee. It looked like a casting call for the next Gorton's fish sticks spokesman. I searched the crowd for a sign of Ashmont or his truck, but saw neither.

If possible, the Reverend looked even less enthusiastic about seeing me today than he had on our first visit. His office was chilly. Reverend Diggins looked up from his desk with a frown when I entered, and the temperature dropped another degree or two.

"I know it's early—I just had a couple more questions, if it's all right."

He nodded to the same chair I'd argued with him from two days ago. I sat. There was a ledger open on his desk, a silver fountain pen on top. He put the pen in a felt case and closed the ledger before addressing me.

"I'm glad that you came, actually," he said, surprisingly enough. "I'm afraid I was a bit harsh with you the other day."

"It happens."

He actually looked amused at that. "I imagine it does. What can I help you with this morning?"

"I thought you might have some old pictures here. Of picnics and special events, that kind of thing."

"Still interested in Rebecca Ashmont, I take it?"

"I'm just curious about her—she caused quite a stir. When I'm writing her for the book, I'd like to have a picture of some kind in my mind."

"You should be careful—you're developing a bit of an obsession."

I looked at him, reminded inexplicably of those old Victorian paintings where the faces remain impassive while the eyes seem to follow your every move.

"I don't think I'd be the first person obsessed with Rebecca, do you?"

"She was an unusual woman. She certainly had an effect on the people she touched, if that's what you mean."

"And did she ever touch you, Reverend?"

The words were out before I could stop myself. The Reverend stiffened. Rather than dignify the remark with a response, he stood and went to a bookshelf on the back wall. He ran a bony finger over the spines until he came to a thick, leather-bound volume.

"This covers the years she was here—you can start with that."

He returned to his desk and opened his ledger once more as I took the album and flipped through. I found what I was looking for after a few minutes of scanning faces and captions. I turned the album so the Reverend could see.

"That's her?"

He nodded, but I couldn't read his expression.

In the first photo of her, a woman with thick, black hair was seated at a picnic table by the water, a single braid hanging loose over one shoulder. Her face was heart-shaped, with high cheekbones and full lips. Thickly lashed, wide black eyes stared back at me. In the first few shots, Rebecca was svelte, with long legs and slim hips. In the next set, she'd gained weight, thickening around the middle, her breasts perceptibly fuller.

"She was pregnant while she was here," I said.

"Was she? It was quite a few years ago—I'm afraid I don't remember it that well."

I let that go for the moment. When I flipped the page, Rebecca stood in front of the church. Something changed about her since her last photograph. It was her eyes—there was something otherworldly about them that I hadn't seen before, like she wasn't quite all there. She held a toddler in her arms—a little boy, maybe two years old. He was dark like his mother, with thick black hair and wide black eyes. I thought again of the blue-eyed angel hidden in Jack's things.

"Do you remember her son at all?"

He shook his head, too fast to have actually given the question any real thought. "No. Rebecca had left the church some time before that photo was taken—she came back to the mainland for a picnic, if memory serves. Before that, I hadn't seen the boy since he was an infant. I never saw him again after that day."

He got up again and returned the photo album to its spot on the shelf. Afterward, he headed straight for the door.

"I'm sorry—that's all I can tell you about the matter. If you'll excuse me, I have morning devotionals to attend to."

I rose without a fight. At the door, I couldn't resist getting in a final question.

"Did you know Joe Ashmont didn't think he was the boy's father?"

He wasn't surprised. "I seem to recall rumors to that effect."

"Any idea who it might have been if it wasn't Joe?"

Much to my surprise, he smiled at me. "Subtlety is not your strong suit, Ms. Solomon. Are you asking if I fathered the child?"

The fact that he was laughing at me took a little of the bite from my interrogation. "Yeah. I guess I am."

We were still sequestered in his office, but the Reverend looked at the door as though confirming that fact. He returned to his desk and sat down. I remained standing.

"I would appreciate it if you didn't tell my son," he said.

"Of course," I lied.

"It would not have been impossible for me to have been the child's father," he said.

"So, you had an affair with Rebecca Ashmont," I said.

He looked a little queasy. When he looked at me again, I was reminded that I was speaking with a scholar of some repute, and not just some Bible-thumping hick. I made a mental note to handle the rest of the interview accordingly.

"I am not unaware of the feelings you and my son harbor toward organized religion. I understand that you find our practices archaic, if not overtly hypocritical. But I take my position very seriously. I always have."

"Which is why you slept with one of your congregation, possibly knocked her up, and then sent her back to her abusive husband, I suppose."

Any trace of amusement vanished from his face. After a few seconds, he managed a placid smile.

"I take full responsibility for my actions. I was under no spell, and I certainly was not under duress."

He paused, considering his words. "With that said, I

would like you to understand that Rebecca was an extremely persuasive young woman who believed herself to be fulfilling a very specific role."

"By sleeping with preachers?"

"People have believed less credible destinies. Rebecca told me once that she believed God spoke to her, mid…" his pale cheeks flushed to a deep pink that climbed all the way to his receding hairline.

"So, Rebecca Ashmont believed she was God's concubine. That's your story?"

"That was *her* story, though not so crudely put," he said. He got up and made for the door one more time. "That's honestly all I can tell you. You should go."

I didn't need to dig any deeper—I knew exactly what the Reverend's spin on the affair would be. It was the story of Eden all over again: an innocent man does his best to lead a godly life only to be led astray by Eve, buck naked with a snake 'round her neck and an evil apple in hand, just begging to be tossed from the garden. I managed to get in one last question before he pushed me out the door.

"So, Rebecca's son—Zion. Where did he fit into this whole delusion of hers?"

I heard footsteps upstairs. Reverend Diggins looked like he was about to be caught in the act instead of just talking about it. His fingers tightened around the doorknob, his lips pressed into a pale, straight line.

"I told you, I only saw them together when he was small. But the way she raised him was not…" he hesitated so long that I thought he might not finish. Someone stopped at the top of the stairs, calling the Reverend's name.

"Reverend Diggins?" I prompted.

He paused to call up the stairs. "One moment please, Alan. I'll meet you out front." He returned his attention to me as the man's footsteps receded.

"Rebecca was not a traditional mother, clearly. Zion was the center of everything. He was a serious baby who grew into a serious toddler, and I expect ultimately became a very serious adolescent. I never knew him as he grew older, but the stories that I heard were that he was somewhat…"

I realized I was holding my breath. "Somewhat…?"

"… Unbalanced," he completed. "There was a rumor that Isaac was grooming him for his position at the head of the church. It is my understanding from accounts I'd heard at the time that Zion took this training very seriously."

"But he was only a kid—he would have been twelve, thirteen years old when Rebecca took him to Payson Isle."

"With Rebecca and Joe Ashmont as parents, I expect twelve years is quite enough time to develop some… eccentricities."

Or go batshit crazy, in other words. I considered this for a moment, still trying to reconcile the image of the black-eyed little boy on his mother's lap in the photo with the man I now believed he had become. Then, something else made me forget that thought altogether.

"Wait—accounts from whom? They'd only been there a month, and everybody out there died. Who talked to you about Zion?"

He hesitated a split second too long, and I knew. I didn't have a chance to ask anything else as he herded me into the hallway. Just before he closed the door on me, he whispered the words I'd already anticipated.

"Your father was concerned. He came to me for counsel regarding the relationship between Isaac, Rebecca, and the boy, a few days before the fire. That's why we were going in—that's why he wanted them off the island. Not just because of Rebecca's delusions, but because of her son's."

AUGUST 17, 1990

REBECCA SITS ON A LEDGE on the north shore of the island, waiting for Isaac. Below, the ocean is a clean, sharp blue, etched with the white lines of a strong surf on a windy day. The ledge provides a perfect vantage, the granite cut as though God himself designed the site for this purpose. Rebecca thinks of the occasional stone masonry Joe used to do in the summers when they were still at the orphanage. She used to imagine Christ wielding a hammer in much the same way, for some reason. Joe would return at the end of the day, covered in fine white dust; she could taste stone in his beard and on his eyelashes.

A voice pulls her from her reverie. It is not the one she expected.

"Beautiful view."

She glances over her shoulder as Adam approaches. "It is."

It is late afternoon, the sun still high in the sky. Rebecca usually meets Isaac in the dark of night or first light of morning, but he suggested an earlier meeting this time. It made her uneasy the way he avoided her gaze when he made the request; Adam's presence does nothing to ease her mind.

He sits beside her without waiting for an invitation. When she looks at him, his eyes are as blue as the ocean below. She thinks for a moment that the name he chose for his new life is apt—he has assumed the innocence, the fresh-boned purity, of someone just stepping into the world. Now that she knows the extent of his deceit, she finds herself unexpectedly impressed with the performance.

"Do you spend much time here?"

She nods, knowing he will continue regardless of whether or not she receives encouragement from her. First man or no, he is still essentially a man.

"Isaac sent me to tell you he can't meet you this evening."

This time, she does turn. There is always something veiled about Adam, a sense that he is hiding some inner darkness behind those eyes of brilliant blue. For an instant when their eyes meet this time, however, the veil falls. She understands suddenly what he sees when he looks at her: A weed. Something unwelcome, something dangerous—a plague to be plucked from their midst before it contaminates the carefully tended garden that is the Payson Church.

She picks up a handful of granite pebbles from the ground beside her and holds them so tightly in her clenched fist that the stones dig into her skin. She attempts a smile.

"Did he say why he can't meet me?"

Adam shakes his head. Doubt darkens his face for an instant before it is gone. "He's busy, I think. Preparing his sermon."

"And you're his messenger."

He nods. The weight of the words she knows he is struggling with are heavy in the air. Finally, she prompts him.

"Was there something else?"

With long, graceful fingers, he reaches for one of the sharper stones on their shared ledge and flicks it in a clean arc through the air. If they were closer to sea level, the stone would have caught the water just right—it might have skipped five, six, seven times before it sank. This high up, it just sails out in a straight line before beginning its descent.

"I just wanted you to know that I understand," Adam says.

She turns to look at him in question.

"I know what it is to want something for your child. I know how becoming a parent changes you—how the world takes on new meaning." He falters when she does not respond. "What I mean to say is, I know how easy it can be to lose yourself—to lose sight of God's plan for you—when you have a child."

"Zion is God's plan for me," she returns simply. It's absurd that she is having this conversation with a man who has allowed his only child to be taken from him, raised by a godless woman on the mainland.

"You've done a good job with him—no one's saying Zion isn't an exceptional boy. I'm just saying, maybe the time has come to start considering your own spiritual well-being."

A fishing boat appears from behind the cove, followed by a dozen or more gulls that dive relentlessly at the deck. She knows immediately that it is not Joe's boat—he kills a fresh gull every morning and nails it to a post at the hull. No gulls follow Joe.

"I'm saved," she finally says.

"The way you conduct yourself with Isaac suggests that you are not." He hesitates a moment when she doesn't respond. "I'm not here to judge your conduct with Isaac. I'm more concerned about his behavior with Zion."

For the first time, she is surprised by his words. "My son has been chosen."

"He's a very bright boy. Gifted. But I'm concerned that Isaac has become somewhat… fixated, on him."

It is only then that she realizes the extent of his envy. Until Zion's arrival, Adam was the sole focus of Isaac's guiding hand, the adored apprentice at the feet of the master. Others attended prayer meetings and Bible study, learned the ways of the Lord, but Adam was the favorite son.

Everything has changed since their arrival.

The silence between them grows sharper. She can feel him struggling with the final words to drive his argument home. He reaches out to her—touches her leg, just slightly, with the palm of his hand. Rebecca flinches, and he looks as guilty as if he'd struck her.

"I think it would be best if you took Zion from this place. Put an end to your relationship with Isaac, take your son, and make a new life for yourselves. Isaac can't do it— you two have some kind of power over him, some sway that he can't seem to fight. But he has built something here, something valuable. All of that has been jeopardized since you and Zion arrived."

Rebecca weighs her response carefully, considering the information Matt passed on to her just yesterday. She hadn't planned on saying something so soon; now, backed into a corner by Adam's design, Rebecca realizes she has no choice. She will not go quietly.

"You say you are concerned with putting the church in jeopardy. If that's true, how can *you* justify living here when your presence is a much clearer danger to the sanctity of this island?"

Several long seconds pass. Seagulls scream and waves crash, but Adam is frozen.

"I don't know what you mean," he says, finally. The words are so weak they make her smile.

"I think you do. I understand the need to separate one's self from the past; to reinvent yourself when it's clear the path you have chosen is not the one God intended. But it seems Isaac and his followers are far better equipped to handle the challenges of one battered woman and her gifted child, than the fury that could reign down upon us all should you be discovered here."

He has gone unnaturally pale, staring at her as though she's already uttered the threat.

"No one knows," he said. "That part of my life is behind me. The people who died, those who survived... It's all behind me."

"Yet you sent your only child away to protect her—isn't that true? To ensure that even if you—if *we*—are found, Erin will be safe. It's a mistake, Adam, to believe I wouldn't go to equally drastic measures to ensure that my son's new life is not threatened."

Before he can respond, a branch breaks behind them. She and Adam turn, and Rebecca is not surprised to find Zion standing at the path. He walks to them with the certainty of a man rather than a child, and comes to stand beside his mother. Still seated, her head reaches just above his hip. His hands fall to her hair, and she nearly closes her eyes at the comfort of her son's touch.

"I didn't know where you were," he says.

It is a lie, but one she can forgive.

"I was here. We're finished now." She looks at Adam, daring him to challenge her. Zion offers her his hand.

Rebecca doesn't hesitate to let him take her full weight when pulling her up, confident he can handle the burden. Adam remains seated. As mother and child prepare to leave, he finally speaks.

"I wish you would think about what I said."

Adam is on the ledge, Rebecca to his right. She doesn't think about where Zion is until the boy has switched places with her, putting himself between her and Isaac's minion. He moves so quickly that he knocks against the older man, his dark eyes hard. Adam grabs hold of a piece of scrub-brush to keep from falling off the ledge and onto the jagged rocks below.

More gulls screech somewhere offshore. Adam gets to his feet, and the two chosen ones—the elder now cast aside, the younger just coming into his own—stand facing one another. Zion looks at Adam tranquilly, his grip tightening on Rebecca's hand.

"You should be more careful," the boy says.

His voice is cool; Rebecca feels a combination of awe and undeniable fear at his confidence. Adam merely nods, but she sees that he is also afraid—of both of them, now. He takes another step away from the edge as mother and son return to their path, hand in hand.

26

AFTER MY CONVERSATION with the reverend, I went straight to the paper to catch Diggs up on everything I'd learned. It was only seven-thirty in the morning, but gray skies and lack of sleep had my internal clock running backward. It could have been noon, it could have been midnight. Hell, it could have been Cleveland for all I knew.

The rain had been heavy enough overnight to cause flash flooding along the coast. Before I could stop him, Einstein swam a couple of laps in an Olympic-sized puddle outside the *Trib*. I did my best to dry him off with a discarded towel in my backseat, and we went inside.

The newsroom was empty when I got there—a sure sign that things had run late the night before. The TV was tuned to the weather channel, and the usual BBC news had been swapped out in favor of the weather radio. Both reports promised winds gusting to thirty knots and seas up to five feet. Not a good day to be on the water.

I was just about to knock on Diggs' door when Juarez called. I thought of the discoveries I'd made since our early-morning rendezvous—the angel in with his things, the photos I'd seen. Reverend Diggins' words about Rebecca's son rattled around in my head: *Unbalanced. Delusional.* The image of Juarez's body flashed through my mind, the taste of his skin. The hammer of my heart when he'd pinned me to the mattress, his dark eyes hard as coal.

I felt no fear with Juarez—but then, I'd never been afraid of Isaac Payson, either. What if that wasn't because Juarez and Payson posed no threat, but simply because I had a spectacularly crappy psychopath-radar? I thought again of Zion Ashmont: an unstable boy who vanished in a fiery blaze of glory, the sole survivor of a congregation he was being groomed to lead...

Who would that boy become, twenty years later?

I answered my phone just before it went to voicemail.

"Any luck?" My voice sounded tight. Jack had been dead on when he'd read me last night; I wondered what he heard now. I turned from Diggs' door and headed for my office.

"None so far." There was a motor running in the background; he had to raise his voice to be heard. "I didn't wake you, did I?"

"No—I had some work to do, decided to get an early start. What's up?"

"I just wanted to find out if you ever got in touch with Sheriff Finnegan?"

Shit. In between rummaging through Juarez's stuff and interrogating the local clergy, I'd totally forgotten I was supposed to be helping save Matt Perkins.

"I didn't, actually—I thought it would be better to wait till morning, since you didn't know exactly where he was." A lie, but at least it was a logical one. "Do you want me to call now?"

"No," he answered, too fast. "I'm still looking—I'll just call him myself once I get a better sense of things."

The call faded in and out, static heavy on the line. "Where are you?" I asked.

"Sorry, the connection's bad—I'm in the car. I'll call back later if I get a few minutes. I just wanted to know if you'd talked to Finnegan. And to let you know I'm sorry—you know, about the interruption last night."

There was no way in hell the motor in the background was a car engine. "Don't worry about it, I understand. Are you in a car or a boat? It sounds like you're on the water."

There was a pause. If my people-reading skills had failed me before, they were working overtime now.

"You're right, sorry—I'm on a boat now. Headed for the car. I'm a little tired, my head's not quite working right. I just took a quick ride around the harbor to see if I could catch up with Joe. I thought he might know where Matt is."

I started to press for more details, but Juarez cut me off.

"I should go, Erin. But stay off the water today, okay? Don't go near the island. Just promise me you'll stay away until the storm clears—at least for the next day or so."

"Jack, what the hell's going on?"

The pause that followed lasted so long I thought we'd been disconnected. When Juarez continued, there was no mistaking the exhaustion in his voice. And something else—something close enough to despair to chill me to the bone. "Just promise me, all right? It's bad out here today."

We lost our connection before I could think of a response.

I sat there with the phone still in my hand, going over his words. *Don't go near the island.* Had he been out there? And if so, what had he found? He was obviously warning me about more than just the weather.

Diggs knocked on my door before I could develop any half-baked theories. He wore a long-sleeved t-shirt with

Curtis Mayfield on the front and the words "Got Soul?" across the bottom. There was a coffee stain on his chest and black ink on the left leg of his blue jeans.

"I thought I heard you in here." He came in and sat down without waiting for an invitation. "Sorry we missed each other last night. Did you make any progress on the case?"

I felt a twinge of guilt. "Not really—though I'd love to run a couple of things by you when you have a second."

"Any word from Juarez since yesterday?"

It was clear from his tone that he already knew the answer to that. "What time did you come home?" I asked, horrified.

"Around two," he admitted. "I figured when Einstein was alone by the fire and your room was empty..." he attempted a laugh, though something in his eyes told me he hadn't been so amused by the situation last night. "I didn't want to interrupt—I figured I'd just come back here and sleep on the couch."

"It's your house, Diggs—that's ridiculous. You could have stayed."

He frowned. "No. I really don't think I could have."

I didn't know what to say. We stood there for a second or two, silent, and then an instant later it was like a mask had fallen. He shrugged, working hard to appear callous. I wasn't fooled.

"I had work, it was just as well. No big deal, Sol. And I still have work, actually—I'm gonna head back to the house and grab a shower and some breakfast, and then I've got a full day here. I just wanted you to know I'll probably be here around the clock for another couple of days with the storm. I'll be keeping a low profile for a while."

"Look, Diggs, it was just one of those things—I don't even know how it happened. And we didn't actually *do* anything. I mean, we might have, if Matt hadn't called, but..." I was babbling. In an effort to stop myself, I took a sharp right turn back to the investigation. "He had to leave. And then, this morning, I found something that made me think—"

Diggs' face darkened. "I'm too tired for a play-by-play, Solomon. I should get going."

Before I could launch into my theory on Juarez and his connection with the Payson Church, Diggs was out the door.

It was clear that I'd be on my own while Juarez was lost at sea and Diggs nursed his bruised ego, so I did my best to come up with a plan of action that involved neither of them. I might not have the scrapbooks I'd taken from Hammond, but I still had the Washington phone number I'd found. This time, I didn't have to wait for fifteen rings before someone picked up. It rang twice before I got a recording.

The number had been disconnected.

Despite everything, I wasn't surprised—if the voice I'd heard had indeed belonged to my father, he'd gone through a hell of a lot to disappear. Disconnecting his telephone seemed pretty minor by comparison.

I regrouped and kept my head in the game. By noon, I'd organized my notes and drafted a new chapter for the Payson book. Kat still hadn't returned any of my calls, and so far all roads tended to lead back to Hammond's investigation and the research my mother had taken from my room.

I had just made the decision to go ahead and drive to Portland to get Hammond's notes back, possibly extracting them from Kat's cold dead hands, when my phone rang.

According to caller ID, the number belonged to a Dr. Maya Pearce. When I answered, the voice was one I didn't recognize.

"Erin? I'm a colleague of your mother's—I'm calling to find out if you've spoken with her recently?"

"She left here last night. Why? She's not at work?"

"She never came home last night, and she was a no-show this morning. No call-in, nothing."

Alarm bells went off and sirens sounded in my head. It didn't matter how pissed off she might have been over our argument, there was no way in hell Kat would miss work.

"Have you called the police?"

There was a pause on the line. "I was hoping things had worked out with you two, and she just needed a little extra time."

Her words from the beginning of the conversation clicked. "You said she never came home—I'm sorry, who are you, exactly?"

Another pause. "Maya—I'm a... friend, of your mother's."

Alrighty then. I stored that tidbit to deal with later and focused on the issue at hand.

"You should call highway patrol—find out if there were any accidents." My mouth went dry just saying the words. "I'll get in touch with the police here and see what I can find out. I'll call you as soon as I know anything."

All I could think of was Hammond's burning house. He died for what he'd known—for the research he'd done. Research Kat had taken from me before I had a chance to make sense of it myself. And now, she was missing.

I called Juarez first, thinking again of his warning to stay off the island. Of his connection with the Paysons. What had he said when he was on the phone with Matt? *You don't need to protect anyone anymore.* Who was Matt Perkins protecting? And what had he done to keep them safe?

Juarez didn't answer his phone. I left a rambling, panic-stricken message on his voicemail, then called back a few minutes later when I didn't hear from him right away. I disconnected without leaving a second message.

My next call was to Sheriff Finnegan. He hadn't heard of any accidents involving a red VW Beetle in the area. It was too early to file a missing persons report, but given Hammond's murder and the link between my mother and the dead man, he agreed to put out an APB on her car. When I mentioned Marine Patrol, Finnegan hesitated.

"In this weather, we can't just send a boat out on a hunch. It seems like you and your mom had a few issues—maybe she's just taking a little time."

"My mother doesn't take time—not away from work. She could ignore my calls till the cows came home and I wouldn't think anything of it, but she wouldn't just ditch the hospital."

"The winds are supposed to die down overnight—how about if I arrange to have Patrol take a ride out to the island first thing tomorrow morning? We'll keep checking the mainland for her, I'll have my guys look for her car, and you can contact the local hospitals. But I promise you, I see this kind of thing all the time. I'm sure it's just a miscommunication. Chances are, she'll turn up fine in no time."

I wished I had half his confidence.

I went to the newsroom next, already on the fence as to the wisdom of bothering Diggs with my mother's disappearing act. One of the reporters whose name escaped me—a smallish man with glasses and a stained tie—intercepted me just before I reached Diggs' door.

"Unless you have a copy of Freewheelin' Dylan on vinyl or Scarlet Johansen's phone number in your back pocket, you might want to wait on that," he said. The way he looked at me made it clear he was protecting Diggs from more than just another work-related annoyance.

"He's that pissed at me, huh?" I said.

"He's tired," he said, not unkindly. "Just give him a little space. I'm sure he'll be fine."

I wasn't so sure about that. Lately, it seemed that all Diggs and I did was argue, while he tried to keep me safe and I fought him every step of the way. It would probably be kinder to just leave the poor guy alone. I walked away without leaving a note, determined to find Kat without his help.

●

Outside, the storm of the century was just gaining steam. Einstein's least favorite thing on the planet was rain, so he wasn't pleased when I forced him out for another quick pee break before we returned to the car. He shook all over the backseat and whimpered indignantly, but—unlike everyone else in my life—at least he was still speaking to me.

I drove through Littlehope going over everything Kat and I had said to each other before she left. I wished it had been the only conversation I'd ever wanted to take back, but the truth was, my mother and I had never really known anything but harsh words and hard feelings. We had nine years together when I was growing up, most of that time colored by a venom I'd never felt for anyone but her. Maybe she drank too much and cared too little in those days, maybe her temper had gotten the best of her more than once where I was concerned, but did that really excuse the way I'd treated her all this time? The fact was, my mother had torn my world apart once when I was nine years old, and I'd been making her pay ever since.

And now, it turned out that I'd had her motives all wrong when it came to that single, defining event.

Your father didn't want you.

And neither had she. But, whether out of guilt or duty or some twisted form of motherly love, she'd stepped up to the plate.

I turned down another of Littlehope's multitude of backwoods roads, scanning driveways and ditches for any sign of a red Volkswagen Beetle.

There were none.

By the time I reached Edie Woolrich's place, it was just after one o'clock—lunchtime. Several residents were gathered around the same dining room table where Noel Hammond, Edie, and I had met just a few days before. Sandwiches were piled high on a plate at the center of the table, tortilla chips in two plastic green bowls on either end. Everyone looked up when I came in. I did my best to appear moderately professional—or at least not on the verge of a mental breakdown.

Apparently I failed, because Edie clearly sensed trouble afoot. She excused herself, shut the French doors behind her, and nodded to the sitting room sofa.

"Why don't you have a seat, hon? Can I get you something hot to drink? You look chilled to the bone."

"I'm okay. I just had a couple of questions. Since you

were so helpful the other day, I thought you might be able to tell me a few things now."

"I'll do what I can."

"When Matt first brought Jack Juarez here, did you hear any talk around town? People must have said something… I mean, a confirmed bachelor shows up with a good-looking teenager to live with him, claiming it was his nephew?"

She got the implication. "Well, you're right about that—people did talk. I think they would've said more about it if Matt hadn't been trying to find him for so long, though."

"Do you remember when he started looking? Was it before or after the Payson fire?"

"After," she said immediately. "Not long after, as a matter of fact. I remember, because your mum and me were working at the clinic one weekend when Teddy Harjula and a couple of his cronies came in, and—" she pulled up short. "But I guess that doesn't really matter, does it?

"Anyway, it wasn't long after the Payson fire that Matt started traveling whenever he had a few days. He'd always come back a little quieter, a little sadder, than when he left. He never was the sanest fish in the barrel, if you know what I mean—I think folks 'round here just figured before he found Jack, that we'd let it alone and nothing would come of all his talk about this long-lost nephew of his."

"Do you remember what Matt said when he talked about him? Before he found Jack, I mean?"

"I don't remember much—just how there was somebody out there, and he had to find him. I only really talked to him about it once. Me and Fred were up at the Grange one night, and Matt came along and tied one on pretty good. He didn't say much—I do remember how he kept saying that he knew the boy was out there, and he owed it to her to find him."

My attention had been waning, but this pulled me back. "Her? Did he say who he meant by that?"

"He didn't. We just figured maybe he had some long-lost sister out there somewhere—whoever was the boy's mum, I imagine."

I tried to piece that in with my hypothetical scenario of what happened on Payson Isle. If Zion had been saved while the rest of the church burned, and then the boy was taken off the island by some third party... Could that have been my father? And if that was the case, then... What? Matt Perkins found out, and went on a quest far and wide to find Rebecca's son and bring back the boy he now claimed as his own blood?

I noticed Edie looking through the doors to the next room. I'd come at a bad time, I knew, and she was just too polite to say anything. "I appreciate you talking to me. I just have one last, quick question."

"Anything I can do to help. What else can I tell you?"

I hesitated. "Do you think Matt's a dangerous man? You've worked with him here for a while now, right? Could he be a danger to others?"

A shadow crossed her usually cheerful face. I thought for a second that she was about to brush me off, insist everything was fine. She didn't.

"Didn't Agent Juarez tell you?" she asked.

I shook my head.

"About three months back, Matt went after Joe Ashmont with one of those big survival knifes you see in the back of Soldier of Fortune magazines—Fred subscribes, that's how I know about them. Anyway, he stuck him in the thigh, probably would've killed him if Joe hadn't been quicker. That's why we called Agent Juarez out here from his job in D.C.—we didn't know what else to do. It was so unlike him… I know Matt's always been a little off, but nobody'd ever seen him like this. Joe wouldn't press charges, but Matt was still in the Togus psych ward for a good month before they'd let him out."

She pressed her lips together as she considered my question. "Whatever demons Matt Perkins is fighting, they've done a number on him. The doctors all said he wasn't a real danger anymore, but…" I waited for her to get down to whatever it was she didn't want to say. "Just between you and me, when he came back I never once left my bedroom door unlocked. There's something not right there."

"If Matt wanted to get away from everyone, can you think of someplace he might go?"

"The islands, I guess. He knows this bay like the back of his hand—if he wanted a break, he'd probably choose one of those little islands out there where nobody ever goes."

I pictured the topographical map of Penobscot Bay we used to have in my elementary school classroom. It had been peppered with tiny, uncharted land masses and a dozen larger, established islands.

"Any one in particular?" I asked hopelessly.

She just shook her head. She looked stricken as realization dawned. "That fire that killed poor Noel the other night—you don't think…?"

"I don't know." I stood before she could ask anything else. "I should go, let you get back to lunch. If you think of anything else, could you call my cell phone? Anything at all."

I gave her my business card and left, trying to figure out where to go from there.

27

AS SOON AS I was back in the car, I called Sheriff Finnegan again. With great patience, he repeated the promise he'd made earlier: if Kat still hadn't shown up by morning, he would call out Marine Patrol. Until then, though, I just needed to sit tight and ride out the storm.

Right.

My next stop was the town landing. It was empty except for a couple of pickups in the parking lot, couples inside the cabs watching as waves battered the wharf and fishing boats bobbed like children's toys on the stormy seas. I left Einstein in the car and walked the dock's rain-slicked planks to get to my speedboat. It had taken on water, maybe six inches in its fiberglass bottom, the seats dripping.

I searched the harbor until I found Noel Hammond's boat, riding the waves at its mooring. Juarez had warned me specifically: *Don't go out to the island today.*

He'd obviously said it for a reason—the more time that passed without hearing from him and the longer Kat was missing, the more convinced I was that Payson Isle was the key. That's where I would find my mother.

The speedboat would never make it the ten miles out there—not in this weather. I needed something more seaworthy… Like Hammond's boat. Hammond certainly wouldn't be using it again. So, if you took the raging winds, stormy seas, and raving madman out of the equation, there really was no reason I *shouldn't* take it. I just needed the keys… Which I didn't have. And of course, the fact that Diggs was probably the one hanging onto those keys now that Hammond was gone didn't make things any easier.

Back at the *Trib* yet again, I pushed sopping hair from my face and, this time, didn't hesitate before I knocked on Diggs' office door. I went in without waiting for an answer.

Diggs took one look at me standing there shivering, dripping rainwater onto his faded linoleum floor, and all traces of his earlier anger vanished.

"Jerry, you wanna grab a couple towels?" he shouted into the other room.

"Don't bother, I'm fine," I said. "I'm not staying. I just need a quick favor—I know you're pissed, but I just…" I kept my eyes on the floor. I just needed to hold it together. How many times had my mother handled situations ten times worse than this? Death and destruction all around on a regular basis, and she rode out every storm as if she'd been born for it.

I met his gaze with a newfound sense of calm. "I need to borrow the keys to Noel's boat."

His jaw actually, physically dropped. I knew there was no way he would hand them over without an explanation, so I gave him an abridged version of events up to that point: Kat was missing, as was Matt Perkins. And Jack Juarez, of course, who may or may not be the psychotic, long-lost son of Rebecca and Joe Ashmont. I told him I thought Perkins had taken Kat, and now they were out on Payson Isle.

Despite my protests, Diggs handed me a towel and made me sit and dry off while he tried to make sense of my story.

"You can't be sure Perkins has her, though," he insisted. Even he didn't look convinced, though. "She could be... lost, or something. Maybe she was just in an accident—a small one," he amended quickly. "She could have amnesia. Somewhere, there's a very surly Jane Doe scaring the hell out of orderlies in some small-town hospital between here and Portland."

"I've called all the hospitals," I said.

"And Finnegan won't budge?"

I shook my head.

Which brought us back to my request.

"So, your plan is to take Hammond's boat—a boat bigger than any you've ever driven before, unless you took up yachting since I saw you last—and brave a violent storm to go out to Payson Isle. And once you get there, how are you planning to get on the island?"

I hadn't thought that far ahead. The mooring was at least a hundred yards from the island itself, and there would be no tripped-out speedboat waiting to take me from Hammond's boat to shore. "I'll improvise," I said.

"Good plan," Diggs said. "That always works. And even if you do make it to shore, what happens then? You find Perkins with Kat and... talk him out of it? And what if Juarez is in on this whole thing, too? You're gonna take out an armed, seasoned FBI man?"

"He's not in on it."

Diggs looked like he felt sorry for me. I bristled.

"He's not," I insisted. I sounded remarkably sure of myself for someone who wasn't sure at all.

Diggs sat down on the couch beside me. I scooted over to the edge, leaving a foot or more of space between us.

Einstein watched all of this from a spot in the corner of the room. He was wet and bedraggled and, thanks to him, Diggs' office now stank of wet dog. I wondered why the hell Diggs had put up with me all these years.

"The guy who attacked you on the island—you said he was a fighter, right? He knew what he was doing?"

I nodded.

"You said he was in good shape. Taller than you. Solid. You don't think it was Joe Ashmont, and it sure as hell wasn't Matt Perkins—if only because you know for a fact that he was in the hospital at the time."

I stayed quiet, staring at my hands in my lap.

"How long did it take Juarez to get out to the island after you called?" I didn't answer. He forged ahead anyway. "Did you have to give him directions to get to the house? Where did he get the boat to get out there?"

I stood. My hands were cold and I had to clench my teeth to keep them from chattering. My clothes clung to me and my hair was still damp. Diggs watched me with quiet resignation.

"So, you won't help me?" I asked.

"I won't send you on a suicide mission, no. I'll talk to Finnegan if you want, though. He's got budget cuts and the governor breathing down his neck, so I don't think we'll change his mind—not until you have something more solid. If I can do anything else, Sol, you know I've got your back."

"I don't need anything else," I said.

I whistled for Einstein, and walked out.

A gale-force winds advisory was issued along the coast at four o'clock that afternoon. Boats were battened down, the harbor deserted. I hadn't heard from Juarez again since his call that morning, and there was still no word of Kat or her car. I'd called Sheriff Finnegan twice more to try and persuade him to send Marine Patrol out looking for Matt, to no avail, and had driven halfway across the county looking for any sign of Matt Perkins, Joe Ashmont, or my mother.

At four-thirty, Edie called. I was in my car on another flooded back road. Tree limbs were down, and power outages had been reported up and down the Midcoast. Einstein had given up trying to figure out any rhyme or reason to our driving route, and was snoring quietly in the backseat.

"Any word on your mum yet?"

I didn't bother asking how she'd found out. "None yet. You don't know anyone who might give me a lift out to the island, do you?"

"Nobody's going out in this, sweetie. You can't blame them—you know what it's like out there in a storm. Nobody in their right mind would be on the water on a day like today."

Which was exactly what I'd been afraid of.

"Did you think of anything else?"

"Matt's doctor," she said. "The psychiatrist who treats Matt at Togus. I thought he might have something he could tell you."

She gave me the number, and we disconnected.

The answering service for Dr. Neil Perry informed me that he wasn't available until Tuesday, but I could speak with someone else if it was an emergency. I assured them that it was, in fact, a huge emergency—but that no one but Dr. Perry would do. They agreed to convey the message, but they didn't sound optimistic. I waited for an hour for a return call, and finally decided to take matters into my own hands.

By six o'clock that night, I was on the road to Augusta.

I'd left more messages for Juarez, spoken again with my mother's…colleague, and had a brief, terse conversation with Diggs that revolved around my lack of objectivity and current level of exhaustion. I hung up on him before the call devolved into a shouting match and one or both of us said something we'd regret.

On a good note, my final call to Sheriff Finnegan that day had infinitely better results.

"I talked to Edie, and she convinced me we should get somebody out to the island," Finnegan said. "I hope you understand why I had to wait this long, though—if I called out the troops every time there was a family spat and somebody dropped out of sight for a few hours, I'd be fired before the day was out. We just don't have the resources."

"But you'll send someone now?"

"I just put a call in to Marine Patrol. Any idea what we should be looking for?"

I'd been thinking about that. "Look for Joe Ashmont's boat. I think if you find that, you'll find Matt Perkins. And my mother."

Thanks to flash floods around the state, a lot of the smaller roads along the coast were impassable. Halfway down Route 235, forty-five minutes into my drive, I slowed at sight of a tree limb across the left lane. I tapped the brake and realized a split second later that the bridge fifty yards down had been washed out.

Adrenaline and fatigue had my nerves crackling like water on an open circuit board. I pulled myself together with a couple of deep breaths, pulled a u-turn in the middle of the flooded road, and retraced my steps back to the main drag.

I kept going over what I knew—the questions Diggs taught me to ask when I was just a cub reporter with a nose ring and a curfew.

I knew the What, the Where, and the When: 34 dead on Payson Isle, August 22, 1990.

I knew the How, more or less: fire.

That left the Who and the Why. Isaac Payson might not have been with the rest of his congregation when he died, but at this point I sincerely doubted he'd been the one to set the fire. Had Matt Perkins been the one to strike the match all those years ago? And what did Noel Hammond and my mother know about any of it, that made them his targets? And, yet again, what did my father have to do with any of it?

I was back on Route 17, half an hour from Augusta, when my cell phone rang. I glanced at the display and grimaced. Diggs.

"Erin," he said when I answered. Not Solomon, not Sol. That alone was enough to make my fingers tighten around the steering wheel.

"They found her," I said. It wasn't a question.

"They found her car. You should come back."

Something tightened like wire inside my chest. "Where was it?"

The second Diggs took before he answered lasted at least a decade. "In the quarry," he said. "They're sending divers down now to see…"

My vision blurred for a split second before I shook my head. I wouldn't cry, dammit.

"To see if she's in the car," I finished for him.

"Take it slow driving home—the roads are bad. I'll be there when you get back, Sol."

I hung up, and turned the car around one more time.

28

THE OLD CALDERWOOD QUARRY was at the end of a dirt road that was more mud than dirt by the time I got there. A pickup was stuck about halfway in, half a dozen rain-soaked locals trying to push it out of the way. I pulled off to the side rather than waiting for them, left Stein in the car, and ran the rest of the way to the scene.

I could see the blur of red and blue lights through the trees, the colors bleeding into one another. Three large, free-standing spotlights had been set up at the edge of the quarry. The light illuminated a sheer granite face and a shine of still black water below. I didn't see any sign of a car in there—my mother's or anyone else's.

Everyone was in motion around me. A small boat with three scuba divers inside was motoring to the center of the quarry.

"They can't bring the car out tonight," Diggs said from behind me.

I turned. He wore a rain slicker, his boots and jeans caked with mud.

"But they can tell if somebody's inside," I said. I was impressed at how cool, how professional and detached, the words sounded.

Diggs nodded. I could tell he was fairly amazed at my demeanor himself. Or maybe disturbed would have been a better word.

"How do they even know it's down there? I can't see a thing."

"I had somebody check it out," he said. "I figured if something disappears in Littlehope, there's as good a chance as any that it's in the quarry. It took some doing to get anybody out here—I had to call in a couple favors."

I turned back to the ledge to watch the activity below. A good five minutes went by before I had the presence of mind to thank him.

"It'll probably be a while before they can get in there and tell us anything. Why don't you let me take you home—just to get warmed up, change into some dry clothes."

I was wearing the same jeans and turtleneck I'd had on since the day began. I stood shivering with my arms crossed over my chest, and shook my head.

"I'm all right."

Diggs didn't say anything to that. It seemed like the rain might be lightening up—or maybe it had just been like this so long I couldn't tell the difference anymore. An indeterminate amount of time passed before Diggs took my hand and pulled me away from the ledge.

"I got these from the Jeep." He produced a sweatshirt and a pair of sweats, with a bright orange poncho on top of the pile. I hadn't even realized he'd gone.

"I'm not leaving," I said.

"So don't." He pushed me toward the edge of the woods gently, handed me the clothes, and turned his back.

"I know you've got an exhibitionist in there somewhere—now's the time to give her a thrill."

Since I wasn't going to win this argument anyway, I found a quiet spot just inside the woods and peeled off my soaking clothes. The sweatpants were too long and the sweatshirt was too big and the poncho came nearly to my knees. Still, they were clean and dry and the fact that they smelled like Diggs didn't hurt matters. I rolled pant legs and shirt sleeves with fingers that had gone numb with cold long before.

"Okay," I said when I was finished.

Diggs turned back around. He smiled faintly when he saw me. "Sorry—I didn't have anything smaller."

"No, this is good. Thank you." I couldn't find the energy to return his smile. With nothing else to say, I returned to the ledge.

Diggs pulled me away from the edge a few inches, which made me think of the afternoon he'd lost his brother here. The day Diggs put away childish things.

There was a crash down below, followed by a flurry of movement and panicked shouts.

"Get clear," one of the techs nearby yelled down. "Christ—what the hell are we doing out here? Somebody's gonna get killed."

I turned in time to see Sheriff Finnegan take the tech aside. The sheriff glanced at me with a quick smile that I imagined was meant to be reassuring.

"Easy does it, boys," he yelled down below. "We don't need any heroes. We're just looking for a clear visual. Take your time."

"That jolt kicked up too much sediment at the bottom," the tech told him. "We'll have to wait till it settles again. It'll be at least an hour."

I felt a wave of nausea. Diggs put his arm around my

shoulder, but I stepped away from him. Away from the ledge. Away from the sirens and the shouting strangers and the shell of my mother's car buried deep in the water below.

When I was eleven, I started working at Kat's clinic after school. My mother was always too busy for family bonding, but some nights we'd order in and sit in the break room eating pizza, talking about the patients she'd seen that day. It was the only time I ever felt close to her—those short hours when we could compare notes on her cases. She would quiz me on what I'd seen, symptoms different patients had presented with, possible diagnoses.

I wanted to be a doctor, back then. Not because of any real interest in medicine, mind you—just because it seemed like ten years of medical school was the simplest way to create any kind of meaningful relationship with my mother.

At the edge of the woods, I took a few breaths and pulled myself back together.

"What's the word from the island?" I asked Diggs when I rejoined him.

He looked confused.

"Payson Isle?" I elaborated. "Finnegan was sending somebody out."

"I don't know if he did, though. I think once we found the car—"

"Matt's still out there—I know it. Whether Kat's with him or not, we still need to find them."

Diggs didn't say anything. I left him and went to talk to the sheriff. Meanwhile, twenty-five feet below, divers continued to search the murky depths for any trace of my mother.

It was eleven o'clock before they got a visual on the inside of Kat's car. I heard the crackle of a walkie talkie, and one of the cops on the ledge responded. The words were hard to make out. Diggs tried to take my hand, but I walked away. The divers had climbed back in the boat, and I could hear the motor starting up again as they returned to dry land. I thought I might be sick before someone finally spoke to me.

Sheriff Finnegan took my arm and pulled me aside.

"The car's empty," he said. I thought of all the ways other people would handle the news—drop to their knees and thank God; burst into tears; embrace strangers.

I just nodded. My throat felt dry, my eyes drier. "Thank you," I said. Finnegan started to walk away, but I ran after him.

"This means he still has her," I said. "You said you sent someone out—you haven't heard back from them yet? They should have been able to get to the island and back by this time, I don't care what the weather is. You're sure they went there?"

"They did—I heard back about half an hour ago. They didn't find anyone."

"How hard did they look?" My voice rose until it was loud enough to hear over wind and rain, sirens and strangers. The sheriff moved closer, with that look cops get when they're trying to placate crazy people.

"They couldn't do a thorough search at night in this weather—we'll go out and look closer tomorrow, just like I promised."

"She'll be dead tomorrow," I shouted.

Diggs came over and pulled me aside, a hand on my arm. "They're doing what they can. You need to stop." He said it as kindly as anything he'd ever said to me. "We're gonna go home and have some food, and then you're going to bed. Just a nap."

I hadn't slept in thirty-six hours, but the thought of stopping the search now was unthinkable. I shook my head.

"I need to talk to the Marine Patrol guys," I said. "Find out where they looked, see if they saw any sign of Ashmont's boat. If they aren't back yet, maybe I can get them to check out some of the other islands nearby." I felt better with some semblance of a plan—like I might actually stand a chance of surviving this night. "Edie said Matt knew all the area islands—he might have taken her somewhere else."

I knew I didn't have much time before Diggs just knocked me out and dragged me, bound and gagged, back to the house—judging by the look on his face, he was entertaining the thought at that very moment. I turned my back on him and chased after Finnegan again, who was getting ready to hightail it out of there along with the rest of his crew.

Before I could reach him, a call came in on his radio.

They'd found Kat.

29

HALF AN HOUR LATER, I stood at the town landing with Diggs. Marine Patrol was on their way in. I didn't know any details about what had happened—not how they'd found my mother, or where, or in what condition. I just knew they had her.

The boat came in at a little after midnight that night. The winds had died down but the rain hadn't slowed, flooding the landing's dirt parking lot. An ambulance was parked at the end of the wharf amid shouting and chaos and lights and an entire world that felt like it was underwater. I couldn't remember ever being dry.

There were too many people around her for me to see Kat when we first arrived—paramedics and cops and strangers in every direction. Diggs saw her first. I heard him whisper, "Jesus Christ" under his breath, and then when I tried to get to her he grabbed me from behind and wrapped his arms around me—one arm across my chest, one across my stomach—and held me back. He didn't budge when I fought him.

"Let them work, Sol," he said, his mouth close to my ear. "They need space if they're gonna help her."

When I finally got to her, Kat didn't look anything like the woman I'd known. She was drenched and unconscious, strapped to a backboard with a head collar and an IV. Her face looked like she'd gone two rounds too many in the UFC. Her left eye was swollen shut, and an ugly purple welt on her forehead still leaked blood that had matted her dark hair.

My stomach lurched and the world tilted. All at once, I remembered nights trailing Kat on cases when I was a kid.

"Keep breathing. It's just a body, the same as all the ones you've seen before. This one's just a little banged up. Don't look away. Don't think about what it should look like. Just think about how we'll fix what we've got."

"You okay?" Diggs asked me. He was still behind me, still holding on, though I'd stopped fighting him.

I nodded. He let me go when I told him to, my voice calm and my eyes still dry.

"I should go with her," I said. "Einstein..."

"I'll take him back to the house and meet you at the hospital," he said. His blue eyes had gone dark, his forehead creased in a way that was usually reserved for tight deadlines and difficult ex-wives. "She'll be okay, Erin."

It was a silly, hollow lie that sounded worse once it was out in open air. I didn't dignify it with a response, and Diggs looked embarrassed for having said it at all. I climbed into the ambulance once Kat was loaded inside. The doors closed.

I'd been in ambulances before, but not for years; I used to do ride-alongs with Kat, back when it still mattered to me that I impress her somehow. I didn't recognize much of the equipment anymore, but I still knew the protocol: stay out of the way.

I sat awkwardly by my mother's gurney. Sirens started

as we pulled away. I took her hand. It was cold and pale. I couldn't remember ever having held it before. I stared at her face, knowing that underneath the bruises and the blood and the swelling, was the woman I had both worshiped and despised for most of my life. It was the face of a victim, now—stark evidence of the fragility of the human body and, most terrifyingly, of the fury and violence I had brought to Payson Isle.

If she died, it would be because I had come back to Maine—I couldn't delude myself about that anymore. Noel Hammond might have died as a result of his own investigation into the fire, but I was the one who called Kat. I brought her back here. I was the one who insisted on digging up memories that almost certainly would have been better left buried.

I didn't say anything on the ride to the hospital. I didn't cry. I sat with my mother's hand in mine and listened to the rain and the sirens and the EMTs on the line with dispatch, shouting orders back and forth. I prayed to wake up from a nightmare that seemed to have no end.

Kat was still unconscious when we got to the hospital. I stood in the ambulance bay while they wheeled her into the hospital. A doctor in blue scrubs approached as soon as I came through the door.

"You're next of kin?" he asked.

I nodded. "I'm her daughter."

"We're taking her straight to surgery—we're concerned that she has swelling that's putting pressure on her brain. We need to go in and relieve that pressure."

Brain surgery. He pushed a clipboard into my hands. Kat was gone now—already wheeled out of sight, doctors and nurses swarming in the sterile, too-white, too-quiet hallway of a hospital that wasn't used to dealing with this degree of violence.

"She's—she has a partner," I said. To the doctor's credit, he didn't look at me like I was two rungs below the village idiot on the ladder of life.

"Dr. Pearce," he said immediately. "She and your mother have done some lectures here. We've already contacted her—she's on her way."

"You know…" I didn't know how to finish that statement. The doctor glanced down at the clipboard in my hand.

"You can call her if you like, but I need you to sign this so we can go ahead with the surgery. Time is of the essence."

I nodded. If I were Kat, I'd have a long list of questions to ask.

"Did Dr. Pearce say this should happen?"

"You should call her—this is her area. She'll tell you everything we're about to do is very standard. And your mother won't survive without it."

My hands were shaking when I signed the release; it didn't even look like my signature. As he was hurrying away, I shouted one more question after him.

"This Dr. Pearce—she's a good doctor? She knows what she's talking about?"

He turned. Something—pity, I think—flashed across his face. "She's one of the best neurosurgeons on the East Coast. You should call her—she can explain the procedure, let you know what to expect."

I nodded. This time when he walked away, I didn't try to stop him.

Except for Diggs, the waiting room was empty when I

got there. There was a drab carpet and wooden chairs with plush floral seats, and three Ikea-style wooden tables with outdated magazines and children's toys. An old episode of Three's Company played on a wall-mounted TV in the corner. Jack Tripper fell over the sofa into Chrissy's lap; the sound was too low to hear the canned laughter that followed.

Diggs was still wet from the rain, two days' beard growth on his chin and his face gaunt with fatigue. If something didn't break soon—or I didn't just give up and go home—I wasn't sure any of us would live to see a resolution to this whole mess.

I sat down beside him.

"They took her into surgery," I said.

"Did they say anything about her condition?"

"Her brain's swelling, they think—they need to go in to relieve the pressure."

He put his arm around my shoulders. I didn't pull away, but I couldn't let myself lean on him, either.

"Did you know Kat's gay?"

He didn't look surprised. "She doesn't keep it a secret."

"She kept it a secret from me."

"Not telling someone something and hiding it are two different animals," he said. "You were busy. Maybe she just didn't think you'd care—it's not like she told you about every new boyfriend she had back in the day, did she?"

It was a valid point. Of course, Kat had changed boyfriends almost as regularly as she'd changed socks.

"Do you know if they've been together long?"

"The first time I saw them together was at a fundraiser in Portland," he said. "That was a little over a year ago. They've done some volunteer work here at the hospital, taught a couple of lectures since then, so I've seen them a few times."

Over a year with a woman I'd never heard of. I leaned my head back against the wall. On TV, Jack had done something to piss off Chrissy and Janet—they were yelling at him behind the same sofa he'd fallen over just moments before.

Diggs leaned down and picked up a wet brown handbag I hadn't noticed before. He set it in my lap.

"One of the guys from Marine Patrol gave this to me— he said it was on the boat with Kat."

Even considering water weight, it was heavier than it should have been. I unzipped the top, remembering days of sneaking cigarettes and stealing spare change as a teenager. In one of half a dozen compartments, I found the source of the weight: gray steel nested among a dozen gold bangle bracelets, though hardly as innocuous. A gun.

I closed the purse before Diggs saw what I'd found. I didn't know what to tell him. Hell, I didn't know what to tell myself.

Eventually, Diggs got tired of trying to comfort a woman who refused to be comforted, and withdrew his arm.

"Can I get you anything?" he asked.

I shook my head.

"What about a change of clothes—I could go back to the house and get something for you. Do you want something to eat?"

"I'm fine, Diggs."

I caught his annoyance at my pat response, but didn't comment.

"Have you been able to reach Juarez yet?" I asked. I knew the answer—I'd been trying to reach Juarez for hours now. Either he wasn't getting the calls, or he wasn't answering.

"I tried a couple times. He's not picking up for you, either?"

"Doesn't look like it."

I leaned my head back against the wall again and closed my eyes. Diggs got up to find a vending machine while I tried to work up the courage to call Maya Pearce. Diggs had returned and I had my cell phone in hand when Juarez himself walked through the waiting room doors.

I put my cell phone back in my purse. Juarez stood in the entryway, holding to the doorsill like he might fall without it. He was drenched and clearly exhausted, but I wasn't feeling especially empathetic at the moment. An unexpected calm fell over me. I stood.

"I'll be back in a few minutes."

I didn't need to see Diggs to know the look he gave me—he'd been giving me the same look for the past week. He was worried. A little hurt, a little angry. I ignored him, tucked Kat's purse under my arm, and grabbed Juarez before he could sit down.

"I need to talk to you."

I walked out of the waiting room, down the corridor, and through the hospital's automatic sliding doors without looking back. The rain had finally slowed to a manageable drizzle, the night black and starless. I walked across a nearly-deserted parking lot to a stretch of pine trees at the edge of the hospital property. When I turned, Juarez was a few steps back. He waited wordlessly while I lit a cigarette and led him to a patch of forest where the hospital's incandescent streetlights barely reached us.

"I lost my cell phone earlier—I just heard about your mother," he said. "I got here as fast as I could. How is she?"

"They don't know—she's in surgery right now." I opened Kat's purse and slid my hand inside. I never took my eyes from Juarez. "Matt did a number on her, though."

A flicker that looked a hell of a lot like guilt touched his face. "She said that?"

"She didn't have to." My voice was steady—no tears, no emotion. Pure steel. I curled my fingers around the grip of the pistol my mother never got the chance to fire. "It was him, wasn't it? That's what he called to tell you—that he'd done something, hurt someone?"

He shook his head. His face was drawn, his dark eyes haunted by ghosts I was only beginning to understand. "I didn't know—he wasn't making any sense when I talked to him. I didn't know he'd go after your mother."

"But you knew he'd go after someone!" I shouted. "You knew he was dangerous—you knew something was wrong. You knew…" I pulled the gun from Kat's purse.

"Erin," he said. His gaze locked on the gun for just a second before his eyes found mine again. He didn't look worried, or even all that scared. Mostly, he just looked really fucking tired. I knew how he felt.

"I found the angel in with your things," I told him. "The one Isaac Payson gave you when you were out on the island. Who helped you escape—who set the fire?"

The fatigue vanished from his face. He stood straighter, his jaw hardened, his dark eyes suddenly cold. I held the pistol more tightly and pointed it at the center of his body as I took a step back. I could hear an ambulance coming, the sirens getting louder the closer it got to the hospital. Jack didn't say a word.

"Who is Matt protecting?" I asked.

Another few seconds, maybe a minute, passed before Jack spoke. "I don't know," he said.

It wasn't the answer I'd been hoping for.

"I mean—I don't know the answers to your questions," he clarified. "I have just as many of my own." Once the words were out, it seemed like he'd used the last of his energy for that single grain of truth.

"I wasn't lying that day in the car—I don't remember my childhood. I don't remember being on Payson Isle, if I ever was. I remember waking up in a Catholic hospital in Miami… I remember the women who cared for me there. When I came to Maine that first summer with Matt, none of it seemed familiar. It's not like it all came rushing back and I suddenly remembered this life."

"And now?"

He shook his head. "I don't know. I don't know any of it—maybe I was Zion. Maybe Rebecca Ashmont was my mother; maybe I was there the day of the fire. Matt thinks I was. He used to slip and call me Zion sometimes—I just thought it was a quirk."

I still held the gun aloft, though it was heavy and my arms were shaking and it seemed almost silly, somehow, to continue with the delusion that I was in control. He took a step toward me.

"I didn't know he would hurt your mother. I didn't know he'd hurt anyone, Erin—you have to believe me."

"What about the day I was attacked?" I asked. I tried to read him and kept my distance, the gun still raised. "How'd you get to the island so fast? How did you even know where the house was?"

It took him a few seconds to follow my train of thought. When he realized what I was asking, he shook his head. "I'd been out there before—a few times since I've been back, trying to get to whatever memories might be locked inside my head. And I got out there so fast because I was worried about you—I was at the general store, so I hitched a ride with the closest fisherman I could find."

It made sense. It could just as easily have been lies, of course—there was no way to confirm any of it, short of finding the fisherman who'd driven him out to the island that day. I could do that later; for now, the only thing I had to go on was my own gut instincts. I lowered the gun. I felt sick, and tired, and the information that I had outweighed the information that I needed by a huge margin. And Jack didn't know any more than I did.

"I should go back in—find out if there's any news," I said when I couldn't think of anything else to say.

He nodded. I slipped the gun back in Kat's purse. Jack stood just a few inches from me now. I believed him, it turned out—maybe I really did have an epically bad psychopath detector, but I couldn't help it. I trusted him. He brushed the hair from my eyes with a cold, cold hand.

"I'm sorry about your mother."

I flinched at his touch. "Don't," I said. Tears rose faster than I could keep them at bay. I turned before he could pull me any closer, stopping just short of a run as I fled for the safety of bright lights and sterile hospital walls.

AUGUST 20, 1990

THERE IS NO WIND. The air is heavy with moisture, thick with rain that refuses to fall. Rebecca's brow and forehead are damp from the humidity and her browned arms and shoulders are dewy with it. Still, the heavens will not spare a drop.

It is dusk, and she is once more in the greenhouse waiting for Isaac. Like the distant storm, she senses that something is coming—something dangerous, something that will change everything. Isaac sent Adam to her earlier in the day, this time to request a meeting between the three of them. The fact that Adam will be there is maddening, but she doesn't dare refuse him. Isaac won't speak with her alone anymore. When she seeks counsel from him, he meets with her in the chapel and schedules her for times when the most people are likely to be present.

The day before, she waited on the greenhouse trail for three hours, hidden in the underbrush like a fugitive. When Isaac finally appeared, he would say only that others were waiting for him; he couldn't speak to her then. His eyes lingered on hers, trailed down her long neck, and she knew then that she still held some sway. If Adam wasn't whispering indictments in his ear, Rebecca is certain she and Zion would be safe.

She needs to be rid of Adam.

When Isaac finally appears on the path, she watches as he makes his way to the greenhouse. He is surefooted and fit, moving with a grace that's in stark contrast to Joe's thunderous assaults on everything in his path. In the past few weeks, she has been pleased to note that Zion is adopting the Reverend's grace as his own.

Rebecca waits until Isaac actually enters the greenhouse before she stands. Adam is not with him. She feels a brief surge of relief before she notes how guarded he looks. She takes a slow step toward him, her hands low and at her sides, as though approaching a wild animal that will spook at any sudden movement.

"Thank you for coming," he says formally.

She forces her lips into a smile. "Thank you for having me," she responds, equally formal. He looks surprised, as though he suspects she is mocking him.

"Adam will be here soon—I wanted a few minutes alone with you first. To discuss things."

"You want me to leave the island."

"I don't believe this is the best place for you any longer."

If he expected histrionics, he is disappointed. Rebecca remains cool and controlled when she replies.

"What do you believe is the best place for me, then?"

It is clear from his relief that he has already considered the question. Of course. His job may be to provide spiritual counsel, but Rebecca knows he is much more comfortable in a world of tangibles. This is the problem; here, then, is the solution.

"I have some money—not a lot, but enough for you to

start over somewhere new. Get away from Joe, away from Littlehope. There's a couple from Boston that I knew before the church—they're good people. They can provide you with food and shelter until you can find a job and make it on your own. Adam can take you to the bus station tomorrow, if you like."

When she doesn't respond, he hesitates before adding, "Or in your own time. Whenever you feel that you are ready."

Rebecca considers this. It takes a moment before she realizes what he is really saying; before the weight of his omission is clear. "And where is Zion to stay?"

His uncertainty returns. He looks out toward the path, where Adam is now making his way toward them.

"I want you to truly consider what is best for your son. You know that he has been called—that he has a God-given gift. To waste that gift because of an earthly love for the child would be a sin. Zion requires the closest attention to fulfill his destiny. I can provide that for him."

"And Adam agrees with this? He believes that Zion staying with you is the best option?" she asks doubtfully. The look on Isaac's face tells her plainly that Adam does not believe anything of the kind.

"Adam knows that the good of the church is my first priority. He has concerns, but he will not stand in my way."

Rebecca says nothing. Feels nothing. She tries to imagine life without her son. Has her purpose been filled? Was she meant to bear the child, help him to grow, watch him suffer, and then simply walk away?

Isaac takes a step forward. They are an arm's length from one another, but he is the last thing on her mind now. Adam arrives and stands just outside the entrance—she senses him but does not turn around. Over a lifetime of abuse and lust and love and betrayal, she has never hated anyone so much as she hates this man.

"You would teach my son," she says to Isaac.

He nods, relieved. He believes he has won. "I will teach him everything he needs to know. Mae and I will raise him, and he will be at my right hand learning God's word from morning to night."

"And I will just…disappear from his life? Tell him I'm going to visit relatives, try a new life in the city, become a missionary in some distant land? What is the story you would have me tell my only child, before you ask that I abandon him?"

Her voice is a whisper, so tight that it is painful. Isaac steps back. His face changes when he realizes she is not as pliable as he would have hoped.

"I… You would tell him the truth. That he has been chosen; that he is meant to stay and study at my side. But that your destiny lies beyond this island."

His eyes soften. For a moment, she believes that he truly sees her for the first time. "Rebecca, you are an amazing, powerful, vibrant woman. You are bright and dedicated— you have the potential for anything. My congregation is filled with people best suited to follow, living out their lives serving the Lord in peaceful obscurity. I don't believe that is your path." He pauses. "Zion will thrive here—you never will. Let him go, and have the courage to believe that God has better things in store for you than this."

She hears children playing somewhere in the distance. Their voices meld, high-pitched shrieks that carry far in the thick air. She knows that Zion's voice is not among them. He is either in his room studying or in solitary meditation in the woods. From the time he was small, she has been his only companion—the only one able to lighten his mood, coax a smile from his serious black eyes.

She shakes her head and turns a hard stare on Adam as he joins them. "You know what has been asked?"

Adam hesitates. She realizes that he is truly afraid of her, and the realization pleases her. Good. Let him quake—whatever may come, she has already decided that if her life on Payson Isle is over, so is his.

"I know that Isaac believes Zion is meant to stay here."

"And you do not."

More hesitation. Isaac starts to intercede, but seems to sense that he is not part of this. He remains silent.

"I believe that sometimes we are too close to a situation to see the Lord's true plan."

"Isaac would have me leave and Zion stay; you would banish us both. Yours is the Lord's true plan, then?"

"In this instance, I think it best that you remain with your child." He looks at Isaac. His gaze appears completely open, beneficence shining in his eyes. "I believe that Isaac and the church need time to mend any bridges that may have been damaged in the past month."

"Since I arrived," she says. She takes a step toward him. He does not back away, but she can tell that he wants to.

"Yes," he says.

"But you do not believe you've done any damage since your arrival on this island."

Adam's eyes flicker from hers to Isaac's and then back again. Rebecca waits for some sign of confusion on Isaac's face at her words. She sees none, and the lack shakes her for just a moment.

"I told you—"

"Yes, you did," she interrupts. "You told me that you had it under control. But Matt spoke with some of the men still looking for you—some of the men who have believed you dead for years now."

His expression is one of pure terror.

"He didn't—"

"They were naturally pleased to find that you had survived when so many others had not."

Adam stands perfectly still, his only sign of life the rapid rise and fall of his chest. "They know I'm here?"

"Matt hasn't given them a location. Yet. But you understand that it's likely only a matter of time."

He wheels away from her and turns on Isaac. "Do you see? Do you see what she is—what she's done? This place is supposed to be a refuge, a healing place. I gave up my daughter to keep everyone safe, but Rebecca isn't willing to give up anything. Anyone. And you can't see what they are doing to you. To our church."

She is tempted to strike him, but holds herself in check. Before he can explain himself any further, Adam turns and walks swiftly from the greenhouse and back down the path. Isaac turns back to her. She realizes at the hardness in his eyes at that moment, that there has been no secret between him and Adam. He has known all along, what Adam is. What he is running from. She pushes unease aside at the knowledge, and forces a smile.

"I'll need to pray before making my decision about Zion. You understand, of course." She smiles demurely and walks away, leaving Isaac alone to think about the wisdom of his request.

30

"WHY IS SHE MAKING ME GO?"

I sit beneath a tree on a part of the island that has always been mine—a glade of evergreens only my father knows about. He won't look at me.

"It's for the best, Erin. You're getting older now—this isn't a good place for you to grow up."

"Why not?" I'm crying—something I almost never do. Dad says I'm like my mother that way. Katherine never cries when people are watching, he told me years ago. I want to be like that—to inspire the awe and sadness that my mother inspired.

Now, I wish I had never heard of her. I wish my mother did not exist.

"Please don't make me go."

He still can't look me in the eye. He stares at the ground and he is crying and my mother—the woman I wish never existed— is a monster.

When I got back inside the hospital, Diggs was at the snack machine talking to a tall, thin woman in scrubs. I didn't even know if Juarez had followed me or simply vanished back into the night. I didn't really care.

"How is she?" I asked.

They both turned toward me.

"Still in surgery," the woman said. She extended her hand. "I'm Maya Pearce. It's nice to finally meet you, Erin."

She had bright blue eyes and short, curly gray hair and an air about her that was both striking and surprisingly unassuming. Her smile seemed genuine, though I wasn't exactly in a position to judge, having never laid eyes on her before.

I shook her hand. "Did they tell you anymore?"

"She's stable. No internal bleeding, no evidence of sexual assault." I appreciated her even tone, the fact that she wasn't falling apart and clearly didn't expect me to, either. No wonder Kat liked her. "The surgery shouldn't take long. Once they're done, we'll just have to wait for her to wake up to find out the extent of the damage."

I nodded. I couldn't think of anything to say.

"Have you eaten?" she asked.

"I'm not hungry."

"Well, of course not," she said, like I'd said something funny. "You're in shock. But you still need to eat. I saw some soup in the doctor's lounge—you can have that."

I started to protest.

"Just humor me, all right? A few bites, then I'll find you an empty room and you can rest your head until Kat's out of surgery."

It seemed pointless to argue. She left for her soup quest, and Diggs led me back to the waiting room.

"She seems nice," I said.

"She is. Keeps Kat in line, which is almost impossible— as you well know. I think you two will hit it off."

The TV in the waiting room had been turned off. I sank

into a chair and gazed at the floor. Diggs sat on one side of me, Juarez—who hadn't vanished into the night after all—on the other. In other circumstances, it might have been awkward; as it was, I barely noticed either of them.

My first night in Littlehope, my mother makes grilled cheese sandwiches for dinner. I've only ever had homemade bread that the women of the church made by hand. This is processed and too sweet and it sticks to the roof of my mouth.

She has already told me I don't need to call her Mom. Dad calls her Katherine, but she says everyone else calls her Kat. She eats too fast and barely speaks to me, and through the entire meal she reads a magazine filled with body parts and skeletons, even though Dad always said it was rude to read at the dinner table.

I eat my cheese sandwich without speaking, already devising a plan to run away at nightfall. I will steal her boat, though I know stealing is wrong. I don't know how to get back to the island, but I don't care.

I'll find my way.

Kat came out of surgery at three-thirty that morning. Maya assured me that she wouldn't wake for hours, but by all accounts the surgery had gone well. Now, it was just a waiting game. She'd either wake up and be fine, or she would not.

Diggs told Juarez to drive me home. He took his jacket off, draped it over my shoulders, held onto the lapels and pulled me close.

"Get some sleep?"

I nodded.

"I won't be long. I just want to drop by the paper, make sure they didn't burn the place down while I was gone."

"It's okay—you should get some sleep too, though."

I thought of the night before. Imagined Diggs coming through his front door to find Juarez and I in the throes of… whatever, in his spare bedroom. My eyes watered. I pulled away and nodded toward the exit.

"Don't stay long. We'll see you later."

In my first two weeks with Kat, I run away seven times. Sometimes, I only make it to the front door; others, I make it all the way out to the harbor. The seventh time, I'm in the process of starting her boat when I see her coming over the hill. She drives an old yellow car, and she drives it fast. She races down the hill, stops in the parking lot, and gets out while I'm still trying to get the motor running.

My heart is hammering and the night is dark and my mother is getting closer. The boat won't start.

Instead of pulling me out as I expect, Kat hops into the boat when she reaches me. She pushes me away from the motor, hard enough that I fall. My head hits the side of the boat with a sharp crack that sounds loud in the stillness. I lay there for a minute staring up at the stars, too stunned to get up.

When I finally stand, Kat has started the engine. It is nearly midnight, but she unties the boat and points it toward Payson Isle. My head throbs and my throat is dry and I am almost positive that Kat is crying as she steers us out of the harbor in search of my father.

Juarez and I didn't talk on the way home. He put in a GLEE soundtrack that he wisely shut off before anyone got hurt, and I stared out the window. The road was flooded in places; we hydroplaned once or twice before he regained control, but I barely noticed. The ride was over faster than

I'd expected, and when we got to Diggs' place I was out of the car before Jack had a chance to put it in park.

I slogged through the mud to the front door. Einstein greeted me like we'd been apart for months, his paws on my stomach, body and tail wriggling. I roughed his ears and snapped on his leash.

"I can do that," Juarez said. I noticed that he'd taken my mother's purse and was keeping it—and her gun—a safe distance from me.

I shook my head, but I didn't say anything as I let Stein lead me back out into the darkness.

"I can't keep her—she hates me."

We are in the Payson greenhouse, where the night smells like soil and tomatoes and flowers in full bloom. My father is in his pajamas—or pajama pants and a t-shirt, the same thing he always wears to bed. He looks tired and sad.

My mother just looks angry.

"She doesn't hate you."

"I do," I say. My head is bleeding from my fall in the boat, and I mean the words more than I ever thought possible. "Don't make me go back there."

He kneels beside me and holds me close. "Your mother needs you," he whispers in my ear. "You can't stay with me anymore, no matter how much I wish you could."

I cling to him with all my strength, my arms tight around his neck until he disentangles himself. He forces me an arm's length away. His eyes are wet when he looks at me, but he does not cry.

"I don't want you to come back here. I'll come visit you in Littlehope when I can—but I can't take care of you anymore, Erin."

He stands. I wrap my arms around his waist and refuse to let go.

"Get her out of here," he says to my mother. "Don't let her come back. Get as far away from me as you can get."

Kat has to pull me away from him, kicking and screaming, my breath coming too fast as panic closes my throat. I scratch her and keep crying until she puts me back in the boat. I don't speak to her again for a week.

I sat down under a spruce tree behind Diggs' house. The ground was drenched, but I barely noticed. How had I forgotten that night? Kat was telling the truth: my father sent me away, she hadn't taken me.

Einstein lapped anxiously at tears I hadn't even realized were falling. I pulled him into my lap, and the flood gates opened.

I cried for the father I'd lost and the mother I'd rejected; for the friends who died on the island and my failed marriage and the baby I'd buried and the children I would never have. Juarez came out at some point and crouched beside me, obviously not sure if I'd had some kind of psychotic break.

"You should come inside, Erin."

I shook my head, but my voice was gone. He stayed and watched me helplessly for another minute or two before he stood and returned to the house.

Why had my father needed me off the island? What did he think he couldn't keep me safe from?

"It's yours, Erin. It means that you belong with us."

Isaac hands me my angel. The paint is still wet, and he's made her with red hair like mine. We're in the meeting room—just Isaac, Daddy, and me. I sit in Isaac's lap and stare into my angel's blue eyes. I'm four years old. Isaac smells like lemonade—we had some for lunch, and it's sweet on his breath. Sometimes, he comes into our Sunday School class and tells stories or plays his guitar. He likes to sing foolish songs that he and Daddy make up together.

"You can trust Isaac," Daddy tells me one day. "You can't trust everybody in the world, there are fakers and fools out there, but Isaac will always take care of us."

I saw the headlights when Diggs came down the road. I was shivering and numb and waterlogged and more than a little nauseous. I was still sitting under the spruce tree behind Diggs' house. Einstein was shivering in my lap, both of us soaked to the bone.

My father had trusted Isaac. That's why I hadn't been afraid of him—not because he wasn't a man to fear, but because my father wasn't afraid. He didn't send me off the island to keep me safe from the Paysons; I was sure of that now. I thought of that night again—the night Kat took me out to the island and begged my father to take me back.

"Get her as far away from me as you can."

Why?

"Erin."

I looked up to find Diggs standing above me. I was still crying—now that I'd started, I wasn't sure I would ever stop. He crouched beside me and gently pried Einstein out of my arms.

"Kat's all right," he said.

I cried harder. "I know," I managed to hiccup in between sobs.

"You're exhausted, Sol—you just need to sleep."

I nodded and kept crying, but I didn't move. Diggs

pushed a sopping, tangled mess of hair away from my eyes. Then, he pulled me into his arms like an overgrown, overwrought child, and carried me inside.

All the reasons I was there, all the stories I knew and all the questions I had, got twisted in my head as the living and the dead chased one another in an endless, indecipherable spiral. I cried into Diggs' neck as he brought me inside. Poor Juarez stood awkwardly at the door looking like he'd rather be just about anywhere else on the planet.

"I started the bath," he said. "Is there anything else I can do?"

Diggs shook his head. "I've got it."

He carried me back to my room with my arms around his neck and my tears dampening his already-damp collar. He set me on the bed like I might shatter more than I already had.

"I'm okay," I said. I sniffled. At least the tears had finally stopped. My teeth chattered and my fingers were frozen. Diggs smiled a little.

"I know, Sol," he said. "You're fine. Jack got a bath started for you—you need to get warmed up."

I tried to undress myself but it turns out twelve hours in freezing rain is hell on your finer motor skills. Diggs pushed my hands away and rolled his clear blue eyes.

"I've got it. It's not like I haven't seen you before, you know."

He gently peeled my clothes off, wet layer by wet layer. If I hadn't been dangerously close to both catatonia and hypothermia, it might have been a little sexy. As it was, Diggs kept his eyes respectfully lowered until I was shivering and nude on the edge of my bed, then handed me my bathrobe and helped me into the tub.

He sat outside the bathroom doorway with the door open and waited silently while I soaked in the warm bath. I'd almost fallen asleep when he handed me a towel and insisted I get out.

"You're getting pushy in your old age, Diggs," I said. I was going for the old, tough-as-nails Solomon, but the words came out sounding broken.

"What can I say—you bring out the alpha in me, kid."

I put on two layers of dry pajamas and a pair of thick socks and I still couldn't stop shivering. Diggs closed the shades against the first glimmer of dawn while I got under the blankets. He kissed my forehead and pulled the blankets up to my chin, but I held onto his arm when he started to leave.

"Stay," I said.

I expected him to argue, or hit me with more of that incontrovertible Diggs logic. Instead, he went around to the other side of the bed, took off his shoes, and climbed in beside me. He pulled me into his arms without hesitation, and we lay there wrapped up in one another until everything slowed to the safe, peaceful rhythm of Diggs' heartbeat.

I slept.

31

IT WAS ALMOST TWO o'clock in the afternoon when I woke the next day, alone in my bed. I tamed my hair into a reasonable facsimile of a ponytail, washed my face, and got dressed. When I emerged from my bedroom I found Diggs reading the paper at the kitchen table, Einstein's muzzle resting on his thigh. Stein rolled his eyes in my general direction and his tail thumped idly once or twice, but otherwise he remained fixated on the cream cheese bagel in Diggs' hand.

"Why aren't you at work?" I asked.

"Took the day off," he said casually, like this was a regular thing rather than the first time this millennium.

I made a face when he pushed the other half of his bagel toward me, but tore off a piece all the same.

"Kat's awake," he said. "No neurological damage, no internal bleeding, no permanent... anything. She'll need physical therapy and it'll be a while before she can operate again, though."

"What's she saying about the attack?" I asked immediately. It occurred to me too late that a better person would probably be more concerned about other things.

Diggs looked at me. I thought of crying into his neck last night, his arms around me. I'd done all manner of ungodly things with him over the years, but I'd never felt more naked.

"She says she doesn't remember," he said.

"What do you mean—none of it? She doesn't remember who attacked her?"

"Maya said it's not uncommon—traumatic amnesia. She may get the memory back in time, she may not."

I didn't say anything. The sun was bright outside, most of the puddles already dried up. She didn't remember. Bullshit. Katherine Everett remembered everything: every surgery she'd ever done, every fight we'd ever had, every patient she'd ever seen. Details that had blurred for me years ago were always fresh in her mind. Once again, all the answers I needed were wrapped up in my mother's tightly clenched fist, and she refused to give an inch.

"What about Jack?" I finally asked.

"He's back out there looking for Matt. No luck so far."

I sat down beside him.

"You look better," he said.

"Yeah, well… Sleep. Dry clothes. Fewer of the, uh, you know…" I gestured vaguely at my eyes. "Sorry about that. The—you know, crying thing. I don't usually…"

"I've known you seventeen years, Sol. I know you 'don't usually…' You don't need to apologize. I'm glad I was here."

I swallowed another bit of bagel. Matt was still out there. I thought of my revelations the night before: the fact that my father had sent me from the island; that he'd asked Kat to take me far away; that whoever he was afraid of, it wasn't Isaac or the Paysons. My exile from Payson Isle happened long before Rebecca Ashmont was part of the church, so it couldn't have been her he'd been afraid of. She'd known a secret about him…

I needed to find out that secret.

"What about Joe Ashmont? Any sign of him?"

"Nope," Diggs said. "They found his boat—that's how they found Kat, actually. The boat was adrift, she was on it. If Marine Patrol hadn't spotted it…"

The statement hung there, unfinished. I pushed the bagel away, no longer hungry.

"I need to get out to the island," I said.

Diggs didn't look surprised. "I figured. There's already a search party out on Payson Isle—we can join them whenever you're ready."

"We?"

"*We,* Sol. Sorry, but I'm not letting you out of my sight until we catch… Somebody. Matt Perkins, Joe Ashmont, or whoever else you may have pissed off enough to incite violence."

"You don't have to protect me," I said. "I was a little overwrought last night, but that doesn't mean I need you to go all white knight on me. I can take care of myself."

He grinned outright. He was showered and shaved and he looked fresher than he had since I'd arrived. Apparently, I wasn't the only one who'd needed the rest.

"I'm not going all white knight, you freak," he said. "But it makes me look bad when my house guests get beaten up and tossed around the harbor willy nilly—I'm just trying to protect my reputation."

"Because you're just that self-absorbed."

"You know me so well. Now come on—eat your bagel and let's go catch some bad guys. It'll be fun."

"You're in an awfully good mood considering all the

death and destruction going on around us."

He gave Einstein the last piece of his half of the bagel and stood. "Stop trying to pick a fight. I'm in a good mood because I realized something last night, and if you're nice I might tell you about it one day. For now, though, eat the damned bagel so we can get out of here."

I decided to give him an easy win this once, and ate the damned bagel.

•

When we got there, the island looked no different than it always did: battered shore, creepy vibe, not another soul to be seen. According to Marine Patrol, they'd found Kat beaten half to death and left to die on Joe Ashmont's boat, which had been drifting about a mile off the southern tip of Payson Isle.

There was still no sign of Ashmont or Matt Perkins.

A couple of guys from Search and Rescue met us at the dock, along with a very pretty hound dog who wouldn't give Einstein the time of day. We climbed up the ridge from there, where Juarez was waiting for us. It was four in the afternoon. Diggs and I may have been bright eyed and moderately bushy tailed, but Jack looked like he hadn't seen a good night's sleep or a full meal in days.

"No sign of Matt?" I asked.

He shook his head. "I'm sorry. We've gone over every square inch of this island. No one's out here."

One of the Search and Rescue guys nodded. "It's true— if anyone was on this island, Annabelle here would've picked up the scent. We caught some cold trails, but nothing fresh."

"And you checked all the buildings? The boarding house, the cabins…"

"Everywhere," Juarez confirmed.

"I'd still like to go back to the house," I said.

Jack hesitated. "We think..." He cleared his throat. I glanced at Diggs, who looked just as clueless as I was. "It looks like that's where your mother was attacked. There's some blood. Broken glass."

So, she had been out here. Or she'd been taken out here—but why? If someone wanted to kick the crap out of her, couldn't they have done it just as easily on the mainland? Unless whoever it was had been trying to get information from her... I thought again of the scrapbooks she'd stolen from my room. Of Hammond's death. My father's voice on the other end of the line, on a stranger's telephone three thousand miles away.

What the hell was going on?

I struck out on the trail toward the boarding house, the rest of the search party in my wake. I might not find Matt Perkins or Joe Ashmont on the island, but I was damned sure going to find something to start making the pieces fit.

Despite my determination, we didn't find anything new on Payson Isle. Eventually, our Search and Rescue duo let Annabelle the Hound off her lead and she and Einstein wrestled and raced while we went through the ruins of the meeting room. One of the windows was broken, blood mixed in with jagged edges of glass and one of my mother's earrings. Upon closer examination, I realized that it had been torn from her ear, a chunk of earlobe still attached.

I went outside and breathed in fresh air until I could think about something other than throwing up. Juarez sat on the back step while Diggs conducted his own investigation of the grounds. By six, I was ready to concede the point:

there was nothing here to find. I'd been over the house from top to bottom, we'd been out to the cabins, Annabelle had trekked through the forest and along the shoreline.

With Ashmont and Perkins still gone and Noel Hammond dead, I was back to square one: Kat was the key.

Once we were back on the mainland, I managed to convince Diggs I wouldn't be in mortal danger between Littlehope and the hospital, so he graciously allowed me some breathing room while he caught up at the paper. Juarez went back to the house to shower and get some sleep, and I ditched Einstein to see if I'd have any better luck questioning Kat when she was on heavy meds and just back from a near-death experience.

Maya met me outside my mother's hospital room at just past seven that night. She didn't look nearly as put together as she had at three that morning, and I had a pretty good idea why.

"They say doctors make the worst patients," I said in lieu of a greeting.

"They don't know the half of it. She's still fairly out of it right now—I don't expect it to get any easier once the meds wear off."

"That's a safe bet."

"She says she doesn't remember anything about the attack."

I caught the doubt in her voice. "But you don't believe her."

"She's been through a lot." She barred the way into the room, though something about her eyes told me she wasn't completely without sympathy for my plight. "I know you two have your challenges, but the Payson fire took something from her, too."

"She told you about it?"

"No," she said. "She doesn't talk about it—the church and your father are off limits, too. But I know something happened, and I don't think she was ever the same afterward."

"It would be easier to buy that if she actually came out and said any of it herself. And it's gotten out of hand now— you can see that, right?" I nodded toward the door. "It's pretty obvious at this point that we're long past the point of no return. People are missing and she almost died, all because of these secrets she refuses to tell. I have to talk to her."

Maya moved out of the way. "Just go easy on her, all right?"

I nodded, but went inside before I made any promises. The more I learned about the fire, the more clear it became that Kat wasn't quite the master manipulator I'd made her out to be all these years—someone else had been pulling a few strings themselves. But if she was keeping a secret for my father, I was damned well going to find out what that secret was.

My resolve got a lot less resolute once I got a good look at Kat, however. Her head was shaved and bandaged, her face bruised almost beyond recognition. Maya hadn't been kidding about her being out of it, either—she looked like she didn't even know who she was, let alone who I might be or the answers to the burgeoning global conspiracy unraveling in our backyard. I sat at the edge of her bed.

"You should see the other guy," she said, her words garbled from pain and medication and swelling. The only way I knew that was what she'd said was because I knew Kat. Of course that's what she said.

"Who did this to you?" I asked. I took one of her bruised and broken hands in my own.

"Don't remember."

She didn't look at me when she said it. She was on enough pain meds to knock out a village, and she was still sticking to her story. Whatever adjectives you might use to describe Kat, weak-willed isn't one of them.

"You don't have to lie to me anymore," I said. I was trying to be gentle, but I wasn't sure that came through. "I know Dad's still alive. I know he was trying to protect me when he sent me away. He was afraid of something, but it wasn't Isaac. It wasn't the church."

She swallowed hard. Pain flared in her eyes. "He's dead. It's over." She closed her eyes before I could argue. "Let me sleep."

Maya walked in then, like she'd been sent some kind of psychic S.O.S. She took my arm.

"She needs her rest."

"I just have one more question."

Maya shook her head, intractable. "Give her a couple of days. She's not going anywhere."

I wasn't so sure about that anymore. My leads were disappearing faster than I could track them down; that didn't bode well for Kat. I thought of the Washington address Juarez had gotten, and the house where my father may or may not be at that very moment. I could book a flight out there, try to find something out that way. If the number had already been disconnected, though, chances were that my father was already back on the run.

But from whom? And why?

I got in my car and headed back toward Littlehope with no more answers than I'd had when I started the day.

I was just getting into town when my cell phone rang. It was dark out, but at least the rain hadn't returned. The name on the caller ID gave me pause, to say the least. I pulled over to the side of the road on Littlehope's main drag and answered.

"Joe?" I said.

Instead of Joe Ashmont, however, a woman's voice answered—low and rough, the voice of a longtime smoker or a veteran phone sex operator.

"Erin Solomon?"

"Who is this?"

"You want to know about your father and the fire?"

My heart stuttered. "I do."

"Bring Zion. Nobody else. Come to the greenhouse—get here quickly. There's not much time."

"Someone almost killed my mother out there last night—why in hell would I come out to the island alone after that? Who is this?"

"The greenhouse," she repeated. "I'll tell you what your father really was. Bring my son, and I'll tell you everything you want to know."

She hung up.

I sat there and stared at the phone like it might come to life and shed some light on whatever the hell had just happened. Sadly, it did not.

Rebecca Ashmont was alive. And calling me from her ex-husband's phone. I went back to the house to get Juarez.

AUGUST 21, 1990

ADAM IS GONE. He's on the mainland with his daughter, ostensibly for her birthday, but Rebecca senses that he will not return. Now that she knows who he is, it will be too dangerous for him to stay—he won't put the church in danger that way. Adam may be a liar and a fraud, but his devotion to Isaac and his congregation is genuine. She is counting on it.

None of this changes her own circumstances, however, as she struggles to decide her own fate and that of her son. Does she leave, or does she stay? Take Zion with her, or let Isaac raise him for the rest of his childhood years? She has prayed, she has meditated, she has searched for a sign. She does not want to go.

It is dusk. The air is heavy, the clouds dark—there will be rain within hours, and Rebecca aches for that release. She sits outside the greenhouse alone and watches the clouds shift and the night fall. The rest of the church—including Zion—are at a service.

She is alone.

What will Zion think of her if she abandons him now? They will stay in touch, of course—write letters, perhaps even have the occasional visit. Whatever she decides, it has to be for him. Leaving him here would be the ultimate sacrifice. She thinks of Abraham, poised to slaughter his son to prove his devotion. This isn't the same: this is an opportunity to prove her love for both Zion and their God.

Her reasons for keeping her son with her are purely selfish—she knows this. A good mother would not put her own desires above those of her child. A good Christian would not refuse the path God has set before her, simply because it may be difficult. She looks out over the quiet field. Breathes in deeply and smells the sweetness of decay, the perfume of flowers and freshly turned earth.

She stands. She will go to the church and get Zion, so that she may tell him of her decision first. Then, later tonight, she will tell Isaac. Perhaps he will see her alone one last time, to allow her an opportunity to explain how much her time on the island has meant.

All of these thoughts and good intentions drain like sand between her fingers the moment she looks up the path ahead of her.

Her heart skids like a frightened rabbit, and the clouds get darker. Thunder rumbles far, far off. He is too close for her to escape, and too mean for her to fight. Rebecca takes a step backward as Joe—the husband she fled from before he could kill her and their son—blocks her path.

He is freshly shaven. His clothes are clean, his eyes are clear, and his smile is the one she remembers from childhood—before the fury took over.

"I'm not here to hurt you," he says.

She swallows past the tremor in her throat. Joe isn't a big man, but he is stronger than anyone she's ever known. She doesn't move, waiting for him to continue.

"I wanted to come here and tell you that they're planning to get you off here tonight," he said. He shoves his hands into his jeans pockets and looks at the ground. Others don't understand Joe Ashmont, but Rebecca always has. It's why she loved him, long ago.

"Who is planning to take me?" she asks. His revelation isn't as surprising as she supposes it should be.

"Adam. Reverend Diggins. I'm supposed to help them, but I thought..." He looks at her. He hasn't been drinking—it's more obvious by the tremor in his hands and the pain in his eyes than the coherence of his speech.

"You thought if you came here, I would be grateful?" she guesses.

"No," he says immediately. "I just thought maybe you could leave first—without Zion having to go through any more shit. I won't stop you. You can set yourself up in Littlehope or you can move to Timbuktu—it don't matter to me. Adam says Isaac's got his sights set on Zion. I just want you two off this rock and away from him."

"Zion is destined for greatness," she tells him. She isn't surprised at the scorn in his eyes, though he tries to hide it.

"He's a good boy," he says. "He doesn't deserve whatever Isaac's got in mind. You two can have a good life."

"We *will* have a good life."

"I know. I just..." He stops. Shrugs. They are standing five or six feet from one another, but she still feels the draw she's always felt with him. Repel and attract, push and pull. Love and hate.

"They won't let you stay—Adam's dead set on getting you off here. Better to just go now, save yourself before you start a war."

"Isaac wants Zion to stay. He will teach him the ways of the church. Help him fulfill his destiny."

For the first time, she sees genuine anger cross his face. He clenches his fists. She moves backward, but Joe does not come any closer.

"That's what we're afraid of, Becca—you can't leave Zion here. Are you fucking nuts? This preacher might seem like an angel to you, but he'll hurt Zion. Open your eyes, goddammit. This isn't where our boy belongs."

As though he'd heard his name, Isaac suddenly appears on the path behind Joe. Her husband turns at the look in her eyes. She expects violence, and moves farther away from the two men.

"Where do you believe your son belongs?" Isaac asks coolly. "Locked up on an island, waiting for his drunkard father to stumble home so he can watch while his mother is beaten half to death, night after night?"

Remarkably, Joe manages to hold himself in check. He keeps his eyes on the ground, his hands clenched at his sides.

"This don't concern you."

"Rebecca and Zion are members of my congregation now—of course it concerns me."

"You're not keeping my son, you fuckin' pervert. You don't go near him again."

Isaac looks past Joe to Rebecca. "I understand that you would think something so ugly, given your past. But your son has a spiritual destiny that won't be denied. I would never do anything to harm him. I only want to nurture his considerable gifts, so that he can one day realize his true potential. For God, and for his fellow man."

Joe looks at Rebecca. "You heard what I said. You know what's coming. We can go get Zion now—I'll call up one of the guys to give you a ride back to the mainland, you don't have to set foot on my boat or see my face again. But leave with me now. You're not gonna like what happens, otherwise."

She hesitates. Over the years, she has seen many sides of her husband: the attentive lover, the doting father, the jealous fiend, the violent drunk. This is new. Isaac ignores him and takes a step toward Rebecca.

"You know Zion's destiny, Rebecca. You know your path. Don't let this man sway you with his lies and paranoia."

It's the final straw—Rebecca sees it snap. Joe lowers his body and charges Isaac. Isaac steps just to the right and twenty seconds later the fight is over: Joe is on the ground, bleeding. Isaac stands above him without a scratch. There is something dangerous about him now; something Rebecca has not seen before. She feels that unwelcome thrill she always feels at the first flush of violence, before fear can take hold.

"Go home, Joe," Isaac says. "Don't come back to this island. You bring violence and ugliness to a holy place, and I can't allow that."

Joe stands. There is a gash above his left eye and his lip is swelling rapidly. He looks at Rebecca and shakes his head.

"I warned you, Becca. I can't do no more than that."

He turns and walks away. Once he is gone, Isaac turns to her once more. The pacifist has vanished; Isaac looks at her with fire in his eyes and something bestial in his smile.

She goes to him.

32

I TOOK EINSTEIN OUT for a perfunctory pee break before I worked up the courage to knock on Juarez's door, back at Diggs' place. I knocked lightly at first, then a little louder when I got no answer. When he finally told me to come in, my hands were sweating and my mouth was drier than the Serengeti. I rubbed my palms on my jeans. Juarez pulled a t-shirt over his washboard stomach and ran a hand through his tousled hair. He'd showered and shaved, so he looked marginally better than he had when I'd seen him last. The boxers and the runner's calves didn't hurt matters.

"I need to talk to you," I said.

He rubbed his eyes blearily and nodded. "Did they find Matt?"

"No—not yet. It's not about that, exactly." I stood there for another twenty seconds trying to figure out where to begin before he arched an eyebrow.

"Did you want me to guess?"

"No—sorry." Jesus. I shook my head. "Rebecca Ashmont called me. She wants us to meet her on the island—as soon as we can get over there."

He showed no reaction whatsoever for what seemed like a very long time. Finally, he blinked.

"Rebecca... I'm sorry, what?"

"I know it sounds nuts. Which is why I'm glad she wants you to come, too—she said she knows about my father. She'll tell me everything if I come out there and meet her. With you." Nothing. "Tonight," I added, in case he wasn't clear on that part.

He pulled his jeans on. "How do you know it was her?"

"I don't. The caller ID was from Joe's phone, though, and she asked me to bring Zion—and then she said, 'Bring my son.' Rebecca Ashmont. They never identified her body with the others—it's possible."

"And you think she meant me when she said to bring Zion."

"If she didn't she's shit out of luck, because you're the closest thing I've got."

"And she wants me out there now?"

"Yeah—she said there's not much time. God only knows what that means, but I'm thinking it's not good." It took a second for his words to register. "Whoa, hang on. Not you—*us*. She asked for me, too."

"I don't know if she's dangerous—hell, I don't even know who she is," Jack countered. He strapped on a shoulder holster with unnerving efficiency. "You're staying here."

"I'll just follow you out there. You know I will."

"Then I'll just call Diggs and tell him what's going on."

I advanced on him. "Screw you—this is mine as much as it is yours. She has information about my father. You have no right to keep me out of this."

I wasn't sure whether he understood my reasoning or sympathized with my plight or just didn't have the energy to fight with me, but he took a few seconds to think about things before he nodded.

"You have to do what I say," he said.

Given the shoulder holster and the almost unnecessarily large gun that belonged there, that seemed like a reasonable stipulation. I nodded.

"And we leave a note for Diggs letting him know where we are, just in case."

I agreed.

Twenty minutes later, we were steering my boat out of the harbor yet again. It was just after nine o'clock. The sky was clear, the moon nearly full. We'd left Einstein behind, along with the requisite note for Diggs. I wore a sweater to guard against a chill I hadn't been able to shake since the night before. Juarez stood beside me at the wheel, his hand at the small of my back while I played captain.

"It could be a trap," he said just after we'd hit the open ocean.

The thought had crossed my mind. I took my eyes off the expanse of deep black sea in front of us and met his gaze.

"I don't want anything to happen to you," he said.

"Yeah, I know—Diggs would never forgive you." I was trying to be funny, but he obviously didn't see the humor.

"I'm not worried about Diggs." The way he looked at me made it clear he was talking about more than just the obvious. I turned back toward the bow and corrected our course, though it didn't really need correcting.

"We should probably stay focused on what we're doing," I said. "Conspiracies, dead parents who aren't really dead… You know, the usual."

"Yeah, you're right," he agreed. Despite the tension I saw

a flicker of a smile touch his lips. "Anyway, it's not like I don't know the score there."

"What score is that, exactly?"

"With Diggs."

We had another forty minutes before we got to the island. Try as I might, I couldn't just let the statement lie.

"What about Diggs, exactly?"

He thought about the question before he said anything. "I'm not anything like him—I know that. I like music that sounds like music; I don't know the latest pop culture references. I don't Tweet. If I never had to touch a computer again, I'd be all right with that."

The seas were calm beneath the boat and our path was clear. Moonlight reflected perfect white light off the water. I looked at Jack and swallowed a shiver that had nothing to do with the temperature.

"So, you're just a simple cowpoke with simple cowpoke ways—is that what you're telling me?" I asked.

He grinned outright at that, a predatory gleam in his eye. "More or less." He paused. "You should watch out."

The shiver returned, a little lower now. "Is that a threat or a promise?" I asked with a sexy smile.

He made a valiant effort not to laugh at me as he nudged me aside and took the wheel. "A warning, actually," he said, nodding toward the sea. "There are some rocks up ahead."

Right. I knew that.

We were both quiet for the rest of the boat ride. We stood side by side in the cool night air, lost in separate worlds. Any concern over romantic entanglements fell to the wayside the closer we got to Payson Isle. A bloated, pale yellow moon hung just over the tree line. We were still about ten minutes out when a thunderous crack shattered the stillness; I nearly jumped out of the boat.

Juarez pushed me down to the deck and followed suit, reaching for his gun. We waited for something else to happen: more gunfire, ghostly apparitions, the sky to fall. There was nothing.

"Was that...?" I asked.

"Definitely."

We had an abbreviated debate over whether or not we should keep going or turn back. I voted to keep going. Despite any chivalrous illusions, I knew that was what Juarez wanted, too. Eight minutes after the first and only shot was fired, we tied the boat at the dock.

Juarez took the lead, and I was only too happy to let him. We both stayed low to the ground. I thought of my mother out here twenty-four hours ago, fighting for her life. A cold wind sang through the trees. The forest was well lit, the path in front of us deep blue in the moonlight. My heart thundered in my ears. We kept going.

By the time we were halfway up the trail to the greenhouse, anxiety had gotten the better of me. There was still no sign of another soul—the occasional, quiet call of an owl out on the hunt, maybe the rustle of a deer nearby, but certainly no more gunshots or threatening figures in our path. I followed behind Juarez and kept quiet.

We both stopped when we reached the edge of the tree line, along the perimeter of an open field surrounding the greenhouse. It was the first time I'd been here since I was a child. The greenhouse was made of granite and glass, though the thick-paned windows had been broken years ago. It stood in stark silhouette, the moon low behind it. I thought of the body my mother said she had found hanging here years ago.

"You came out here today?" I whispered to Juarez,

thinking of the search party that had been on the island earlier.

"Yeah—we didn't find anyone, though. Obviously."

Of course not. Whoever we were looking for—whether it was Rebecca Ashmont or someone else—must not have been on the island earlier. Juarez touched my arm and nodded toward the greenhouse, now about fifty yards away.

"Stay low and keep close."

I nodded. The field was overgrown, but we wouldn't be nearly as well hidden as we'd been in the woods.

"You have your phone?"

"Yeah," I said.

"Good. Call Diggs."

"But—"

He held up his hand to stop me. We were close enough that I could feel his breath in my ear when he spoke, the warmth of his body against mine.

"It will take them some time to get here—whatever's about to happen, it'll already be over by then. Just call."

I made the call. Diggs answered on the first ring. I told him where I was and what was happening, then hung up while he was still trying to get his head around what I'd said. Juarez looked at me, then nodded toward the greenhouse.

Now or never.

Since the gunshot we'd heard while we were still on the water, everything had gone eerily still. Other than the distant surf and the occasional, mournful call of an owl out for its nightly hunt, the woods were silent. I swallowed past my fear. Juarez squeezed my hand. He got down low with his gun close to his body and went out first. I followed.

Nothing happened. The field was thick with blackberry brambles and burrs and other things that cut and caught at us, but other than a few scratches and scrapes our run across the field was uneventful. When we got to the open, stone archway leading into the greenhouse, Juarez went in first. Looked around. When he was sure that it was safe, he gave the all clear. I went inside. Shattered glass sparkled like rare gems in the moonlight. I picked my way between broken plant pots and stray seedlings that had taken root between cracks in the floor, fallen sculptures and an old birdbath filled with algae and muddy water.

There was no one there. Juarez paused to look out one of the broken windows. I gave him his space. He'd straightened somewhere along the line; my spine popped when I followed his lead, grateful to walk upright again. I thought of the hours I'd logged out here with my father years ago, just the two of us watching the sun rise while we tended the plants and he taught me the finer points of making things grow.

"You'll always be my magic bean, baby."

I joined Juarez at the window. We didn't touch, we didn't speak. There was nothing outside, either: No Matt, no Joe. Certainly no Rebecca Ashmont.

"We should go to the boarding house," he whispered in my general direction.

I didn't say anything. Now that we were here, alone and vulnerable on a moonlit night with no sign of whoever had lured us out in the first place, I realized that I didn't want to go back to the boarding house. In fact, I didn't want to be here at all. What the hell was I looking for? What did I expect to find?

Rebecca Ashmont, or someone claiming to be Rebecca Ashmont, said she would tell me all my father's secrets. Secrets my mother knew and refused to share; secrets Noel Hammond and possibly the entire Payson Church had died for.

"Do you think it was really Rebecca who called me?" I asked.

"I don't know. But someone wanted us here... And we didn't imagine that gunshot."

No, we didn't. I thought of Diggs' voice on the phone; the fact that he was on his way here now. For what?

"So—boarding house next," I finally agreed.

"It makes the most sense."

Right. I started to walk away, but he caught my arm. I turned. He held up his hand before I could ask what he wanted. I stopped. Speaking, moving. Breathing.

A low moan rose on the cold night air, traveling like fingernails up the base of my spine.

Juarez pushed on my shoulder and I crouched down again. He did the same. I stayed that way, trapped between the cold stone wall and Jack's warm body, for another thirty seconds or more before the sound stopped just shy of a wail.

The world went quiet again.

"What the hell was that?" I whispered when I could speak again.

"No idea," he whispered back. He backed away from me but stayed low against the wall. He nodded in the general direction of the field. "I think it came from out there."

Of course it did.

I followed him back outside, as much because I didn't want to be left alone as anything. We'd come from the right before; now, Juarez went in the opposite direction. I kept two steps behind, looking over my shoulder for any sign of the monster I was sure lurked in the shadows.

We were back in the field, fighting our way through a dense thicket of thorns and brush, when Juarez stopped. He pointed up ahead. It took a second or two before my eyes adjusted enough to sort out the shapes and make sense of what I was seeing.

Another two or three yards, and the thorns and brush cleared to open field again. Someone was there. Dressed in black, barely discernible in the high grass, a figure lay on the ground.

Whoever it was, he—or she—wasn't moving.

Juarez and I crept closer, his gun trained on the inert form.

The second we were close enough to see who it was, Juarez dropped his gun to his side. He ordered me back and rushed in without so much as a glance in either direction to make sure he was safe. I waited with the blood rushing in my ears while he knelt beside Matt Perkins and checked for a pulse.

Apparently, he found one because a minute later Jack took off his jacket, wadded it up, and put it under Matt's head. I got closer. The front of the old man's shirt was stained with blood, his eyes wide and his face twisted with pain. He stared at Jack like he'd never seen him before.

I took a step back and tripped on something lying beside him, barely managing to right myself before I fell.

A shovel. While Juarez tended Matt, I focused on the site where we'd found him. A few feet away was a hole maybe four feet long, some spots deeper than others—like Matt had been searching for something buried there. I looked closer. It didn't take long to find what that had been.

At the far end of the hole, the moonlight reflected off something hard and pale white. I got closer. Knelt in the cold, damp earth, and brushed the dirt away.

A human skull.

"Jack," I said. I forgot to whisper. The sound of my voice was almost as jarring as the gunshot we'd heard back on the water.

He didn't answer.

I swept away more dirt until the entire head was exposed. If I was Kat, of course, I could tell something from the skeleton—male or female, age, race... Something. All I saw was a human skull with a very prominent hole in its forehead. I turned to look at Jack. He was kneeling over Matt, but I caught the confusion on his face when he looked in my direction. I turned back to my own task as he returned to his.

A skeleton. It wasn't an infant, but other than that I couldn't tell anything. I was trying to clear more of the dirt when my finger snagged on something sharp. I pulled it back as blood dripped from a cut in my index finger. I ignored the blood and the dull pain and the imminent threat of tetanus, and set back to work until I'd fully excavated what I had found.

A glass crucifix.

Rosary beads of bone.

I rubbed the dirt from the rosary until I could make out the name etched in the glass:

Zion.

AUGUST 22, 1990

THE RAIN COMES LATE that night—well past midnight, while Rebecca waits inside the greenhouse for whatever is about to happen. She still smells Isaac on her, is raw from his caresses and the violence of their union after Joe left. In the moment, she had thought it would change something, being with Isaac like this again. Now, she realizes that is not the case—there was a sense of finality in their parting that she can no longer ignore.

Now, she is back to the decision she had hoped she would not have to make. She thought once her mind was made up she would feel some sort of peace at the resolution, but all she feels is sadness.

She will go. Zion will stay.

Isaac returned to the house a short time ago, but Rebecca remains, waiting for the rain. The heavens open and the skies weep with a fury she understands all too well. She is exhausted. Confused. Bitter, when she knows she should not be. Isaac will guide her son. She will find her own path, whatever that may be. She sits on the ground inside the greenhouse with her back against the cold stone. By the time someone finally comes, she is nearly asleep.

The man who stands in the doorway isn't the one she expects, however, and apprehension wells in her chest at sight of the boy at his side.

"Matt?"

"What's going on, Mom?" Zion asks. His hair is wet, and rain washes down his cheeks in rivers. His eyes are still bleary from sleep. "Uncle Matt said you needed me."

She stands and goes to them. They come in out of the rain; outside, the sudden onslaught after the long drought has washed away topsoil and already flooded the path in places. Matt is soaked. He looks drawn and frightened, but resolute in that way that always meant trouble when they were younger. When Matt makes a decision, few can sway him.

"You talked to Joe?" she asks.

"He said you won't come. I told him maybe this time you need somebody else to make the choice for you. Adam and Diggins aren't part of this—it's none of their business. It's just us. Like always. I'll take you somewhere safe—Joe says he won't stop us."

Zion looks bewildered, more childlike than she has seen him in years. "Take us? We're happy here. Isaac is teaching me. This is where we belong now."

"You don't belong with a degenerate who's twisting your minds," Matt snaps. Zion backs away. Matt has always been unpredictable—affectionate one moment, troubled and broken the next. Though she has never been on the receiving end of his ire, in many ways Rebecca still prefers Joe's violence to Matt's. There is at least some semblance of control when Joe lashes out. The world makes her husband angry, but demons drive Matt.

"Let him go," she says quietly. It is an order, simple and clear. Matt hesitates only a moment before he obeys.

"Zion, go back to the house," she says.

"You should come with me," Zion says. She notes that he does take a few steps away from Matt, however, until he is standing just out of his reach.

"I'll be there soon. You need sleep."

"You'll come say goodnight?" he asks. The doubt is plain in his voice.

"Of course," she lies. Zion looks at her, rain dripping down his face, and she can see that he does not believe her. He turns, regardless.

"Goodbye, Uncle Matt."

Before he can go far, Matt reaches for her son again. This time, all trace of uncertainty is gone—he holds tight to Zion's arm and takes a step toward Rebecca. A crack of thunder rocks the night. Lightning flashes just seconds later.

"You have to come with me," Matt says. He pulls Zion into the greenhouse. Closer to Rebecca. Farther from the church. "We have to go. I came here for both of you."

"I'll go with you," Rebecca says. "Zion has to stay. He has a destiny."

There isn't a trace of surprise on Zion's face when he meets her gaze. "You don't need to go with him," her son says.

"I do." She doesn't cry, and she doesn't waver. "You belong here. I don't. We'll write; I'll visit. You will do great things."

Matt still has hold of Zion's arm. His fear breeds desperation, a darkness to his eyes that all but obliterates the gentle man Rebecca loves. Zion starts to struggle, intensifying his efforts at the first traces of fear on his mother's face. An instant later, his struggling ceases when a familiar voice intercedes.

"Let him go."

Isaac stands tall, silhouetted against the gray night and driving rain. As though too stunned to argue, Matt releases the boy's arm. Zion races to Isaac's side.

"You can't have him," Matt says. There is a tremor in his voice and fury that borders on madness in his eyes.

"I am merely God's instrument," Isaac says smoothly. "Zion is here for a reason. You cannot stand in the way of the will of God."

Zion takes Isaac's hand. "He wants to take my mother. Tell him she must stay, too."

Isaac says nothing. She can see the moment when Zion understands the reality of what is happening; that Isaac has banished her. That she will leave and he will stay. Tears mix with the rain still washing down his cheeks.

"You have a destiny, my son."

Zion shakes his head roughly. She can't remember ever seeing him cry like this. "Not without my mother. She has to stay. She has no one else to protect her—she'll die without me."

Isaac puts a hand on Zion's shoulder. Rebecca has been so absorbed in their reaction that she's nearly forgotten about Matt. His gun is already raised by the time she realizes his intent.

"Leave us!" Zion shouts, his rage directed at Matt.

Isaac's hand flexes on Zion's shoulder, holding him still. "Matthew, I know there are demons that haunt you."

"Shut up," Matt whispers.

The preacher takes a step closer. "I know the voices of those you struck down cry to you in the night—I was there, Matt. I lost my way, too. War changes a man; makes him see the worst in people. I'm here to tell you there is still good in the world. Zion exemplifies that good."

He takes another step forward. Matt steps back, the gun still raised. He is trembling.

"I want you to take Rebecca and leave this island," Isaac says. Zion flinches as though a blow has been struck.

"No!" her son cries.

Isaac holds up his hand. Turns on the boy. "God has made his wishes plain to me. He has told me what your path holds."

"I don't care about God's plan, then," Zion says. His voice is choked with tears. Isaac ignores him and advances on Matt, faster now, his hand outstretched.

"Give me the gun, Matthew," he says. "Leave here. Take the woman and don't return."

Zion tries to run past them both to get to his mother, but Isaac holds him back. Rebecca takes a step toward him. The wind rises and the trees moan and the heavens rain down. Isaac is smiling. Zion is possessed. Matt stands perfectly still, terrified. Something is about to happen—she feels it in a bone-deep pause, as though God himself is holding his breath. Waiting.

There is another crack of thunder, another flash of lightning that illuminates the night. A scream dies in Rebecca's throat when she sees the man standing to their left, at the very center of the greenhouse. He is dressed in black, a hood up around his head, a cruel smile on his thin lips. The Angel of Death, Rebecca thinks suddenly. Has he been here the entire time?

Matt turns toward her to find out what's wrong. Isaac takes the opportunity to wrest the gun from his grasp, still holding Zion close. Rebecca watches and she knows in the way that mothers always know, the moment that Matt's finger grazes the trigger. The smile vanishes from Isaac's lips. A crack that sounds like the end of the world tears through the night. Matt cries out.

Zion does not.

33

NURSING MY BLOODY FINGER, I crawled back to Jack and Matt. When I reached them, Jack looked at me like he'd forgotten I was there. The old man's chest rose and fell in shallow, useless gasps—the final breaths of a dying man.

"Matt, who killed Zion?" I asked.

He blinked. His face was wet with tears. "I did," he whispered. Jack stared at him.

"Just the body," Matt said. "I killed the body—he'll rise. I thought I found him." He looked at Juarez with madness shining in his rheumy blue eyes. "I thought I found him, but it was a lie—I was wrong. She told me you were him. We believed. But if you're him, he can't still be in the ground. Joe says he's dead."

I tried to think of a question. As it happened, I didn't need to; now that he'd started, Matt continued without being prompted.

"Everything got jumbled that night—everybody was moving. Isaac wouldn't let us go. Zion wouldn't leave Becca; Isaac wouldn't let us take him." More tears leaked down his face. He coughed and a trail of bloody spittle flowed down his chin.

"I shot them both," he said.

"You shot Isaac?" I asked.

"Shot him dead. And Zion. Two birds with one stone."

"Then who am I?" Jack asked. "If I'm not Zion...?"

Matt looked like he'd just been presented with some indecipherable riddle. "I don't know who you are," he said finally. "A boy who looked like Zion, grown to a man with no past. I thought you were him."

I was still trying to put everything together when a branch broke off to the left. Juarez went for his gun. Before he could fire, Joe Ashmont emerged from the brush and stood tall at the edge of his son's grave.

He was limping, a rag tied tight around his right thigh. His clothes were wet, his face black with grime. He held his shotgun in both hands, as though it would be too heavy otherwise.

"You knew all this?" I asked. "That Zion was dead? You knew what happened the night before the fire?"

Joe nodded. "I knew all Matt's secrets. Just learned everybody else's, though."

"Why did you try to kill my mother?"

He ignored the question. "I've been telling them for years the boy was dead—I was there, I watched him die. But Becca had it stuck in her head that he was coming back, and anything Becca was selling Matt always bought. Right, Matty?" He leaned forward, eyeing Matt's bleeding form.

"He dead?" Ashmont asked me.

Matt coughed. Something that looked a lot like relief crossed Ashmont's face before it vanished.

"So Rebecca's still alive?" I asked.

"Not now," he said. Fast, short. Grief or anger or some combination of the two made him look away from me for a second or two, while he got himself back together.

"You killed her," I said.

"Who the hell do you think I am—you think I just go around murdering every woman I see? I didn't touch Becca. Twenty-two years, I've kept her secrets. Fed her, nursed her, kept outsiders from coming in here, while her and Matt kept on with the delusion that her fuckin' kid was the second coming. He's in the ground, Matty," he said, addressing his old friend. Matt stirred.

Ashmont shook his head.

"Batshit crazy—both of 'em," he said, half to himself.

"Did you know my father's still alive?" I asked. "Do you know where he is now?" He barely acknowledged me—I might as well have been talking to the air.

I looked back to Matt for more answers than Ashmont had provided thus far. Juarez had brushed the hair from the old man's forehead. He prayed quietly, while Matt continued to leak blood and gasp for breath.

"What about the fire?" I asked Matt. "And my father—Rebecca said she knew a secret about my father. Do you know what she was talking about?"

A flash of panic crossed the old man's pain-filled eyes. "They killed Becca. They warned us—it's what happens when you start telling secrets."

Matt closed his eyes. I turned to Ashmont, who was watching all of this with only mild interest. He'd dropped the shotgun to his side and was using it to prop himself up.

"Who's they?" I asked. I took a step toward him, no longer mindful of staying out of sight. Ashmont just smiled. "Who set the fire, dammit? Who attacked my mother?"

He looked past me, straight into the woods. Matt started coughing. Jack knelt beside him and tried to staunch a fresh flow of blood.

"I tell you and you're dead," Ashmont said. He still wasn't looking at me. "Just like the rest of us—Matty's almost there. They'll get you too, one way or the other. Becca said it was the Angel of Death that struck the match, but you and me know better. He ain't no angel; I don't know who the fuck he is, but he's just a man. Adam wants to pretend it never happened, and Kat's the only thing standing between you and a bullet that's had your name on it since the day you was born. There's a stack of bodies a mile deep and they keep piling up—you really think it's worth all that?"

I hesitated, but only for a second. "I need to know what happened."

His eyes flitted to mine for just a second before they returned to the trees behind us. Jack was oblivious, now doing CPR on a dying man whose bloody past would chase him to the grave. I turned around. The world slowed to a series of freeze frames that my brain could barely process.

Twenty yards away, a man stood with a rifle pointed at us. He looked directly at me. In the moonlight, I could make out high cheekbones and a thin, sharp nose.

He fired.

Ashmont never flinched. Never ducked. He fell into the grave where I'd just uncovered Zion's body, and he didn't move again. I was dimly aware of Juarez shouting for me to get down, but I ignored him.

When I turned back to the tree line, the cloaked man from my nightmares had vanished into the woods.

I got to my feet and ran after him—through the woods, past the boarding house, down the trail to the ocean. I ran through a blue forest toward the deep black sea and I didn't stop. Didn't slow. The ground was rough beneath my feet. I tripped and landed hard, skinned my knees and jarred my bones. I tore my face on a bramble of thorns I couldn't get free of, while just up ahead the man with all the answers I'd been looking for since childhood ran like a specter through the night.

Except I didn't believe in ghosts.

I kept running.

He broke off from the path somewhere along the line; I caught glimpses of him through the trees, but he was always out of my reach. He was leading me toward the south side of the island, where the cliffs were high and the drop to the ocean below was fifty feet of hard edges. I couldn't see him anymore. Heard nothing. Somewhere far off, Juarez was calling for me.

"Ssh," my father says. It is night in the woods. We are alone. "Don't make a sound. Hold your breath. Listen to the forest. You can hear a mouse creep, if you listen hard enough."

I stopped running and held my breath.

Five seconds passed. Ten. Nothing but the wind in the trees and the distant surf, Juarez's voice sounding more and more panicked as he shouted my name. And then...

Footsteps, moving fast. I followed the sound, running faster than I had ever run in my life. I saw him up ahead—a black silhouette racing like he couldn't be stopped. I didn't slow down when he led me off the path again, where the trees grew thinner and the wind got colder. We cleared the forest and reached the cliffs.

He kept running, leading me dangerously close to the edge. I could hear the waves crashing below, could feel a vast emptiness to my left. A single misstep and I'd be gone. The cloaked man was ten feet away, maybe less, when he turned toward me. He stood at the edge of the cliff and smiled. He held a long, bony finger to his thin lips.

"Ssssh."

He turned to face the abyss.

An instant later, he was gone.

I ran after him, stopping short at the ledge. Below, I could see him make his steady way down the sheer face, hand over hand down a rope anchored into the granite just a foot down from where I was standing. A boat was idling in the waves below. I couldn't see details, but at least one other person waited for him.

I stood there gasping for breath and watched as the cloaked man, the man in my nightmares, the man who had been a ghost but was now once and for all incontrovertibly proven flesh and blood, climbed into the boat. He disappeared into the night.

I found Jack in the woods fifteen minutes later, calling my name. Blood coated the front of his shirt. When I finally appeared on the path in front of him he stopped short, his breath coming hard. He wiped blood, sweat, and tears from his face with the back of his hand. I'd never seen him so angry.

"Diggs is right—you do have a death wish. What the fuck is wrong with you?"

I swallowed past the boulder-sized lump in my throat. I'd sprained my ankle and scratched my face. My jeans and jacket were torn.

"I'm sorry—I wasn't thinking. I just… I had to try and catch him. I'm sorry," I repeated. "Matt…?"

"They're both dead," he said numbly.

There's a stack of bodies a mile deep, and they keep piling up, Ashmont had said. Matt might have killed Zion and Isaac all those years ago, but were the rest of the deaths really on my father's head?

"I didn't find Rebecca," he said.

I nodded again. I took his hand and led him back down the path. "I think I know where she is."

AUGUST 22, 1990

JOE APPEARS AFTER THE shot is fired. He is not there, and then he is. The last remnants of coherence in her tangled brain tell Rebecca that he has been lurking in the background, waiting to intervene when he was needed. He is too late.

Isaac falls. He sinks to his knees, his eyes wide. The bullet hit him in the chest; the blood soaks his shirt and the ground beneath and he dies almost immediately. Rebecca barely notices, however. Her attention is fixed on Zion. He falls backward, hard, and she worries about him bumping his head until she gets closer and sees the gaping wound in his forehead. His face is still wet with tears, but his eyes do not see. She falls to the ground beside him. Pulls him into her arms.

Matt is screaming—the scream of a madman who will never be silenced. Joe is the only one who is calm, though she can see that he is barely holding on. He takes Matt by the shoulders and steers him away from them. Gives orders that Rebecca only half hears:

"Stay with her, Matty—I'll come back for you. Just stay here till I can get back. I'll take care of everything."

Matt becomes very quiet. Joe takes his gun. He kisses Rebecca's head and wipes away her tears, but he can't get her to move away from their dead son.

"I'll be back, Becca. I'll take care of you."

He leaves her there with her dead child and her dead lover and the man who took them both. Matt stands. He is still weeping. He goes out into the rain and disappears down the path. Rebecca is certain she will never see him again.

She hopes she will never see any of them again.

She sings to her son, lying broken in her arms.

The Angel of Death reappears. His brow is furrowed. He touches Rebecca's head. "What a mess you've made," he says. He smiles at her.

He goes to Isaac's body and lifts it easily over his shoulder, as though it weighs no more than a sack of flour. He carries the dead preacher down the path, paying no mind to the rain or the blood that drenches his cloak. Rebecca blinks away tears, wipes away her son's blood. The Angel turns back.

"Your son will rise. If he is chosen, he will rise. Leave him. Come with me."

She kisses Zion's lips. Arranges him as carefully as she can on the granite floor. She stands and crosses herself in a way that Isaac would disapprove of, though the priests she knew as a child would find it only fitting.

She follows the Angel of Death into the rain.

They go to the chapel. The sun is just coming up, and the congregation has already gathered for their early-morning service. Candles are lit, and churchgoers are singing inside. Their voices are hazy—the chorus of drunken sailors rather than a choir of angels. Her Angel of Death drops Isaac's body at the bottom of the stairs leading up to the chapel.

She watches as he latches the door to the chapel, and places a heavy iron padlock on it.

"It is God's will," he tells her. "You are here as witness to God's fury."

He goes to the back of the barn. When he returns, he carries a metal container of gasoline.

"You can't—" she says. She feels the first vestiges of reality seeping in. Her son lies dead. And now…

"I have no choice," he tells her. "This is what's required. We sacrifice the flock to resurrect the Lamb of God." He smiles at her again. There is something insincere about the smile; for a moment, she feels as though he is laughing at her.

Sacrifice the flock to resurrect the Lamb of God.

She stands outside in the rain while the angel completes his mission. The congregation is still singing upstairs. Someone is speaking. The Angel of Death returns to her side. He holds up a lighter.

"I'll go. You stay here. Wait for your son to return to you. Hide from the world until he does." He moves closer and presses a kiss to her cheek. He smells like blood and gasoline and the fury of a vengeful God. "Tell Adam that Father is watching," he whispers.

He curls his body around the lighter, shielding it from the wind and rain until a flame appears. It takes three attempts before the gasoline catches and the fire starts. Someone screams inside the chapel. Children cry. When Rebecca looks around again, the Angel of Death has vanished.

She returns to the greenhouse to wait for Zion.

34

WE FOUND REBECCA ASHMONT in my father's cabin, where I suspected she'd been staying since my father left the island. She lay on my father's bed with her hands crossed over her stomach and her eyes closed. Her once-dark hair had gone silver and there were obviously more wrinkles than there'd been in the photos I'd seen, but she was still a striking woman.

Jack checked her pulse, though the ligature marks around her neck made it clear what he'd find. I thought of the man I'd just chased through the forest; the man I was now positive had attacked me that morning at the old Payson house.

Rebecca and Joe Ashmont; Noel Hammond; Matt Perkins—all dead now. Ashmont had said Rebecca had seen an Angel of Death—that that Angel was the one who burned the Payson Church to the ground. There was nothing supernatural about this man, though; I'd looked in his eyes twice now, and he was nothing if not flesh and blood.

I touched Jack's arm and motioned him outside. We watched the sun rise over the ocean and waited in silence for Diggs to arrive with the police.

It was late afternoon the next day before I got back to Diggs' house. I'd been given a clean bill of health at Kat's old clinic, then sat through several hours of questioning with Sheriff Finnegan and a multitude of much less friendly faces from the state police, while we tried to sort through everything that had happened. Without much luck, as it turned out.

Diggs' Jeep was gone when I pulled in, but Jack's Honda Civic was parked out front. The hatchback was open and a couple of boxes were already packed inside. Einstein bolted past Juarez when he opened the front door, and we had a brief but heartfelt reunion before Stein took off to christen a few bushes in my honor. Juarez approached.

He'd showered and shaved and presumably gotten a couple of hours' sleep. All things considered, he looked a hell of a lot better than I'd expected. Still exhausted, still haunted, but there was a resilience about him that pleased me. It would take a lot more than a few dead bodies and an amnesic childhood to keep Jack Juarez down for long.

He set down the box he'd been carrying. "Police all done with you?"

"For now. They didn't learn much—since I don't really know anything."

"You know who killed them; that's something."

"I saw who killed them—but I don't have a clue who he is, or what he has to do with any of this. My father's alive, but I don't know how to find him. More people died because of this thing—whatever it is—and I don't know why." I couldn't keep the frustration from my voice, try as I might. "I'd say that's not much of anything, actually."

"It's more than I have," he said quietly. I looked at

him and saw the same frustration I was feeling, though considerably magnified. At least I knew where I came from; at least I had a place to start.

He touched a scratch on my cheek. "Aside from that, you survived relatively unscathed this time, right?"

"Nothing that time and a little concealer won't heal. What about you?" I looked him in the eye. He wavered for just a second before the weakness passed and he smiled. It wasn't so much an attempt to hide the pain as a refusal to give in to it. I liked that.

He shrugged. "I'm fine. Scratches, scrapes, a bruise or two…"

So, we weren't talking emotional scars today. Fine with me. He moved in a little closer and ran his hand through my hair. I backed up until I hit the Honda Civic. Jack followed me.

"So, you're leaving?" I asked.

"I've gotta get back—I'm starting to forget what I've got waiting for me."

"Which is?"

He took a little while to think on that. "A job I love. Good friends. A bed that's been empty too long." He looked at me meaningfully. "What about you? Are you sticking around Littlehope, or can I tempt you out to D.C. now and then?"

The afternoon was quiet and his body was warm and, honestly, what the hell else was I going to do? I swallowed hard and looked deep into his dark, dark eyes.

"I don't really know what I'm doing. But maybe a trip to D.C. could be arranged." I hesitated. "It might be nice to spend a little time without quite so many distractions."

"If those were distractions, I'd hate to see what qualifies

as a real disruption in your life."

I laughed. "Not just the death and mayhem. The whole thing with Diggs…"

There was barely room to breathe between us, but he moved closer. "I told you before," he said. "I'm not worried about Diggs." He leaned in and kissed me. I kissed him back, pressed against the car in the bright sunshine. The world was disappointingly lacking in electricity when he stepped away from me.

"I like you, Erin," he said. "I think you're tough and smart and sexy as hell. If Diggs is too scared of what people might think to admit he's been in love with you since you were sixteen, that's his loss." He grinned like he knew full well the kind of bomb he'd just dropped, and didn't really care. "I'm a good guy—but I'm not so good that I'll just take a step back till he comes to his senses."

The world got very, very quiet after that. Crickets, and so on.

"Diggs isn't…" I started.

He gave me a look that implied arguing the point would be useless. I couldn't explain the thing with Diggs to myself, let alone anyone else. Why bother even trying?

"So, you really want me to come out to D.C. sometime?" I asked instead.

"Name the weekend and I'll show you the city." He got close again. Leaned in and kissed my neck. "Among other things."

We may have broken a few of your tamer public decency laws before we both came up for air. He had a flight to catch. I had thousands more questions that needed answering and a whole lot of sleep to catch up on. We kissed one more time, he promised to give me a call once he was back in

D.C., and I watched him drive away.

I went back inside when he was gone, took a cold shower, and crawled into bed with Einstein.

I didn't get up again for twenty-four hours.

●

While I slept, I dreamed of the Angel of Death—the mysterious hooded man who chased me across Payson Isle twenty-two years ago, and who now took up almost as much space in my head as my missing father. He was chasing me again in the dream—so close behind that I could feel his fingernails at the back of my neck when he reached for me. I woke in a tangle of sweaty sheets, my head filled with unanswered questions.

Who the hell was he? And what did Kat know about any of it? What the hell kind of secret did my father have in his past that a creepy lunatic in a cloak would come to town after all this time and murder anyone who might reveal whatever he was hiding? And if that was the case, then why hadn't he killed me when he had the chance? I went in the bathroom and brushed my teeth, still going over everything in my head. I'd solved one mystery: who set the Payson fire. But how many others did I stir up by answering that single question?

I went to see Kat in the hospital that afternoon. Juarez was back in D.C. I'd managed a couple of sleepy exchanges with Diggs, and been called in for more questioning with another half-dozen agencies now looking into the Payson fire and the most recent deaths on Payson Isle. So far, Maya had been adamant that no one be allowed to question Kat until she was on her feet again, but I personally didn't think that would make any difference.

My mother wasn't talking.

I went to see her anyway, just in case.

When I got there, she was sitting up in bed trying to type on her laptop with only one hand. Her face was less swollen but no less alarming, and judging by the look in her eye she'd cut off the painkillers about a week too soon.

"You heard what happened?" I asked.

She looked up. "Are you all right?"

"I'm fine."

She pushed the wheely cart holding her laptop aside and nodded me closer. "Sit."

I sat on the side of the bed.

She poked at my cheek and made a face. "Blackberry brambles?"

"I think so, yeah. It was dark—hard to tell."

"You're limping."

"I sprained my ankle. I'm okay, Kat."

I got off the bed and pulled up a chair instead. I looked her in the eye. She didn't look away, which I took as a good sign.

"Dad's still alive."

"We buried your father," she said.

"I don't know who you buried, but it wasn't Dad. Joe Ashmont told me you're the only thing standing between me and a bullet," I said. "Why would he say something like that?"

"Joe Ashmont was a fool and a drunk to boot. How the hell should I know why he said anything?" I noticed that she'd stopped looking at me, though.

Clearly, this was getting us nowhere. I took a deep breath

in a vain attempt not to throttle her in her hospital bed.

"Okay, let's try something else. I'll tell you what I know. Maybe you'll have something you can add."

She didn't look enthusiastic, but she didn't stop me, either.

"Isaac Payson helped Rebecca Ashmont and her son escape from Joe, because he was beating the tar out of them. But then Rebecca got out to the island and started sleeping with Isaac, which Dad didn't like. And Isaac started paying a little too much attention to Zion, who may or may not have been off his rocker himself."

She smiled faintly at that.

"So, Dad went to Reverend Diggins to get some advice on what he should do. And of course Daddy Diggs decided the best course of action was going out there and staging an intervention. They recruited Joe to help—I'm guessing because Rebecca said she wouldn't go no matter what, and she was threatening Dad with whatever secret she knew about him. So, he needed her off that island."

I looked at Kat to see if she would argue any of this. She waited for me to continue, sitting there like a very battered Queen of Sheba.

"So, Matt decided he would have a go at getting her off the island before anybody else went out there—maybe to play white knight, or maybe there were other motives at work. I don't know. But things went wrong. Isaac showed up. Things got confusing. Matt's gun went off, and he took out Isaac and Zion in one fell swoop."

She lowered her eyes. So, she hadn't known that part, at least.

"Where I get lost is after all that went down," I said. Frustration was starting to bleed into my voice. I tamped it down; losing control would never get Kat to see things my way. "Because after the shooting, Dad got a call from Joe telling him they weren't going after Rebecca. That he should just forget it. So, Dad called Reverend Diggins, and then...?"

I looked at her. She stared at her hands for a long time before she finally met my eye.

"He came to see me," she said.

Things got quiet. "You said you didn't see him that morning. That if you'd known he wasn't coming back for me, you would have gotten me yourself."

"I lied," she said simply, and I knew that for once she was telling the truth. "He came to me to ask what he should do. He was in trouble—he knew that. Rebecca saw to it. So, I told him to leave."

"Leave where?"

"Payson Isle. Littlehope. Maine. The U.S., if he could. I was on my way to get you when Diggins called to tell me Joe was there, drunker than a skunk and talking crazy. And he was: beaten to hell, crying, covered in blood, babbling about something I didn't understand." I could imagine Ashmont seeking refuge at the bottom of a bottle after his son had been killed, maybe getting the snot kicked out of himself somewhere along the way. "He said Matt was still out on the island," Kat continued, "and he needed to get back out there. I dosed him with sleeping pills and he passed out."

"And when he woke up, you found out the island was burning," I guessed.

"Your father came back—I don't know how he heard. He went and got you." She rolled her eyes. "Took you out to that fucking island where dozens of people were already dead, because he was afraid to leave you alone once he knew what happened."

I held my breath. "And what happened, Kat?" I finally managed.

She wet her lips. Looked me square in the eye. "There was a fire," she said. "People died. That's all you need to know."

"The hooded man—the one you always said was a figment of my imagination? I saw him again. He was the one who attacked you out on the island, wasn't he? You and Joe and Matt—what the hell were you up to? Did he come for you, or did you go looking for him?"

"There was a fire," she repeated. Her eyes had gone cold, but there was still a tell-tale spark of fear lingering there. "I'm telling you: that's all you need to know, Erin. Stop looking."

Maya came in before I could get the water boarding under way.

"You two are still playing nice, I see," she said. She wore jeans and a pretty green sweater and she looked more chipper than my mother on her best day. Kat smiled at her—actually smiled. I'd forgotten she could even do that.

"Just catching up, but Erin has to be going."

"Did you tell her our news?" Maya asked. She sat down on the edge of the bed, her hand resting absently on my mother's knee.

"What news?" I asked. If there was suspicion in my voice, I felt it was entirely justified.

I sat with my hands folded in my lap while Maya gave me the skinny on my mother's future plans. They would stay in Littlehope—just for a while, Kat assured me. Take over the clinic while she recuperated. Take things slow. I tried to read my mother in all of this; the woman who had despised Littlehope almost more than I had when I was growing up. She might have been bruised and swollen and just back from the brink of death days before, but she looked surprisingly pleased with the decision.

Maya gave me a hug before I left, while Kat just told me to put ointment on my scratches and get a damned haircut already. I got back in the car and drove Einstein to the local dog shop, where I sat and watched him wrestle with a shepherd named Chuck while I checked out premium dog foods and thought about the bizarre bastardizations of love that manifest between parents and children, and all the ways they'll bite you in the ass in the end.

Then, I bought six tins of Loyal Biscuit premium dog biscuits, packed my mutt back in the car, and buckled him into his brand new doggie seatbelt.

I went to find Diggs.

Einstein trotted happily beside me once more when we returned to the *Trib*. The sun was out, the sky was clear. Diggs smiled when I came into the newsroom, nodding toward his office before any of the roving reporters could question me about the alarming number of people who seemed to meet a terrible end shortly after they crossed my path. Diggs sat in his chair; I sat on the corner of his desk.

"You got some sleep," he said.

"Lots of sleep."

"Come up with any answers to the mysteries of Payson Isle?"

"Other than the basics? Not really. I need to know who the Angel of Death is, though."

Diggs looked uncomfortable at that. The day before, I'd finally given him an abbreviated version of my story about the hooded man who had chased me the day of the Payson fire, and the role I suspected he'd played that day and over the past week. I hadn't been able to tell at the time whether Diggs was skeptical of my tale or just plain terrified.

"What? You think I'm still making him up?"

"No," he said quickly. "I think three people were murdered out on Payson Isle yesterday, and you and Kat almost joined that list. I think your father's hiding out for a reason you might not be ready to know, and this nut job in the hood isn't just gonna drop everything. Not if you keep pushing."

I had actually considered all of that. Someone saner might have just let the whole thing go, but I knew I couldn't. Diggs read that without me having to come out and say it and moved on to the next topic.

"And you still don't have a clue where your father might be."

"Washington, I guess—I mean, that's where the phone rang, anyway. I'm booked on a flight tomorrow."

He didn't look happy about that, but he didn't look that surprised, either.

"Did you know Kat and Maya are moving back here?" I asked.

Based on his reaction—or lack of one—I was guessing he did. "What about you? Are you sticking around the old hometown for a while?" he asked. "After the Washington trip, I mean?"

"Maya asked if I wanted to take care of their place in Portland. I think I'll do that, actually."

There was a flicker of what might have been disappointment before he nodded. "Good—it'll give you a chance to establish yourself, get back on your feet. Maybe go a few months without a life-or-death struggle for truth and justice."

"Just truth," I said. "Justice is beyond my scope."

He smiled at that. "What about Juarez?" he asked. "Any word from the Cuban commando?"

I thought of Jack's words, and focused on drawing intricate patterns in my jeans so Diggs couldn't read me. *...been in love with you since you were sixteen.* Yeah.

"I'm sorry about that whole thing," I said. I managed to divert my attention from my denim etchings back to his face. "I know you and I aren't...whatever, and you obviously don't think of me that way anymore, which is totally understandable given, you know, everything. But it still wasn't fair putting you in that position."

He didn't say anything for at least twelve Mississippis, but his smile was one I remembered from another life. He put his hand on my knee and stood up. Situated himself between my legs and got a lot closer than two BFFs typically get. The look he gave me was anything but brotherly.

"I didn't say that," he said.

"Didn't say what?" It was suddenly much, much warmer in his office.

"I didn't say I don't think of you that way anymore."

I blinked at him stupidly. "What do you mean? Yeah you did."

"I didn't say I didn't think of you that way—I said we shouldn't go down that road. Then I got married. And I got divorced. And *you* got married. The timing was always a little off."

He tangled his right hand in my hair and gave me a bemused half-smile.

"I never said I don't think of you that way anymore, Solomon," he repeated softly.

"But the other night... This whole visit—"

He rolled his eyes, but he still didn't let me go. "Your

marriage just fell apart. You just lost a baby, for Christ's sake. You've been working twenty-eight hours a day trying to solve a mystery that's been dogging you since you were a kid. Maybe I'm old fashioned, but it didn't seem like the best time to make a move."

I tried to remember the basic mechanics of breathing in and out. "And now?" I asked.

His lips hovered just a milli-second from mine. "I guess we'll see," he said.

The conversation was clearly headed in a direction I hadn't expected. Before we could get there, my cell phone rang. Diggs looked mildly amused.

I let it ring once more.

"You should probably get that." He took a step back so I could dig through my purse. My knees were shaking and a lot of parts that had been solid before I walked into the office had liquefied in the past five minutes.

It was Juarez. Now, Diggs looked *really* amused. He grinned, eyes sparkling when I answered.

"Are you at a computer?" Juarez asked without preamble.

I was still stuck at the part where Diggs had me pressed against the desk, so it took a second to switch gears. Once I had, I pushed Diggs out of the way none-too-gently and turned his laptop toward me.

"I just sent you something," Juarez said.

I checked my e-mail and clicked on a link he'd forwarded. It led to a breaking news story in Olympia, Washington.

Former Senator Jane Bellows Found Murdered In Her Home.

I froze. Diggs scanned the headline over my shoulder.

"That's the woman, right?" Juarez asked. "That was the phone number Noel had written down with your father's name next to it?"

"Yeah. That was her."

A former senator.

"I'm booking a flight," Juarez said. "Are you coming?"

I looked at Diggs. He nodded like he knew exactly what was happening.

"Yeah," I said. "I'll be there."

I hung up the phone.

Diggs glanced at his watch. "When do we leave?"

Looking for more Erin Solomon?
Turn the page for a free excerpt from
the next novel in the critically acclaimed series,
SINS OF THE FATHER.

1

I FIRST MET HANK GENDREAU at the Maine State Prison in Warren, twenty-five years into a life sentence. It was hotter than hell in Midcoast Maine, and I was damp from the humidity and cranky from spending an hour and a half in summer traffic, crawling along a bottle-necked stretch of Route 1 that ran the full thirty miles from Bath to Waldoboro.

When I finally hit Warren, I parked Einstein—my faithful canine compadre—with a sympathetic neighbor I knew from back in the day, thus saving him from baking in the hot car while I went about my business. Then, I drove another half mile up Route 97 and turned right at a section of brick wall taken from the original state prison in Thomaston, before it was replaced by the fifty thousand-square-foot "Supermax" I was about to enter.

According to the official prison visitor's rules of conduct, shorts and a tank top are too much for the average lifer to handle, so I opted for khakis and a button-up blouse. The ensemble was cooler than jeans, but still too warm for the dog days of summer. Once inside the building, it took forty-five minutes to get through the metal detector, a lengthy list of questions, and a frisking more intimate than any date I'd been on in recent memory, before I was allowed into the belly of the beast. The sun was blazing outside, but that light didn't make its way into the stark visiting chamber where Gendreau waited for me.

A few other inmates were already scattered throughout the room, visiting with friends and family. Gendreau sat behind a wood-veneer table with his hands folded and his eyes on the clock. Unlike movies or TV, there was no protective glass between us. He wore a blue denim shirt with faded jeans. No shackles. His hair was graying at the temples, and his brown eyes were clear and soulful. At first glance, they didn't look at all like the eyes of a man who'd tortured and killed his seventeen-year-old daughter in a hallucinogenic frenzy.

I sat down in a plastic chair on the opposite side of the table. He smiled, his teeth even and surprisingly white. In another life, he would have been an attractively innocuous sixty-year-old man living out an attractively innocuous life. Someone you might remember for his good manners, but not much else.

I introduced myself and managed a good two minutes of small talk—a personal record—before I got down to business. The guards had confiscated my bag before I was allowed inside, but they let me carry a letter in with me once they'd assured themselves I wouldn't pull some kind of Ninja death-through-origami stunt.

"I know your final appeal was just denied. I'm not sure what you expect me to do about that," I said. I tapped the letter with my index finger. "What did you honestly think you'd get by writing me?"

He didn't seem ruffled by my tone. "You came. That's something."

I opened the envelope and took out the blurry photo I'd received with it two days earlier. Someone had scrawled the words *Jeff, Will & Hank, Summer 1968* in sloping penmanship on the back. In the photo, three boys mugged for the camera. Two were dark-haired, the other a redhead, probably between fourteen and sixteen years old. The picture was too out of focus to tell much beyond that, however.

"I've had that for a long time," he said. "But it didn't click for me till last week, when I was reading a story about the Payson fire in the *Globe*. They had a picture of you and your father in there, when you were younger."

I'd seen the article; it was one among many these days. Three months earlier, I'd bungled my way through an investigation that had ultimately proven the alleged cult suicide by fire of the Payson Church of Tomorrow—the religious community where I spent the first nine years of my life—hadn't been suicide at all. In the process, I'd learned that my father had been harboring a secret that, for reasons I still didn't understand, had inspired him to fake his own death ten years later. For the past three months, I'd been searching for some hint as to what that secret might have been… And where, exactly, my father was now. Gendreau's letter was the first lead I'd gotten with any real potential in months.

"And you recognized him after all those years?" I asked.

"I wouldn't have if you hadn't been in the picture with him. But you looked just like him when he was younger." I didn't care for the way he was looking at me: like I was some ghost of Christmas past, come calling in the dead heat of summer.

"I don't know how you think this picture would convince me of anything—I can barely tell these kids are kids, much less that one of them might have been my father forty-five years ago. Besides which, my father's name was Adam, not Jeff."

I waited to see if he took the bait. I knew full well my father wasn't born Adam Solomon. I just needed to know if Gendreau did.

"Maybe he was when he had you—after he joined that church," he said evenly. "But when we were kids together, it was Jeff. He had a birthmark behind his knee shaped like South America, and a scar on his left forearm. You remember?"

I nodded, but said nothing.

"He got that scar when we were out fishing one day—we were about fifteen," Gendreau continued. "There was this pond with some of the best trout in the County, but we had to climb over a fence to get to it. Somebody saw us. While we were trying to get away, Jeff got his arm snagged on the barbed wire. I'm telling you the God's honest truth: the boy in that picture is your father."

I'm not above taking the word of a crazed psychopath, but I try not to make a habit of it. Facts don't lie, though: my father did have a scar on his left forearm, and he'd told me almost exactly the same story about how he'd gotten it. And while as a kid I'd always thought the birthmark behind his knee looked more like a dancing hippo than South America, I could see where someone might get confused.

"In your letter, you said you could give me answers." I hesitated. There were a couple of prisoners at a neighboring table seemingly lost in their own conversations, but I'd learned the hard way that there was a very determined, as-yet-unidentified faction out there who'd go to great lengths to keep me from finding the truth about my father. I leaned in closer and lowered my voice, comforting myself with the knowledge that it's only paranoia if there's no one out to get you.

"How did you know him? Where did you two grow up?"

He pushed the letter and photo back toward me and wet

his lips. Like that, his eyes changed. Either thirty years in prison had made that pleasantly innocuous sixty-year-old a hell of a lot harder than he would have been otherwise, or I was getting a rare glimpse into the true Hank Gendreau. He never took his eyes from mine.

"I'll make a trade," he said.

"What kind of trade?"

"I don't have any money left to hire anyone. My last appeal's been denied. But I read about what you did with the Payson fire—how hard you worked to find the truth." He looked like he expected me to argue the point. I kept quiet. "If you'll look into my daughter's murder, I'll tell you about your father. Whatever you want to know."

"What was his last name?"

"Not until you bring me something. Will you look into that day?"

I'm not an idiot—I knew he could be lying. Maybe he and my father had known each other when they were kids, and that was the end of the story. Maybe he'd never known my father at all.

"What if all I uncover about your daughter's murder is that you did it?"

"I didn't," he said. His eyes hardened, but he didn't flinch and he didn't look particularly offended by my words. He looked around for the guards, then waited a second or two, until he'd assured himself they weren't listening. "There's something else," he said. "Something I didn't mention in the letter."

I waited for him to continue.

"Did you hear about the bodies they found up at the border last week?"

"In Canada?" I asked. "Sure, who hasn't?"

A week before, a couple of hunters had gotten off track in the deep woods along the border between Maine and

Quebec. In the process, they stumbled on a shallow grave…
and then another one. And another. By the time they made
it back to civilization, they reported that they'd found half
a dozen of these unmarked graves. It turned out that all six
belonged to high school and college girls who'd gone missing
sometime in the '80s. There weren't a lot of details beyond
that yet, but the story had been getting plenty of air time
ever since.

"You're telling me that whoever killed those girls is the
same one who killed your daughter," I said. I didn't actually
come out and say he was full of shit, but it was certainly
implied.

"They were all Ashley's age. All tortured. Strangled."
He stopped. The hardness vanished from his eyes. "They
all died the same way," he said. "Five of the bodies have
been identified as girls who'd gone missing from central and
northern Maine at around the same time Ashley was killed."

"According to the stories I've heard about this case, you'd
taken three tabs of acid the day your daughter was killed," I
said, unmoved. "They found you with the body, covered in
her blood. And correct me if I'm wrong, but there's the little
matter of a confession that keeps cropping up in all these
appeals you've been filing."

"I didn't know what I was saying—I was out of my mind
by then. The drugs were still in my system. And even if they
hadn't been, finding Ashley that way…" His eyes filled with
tears. If his grief was an act, Hank Gendreau deserved an
Oscar. "I was out of my mind," he repeated.

"So, what changed?" I asked. "How are you so sure of
what happened now, twenty-five years later? How do you
know you didn't stumble across your daughter on a path
in the woods that day in the middle of some epically bad
trip and just lost control? And then when you came to, the
reality of what you'd done was so horrifying you just blocked

it out."

"I didn't kill my daughter," he said. "You don't have to believe me—take a look at the evidence. The DNA and blood samples as much as prove it."

I'd heard rumblings about this, but I wanted to hear the details from him before I formed any opinions. "If you have DNA evidence proving you're innocent, why are you still in prison?"

"The judge says it's tainted; he ruled it inadmissible. But I had tests done. There were blood and skin cells under my daughter's fingernails. They weren't mine."

"They can't tell whose they were?"

"There wasn't enough to come up with a match—most of the evidence got tossed after the first trial. But it didn't come from me; that much has been proven. Someone else did this. I couldn't do something like that."

I took a few seconds to think about that. The room was hot and overcrowded. There were sweat stains at the neck of Gendreau's denim shirt and under his arms. A little boy with dark hair played with a plastic truck in one corner of the room, a rail-thin, dark-haired woman not far from him. She chewed gum and held hands with a built blond guy with some seriously disturbing tats extending from his upper arm all the way up his neck. He caught me staring and met my eye. Smiled. I looked away.

"I'm not a detective," I said, my attention back on Gendreau. "I'm a reporter. Which means whatever I find, chances are good that I'll shout it from the rooftops. You're prepared for that?"

"That's part of the reason I contacted you. You think if I had any doubt about whether or not I'd done this, I'd call a reporter to investigate? Would I order DNA tests if there was any question in my mind that I might've just blacked out? I'm telling you." He leaned in so close that I saw one of the guards take a step toward us. "Find the man who killed those girls and buried them in Canada, and you'll find Ashley's killer. He did this."

"Look, Mr. Gendreau—" I began.

He held up a hand to stop me. "Whoever murdered my little girl is still out there. I have two other kids I watched grow up from behind prison bars. They won't speak to me. My wife filed divorce papers an hour after I was convicted. I lost everything the day my daughter died."

I glanced at the photo again, not sure how to respond. It took maybe fifteen seconds before I'd made up my mind. "If I do this, I'm doing it my way."

"That's what I expected," he assured me. "And for every piece of information you bring me, I'll answer anything you want about your father."

"I won't do anything until you give me at least one scrap about my dad," I insisted. "Last name. Where he was from. Something."

"Black Falls," he said. "That's where I met him. You want to know more, you'll need to work for it."

I got the same sweet-as-sugar rush I always get when I have a lead, and stood. Black Falls. "Fair enough. I'll be back in a few days."

He nodded. Something about his story still bugged me—aside from the fact that if Hank Gendreau really was innocent, the wheels of justice had skidded horrifically off course. Or maybe it was just something about *him* that bugged me. At the very least, I didn't trust him. The guard who'd been about to intervene on my behalf a minute or two earlier flashed me a smile as I left the room. When I looked back over my shoulder, Gendreau was sitting where I'd left him, his gaze fixed once more on the seconds ticking by.

•

After I'd retrieved Einstein, my next stop was to the *Downeast Daily Tribune*, where I cut my teeth as a reporter way back when I was still wearing combat boots and too much eyeliner. That meant returning to Littlehope, of course—the hometown I'd been avoiding since the aforementioned horrifically bungled Payson investigation in the spring. The second we crossed the town line, Einstein was on his feet, whining at the window. He darted past me as soon as I opened the car door in the *Trib* parking lot, made a quick rest stop at a nearby shrub, and headed straight for the front door without me.

I wasn't feeling quite so eager. I wiped my sweating palms on my khakis, checked my reflection in the glass door, and did what I could to wrangle my red hair into some kind of discernible style. That never actually panned out, so I eventually gave up and pulled it back into a ponytail, straightened my top, took a breath, and went inside.

The *Trib* is a no-frills operation—most days, you're just grateful the plumbing works, so A/C is out of the question. The concrete walls were sweating and the linoleum was slick with humidity as I headed down the hall to the newsroom. Not a soul was in sight.

I was still a few feet from my destination when the newsroom door opened and Daniel Diggins, editor-in-chief, stepped outside. He had his head down, focused on some paperwork in his hands. Einstein gave a hysterical yelp of joy and was off like a bolt of furry lightning as soon as he caught sight of him. Diggs looked up from his papers, then just stood there for a split second, like he wasn't sure I was actually there. Once he'd assured himself I was no mirage, a smooth, slow grin touched his lips.

He knelt to give Einstein a proper greeting while I bridged the distance between us. He had on shorts and an Arcade Fire t-shirt, his wavy blond hair as untamed as ever. His blue eyes sparkled when they met mine. Diggs is eight years older than me, and forty has never looked so good as it did on that man. He straightened. Stein wandered off to make sure all was copasetic with the rest of the paper.

"I wondered when you'd show your face around here again." He said it with a smile, no trace of the awkwardness I was afraid I might find.

"I've been busy. You know how it goes."

He looked amused, like my absence was exactly what he'd expected, my return right on schedule. I felt a flash of irritation that vanished when he took a step closer and tucked a tendril of hair behind my ear.

"You look good, Sol," he said.

If I hadn't been about to melt from the heat before, the look in his eyes was enough to finish the job. "You, too," I said.

My voice didn't sound like mine and the flush in my cheeks didn't have a thing to do with the weather. In the good old days, we would have hugged hello and he would've given me hell for staying out of touch so long. Now, thanks to a two-minute conversation while I was pressed against his desk in this very building three months ago, I was blushing like a virgin bride.

I cleared my throat and took a step back. "I was in town on a story—figured I'd pop in."

"And steal our Wifi?" he guessed correctly.

"I'll buy you lunch for it; that's not stealing."

"Deal." He nodded toward the newsroom. "Snag a desk, or you can set yourself up in my office. I'll be back in ten."

He didn't tell me where he was going, and I didn't ask. After three months without so much as an e-mail to let him know how I was, I figured I didn't merit much in the way of explanations.

Einstein and I went into the *Trib*'s newsroom, but the heat and the faint smell of sweat and stale Cheetos drove me straight to Diggs' door. His desk was uncharacteristically neat, complete with a labeled inbox, a new computer monitor, and a jelly jar of wildflowers looking somewhat worse for the wear. Diggs isn't really a wildflowers kind of guy; the sight didn't sit well with me.

I set myself up with my laptop on his leather sofa so I could make the most of the tiny bit of relief provided by an old box fan in the window. I'd already logged into the network and was looking for everything I could find on Hank Gendreau by the time Diggs returned.

He tossed a plastic-wrapped sub sandwich on my lap and handed me an extra-tall iced coffee.

"I thought I was buying lunch."

He waved me off, his attention already on my computer. "Next time. So, what's the big story?"

I set the laptop aside for the time being. The sub was from Wallace's—the town general store—which meant it tasted like the best thing this side of heaven but probably took five years off my life. Einstein parked himself at my feet with his chin resting on my foot, gazing up at me with profound faith that I'd do right by him. I tossed him a pickle.

"What do you know about Hank Gendreau?" I asked.

Diggs perked up. "The guy who claims he was framed for raping and murdering his own daughter? That's who you were visiting?"

"I got wind of some anomalies in his case, heard there might be a story there," I said. "I figured I'd talk to him first and see what I could find out. And there was no rape," I added. "His daughter was tortured and strangled. No sexual assault."

"Ah. Well, I guess if all he did was torture and strangle her, it's no big deal." He bit into his veggie burger and took his sweet time chewing before he continued. "They just turned down his last appeal, didn't they?"

"Yeah. But there's been a lot of interest in his case over the years. There's some DNA evidence the jury never heard about, apparently."

Diggs got that look he always gets when he sees more than I intend on showing. "What's your interest? I thought you were focusing on your dad's story for a while."

"I still need to pay the bills." It was the truth. Basically. "People eat this shit up, you know that. So, what's your take—is there a story or isn't there? Do you think he did it?"

"They got a confession from him, right? He was in the woods tripping balls the day it happened, then they found him later covered in his daughter's blood. Definitely a slam-dunk case at the time."

"He says they found someone else's DNA under her fingernails."

Over the course of his career, Diggs has somehow managed to retain the details of just about every news story on all seven continents for the past century—something I tend to view as either incredibly helpful or just plain annoying, depending on circumstances. He didn't even blink at what I considered fairly weighty evidence in Gendreau's favor.

"There've been a couple of cases in the news about that lately," he said. "The thinking now is that the nail clippers CSU used back then might have been contaminated from other victims."

I read farther down before I shook my head. "They were using disposable clippers by then, for just that reason. Whatever scrapings they found had to come from under Ashley Gendreau's nails."

Diggs scratched his stubbled chin, thinking that over.

"Have you met him?" I asked.

"Gendreau? Once. I was doing a story on one of the job programs he spearheaded over at the prison. He's done a lot of good work in there."

"Everyone I talked to so far over there loves him," I said. "Maybe times have changed, but the last I checked, guys accused of torturing and murdering their own kids aren't real popular round the cell block. The consensus on the inside is he got railroaded."

"Maybe he's just a good actor," Diggs said. He sat back in his chair and finished his burger. "He could be a sociopath. Split personality. Anything's possible."

"He's seen shrinks for the past thirty years. You don't think one of them might have picked up on that?" I pulled up the story Gendreau had turned me onto during our visit.

"And then there's this," I continued. I read aloud from the screen. " 'Five of the six bodies discovered buried in the woods along the Maine/Quebec border have now been identified as young women from the central and northern Maine area reported missing in the early '80s.' "

"And you think whoever killed these girls is the same guy who killed Ashley Gendreau?"

"It's a theory. They were all the same age. All kidnapped, strangled, and buried."

"Except Ashley wasn't buried."

"Maybe her father interrupted the killer. Whoever did it had to run before he could haul the body away to his burial ground."

He arched an eyebrow. "You're reaching, Sol—this guy's desperate. Since when did you become such an easy mark?"

I bristled. "I'm not an easy mark. There are plenty of unanswered questions here—I'm not alone in thinking maybe Gendreau got caught in a shit-storm with a bunch of cops out to string up the first suspect they found after they saw everything that had been done to this girl. You honestly think anyone could have been impartial after seeing that?"

He thought that over for a few seconds, then settled in behind his desk and fired up his own computer. "So, this mysterious killer who was murdering girls in the '80s... Do they have any leads on who he is? Any clue where he might be now? Or why he just stopped killing for no apparent reason?"

"How do we know he stopped?" I asked. "He could have more burial sites than just the one they found. Or maybe he got caught. Maybe he died."

We both fell silent, scanning the innumerable websites that detailed the brutal slaying of Ashley Gendreau in 1987. At the time, the public had been ready to skip Gendreau's trial entirely and get straight to the lynching. He'd gotten hate mail, death threats, been segregated from the general population...and yet, despite all that, somehow over the years he'd been able to change a lot of minds while he'd been inside. I wasn't ready to dial up the governor for a pardon just yet, but looking into the matter didn't seem like quite the colossal waste of time I'd thought it was when I first got Gendreau's letter.

I spent the afternoon and evening in Diggs' office researching the Gendreau murder and the discovery of the bodies in Quebec. Hank Gendreau had given his lawyer permission to talk to me, so I set up a meeting for the following day. I checked the map to figure out where his daughter was killed and sketched out a time to visit the site later in the week.

I was in the middle of jotting down notes on the other victims when Diggs got up from his desk and turned off the fan.

"All right, Sol, I'm closing up shop."

I glanced at the clock on my computer screen. "It's not even seven o'clock—what happened to burning the midnight oil?"

"Not tonight. Your mutt's wilting, and I'm teetering on the brink of heat stroke over here. First we swim, then we eat. This'll wait until tomorrow."

Einstein was looking pretty sad, and I was feeling a little damp myself. I peeled myself off the furniture and packed up my stuff. So far I hadn't broached the subject of where I was planning to crash for the night—another thing that had changed since my last visit. I glanced at the flowers on his desk again. Usually, it was a given that Diggs would be putting me up during my stay. I wasn't so sure about that anymore.

"I was thinking about giving Edie a call, and maybe spending the night there tonight," I said, like it was no big deal at all.

Diggs flashed a brilliant smile my way, amused. "Oh?"

"It's not really fair of me to just show up out of the blue like this, and expect you to...you know."

He folded his arms over his chest and leaned back against the doorsill, clearly enjoying himself. "No, I guess it isn't."

"You're not gonna make this easy, are you?"

"Not if I can help it." He straightened, grabbed my backpack, and tossed it over one shoulder. "Come on, Sol— I'll race you to the car. We can fight about it there."

Einstein was already out the door, hot on Diggs' heels, while I was still trying to figure out my next move. It was pretty much a foregone conclusion, though: I'd been following Diggs since I was knee high to a toadstool. I wasn't about to stop now. I grabbed the rest of my stuff and locked the door behind me, feeling undeniably nostalgic for those hot summer nights of my youth.

More Mysteries from Jen Blood

In Between Days
Diggs & Solomon Shorts
1990 - 2000

Midnight Lullaby
Prequel to
The Erin Solomon Mysteries

The
Payson Pentalogy
The Critically Acclaimed 5-Book Series
Readers Can't Put Down!

Book I: All the Blue-Eyed Angels
Book II: Sins of the Father
Book III: Southern Cross
Book IV: Before the After
Book V: The Book of J

And the First Novel in the Jamie Flint
K-9 Search and Rescue Series

The Darkest Thread

ABOUT THE AUTHOR

Jen Blood is a freelance journalist and author of the bestselling Erin Solomon mystery series. She is also owner of Adian Editing, providing expert editing of plot-driven fiction for authors around the world. Jen holds an MFA in Creative Writing/Popular Fiction, with influences ranging from Emily Bronte to Joss Whedon and the whole spectrum in between. Today, Jen lives in Maine with her dog Killian, where the two are busy conquering snowbanks and penning the next Erin Solomon mystery.

For regular updates, free short stories, contests,
and giveaways between book releases,
visit http://jenblood.com/,
and like us on Facebook at
http://facebook.com/jenbloodauthor/

Made in the USA
San Bernardino, CA
18 February 2017